STAY GONE DAYS

STAY GONE DAYS

a novel

Steve Yarbrough

PUBLISHING

NEW YORK, NY

Ig Publishing
Box 2547
New York, NY 10163
www.igpub.com

ISBN: 978-1-63246-13-5-3

PRINTED IN THE UNITED STATES OF AMERICA
FIRST EDITION | FIRST PRINTING

for Ewa
once more with feeling.

The Cole Girls

IN ELLA'S RECOLLECTIONS, THEIR HOUSE stands on the east side of the gravel road, a cotton field to the north, an orchard to the south. It's a boxy little two-bedroom with Sheetrock siding, hot in spring and summer, cold in fall and winter. They had a window unit, but it mostly just made noise. They had a fireplace, too, but it stayed boarded up because one time they found a dead snake there.

The orchard wasn't really an orchard, that's just what her father chose to call it. About halfway between the house and their neighbor's soybean patch languished a lone Bartlett pear. Some years the fruit was fit to eat but most years not. She thinks the plot used to be a garden, that maybe at one time their parents grew watermelons and tomatoes and whatever else people in the Delta liked to eat: Okra, possibly. Black-eyed peas.

Her father was not officially a farmer then, though he used to be. He drove a propane truck during the day but studied electronics at night via correspondence course through the Cleveland Institute, which was not up the road in Cleveland, Mississippi, but hundreds of miles away in Ohio. Whereas he once spoke the language of agriculture, tossing around terms like "hill-drop," "strict-middling" and "string-out," he'd recently adopted a new vocabulary, talking constantly of "triodes," "diodes" and "electrodes." One day he went to Jackson to take an exam and returned with a certificate that pronounced him a Certified Electronics Technician. From that moment on, whenever he composed a letter, he typed his name at the bottom, followed by a comma and C.E.T.

On the weekends, he repaired people's televisions, stereos and radios. Years before she knew the term CD she knew CB. CB stood for Citizens' Band, the kind of radio that only he seemed able to work on. Why he failed to place periods in this particular initialism she never understood. She accepted it on faith, along with so much else he said and did.

> Dear Mr. Stark:
>> This invoice is a reminder that you still owe $17.50 for fixing your CB on 10/12/74. Please remit at your earliest convenience.
> Sincerely,
> Alton Cole, C.E.T

The reason she knows what he wrote in those letters is that he kept carbon copies of all communications, storing them in the attic, in a large metal lockbox, which she found right before they moved out. She placed it sideways on the floor, on an afternoon when she was home alone, and hit it hard with a pipe wrench.

She often thinks of the box, how thin the metal was, how it crinkled from a single blow, how little protection it offered in the end, allowing to come to light so much that he would have preferred to keep hidden in the attic of a house soon to be abandoned.

.

They went to a private school. This sounds impressive, as if they were people of means. At various times, Ella's younger sister Caroline, who after leaving home began to call herself Carin and later on Caro, would with practiced offhandedness remark: "Down south, I attended a highly ranked private school."

The truth is less savory. Paying the tuition left their parents constantly broke, but the only thing highly ranked at the school was the football team. And it would not have been highly ranked either if it played teams from public schools, which by then the courts had forced to integrate. The school existed for one reason: the maintenance of segregation. All the white kids went there whether or not their parents could afford it. To do otherwise would have incurred disgrace.

The colors were red and gray, the nickname the Rebels, the fight song "Dixie." There were no buses, and many students drove themselves to school in nice cars. She and Caroline were among those that didn't. Their mother, who operated a cash register at United Dollar Store, dropped them off just before eight, then drove downtown, parked behind the store and waited until the manager showed up and unlocked the door. In summertime, when it got hot early, she often had to drive back and forth in the parking lot to keep the air conditioner running. Ella did not learn about this practice from their mother but from a high school classmate named Kim Taggart.

The new biology teacher had assigned them to dissect a frog together. This particular teacher would last only one semester, getting fired right before Christmas. She just didn't understand how things worked, people said, shaking their heads. Every time a student used a racial slur, she issued a public reprimand. This kept her pretty busy.

One of the things she didn't understand was that a girl like Kim Taggart should not be paired with one like Ella Cole. The Cole sisters were poor girls from the countryside, the kind who up until second or third grade had said *fanger* for *finger*. When their mother took them to the circus, they didn't sit in the reserved seats but at one end of the oval ring, where a single strand of seagrass rope separated them from the small number of black people who could afford general admission. Kim, on the other hand, was the daughter of "Tag" Taggart, a former Ole Miss baseball star and local attorney who'd become rich representing agricultural interests, sometimes traveling on their behalf to Washington, D.C. Their house held a commanding position on Bayou Drive. A plantation-style affair with white columns and a rotunda, it was spot-lit every night. Thomas Jefferson might have felt at home within those walls. They owned another place, too, in the New Orleans Garden District. Word was that when Kim graduated, they'd sell their local home and move on. The town was too confining for people like them, even if they'd been born and raised there.

Each two-person team had to pay for its own dissection kit and frog. Ella, newly resituated up front beside Kim, reached into her bag to withdraw the two dollars her mother had given her that morning. But Kim, a glittering girl with long blonde hair that lay regal on her shoulders, said, "That's okay. I've got us covered." She stood and walked up to the teacher's desk, handing her a ten and waiting patiently for change. She wore the kind of plaid wool skirt fashionable at the time, along with a white wool blouse. On her wrist, a hammered heart charm wrap. For days people had been trying to figure out who gave it to her. She wouldn't say. Kim Taggart valued discretion. She was Tag Taggart's daughter.

The dissection began smoothly, Ella spreading the frog out on the tray and holding its limbs in place while her partner pinned them down. She'd once watched her mother and grandmother remove the eyes from the head of a newly slaughtered pig, then place it in a brine pot to make head cheese. She hadn't felt squeamish then, and she didn't now. Neither, apparently, did Kim. While most of the other girls as well as a number of boys wrinkled their noses and voiced disgust, Kim proceeded methodically, her gaze narrowing each time she pushed a pin in. "I probably ought to be wearing contacts," she said. "I think I inherited my dad's vision."

Mr. Taggart, Ella recalled, wore wire-rimmed glasses with thick tinted lenses. "He's got bad eyesight?"

"Without those awful glasses, he couldn't even drive."

"What about your mom?" Until now, they had never exchanged a word, though they'd been in so many classes together that Ella had lost count.

"My Mom can see to Memphis and back. If there's a speck of dirt in the corner of the bathroom, she finds it. It's a rare day when she doesn't make me plod downstairs and grab the vac."

"Really?"

Kim pushed the last pin into one of the frog's webbed feet. "You assumed we didn't do our own vacuuming. Right? Well, I do all the cleaning. She makes me use a toothbrush on the shower grout. How do you think folks with money stay rich?"

"I don't know how they stay rich. And more importantly? I don't know how they get rich."

The other girl laughed and touched her forearm. "I don't know how they get rich, either. It happened before I was born. How they stay rich is to make sure they don't spend one unnecessary dime. My mother carries a calculator everywhere. She conducts spot audits of stuff like the sales receipt at the grocery store. She once pulled the thing out at Commander's Palace, and while my dad looked on horrified she re-tabulated the check. She is the stingiest human being you will ever meet."

Ella had never heard of Commander's Palace. As if she'd read her mind, her partner said, "Commander's is a restaurant in New Orleans. It costs a lot to eat there. If you ask me, the food's often nauseating. Can you imagine turtle soup?" She gestured at the newly impaled frog. "It wouldn't surprise me to see our poor friend on their menu."

The thing was, Ella had eaten frog meat. Her father and her uncle went gigging, then stewed frog legs for supper. Her aunt and her mom and Caroline refused to eat the stew and had baloney sandwiches instead. To Ella it tasted neither bad nor good. It was food. You ate it.

She knew, in the way she knew all sorts of things without having them explained, that at this point it would not be wise to reveal her culinary history. It seemed like something unforeseen might be happening between her and Kim Taggart, and she wanted to find out what it was. "You're my curious one," her father liked to say, "and curiosity's okay. Now, some folks'll tell you it killed the cat, and maybe it did. But what they don't want you to know's that the cat's got nine lives."

Please remit: one life for one surprise.

•

"Kim fucking *Taggart*?" Caroline says that evening from the bunk below hers. "Are you shitting me? She invited you to *dinner*?"

Her sister is a year-and-a-half younger. When she was little, she slept in the upper bunk, but then she began to complain about feeling claustrophobic, so Ella agreed to switch. Nobody beyond the family knows this, and most would be stunned by it, but Caroline is prey to many phobias. She's terrified of cottonmouths, which is perfectly reasonable, but also of dust particles, which is not. She's afraid of getting food poisoning, though she's never had it, and is always checking the dates on everything in the refrigerator and occasionally discarding stuff like buttermilk and orange juice a few days in advance, and this drives their father half-crazy. She's afraid of dogs but pines for a cat, which he won't let her have. More than anything, she's afraid of the dark. Beneath her bunk she keeps a small lamp that burns all night. Sometimes Ella has to wear a mask.

"You have a truly foul mouth," she observes. "Has anyone ever told you that?"

"You've told me that like maybe about five hundred fucking times. I find profanity sublime. That's what I'm doing when I use it. Sublimating base urges."

"What base urge are you sublimating now?"

"To be frank? I'd like to kill Kimberly Faye Taggart."

"Kimberly Faye? When did you hear anybody call her that?"

"Actually, I saw it on her driver's license."

"You saw her driver's license? How?"

"Well, to be completely forthcoming, Els? For a while, said document was in my possession."

Some statements take time to sink in. This isn't one of them. Six or seven weeks ago, during sixth-period gym class, several items were pilfered from the girls' locker room. The principal made an announcement over the PA system, demanding that anyone with information about the thefts come forward. But as far as Ella knows, no one did. "Oh, Jesus," she says now. "Surely, you didn't."

"I hate to disappoint you."

"No, you don't." She rips off the mask, swings her legs out of bed and bangs her head on the ceiling. She doesn't bother with the rickety ladder. Her feet hit the floor with a thud.

Her sister is propped on three or four pillows, her smooth face serene, the tiny mole near the corner of her mouth scarcely visible in the glow from the night lamp. Though neither of them knows it, there's a running debate among a contingent of high school guys about which of the Cole girls is hottest. Most would vote for Caroline. It's the dirty language, the wild red hair, the piercing green eyes, the bad grades she doesn't give a damn about, the rumor about what happened one night behind the old abandoned brick yard and was said to involve the entire first team-offensive line and the backup tight end. An air of danger surrounds her, and the guys who wage the debate love danger, even as it scares them. Nobody thinks Ella is dangerous. She makes straight A's, has pale skin and hair so blonde it's nearly white, and she's got the placid demeanor of a Christmas tree angel. Which probably means, according to minority opinion, that if you could just get a few drinks in her, she'd fuck you up one turnrow and down the other.

That her sister finds satisfaction in her dismay would be impossible to miss, even if she'd never noted it before. But she has. She detected the same sort of amusement last week when Caroline, having been caught cheating on a test in the only class they've ever taken together, announced to their teacher: "That's the last time I'll ever lift a finger trying to pass Algebra." Caroline's pleasure is bound up with her own discomfort. It has been this way for quite a while. Before that, they were everything to each other. But things change. Ella has not expended much effort wondering why.

"You stole from Kim. What did you take?"

A shrug. "A few dollars. The driver's license. Her car keys."

"Jesus. You weren't . . . You didn't plan to steal her car, did you?"

"Hell no. That could lead to some truly bad shit. Now, I'll admit I fantasized about pouring a quart of Daddy's Valvoline on the leather seats. But he'd probably miss it. And, of course, if that happened, you know who would catch hell."

This is her self-defined position in the family: she's the bearer of blame, the beast onto whose back all burdens are strapped. She's presumed guilty until she proves herself innocent, and such proof is hard to produce when you're nearly always at fault.

"What have you got against Kim Taggart?" Ella asks, keeping her voice down because she just heard their mother step into the bathroom. "What did she ever do to you?"

"You know something, Els? If you aren't careful, Momma's worries about you are gonna come true. She's scared you'll turn into somebody's doormat. I heard her say so to Grandma right before she died."

Ella reaches for the ladder, locks her hand around a rung. "What did Kim Taggart do to you?" she asks again.

"Do you know what was in her fucking purse? A hundred and forty-three dollars. Momma probably makes less in a week for standing on her feet eight hours a day."

"That still doesn't make it right to steal from her."

"I bet you she didn't even *know* how much she had. You wanta hear what else was in there? I mean, besides the keys to her hideous little BMW?"

She ought to say no, and she intends to, but words fail to emerge.

"Two condoms, still in their packages. Two of those little bottles of whiskey they give people on planes. And—get this—a note saying *Brad, there's much more of me where last night came from.*"

Brad Moss is the quarterback, the most popular guy in town, reputedly being recruited by both Ole Miss and Auburn. People think he's the one who gave Kim the charm bracelet. He recently broke up with his girlfriend.

Ella turns loose of the ladder and sits down on her sister's bed. "Why are you telling me this?" she asks. "Why now?"

"Because," her sister says, her mouth beginning to quiver like it used to when in an effort to win attention she'd posed a silly question—*Is snow made out of cotton?*—only to be met, yet again, by their father's derision. "I don't want you to become one of her play-things. She already has plenty of bright toys. What have you got? What have I got? Who in the hell are we?"

"WHEN WE WERE BUILDING THE HOUSE," Mr. Taggart said, "we had some . . . well, let's just say *spirited* discussions about whether the dining room ought to look onto the street or the bayou. I'll be the first to admit that a case could be made for either one. But I argued that every December, when the Christmas floats go out, we'd regret it if we'd put it up front."

"And of course, being a lawyer," Mrs. Taggart said, sipping from her fourth or fifth glass of red wine, "my husband won."

"That's a simplification." Mr. Taggart gestured over his shoulder at the bayou, where a brightly-lit Santa manned a sleigh pulled by a pair of neon-antlered reindeer. "In my profession, it's often necessary to arrive at a compromise. So yes, we put the dining room where I wanted. But notice whose back is turned to the window so he can't enjoy the sights. Seems fair to me. Don't you think so?"

Later, after she saw the news about Tag Taggart in the local paper, she would feel no small measure of sympathy for Kim's mother. But that night, she couldn't muster a shred. If Mrs. Taggart kept drinking, it wouldn't be long before the lights and the float dissolved into mist, if they hadn't already. On her the view was wasted. "Yes sir," Ella said. "That seems like a reasonable solution."

Mrs. Taggart smiled into her glass. She lacked, people said, her husband's charisma. The only person Ella had heard say a kind word about her was her own father. "In high school, Louise was a real friendly girl," he remarked a little while ago, on their way into town. "Even back

17

then, that damned Tag was just as slick as if you'd rubbed him in bacon fat. I wouldn't trust that scutter as far as I could punt him."

When dinner concluded, Mr. Taggart pushed his chair away from the table and said he'd better get on down to his office, that he was working on an important case and needed to put in several more hours, even though this was Friday evening and Christmas only ten days off. He said good night, and before they heard the front door close, Mrs. Taggart had drained her glass. "Well, girls," she said, "good luck with the dishes." She rose, picked up the corkscrew and an unopened bottle of wine that waited on the sideboard, and headed upstairs.

Kim studied the remains of her dessert, a chocolate torte. For reasons that she would not have been able to articulate, Ella wished she felt free to reach across the table and pat the other girl's hand. That she didn't do it will bother her, off and on, for the remainder of her life. She will recall it more than forty years from now in a Boston hospice.

Kim finally made eye contact. "Well, child," she said, not quite mimicking her mother's tone, "let's get in there and see if the dishes bring us luck."

•

What did they do that night, she and the girl who would soon, if only for a short time, become her best friend?

To begin with, they washed dishes. Or to be more precise, they rinsed the dishes and lined them up neatly in the dishwasher and Kim closed the door and turned it on. Ella thought maybe the evening had reached its end. She'd been invited to dinner, and dinner had come and gone. Better get ready to phone her father.

"Want to head upstairs? We could put some music on."

Kim led her out of the kitchen and down a hallway, onto which several rooms opened. When she'd wondered what this house would look like from inside, Ella had thought in terms of objects: vases fashioned from hand-blown glass, brass andirons, Persian carpets, original paintings by long-dead artists. But except for some furniture, which didn't look all that special, the parts of the house she could see were nearly empty. The only thing hanging on the hallway wall was a photo of Mr. Taggart's law school class.

At the foot of the staircase, Ella paused, stepped out of her flats and picked them up—to discover that Kim had halted too and was watching her. "You don't need to do that," her host said.

For the first time all night, she felt as if she'd committed a *faux pas.* "My mom made me do it when I was little. I don't remember who we were visiting. Somebody with a two-story house, obviously." She started to bend and put the shoes back on, then thought better of it. "If you don't mind, I think I'll just stick with tradition."

Kim was standing on the bottom stair. She swept her hair out of her face, then leaned over and kissed Ella on the forehead. The kiss only lasted a second, but the confusion it caused lingered much longer.

"You're a sweet girl," her new friend observed.

It seemed to Ella that she could hear herself swallow and that Kim must have heard her too. "So are you."

"Nope. The jury's rendered its verdict that I'm the most heartless bitch in town. Junior division, anyhow. My mom's got the overall title nailed down."

Her room was directly above the one where they'd dined. There wasn't much in it either, just a bed and desk, a bookshelf and a stereo. Kim walked right through it, opened a French door and led Ella onto a small balcony, where they achieved a perfect view of the bayou. "Which of the floats is your favorite?" she asked.

"Probably the manger scene down there by the Main Street bridge. What's yours?"

"Mostly, I don't like them. But then mostly, I don't like Christmas."

"Why?"

"That's a hard one." Kim hugged herself. It was a chilly evening, temperature in the high thirties, a few wisps of fog rising off the water. Supposedly, tomorrow promised a slight chance of snow. "You know that John Denver tune? 'Please, Daddy, Don't Get Drunk This Christmas'?"

"Yeah. It's that what your dad does?"

"No, that's what he ought to do. I would. I do."

"Get drunk at Christmas?"

"Get drunk at every opportunity. What about you?"

She'd had a couple of drinks a few weeks ago with another junior named Irwin, who'd invited her to the Halloween dance. He was quiet and shy, the sort of boy who got sent into a football game in the fourth quarter, after it was safely won or irrevocably lost. His father, like hers, worked for Barkley Petroleum. She'd been seeing him at company parties as far back as she could remember. They'd once ridden a seesaw together for half an hour at the lake house that belonged to their dads' boss.

After the dance, he asked if she'd like to try some Boone's Farm. He said he had a fifth of Strawberry Hill. She said sure, so he parked the pickup on a turnrow south of town and screwed off the top. The first thing that surprised her was that he drank direct from the bottle. The second was that he killed about a quarter of it before handing it over.

He hadn't bothered to wipe it off, and she decided that doing so herself would be rude. In the end, it wouldn't have accomplished much anyhow, because when they finally finished the wine, he scooted across the seat, threw his arms around her and pressed his lips to hers. This was not the last time a male would reward her with unwanted attention, but it was the first, and she behaved more or less as she would in similar circumstances for the rest of her life, on nearly every occasion. She shoved her fist into his ribcage, prompting a startled cry that sounded like nothing so much as *oink*. "Don't *do* that," she said.

In the dark he looked unmanned, like he'd just missed an open-field tackle and been confronted by his coach. "I'm so sorry. Please don't tell anybody. I'll never do it again. I promise. Not *ever*." It sounded as if he intended to take priestly vows.

"I'm afraid," she told Kim now, "that I've never been drunk."

"Is that by design? Or due to lack of chance?"

"I guess I had a chance that I didn't take."

"That was probably a mistake."

"Maybe so."

Kim turned her back to the bayou, resting her elbows on the railing. The lights from Santa and the reindeer added red and green tinges to all that blonde hair. "If you had another chance, would you take it?"

There are things you can't imagine about yourself until the moment

20

imagination is no longer called for. Until three days ago, she'd never suspected she'd set foot in this house that she'd been riding by her whole life, that she would be standing on a balcony at night with the girl who lived here. Nor had she imagined she would say what she was about to: "With you I would."

The other girl's smooth face didn't reveal much, but for a few seconds Ella felt as if she were being appraised. Finally, Kim opened the door and went back inside, and she followed.

When she got to the bed, Kim lifted the spread, jammed her hand between the mattress and box spring and pulled out a pint bottle. "Nothing beats Four Roses," she said, "on a cold winter's night." She reached for the wall switch and flicked off the light.

She'd mentioned music but never put any on. Instead, she sat down on the floor, her back against the bed, and Ella joined her.

"I'm guessing you don't know what whiskey tastes like."

"You guessed right."

"Tonight, I'm a prophet. This one'll burn you pretty good. But at least it's better than Scotch." She turned it up and took a swig.

"If you don't like it," Ella said as she accepted the bottle, "why do you drink it?"

"Ask me again in an hour."

The taste was not as bad as she expected, but the burning was much worse. She coughed three or four times, and her nose began to run.

"Wasn't that fun?"

"Not exactly." She handed back the whiskey, promising herself that she would only take one more sip or, at most, two. Three at the outside.

"Do your folks drink? They probably don't, do they?"

"My mother doesn't. I think my dad does, but he hides it."

"He's ashamed?"

She'd often wondered why he didn't do it openly. Neither of her parents went to church anymore, so it wasn't like he feared Baptist condemnation. "I think ..."

"You think what?"

"I think maybe he just likes to hide things."

"That's interesting. I like to hide things too."

Kim didn't slug alcohol like Irwin, just took a good-sized swallow every five or ten minutes. When she offered the bottle, Ella did the same. After a while, the burning stopped bothering her, and she began to look forward to her next turn.

Upon waking the following day, she wouldn't remember precisely what they talked about, but she knew they'd shared many secrets and the conversation had grown profound. She also recalled how comfortable she felt sitting on the floor beside Kim Taggart. At some point, Kim had kissed her again, this time on the mouth. It didn't seem strange there in the dark. It didn't even seem all that strange the next morning.

TODAY, CAROLINE DETERMINES, WILL BE a Stay Gone Day. She'll leave school on the sly and stay gone until tomorrow.

She reaches this decision during her sophomore English class where, as usual, chaos reigns. Some folks are doing homework, a couple taking naps, the majority relaying gossip. The teacher, a woman in her sixties named Mrs. Batch who affects a British accent and loves words like *ubiquitous, obsequious, urbane* and *germane,* is fluttering her eyelashes at Brad Moss and two other senior guys, who have again barged in to go over the forthcoming edition of the *Rebel Times,* for which the old lady is the faculty advisor. "One never alters the essence of any given situation," Caroline hears her say, "by exercising a timorous voice. Would you like to know why?"

Moss, first in all things, beats the others by a second. "Yes, ma'am."

"*Panta rei,*" she intones. "As Herclitus told us, 'All flows.' You can't step into the same river twice, etcetera, etcetera. If you wish to impede the movement of an established waterway, you erect an impermeable dam. Concomitantly, if you want the junior-senior banquet to occur on Saturday night rather than Friday, you don't compose an editorial meekly requesting 'reconsideration.' You issue a stern condemnation followed by a robustly-worded demand."

Caroline doesn't ask for a pass to visit the restroom. Instead, she just slips out the door. Nobody notices. Nobody cares.

Except Coach Raleigh, who teaches driver's ed and coaches the running backs. He's parked halfway down the hall near the cafeteria, the fifth-period monitor. Across his lap lies a baseball bat, sawn in half, the flat side sanded down and waxed. It serves as his paddle. So far, he's only applied it to male posteriors, though he keeps threatening to employ it on her.

Can eyes really undress you? His can. His do. "Cole," he says, "where's your pass?"

He calls everybody by their last name, even some of the other teachers. Mrs. Batch hates his guts. "Coach Raleigh," she told Brad Moss some days ago, speaking loudly enough for the whole class to hear, "is both perfidious and invidious. Look them up."

Caroline stops three or four feet away. Word has it the coach was once engaged to a rich girl from Jackson, whose parents, after meeting him, monkey-wrenched the whole thing. "I'm looking at my hall pass," she says. "You're it."

His face turns crimson, the way it did the last couple of times she left without permission. He glances left, then right, then straight ahead, toward the principal's office. Back at her. "Cole," he says, "there's a word for girls like you."

"There's a word for men like you too."

The first time she left, right before Christmas, she let him study her longer than she will this afternoon. That day, when he asked for her pass, she said, "Coach, to be perfectly honest, I don't have one. But I'm bored half insane by Mrs. Batch, who says bad things about you, from time to time, by the way, and I'm dying to get some fresh air. This is fifth period. I've got gym next. Maybe you'd let me go? I don't think anyone will ever know. And I'd be eternally grateful."

He asked her what Mrs. Batch said about him, and she relayed a few comments, a couple of which were true. When she'd finished, he said, "About all that's wrong with her last name is the 'a.' It should have been an 'i.'"

"Many of us think so."

"All right," he said, "go on and carry your swishy tail elsewhere. But stay out of trouble."

She took a couple of steps toward the door, giving him a little space. "Hey."

She turned.

He dropped his voice. "You know where I live?"

Slowly, she delivered her line. "Two . . . seventeen . . . Loring Avenue."

"Stop by sometime."

She can tell from the way he's looking at her now that he'd love to choke her. That's because about two weeks ago, on one of those warm, springlike Delta Saturdays you occasionally get in February, she did as he suggested, appearing on his porch. She'd ridden in with her mother, claiming she needed to go over to the public library to conduct research for a paper. He came to the door in a bathrobe, rubbing sleep from his eyes. "What are you doing here?"

"You invited me."

He looked over his shoulder. For a moment she thought maybe someone was back there in his bedroom, her bare haunch poking out from under the covers, messy hair spread out on a pillow. Maybe, after all, he had a life.

"This is not a good idea," he said.

"Okay." She made as if to leave.

"Wait a minute." His eyes scanned the street. "You want something to drink? A Coke maybe?"

"Sure."

He stepped aside to let her enter.

She quickly catalogued the room's contents: a brown sofa pushed against one wall, the fabric on both armrests frayed as if a persistent cat had applied its ingenuity, though no cat was visible; the bench-press near the fireplace, black weight plates strewn about the floor; on the mantle, a framed photo of him in a blue and gold football uniform, his hands extended as if to catch a pass; a Sylvania TV resting on a wobbly-looking table, beneath it a pile of magazines. Finally, as she took a seat on the sofa, her gaze settled on the detail that sang, the one that nobody could make up. Through an opening into the hallway, she could see another room. On a desk sat a big green ceramic frog with a penis that must have been a foot long. A couple of rubber bands dangled from the shaft.

"You want your Coke with ice?"

"Is it in a can or a bottle?"

"What difference does that make?"

"If it's in a bottle, I don't want a glass. If it's in a can, I want ice and a glass."

"That's weird."

"Microscopic particles rest on top of cans."

"Who told you that?"

"We learned it last year in biology. From Mr. Vacarella."

"Vacarella's a fag. That's why they got rid of him." He stepped into the kitchen.

A stack of mail lay on the coffee table. She quickly thumbed through it. A phone bill, a light bill, a renewal notice from *Sports Illustrated,* and a flimsy-looking envelope edged with red-and-yellow stripes. Addressed by hand to Milton A. Raleigh, it had come from someone named Adelina Carrillo Hernandez, whose address was apparently 10-3°, 26400 Calle del Almendro, Madrid, Spain. She tucked it into her blouse.

The coach returned carrying a bottle of Coke and a long-necked Bud. He handed her the Coke, then sat down in a nearby armchair. He must have been self-conscious about his legs, which were pale and all but hairless: when he saw her looking at them, he re-arranged the folds of his robe, covering as much as he could. "Does anybody know you're over here?"

She tipped up her Coke and took a couple of swallows, then set it down on the coffee table. "Nope," she said. "Not a soul."

"Didn't you mean to say 'No, sir'?"

"No, sir. I meant to say 'nope.'"

"You've got quite a mouth on you, don't you?"

"Yep."

"Why don't you tell me why you came here today?"

"Well, like I said a minute ago, you invited me."

"I don't recall that. That's what my response'd be, by the way, if anybody ever asked."

"What would you say about letting me leave school?"

"I'd say it didn't happen."

"And I'd say it did."

He smiled. It was an unusual smile, closer to a smirk, and she would remember that look more than twenty years later, when she watched an American president being interrogated by a special prosecutor about alleged sexual improprieties. The president smiled in similar fashion each time he dodged a question. "Thing is," Raleigh said, "nobody'd believe you. Not after you got your ass caught cheating in Algebra."

She knew when she was looking vulnerability in the face, having glimpsed it in many a mirror. Her guess was that he didn't know when he was looking at it. When he looked in the mirror, he most likely loved everything he saw and, if he questioned anything at all, it was probably the failure of others to be equally impressed.

She chugged the rest of her Coke and set the bottle down. "So long," she said, rising. "See you in the halls." She was halfway to the door before he leaped out of his chair.

"What did you say?"

Her pulse sped up. Why lie to herself? He could hurt her, he had it in him whether he knew it or not. She threw the door open, bounded down the steps, took off running and didn't look back.

Please do for yourself what you do before, said the letter from Adelina Carrillo Hernandez, in Madrid, Spain, *when you see the last picture I send*. To aid Milton A. Raleigh's efforts, she'd enclosed another photo.

This lingers between them in the air of a high school hallway, along with the smell of Lysol and damp socks and the coach's fear, desire and loathing. "Get out of here," he says. "I can't wait till you graduate."

"If I flunk Algebra," she warns, "I'll be here forever. Better burnish your resumé."

•

The local library is four blocks away, on a quiet street just east of downtown. This is where she goes each time she escapes school, coming in through the rear entrance, which opens onto the parking lot. That entrance has existed for about two years, since the library expanded. If you enter from this direction, you don't have to pass circulation. Apparently, it never occurred to anyone that such an arrangement would make it easy to steal books. Or maybe they just assumed nobody would want one enough to swipe it.

She does want books. At home they have only two shelves worth, mostly belonging to her dad. He reads indiscriminately. Ernest Hemingway one day, Zane Grey the next. Two or three years ago she found a novel there that she loved: *Appointment in Samarra*. It was set in a Pennsylvania mining town, and everybody in the book acted drunk even when they weren't, though typically they were, and all of them seemed to be standing at a precipice. The question was not whether they would fall, only when. She tried to discuss it with her father: "Daddy, have you read this one?"

He lay diagonally across his bed, both feet dangling off the corner. He still had his work clothes on, and his face was pink, as if he'd been drinking, and the skunky stink of propane hung in the air. He was reading something himself, a small white paperback. *Force Ten from Navarone*.

He put it aside and squinted at the one in her hand. "*Appointment in Samarra*? What are you doing with *that* thing?"

"I read it."

He planted his palm on the mattress and pushed upright, then reached out to seize the novel. That was when she made the sort of mistake she couldn't seem to avoid in his presence, taking a single step backwards, simultaneously protecting the book.

"Goddamn it!" He bounded off the bed. "Give me that nasty piece of smut!"

That was when she made her second mistake. "If it's smut," she cried, "what's it doing on our book shelf?"

He jerked it out of her hands, then spun her around and smacked her on the bottom. "Go to your room."

She didn't run. She didn't cry. But she did, for an instant, wish she could die.

Ella sat at their desk, her back to the door, doing her homework. In those days she was always doing homework, the flaxen-haired embodiment of duty and obedience. She made the greatest grades, she sang in Concert Choir, male teachers got misty-eyed every time she soloed.

Caroline closed the door and leveraged herself into the lower bunk.

"What was Daddy hollering about?"

"He got mad at me for reading a book." Even she knew that was only part of the truth.

"What book?"

"Never mind."

He sister's pencil kept moving. "Would I like it?"

"Probably not."

"How come?"

"It would depress you."

"I'm pretty hard to depress."

That ain't just the truth, their grandmother used to say. That's the God's-honest-truth.

"Someday," Caroline predicted, "trouble's gonna smack you right upside your pretty blonde head."

Her sister flipped the page of whatever textbook she had open. "And you no doubt hope you'll be standing by to observe the effect."

"Actually, I do. But not for the reason you suspect."

"So what's the real reason?"

"You're going to need me."

"Indubitably."

"You learned that word from Miz Bitch. Do you know what it means?"

"More or less."

Less is more, their grandmother sometimes said, when you look at it upside down.

•

The book she carries into the library's rear entrance after slipping away from school is a big leather-bound volume, George Eliot's *Adam Bede*. She stole it two weeks ago. She never intended to keep it, just wanted to read it, and you never know when the sour-faced head librarian will tell you this or that book is "inappropriate" for someone your age. She's glad she swiped it, because she lost herself in the passions of Hetty Sorrel. The only part she didn't like came at the end, when Hetty's life sentence for child murder was commuted to penal servitude. The poor girl had been a prisoner since the day she was born.

A couple of old men are sitting on couches, reading magazines. One of them, whom she doesn't recognize, has what looks like snuff stains on the front of his shirt, which is also missing a button. The other man used to be the postmaster. Last year his wife died. Since then, every time she's been here, she's seen him. When she passes him today, he looks up and says, "Hello, Caroline." He knows the name of everybody who ever mailed a letter or bought a stamp.

"Hi, Mr. Langley."

"Shouldn't you be in school, hon?"

"Yes, sir. Technically."

He laughs. "Well, we don't want to get fixated on technicalities, do we? You can get a perfectly fine education in here."

"Yes, sir."

"Assuming you want it, of course."

"Yes, sir. I do."

"Good for you."

She tells him bye, then walks into the fiction stacks. There's still an empty space waiting for *Adam Bede*, which was last checked out in 1959. After placing it on the shelf, she closes her eyes.

She feels her way down the aisle, running her hand along book spines. When she reaches the end of the row, she turns the corner into the next aisle, walks until she's about halfway down it, then lets her hand settle on a book and opens her eyes. If you don't know much about anything— and she understands that she doesn't—one thing *could* be just as good as another. This is why she lets books choose her. It's how she found all the ones she liked as well as several she hated.

The Naked and the Dead, the spine says. She likes naked. She even likes dead. The two together sound sexy, provocative. The jacket is missing, so she can't tell anything about the book except the author's last name. Even if the jacket were there, she wouldn't read the description. It's against the rule she made for herself. She won't have the slightest idea what the book is about until she reads the first line, and she won't do that until she's someplace quiet, where nobody can disrupt her concentration.

She slips it into her backpack, then starts toward the door. When she steps out, the head librarian appears from nowhere and grabs her arm.

She's a big woman, there's no point in putting up a struggle.

"I knew it," she exults, her other hand pawing through the backpack, which Caroline didn't even bother to zip up. "Young lady, when I get through with you, you'll rue this day."

Might as well inflict whatever damage she can. "I think you missed your calling," she says. "You should be playing tackle in the NFL. You've got the perfect body."

IN THE LOT BEHIND THE LIBRARY, her mother sat silently, not bothering to start the ignition, her eyes studying the bayou just as Caroline studied her. She'd recently turned forty. Her hair, once the same color as Ella's, was streaked with gray. It seemed as if there were a few more strands each day.

"I'm really sorry, Momma," she said, and she really was. In exchange for agreeing not to summon the police, the librarian had permanently banned her. The woman would have to drop dead before Caroline could again set foot in the stacks. The pathetic little library at school wasn't worthy of the name, and this sad excuse for a town couldn't even support a bookstore where she might've been able to shoplift some decent reading material.

"Do you know what would've happened if she'd called the cops? On Thursday your name would have appeared in the *Weekly Times*, where they list everybody that's been charged with a crime."

"Actually, you're wrong. I'm still just fifteen. It would have said something like 'An under-aged female was arrested at the Loring Public Library for book theft. Police refused to identify the suspect.'"

Now her mother faced her. She could tell that in her mom's eyes, she had just gained stature. Why this should be so, she didn't know, but it didn't surprise her.

"'Police remanded the accused to juvenile court,'" her mother said. "That would have been the next sentence. Of course, by then, everybody in the county would already know who 'the accused' was. And at least one of them, if not several, would have had a conversation with your daddy. They wouldn't actually *tell* him about it, understand. They'd just say something along the lines of, 'Sure do hope Caroline's okay. Everybody gets in a little mischief growing up.' The first time he heard it, he wouldn't be able to stop himself from asking what they were talking about, and then they'd act mortified to be the one that told him, and that'd make him even madder. You'd be in a pretty fix when he got home. Wouldn't you?"

"Yes, ma'am, I guess so." She couldn't resist adding: "But not for the first time."

Her mother turned the ignition. The old Galaxy coughed once or twice before the engine started. "I hate this car," she said. "It was ready to quit the day we drove it away from Discount Auto."

She pulled out of the lot. It was only 3:45, and Caroline assumed they'd drive downtown so her mom could operate the checkout stand until a quarter till six, at which point Mr. Wayne, the manager, would trade places with her so she could "check up." Either he lacked the math skills or was too lazy to perform the task.

To her surprise, they headed away from downtown, toward Highway 49. They didn't turn onto the highway, though, just crossed it, hugging the south bank of the bayou until they passed the city limit. She couldn't imagine where they were going, or why they were going there. The only thing for miles around was a bunch of barren fields.

Before long they crossed the Sunflower River, on a badly rusted bridge that she didn't even know existed. Her mother drove for several more minutes, then pulled onto the shoulder and stopped. They were probably eight or nine miles from town.

"Your daddy's got some extra deliveries to make this evening. At least that's what he says. I don't expect him home till late. Your sister's spending the night with her friend in the castle."

"This is a *week* night."

"Louise Taggart called, maybe fifteen minutes before the librarian. She said your sister and the princess needed to work on some project. One of my girls has access to the penthouse, the other one's bound for the pen. Unless I head it off. Which this time—thank Jesus, Mary,

Joseph and their donkey—I did. The thing is . . ." She'd always been good with pauses. She was a regular Paul Harvey. " . . . if I made a list of stuff I'm tired of? You staying in hot water with your daddy would be close to the top. Understand, it wouldn't be *at* the top. Just close. Open the door and get out."

"What?"

Her mother reached across her thighs, released the latch and shoved the door open. "Get out."

If her father had told her to do that, she would not have complied. He would have had to kill her and throw her body from the car. But she did as her mother ordered, stepping onto the shoulder.

In town, it hadn't seemed like a particularly cold day, but now it did. As far as she could see, there was nothing but empty gray fields. Dead cotton stalks whistled in the wind.

"I'm going back to work," her mother said. "I'll have supper on the table at seven. I hope you're there to eat it with me. If you intend to keep getting in trouble, might as well learn to get out of it without my help." She pulled the door closed, made a U-turn and headed toward town.

•

Caroline walked into the house at 6:57.

The guy who'd finally picked her up—after she slogged back roads for more than two hours, hoping nobody she knew would see her—had let her out, as requested, in front of another family's house about a mile from her own. The driver was a nice man, a big red-faced guy in a flannel shirt, who had a can of Miller Lite clamped between his enormous thighs. The bed of his pickup was filled with burlap sacks, cattle feed, he said, for his herd of Black Angus. He told her he lived near Leland and said that she should *ab-so-tiv-ly not* be walking down a country road by herself after dark. If he caught his daughter doing that, he'd ground her for at least six months. She started to tell him a big tale about how her father was dead and her mother was hospitalized with pneumonia and her sister had run off to join the Symbionese Liberation Army, but she couldn't quite form the first sentence. Instead, she said, "I'll be fine.

I really appreciate the ride." He didn't drive away until he saw her step onto the neighbors' porch, which of course stirred up their dogs. As soon as his pickup began moving, she took off for home.

The house smelled of fried potatoes, collard greens, black-eyed peas and chicken fried steak. In the kitchen, her mother was untying her apron strings. "Wash your hands, hon," she said. "They're probably covered in dust. On the road a person can't help but get filthy."

THEY COULD ONLY IMAGINE A typical morning in the lives of their parents that last year when they were all together. By design they never saw them eat breakfast except on the weekends, and those were carefully managed.

Their mother stands at the stove frying bacon. She's wearing the robe they pooled their resources to buy her two or three Christmases ago. As her hand rises to brush a bead of sweat off her forehead, she looks out the window at the pump house. If the temperature drops much lower, she might be thinking, their father may have to take his shotgun out there and fire it into a pipe to keep their water from freezing—that's happened before. Beyond the pump house is the smoke house, where you could cure bacon if you had hogs, but by this time they don't. Beyond the smoke house is the barn, where you could keep cows, but they don't have those either. Both buildings are just standing there waiting to fall down.

Their father enters, fully clothed for work in regulation gray Dickies. On a white patch above his heart his name scrolls out in red. He looks like a garage mechanic, which briefly he used to be, though neither of them remembers it. He farmed, he repaired cars at Loring Motors, he farmed again, now he drives the propane truck and fixes those radios and TVs on the weekend. An entire room is filled with them. He's made noise about converting the smoke house into a shop, but when would he do it? And who would help him? Their uncle lost his right hand last year while working at a cotton gin. They are the kind of people things like that happen to. You lose your hand, you get shot behind the counter at a liquor store, you eat too much Crisco and have a heart attack and die at forty. One day they'll be the subject of hill-billy elegies and Harvard dissertations. Now they're just folks who, for the most part, escape notice.

Which is how their mother likes it. By this time in her life, she doesn't want to be noticed. Mr. Wayne notices her. Mr. Burns, the regional boss for United Dollar Stores, whose thick bushy moustache, deep-set eyes and heavy eyebrows evoke G. Gordon Liddy—he notices her too.

Their father craves notice. He writes letters to the local paper, on subjects such as the failure of the county supervisors to properly grade gravel roads like the one they live on, the reported sighting of a nutria in Loring Bayou, the dangerous propensity of crop dusters for flying under power lines. He likes to get his name out there.

Just yesterday he received two boxes of business cards that he ordered from an office supply store in Jackson.

> *Alton Cole, C.E.T.*
> TV, Stereo and Radio Repair
> (Specializing in Citizen's Band,
> 27 MHz (11 meter)
> *Route 2, Box 79*
> Lording, Mississippi
> 601-887-2959

This morning he walks over to the stove and tries to hand her a small stack of them, maybe ten or fifteen. "Pass these out at the store," he says. "Give one to Mike Wayne and Tommy Burns and anybody else you think might need it."

Methodically she flips the bacon: two slices apiece for her and the girls, four for him. "Why would anybody need one?"

"Because folks know I'm doing it, and they know they can count on me to do it right."

"If they know that, why'd you have to spend fifteen dollars on cards to remind them?"

"Because the version of me that runs his own small business, as opposed to the one that drives that damn propane truck and comes home smelling like a walking fart, has to be aggressive."

She turns and examines the top card. "There's a missing parenthesis mark."

"No, there's not."

"Yes, there is." She taps the card. "There's an open parenthesis before the word 'specializing,' and then down on the next line there's an opening mark before the number '11' and a closing mark afterwards, but there should be two. Parentheses within parentheses. And by the way? Somebody misspelled 'Loring.' It says 'Lording.'"

There he stands, their father, bathed and groomed and not yet smelling like the gas he will spend the rest of the day delivering, driving around the county on farm roads, his only company the voices he hears on the E.F. Johnson White Face CB that he installed below the dash. Men with handles like "Pork Chop," "Coon Tail," "Double D," "White Knight." A woman who calls herself "Amazing Grace." As he studies the business card, marred now by mistakes, his face falls. It falls so far, so fast, that the collapse encapsulates both the lowness of his origins and the paucity of his aspirations. Anybody with even a measure of objectivity would feel a touch of pity.

But when it comes to their father, their mother is anything but objective. She turns back to the stove, to prevent him from seeing the faint smile she knows has appeared on her face—that's all the charity she's got left. "Fifteen dollars," she says. "Let's see." She shuts her eyes to do a little math. "At two dollars and ten cents an hour, I worked about seven hours and fifteen minutes to pay for those cards. Or to put it another way, you drove the truck five hours to buy them. Understand, that's leaving out taxes."

Except for spanking Caroline, their father has never been violent. Which is a good thing. If he were a violent man, he would clamp his surprisingly small, soft hands around her throat and choke her. He would squeeze all the breath from her body, then shove her face into the skillet to fry with the bacon.

A plate of freshly baked biscuits waits on the table. He grabs two of them and shoves one in each shirt pocket, fills his travel mug with steaming coffee, then walks out of the kitchen without saying goodbye.

This is the kind of thing that happens at Route 2, Box 79, early on a weekday morning before their mother knocks on their door and says "Time to rise and shine." Both of them *know* it, even though they don't know it.

JACKSON. A SATURDAY NIGHT in the spring of '75.

The bus pulls to the curb beside the Hotel Heidelberg, which is no longer a hotel but a place where meetings and competitions are held. Their music teacher makes the singers remain in their seats while Brad Moss and the other instrumentalists step off and collect their equipment from the baggage compartment.

Ella and Kim are dressed like all the other girls: lime-colored blouses and matching skirts, sleeveless emerald cardigans. Their music teacher got into a mini-spat with some of the parents at a recent PTA when they expressed displeasure that the school colors, red and gray, had not been chosen. She walked to the podium, said a single sentence— "Concert choir and the Madrigal Singers are not an extension of the football team"—then sat back down. She can get away with that kind of behavior. Her father is the mayor.

By design, they're sitting at the back of the bus. In her purse Kim has a half-pint of 'Roses, as they have come to call it, and both of them took a sip on the short drive from the motor inn where they're all spending the night. Earlier, on the two-hour ride down Highway 49, they each had a couple of swallows too. Kim believes in moderation, at least up to a point. "I just want that golden glow," she likes to say. "I don't want canary yellow." Ella is glad for the glow tonight. She was chosen to sing a solo.

She and Kim have been spending a lot of time together. Most afternoons, Ella goes over to study and talk and sip a little whiskey, and sometimes she stays for the night, even on weekdays. When she does go home, Kim drives her out in her little BMW, though she's never set foot inside the house. It's as if both of them understand this would lead to mutual embarrassment.

Three or four times, always on a weekend, they've ridden over to Greenville to watch a movie. Last Saturday they saw *Brannigan* and, on the way back, took turns imitating John Wayne.

That'll be two eggs lightly fried on both *sides, a rasher of bacon, and a modest stack of pancakes. . .*

Angell, you're a real bush-leaguer. . .

Kinda strange, havin' two cops advise you on what's in your client's best interest. . .

Her mother doesn't seem to mind that she's gone so often, and her father acts proud. Maybe one day, he says, she'll have a house like Kim's herself. He sees college in her future, Ole Miss or even Vanderbilt. She's got the grades and the gumption too. There's nothing his girl can't do.

Her sister has all but stopped speaking to her, and she has all but stopped caring. At night, Caroline bangs into the room, slamming the door behind her. In bed she doesn't roll over—she hurls her body from one position to the next, making the upper bunk quiver. In the hall between classes, she walks right past, chin tipped up, eyes trained on the end doors like she's plotting another escape. She's a moving mass of resentment.

Through the bus window, Ella sees Brad Moss step onto the sidewalk with his trumpet case. He plays saxophone and flute, too, as well as piano and guitar, and he can draw and paint and act. When they were handing out talent, Brad showed up with an eighteen-wheeler. He's been offered football scholarships by Ole Miss, Mississippi State, Southern and Auburn, but he chose Ole Miss because they also agreed to let him play baseball. At the dinner table last week, she heard Mr. Taggart say that he called the athletic director on Brad's behalf. "I said listen, if you want this kid to play ball for you, you're going to have to play ball with him. So he misses a few days of spring training to go across the street and chase flies in centerfield. So what?"

"I'll bet you he never starts one game for Ole Miss," Mrs. Taggart said with surprising vigor.

"I guess you know better than the coaches and the athletic director, since they want him pretty bad."

"I may not know football better than they do, but I know an immature cry baby when I see one. The first time he gets hit by a hungry black kid, he'll quit being Brad Moss and turn into Chicken Little."

Mr. Taggart changed the subject, but later that evening, on the way to brush her teeth, Ella heard raised voices coming from the master bedroom.

"I think I was conceived here," Kim says now.

"In Jackson?"

"In the Hotel Heidelberg. My folks spent their wedding night in there. They got married at the Loring Country Club, and they were on their way to Gulf Shores for their honeymoon, but just as they pulled into Jackson the radio broadcast a tornado warning. So they headed for the closest decent hotel, which happened to be this one. I was born eight and a half months later." She leans closer and drops her voice even lower. "I'm pretty sure my mom was a virgin when they married. Do you think yours was?"

"I don't think about such things."

"You're lying."

"That's true. It'd probably be more accurate to say that I do think about them, though I try not to, and that what I really don't do is talk about them."

"Not even with me?"

"Not even with you."

"I bet I could get you to."

"I doubt it," Ella says because she suddenly, badly, wants her to try.

"For instance . . ." Kim says, but their music teacher tells them it's time to get off the bus, go inside and set up.

Kim rises but lets the pair of sophomores in the seat opposite theirs step into the aisle first. As those two head toward the front, she says, "For instance, what if I told you that Brad has the hots for your mom?"

"My mom is *forty*."

Her friend stands between her and the aisle. She's two or three inches taller than Ella, and her wrists and knees and shoulders are bigger than they look when you see her in the classroom. She's a person whose corporeality—another of Mrs. Batch's words—cannot be ignored. "Brad fantasizes about making it with her," she whispers, "in the backseat of that old Galaxy. Right out there behind the United Dollar Store in broad daylight."

"Brad told you that? He said that about him and my mom?"

Everybody else has gotten off the Greyhound. The driver is looking over his shoulder.

Kim steps into the aisle, then laughs. "He didn't have to tell me. I know what he's thinking. I know what *Brad* wants."

•

The grand ballroom, if that's what it used to be, looks shabby now. A threadbare brown carpet covers the wooden floor, visible where the fabric is particularly frayed. A stage has been erected at one end of the room, and in front of that there are fifteen or twenty rows of mostly empty metal folding chairs. Notes have been taped to five seats in the front row. *Reserved for Judges.*

Groups from numerous schools are assembling, and it doesn't take long for the scene to turn cacophonous. The guitarists and bass players locate unclaimed outlets, plug their amps in and start playing riffs, the horn players begin honking and squawking, and on the stage the percussionists start assembling their drum kits and arguing over space, which is going to be at a premium with this many contestants.

Kim rolls her eyes toward the ceiling, where fluorescent lighting has replaced the chandeliers that must once have hung there. "Just imagine," she says. "Somewhere on one of the upper floors, in a bed that probably went to a discount furniture store when this place closed down, my mother and father took part in carnal congress."

"You make it sound like an act of legislation."

"Well, that's what it was. They legislated me into existence. And if it weren't too late, my mom would try to repeal me."

"You don't really think that."

Creases begin to form around Kim Taggart's eyes. Her nose wrinkles, and her lips jut into a duck's beak. One sob, all the more persuasive because unaccompanied, escapes. "Yes. . . I really do."

Before Ella can put an arm around her, Brad Moss materializes with his sparkling trumpet, banishing every last trace of her friend's dismay. "Y'all need to hustle up. Miss Young says time to go backstage."

For the remainder of the proceedings, there in the building where Kim believes she was conceived, she never once meets Ella's gaze. Their troupe is last on the schedule, so there's plenty of idle time behind the curtains, but she spends it in a corner with Brad and a couple of other senior guys chattering with a group of girls from Jackson Prep, the ritziest school in the state. Rumor has it Brad started dating a Preppie after he signed with Ole Miss, which makes it all the more surprising to see Kim so engaged. Until today, though they've talked about all kinds of things, and lots of different people, Kim had never said Brad's name. Ella assumed he was out of the picture. Now it looks like he's back in it.

Finally, it's their turn to perform. They sing "Vehicle," "The Way We Were," "Hooked on a Feeling" and a couple of choral numbers. Then it's time for her solo. Even though Kim is standing on the rafter right behind her, she fails to wish her good luck as she steps down to confront the mic. How much could a whisper have cost?

The only instrument Ella owns is the one she was born with, and while she would love to play the piano, she has always made do with what she's got. A five hundred dollar scholarship is riding on her performance. Win it this year and next, and she'll have a year's tuition at State or Ole Miss. That's why she was so unhappy when their music teacher chose "Moon River" for her solo. Everybody's heard the song so many times that they will probably tune out when she sings the first words.

But they don't. They hear what she can't, a pronounced lack of affect. She forgets about her diaphragm, her lungs and her ribs, she neglects to flex her facial muscles. Rather than look at the audience, which has grown to a few hundred people, she stares at a large photo mounted on the rear wall: the Hotel Heidelberg in its heyday. Against a black sky, it's lit from within, the lights on in every room, cars like those in gangster movies clogging the streets. A safe place to shelter from the deadliest of storms, to curl up in bed with someone you love, if you've got someone to love. But she doesn't.

"I think," the head judge will intone fifteen minutes from now when he hands her the gold medal, "that what did it for one of my colleagues . . ." a glance at his notes . . . "was the 'effortless chromatic glissandos.' She's a little more erudite than I am. I voted for you because of the lump I felt in my throat when you caressed the words 'my huckleberry friend.' I've had a huckleberry friend or two myself." He waves his notes at the audience. "I bet everybody here has. Congratulations, Miss Ella Cole. The check, as they say, is in the mail."

.

Because the scholarship winners in each category had to fill out forms listing their names and addresses, she was the last one to reach the Greyhound. She expected to find Brad seated next to Kim, but for some reason he wasn't on the bus at all. Kim beckoned from the back. On her way down the aisle Ella received congratulations from three or four people, all of them guys. A couple of girls that she'd always gotten along well with averted their eyes. Being friends with certain people has an upside and a downside.

"You were great," Kim said, sliding over to make room. The bus doors closed, and the driver pulled away from the curb. Kim didn't even bother to conceal her bottle, raising it and taking a much larger swallow than Ella had ever seen her take before. "Here," she said. "Hit it hard. You deserve it. And by the way? There's another one in our room. I hid it in my suitcase."

She felt fabulous. Brad Moss was nowhere to be found, she'd won a chunk of money to spend on college, her talent had been recognized, and she was with the coolest girl around. She deserved the drink. She deserved as many as she wanted, and she wanted quite a few. She swallowed once, and when it had gone down she drained the bottle.

"Atta girl," her friend said. "We're going to raise ourselves some hell."

They were staying at a motel on Lamar Street called the Sun 'n' Sand. Though she wouldn't know this until she decided to Google it thirty years later, in the early '60s it had served as the Jackson base for many state legislators, who favored it because a reliable bootlegger lived close by. After they legalized booze in 1965, it got the first liquor license in town.

By the spring of '75 it was starting to look rundown. An E-shaped structure arranged around a pool with no sand in sight, it had rooms on both floors. Something that hadn't registered earlier, due perhaps to her anxiety about the competition, was that the room she and Kim were sharing was in a different wing from all the others, and it was upstairs, whereas the others apparently were on the ground floor. As they climbed the stairs, she asked her friend about it.

"My dad arranged it," Kim said. "I told him you were nervous about performing and needed a quiet place to relax before the competition." She mentioned the names of two other girls. "They were supposed to be in here with us, but he got them their own room too."

Ella paused on the next to last stair. "Does Miss Young know?"

"Of course. He told her about it. I don't think she liked it. But so what? What can Miss *Young* do?"

"Her father's the mayor."

"Who do you think bankrolled his last two campaigns?"

Number 210 was at the end of the hall. While she went to the bathroom, Kim messed with the clock radio. "Something's wrong with this thing," Ella heard her say. "No music tonight."

It had occurred to her some time ago that Kim didn't especially enjoy music. Despite singing in Concert Choir and the Madrigals, she had almost no vocal range and was plagued by pitch problems. She never turned music on when Ella slept over, though she always said she planned to.

Ella washed her hands and stepped out of the bathroom. "Well, we've had nothing but music all night long. I wouldn't mind a little silence. Where's your other bottle?"

Kim pulled the cardigan over her head and tossed it on a chair. She sat down on the bed closest to the window and propped herself against the vinyl headboard. From beneath the cover she withdrew a half-pint of Four Roses. "Actually, I have not one but two bottles. In other words, an honest to Jesus pint of pure unadulterated whiskey. But I've also got something to tell you, Ella." She paused and studied her for a moment, then continued, "And I think I might as well go ahead and get it said now. It feels like the honest thing to do. I mean, we're friends, right? And friends need to be straight with each other. That's how I look at it."

The distance between them could not be measured by conventional means. She had known that last fall, up until the day when they went to work on that poor frog. Since then, she'd let herself start thinking they were almost equals. Though Kim was a good student, she'd made a couple of Bs, whereas in her entire life Ella had never earned less than an A. She could sing, and Kim couldn't. She'd learned French, and Kim hadn't. Her face and hair were about as nice as her friend's, and she didn't have the worries about weight that she knew visited themselves upon Kim from time to time. Kim had one thing she didn't: the confidence that came with her last name.

How long she stood there with a stricken look was something she'd wonder about later. Tomorrow it would seem longer than it did tonight, and next week it would seem longer than it would tomorrow. A year from now it would seem like forever. Some moments, if you let them, stretch into infinity.

"The second bottle," Kim said slowly, "is not W-H-I-S-K-*E*-Y. It's W-H-I-S-*K*-Y. In other words, baby, I'm sorry to admit it's Scotch." Grinning, she pulled a half-pint of Cutty Sark from beneath the covers and laid it beside the Four Roses. "Fooled you, didn't I? You thought I'd tell you Coach Raleigh got me pregnant, or something even worse." Patting the mattress, she said, "Let's drink to your stupendous success."

They'd eaten dinner before the competition, a good five and a half hours ago, and because her stomach was full of butterflies she hadn't done much more than pick at her food. She was not very big, and the booze she'd chugged on the bus had already begun to affect her. She knew she ought to be careful. She also knew she might never again be where she was tonight. What she didn't know was whether two years from now she'd be in a dorm at Ole Miss or Vanderbilt, or behind a cash register at Piggly Wiggly or the Delta Diner or maybe even United Dollar Store. This might be the only success she'd ever have to drink to.

She walked over and sat down on the bed beside her friend, her back against the headboard. They started with the 'Roses, drinking faster than before. Time must have been passing like time always does, but she didn't sense one moment turning into the next. She had not yet learned that there are no mile markers on the road to oblivion. When the first bottle was empty, Kim uncapped the Scotch.

If they talked about anything important, she wouldn't recall it the next day. She remembered the TV on the dresser and how, at some point, Kim said, "Wouldn't it be great if we could see ourselves there, if we could watch ourselves watching ourselves? Wouldn't you like that, Muffin?" She didn't understand why Kim called her "Muffin," since she'd never called her that before, and she didn't understand what would be so great about watching themselves on the TV as they sat guzzling whiskey.

There were still a few swallows left in the second bottle when Kim reached over and turned out the light. It was as if they'd both been waiting for these hours in a rented room that nobody else had a key to. It was all very gauzy—that was how she'd describe it many years later in the office of a Back Bay therapist, on a day when a winter storm morphed into a full-scale blizzard, burying Boston beneath three feet of snow and forcing her to spend the evening right there on the couch, wrapped in a couple of blankets.

Kim's kisses were aggressive, nothing like the gentle ones she'd given her when she visited the Taggarts' house. She only let up to say things that made little or no sense.

I hate my life.

One day I'll be fat.

I'm drowning. Are you?

You are, aren't you? Aren't you drowning too?

The night called for the subjunctive mood. If she were to offer answers, what might they be? If she were to resist, how might she do it?

If she were unhappy, wouldn't she know it?

If this were to last forever, mightn't that be nice?

How long it lasted, she couldn't say, but it was a far cry from forever. One moment she was wild with wonder, the next moment filled with lassitude, disinterested in everything except closing her eyes. She fell asleep on her side, Kim behind her, one arm locked over her ribcage. She couldn't have escaped if she wanted to, which she didn't.

·

When she woke, Kim's arm was gone. The bedside clock said 3:21 AM. The spot where her friend had been was empty but still warm.

Her mouth was full of acid, her head pounding. She believed it might be in her best interest to get to the bathroom as fast as she could. The problem was that something seemed to be happening in the other bed. Rhythmic breathing, creaking springs. At first, all she could see was a moving gray lump. Gradually the outlines of not one but two heads took shape. One above the other.

"Fuck yeah. Hell fucking yeah."

"You and your little Preppie. I ought to cut your balls off."

"You wouldn't dare."

"I will one day."

"Yeah?"

"Yeah. I'll crack your eggs open and froth 'em for an omelet."

"You know where I'd like to fuck you?"

"Where?"

"In a cotton trailer."

"I'd get burrs up my ass."

"You'd love it."

Ella pulled the covers over her head, burying her face in the pillow. If only she were deaf. Or maybe even dead.

The sounds finally stopped. She realized she'd been holding her breath, that she was about to suffocate, but she was scared that if she inhaled it would result in an audible gasp. She let a little air in, then let it out. The bed had grown damp from her sweat.

In a few minutes, the springs squeaked again. Someone rose and padded across the carpet. She heard water splashing, then the toilet flushed. Once more the sound of soft footsteps. Then a hand pulled the covers off her head, and Brad Moss lay down beside her.

What he might have said, if he would have said anything at all, she would never know. She rolled off the opposite side of the bed, slammed into the wall, then ran toward the door. She felt for the light switch, intending to turn it on so she could see where he was, but then she realized she was naked.

Brad Moss was not used to hearing the word No, but that was what she said. She said it in the firmest possible way, in a voice as calm and steady as she could make it. "No, Brad. No."

He switched on the beside lamp. He sat staring at her as if she'd lost her mind. His chest was completely hairless, not at all like her father's. He was already erect again. She didn't know it could happen that fast.

"No?" he said. He looked from her to Kim, who'd thrown an arm over her eyes, as if to shield them from the glare. Back at Ella. "You're lucky to be here, you know that? Your momma works at the Dollar Store, and your daddy drives that old gas truck." He rose and walked toward her, grinning and bouncing his penis off his palm.

Mrs. Taggart was right about his future. He would never start a football game at Ole Miss. He'd ride the bench for two years and then quit and serve mostly as a backup in baseball to hang onto his scholarship. After graduation he'd enter law school at Tulane and, once he'd earned his degree, he'd remain in New Orleans and go to work for a corporate law firm. He'd quit that when he was thirty-five and begin a new life as a public defender. When Katrina hit, he would spend a couple of days helping rescue people from flooded homes in the Ninth Ward. She'd see his photo in the *Boston Globe*, pudgy bald Brad in a fishing boat filled with black children.

Tonight, though, he was not pudgy and bald, he was tall and he was hard and there was nothing he might not do and nothing she could do to stop him. So she threw the door open and dashed into the hall.

Brad Moss stuck his head out, laughed loudly and slammed the door shut. Over the sound of her own pounding footsteps, she heard the deadbolt click.

THE HOUSEKEEPING CLOSET WAS NEAR the snack machines and ice maker. Filled with buckets, mops and cleaning supplies like Comet and Lysol, it should have been locked. But it wasn't. Once inside, when she tried to lock it herself, she discovered why. The strike plate was missing. So she shoved a couple of buckets against the door, knowing they wouldn't stop anybody determined to enter, then sat down on a small footstool and wrapped her arms around herself. Before long, she was shivering. She looked for something to cover herself with, but the only piece of fabric she saw was a grimy towel that smelled like paint thinner and wasn't large enough anyhow.

"Ella can go to sleep everywhere," her future husband would say. "In a taxi, on a plane, on the subway, at Fenway. I don't know how she does it." She didn't know how she did it either, especially while naked and half-frozen, but that was what happened. She was still sitting on the footstool hugging herself, her head lolled back against the cinderblock wall, when suddenly the door creaked open. She heard somebody cry, "Lord Almighty!" At first she thought it had come from her own throat, but when she opened her eyes, she saw a black woman framed in the doorway.

She was tall and about fifty, in a white skirt and blouse that made her look like either a waitress or a nurse. She had long, black hair of the type that Ella had heard her grandmother and others call "straightened." She used to wonder how they could know it had been straightened, unless of course they asked, which seemed unlikely.

On top of her blouse the woman wore a thick wool jacket. She pulled it off, stepped over to Ella and threw it around her shoulders. "What're you doing in my closet in this shape? Somebody been messing with you, hadn't they?"

There didn't seem to be much point in denying the obvious, especially since this black woman dressed in white represented her only sliver of hope. "Yes, ma'am."

"I bet that's the first time you ever told a black lady yes ma'am. Am I right about that?"

"Yes, ma'am."

The woman didn't exactly smile, but it seemed like maybe she considered it. "I guess that's what we need. A bunch of naked white people looking for their clothes. You know where yours are, I suppose?"

"They're in room 210. Or, anyway, they were."

"And who's in room 210 with them?"

"This friend of mine. And a guy."

"The guy not your friend too?"

"No, ma'am."

She pulled a ring of keys from her skirt pocket. "With my luck, she'll be the granddaughter of Jim Eastland, and he'll be the governor's boy. But I'm going and see can I get 'em for you. The college boy down there pretending to be a night clerk, he won't want to deal with it, he'll just call the Jackson police, and then you'll end up in trouble with whoever should have kept you from putting yourself in this situation to start with. You believe in God?"

Ella wasn't sure. "Yes, ma'am."

"Then you better say a prayer that when I bang on their door, they don't call me you-know-what. They do, we'll both end up in trouble. And I can't afford that. I don't know about you."

The woman left. Ella waited there on the stool, all but certain that Brad and Kim would ignore her knock, force her to unlock it with one of those keys, and then Brad would call the woman you-know-what, and then the woman would say something back, and a scene would erupt, lots of hollering back and forth. Folks on the floor below, including Miss Young, would hear the fracas, and in no time she would be found hungover and naked, and come Monday the school, if not the entire town, would be talking of nothing else. That would be bad enough. But what hurt more was that she wouldn't be able to seek comfort from her friend, since her friend was the cause of her misery. She couldn't talk to her sister about what had happened, either, because her sister felt abandoned, and she couldn't talk to her mom about it, because her mom would tell her she'd been a fool, which was true. She couldn't talk to her dad, for fear he'd kill Brad Moss. All she could do was hope things worked out better than she expected, that in a few moments the woman would come back with her clothes.

To her surprise, that was exactly what happened, and it took next to no time. She hadn't heard a thing.

"Here you are," the black lady said. She handed over her shoes and travel bag and said the clothes and her toothbrush were inside it. "That boy down there," she said, "he act just like a lamb, did everything but bleat. I told him I called the police, that he better not get caught with your clothes when they show up. Now what I want you to do's put them on and get out of my closet." She turned her back to allow her to dress unobserved.

When she got her clothes on, she started to leave, then stopped and said, "Thank you so much." That was when the tears finally began their sad cascade.

She thought maybe the woman would hug her, and she wanted her to as badly as she'd ever wanted anything. But no hug was forthcoming. Instead, she pulled a wad of Kleenex out of her pocket and shoved it into Ella's hand. "Don't let me see you squall," she said.

BETWEEN THAT THING AND THE next thing—the thing that can't be undone or looked back on through gauzy nostalgia—there's a blank spot. It will remain blank for years. Ella sees it as a sheet of stationary, nearly always lavender. Why lavender? Who has lavender-colored stationary? Why not just a plain white sheet of paper? Why color it and invest it with attitude, meaning, significance? Yet lavender it usually is, except a couple of times when it turns the same shade of orange as the sherbet their grandmother used to buy them at the Walk-In. *Share*but, they learned not to call it by the age of nine or ten after the other kids made fun.

One day she will pay a lot of money in an effort to recover some of what transpired in that three-week gap. But Caroline will have no such problem. For Caroline, the blank is filled in. During the daytime, her sister behaves as if everything is normal, doing her homework, going to school, making those straight-laced A's. Yeah, she's even quieter than usual, and she walks with her head down, and she never goes over to the house on the bayou anymore, but if she is aware of the rumors, there's no visual evidence.

Caroline hears what people are saying in the hallway. They like to say it when she's around, pretending to drop their voices to a whisper. Word is that down in Jackson, Kim and Brad Moss were in the motel room getting it on when the Christmas tree angel tried to get involved. People are saying that Kim and Brad were both revolted, that Brad shoved her into the hall and told her to carry her sick white-trash ass elsewhere.

Brad, word is, has taken some ribbing about it, but every time one of his buddies brings it up, he says: "I wouldn't fuck her if you let me use *your* dick," which always elicits the same response: "I wouldn't let you use my dick if I knew you aimed to stick it in *her*." Some say she was found passed out naked in a broom closet, that a janitor threatened to call the police. What's not open to conjecture is how she got home: she rode alone in the back of the bus, her face turned to the window, her moment of glory at the vocal competition drowned beneath a wave at the Sun 'n' Sand.

Caroline doesn't know what did or didn't happen, and the possibility of discussion and commiseration no longer exists. What she believes, though, is the evidence she hears with her own ears, when she lies in the lower bunk unable to sleep, dreading the next day and the day after that and all the days in all the years that stretch out ahead of her like a long ribbon of blacktop, a road that sometimes bisects a desert, sometimes snakes its way through a gorge, sometimes curls around the shoulder of a mountain in a hairpin turn that you'll have to take on faith if you can find some. It's a single word that she hears coming from the bunk above her own, always the same one, sometimes a sigh, sometimes a cry, sometimes in disbelief with a question mark attached, the same word again and again.

Kim. Kim! Kim?

ONE MORNING, ONE MORNING, ONE morning in May.

They're sitting in Algebra when it happens, together again in the only class they share, Ella on one side of the room, Caroline on the other. The teacher is explaining why *Pi* can never be expressed as the quotient of two integers. Neither girl is paying attention. Ella is gazing at the back of the girl directly in front of her, willing herself not to look at the first row, where Brad Moss is sitting in the seat she used to occupy. Caroline is reading the paperback novel hidden behind her open textbook, something called *One for the Gods*, about a romantic triangle between two men and a woman who yacht around the Mediterranean screwing fore and aft. She can't imagine how this wretched book found its way onto the book rack at Mr. Quik, but it did, and she appropriated it a couple of days ago. Sometimes you have to make do.

The intercom crackles, and the principal's voice—oddly subdued—says: "We need the Cole girls down in the office."

Twenty-four pairs of eyes watch the two of them rise. Each of the sisters resists the urge to glance at the other, both of them knowing that whatever led to this summons can't possibly be anything good.

•

I Believe in Propane.

That's what the sign on the wall behind the desk of their father's boss says. Everybody in town knows this, though few of them have seen it. They only see what you see when you enter through the front to pay your bills. There are always limits to what the public knows. The public finds out some things and invents the rest, depending on the story it wants to tell itself. In the months and years ahead, Ella will invent her own version of this May morning, too, a version that will be revised many times, depending on numerous factors, chief among them her mood in the moments in which she re-imagines it. The only thing that never changes is the ending.

As she sees it, their father walks into the office at the rear of the building to learn that for the third time this week, Mr. Barkley chose to sleep late and hand the morning's duties off to his son William. All of twenty-two, William is wearing a crisp, white long-sleeved shirt and a blue tie that looks like real silk. His dad's making him work at the plant for a year before he returns to Vanderbilt to earn his MBA.

"How are you this morning, Mr. Cole?" William asks.

"Just fine, William. What about you?"

Young Barkley lifts a stack of papers, taps it against the desktop, then lays the stack right back where it was. "Franklin woke me at four-thirty. I don't know what set him off."

While it's not strange to know the name of your employer's German Shepherd, her father might be thinking, it is odd for his son to assume that you do—or that if by chance you don't, you should. "Probably a cat," he helpfully offers.

"Maybe so. To make matters worse, Mr. Majori's not feeling well. He called in sick."

Mr. Majori is the father of Irwin, the boy who kissed Ella on the turnrow. "I bet it's his gall bladder," she hears her father say. "It's been acting up." Ricky Majori, her father once told her mother, would love to have his gall bladder removed, just as he would love to have his prolapsed discs repaired, but he has no health insurance. Barkley Petroleum doesn't provide it. Like her parents, he's insured his kids, but that's about all he can do.

"At any rate, some of his scheduled deliveries are pretty pressing. This lady . . ." Ella sees William Barkley consult a scrap of paper, then point at the name on it with a neatly clipped nail. ". . . She's been pretty insistent, three calls since last Friday. Mrs. Pace. Oh, my, look at that."

A giggle. "Grace. Grace Pace. And she lives on the Quiver River!" Still grinning, he looks up at her dad. "That's so funny. Don't you think?"

Did her father, as William will report to Mr. Barkley and numerous others, really get a strange look on his face before replying, "Yeah. It's doggone hilarious."

•

Nearly forty years from now, she will finally gaze upon the remains of the Paces' farmhouse, on the east bank of the Quiver River. Anybody inclined to disbelief, assuming they have access to an old phone book or the inclination to research county records, can look up the address. Grady and Grace Pace, 100 Quiver River Road, Loring, Mississippi.

At one time, her father knew that house as well as his own. He and Grady Pace went to school together. They played football and baseball together, and neither of them was very good. They both served in Korea. That was where their respective fates diverged. Alton Cole joined the navy and never heard a shot fired. Grady Pace, on the other hand, could not swim. Inducted into the army, he ended up in Task Force Faith and became one of the unit's 385 infantrymen who survived the Battle of Chosin Reservoir—the *Weekly Times* published an article about him after he returned. Unfortunately, frostbite cost him three toes on one foot, two on the other, and much of the equilibrium that comes from having five on each.

Grady Pace used to fall a lot. It began to happen as soon as he returned home to help on his father's place. He'd climb down off their Allis-Chalmers and fall on his face. That was bad enough, but at least he could put his hand out to lessen the impact. Finally, a little more than ten years before the day William Barkley dispatched her father to deliver their gas, Mr. Pace fell over backwards. It wasn't out there on their farm, it was in the sanctuary of Quiver River Baptist Church, while he and another deacon moved along the center aisle picking up the collection plates and handing them to people in the next row. He banged his head on a hardwood pew. Now—on this particular morning in May of '75— his brain is no longer able to send certain signals to his legs. He's been confined to a wheelchair since November of '64. You could read about that in the *Weekly Times* too.

Her father has never made a delivery to the Paces. Before they were on Ricky Majori's route, they were on someone else's. But due to Mr. Majori's gall bladder, which he can't get rid of because the Affordable Care Act is several decades away, there's nothing to do but head out there. With any luck, he must be thinking, he'll be able to fill their tank and escape unnoticed. The tank's not all that close to their house.

She sees him climb into the old bobtail. Soon he's out in the countryside near where he was raised, driving down a narrow gravel road. The land out here's some of the worst in the county, too much acid in the ground, she once heard him say. The only things that grow well are red vines, tea weed, cockleburs and Johnson grass. It's hard to forge a life out here farming, but Grady and Grace Pace have attempted it, with predictable results.

He crosses the rickety bridge over the Quiver. Normally, the first thing he does after starting the truck is to turn on his CB. Did he do that this morning? Has he already heard her voice crackling over the Johnson White Face? Amazing Grace. KBR-7945. He's been hearing her for years.

Ella watches the bobtail slow down as he approaches their place. He drives past the house toward the tractor shed and nearby storage tank. He pulls up to the tank. He shuts off the motor. He jumps out. He slams the door.

It isn't as if he never encounters her. One Saturday last fall, according to the owner of Loring Hardware, her father was in the store, trying to find a part for their leaking toilet, when he heard her voice: "I need a box of Remington .20 gauges. Birdshot'll do. An old stray's been hanging around. I don't want to kill it if I can run it off." Word will have it that her dad hunkered down in the plumbing section, pretending to examine various wax rings until she left, that he remained there for over half an hour, probably hoping she'd be in the pickup and gone by the time he reached the street. He walked out without buying anything, which amused the hardware owner.

At home, in a safe spot, where he thinks they will never be found, her dad has all the letters he wrote to Grace when he was in the navy as well as the ones she wrote him. When she she returned the ones he'd written, did she ask for hers back? If so, he must have lied and said he'd lost them, or destroyed them, or whatever. The other thing he has is a handful of letters he wrote her years later, after Mr. Pace was already in the wheelchair. It will subsequently emerge that she gave those letters back only after Mr. Pace learned of their existence.

Her father must have created commotion pulling up to that tank. The Paces have a dog, which has crept out from under their house and is barking his head off. The dog no doubt annoys their father, who must have been hoping that he could complete the task he was sent to perform and escape without confrontation. She sees him hurry to the rear of the truck to release the filler hose. She watches as temptation gets the best of him and he risks a single glance at their house. Grace Pace is standing on the back porch staring at him. She's got on a pair of faded jeans and a tie-dyed tee shirt like she's some kind of hippy though she's forty-two years old. Even from this distance he must see the freckles that cover her arms and face. Her hair's still short and still reddish-orange and she's still puffing Pall Malls, because when was she not? That's one thing everyone can agree on, even Mr. Pace.

Mrs. Pace continues to stand there observing their father as he reels out the hose. What's going through his mind? Is he thinking that if she were to say *Come on, Alton, let's jump in that truck and take off, cross the big river and never look back*, he'd climb into the bobtail with her and disappear, leaving his wife and daughters behind? Or is he thinking that in life you have to make choices, that as bad as he wants her, he made his choice and plans to honor it? Either is possible. It's wrong to exclude the latter just because the former yields more drama.

Grace opens the screen door and steps off the porch. Alton Cole holds that hose, watching her walk toward him.

When she's close enough for him to see sunlight glinting off both her damp cheeks, she says, "Where's Majori? You're not supposed to be here, Alton. You *know* you're not supposed to." She gestures over her shoulder with her cigarette. "Grady saw you out the window. He's fit to be tied."

Who in God's name needs to be tied when he's already stuck in a wheelchair? "Ricky had a gall bladder attack," Ella hears her father say. "You've been hollering for gas, and I'm the only driver available. What do you want me to do, Grace?"

The world is so goddamn unfair, she believes her father is thinking. Not only can he not have the only woman he's ever loved, he can't even get a business card printed right. "Just let me do my job," he says. "Leave me the fuck alone, and I'll be away from here and gone."

He gives the refill hose a mean-spirited jerk, slamming the brass nozzle against a badly corroded release valve. Vaporized propane shoots from the tank that Grady Pace will tell the *Weekly Times* he and Alton Cole used to straddle as boys, pretending it was a stallion they could ride to kingdom come. Grace has just taken another puff of her cigarette when the gas hits her in the face and she and Ella's father both go up in flames.

THE FUNERAL HOME WAS DOWNTOWN, across from the Methodist Church. Caroline had been inside it once before, when their grandmother died. She hadn't cried that day, though she'd felt like it. This morning, the impulse was missing. Why pretend her father ever gave a damn about her? He didn't. He couldn't. Why, she'd never know. Her grandmother's explanation—*Y'all are too much alike*—never made any sense, though nearly all her other observations did. In a way it might be a relief not to have to keep wondering why he didn't love her. She didn't yet know the wondering wouldn't cease just because his heart no longer beat.

His body, properly speaking, didn't even exist anymore. The coroner, quoted yesterday in the newspaper, said, "It wasn't a whole lot different from what happened at Hiroshima. One minute they were both here, and the next minute they weren't." The casket, which rested on a portable pedestal in the visitation room across from the chapel, remained closed. A wreathe from Barkley Petroleum winged it on one side. On the other, a much larger wreathe with no note attached.

Scandal thickened the air. Coming out of the restroom a few moments ago, Caroline overheard a snippet, the coroner and her father's fellow driver Ricky Majori talking with their backs turned. "I hear Grady's planning to sue y'all," the coroner said.

"He ain't suing me. When it happened, I was on my knees at home puking."

"You know Alton and Grace used to . . ."

"Yeah, I know."

"Word is, they never quite quit."

"Yeah, I know that too."

"Seems like maybe it runs in the family. Both of them girls of theirs ... well, I imagine you've heard about them."

"Hasn't everybody?"

"You think Alton blew himself and Grace up on purpose? That's what Grady claims. Poor bastard watched 'em through the window."

"I don't have no opinion. Only thing I can say for sure's I was busy puking."

Her sister had been doing the same thing, even though her most recent meal was days ago. Last night the doctor finally gave her a shot and knocked her out. Now she was sitting on a couch opposite the casket, her jaws lank, her eyes gazing at the floor like she wished she were underneath it.

Their mother emerged from an anteroom, holding the arm of an ancient preacher. Caroline wondered where he had been unearthed. He wore a gray suit and had a few threads of gray hair. Even his face was gray. He looked like a Confederate monument. "I'll ask the rest of the family to join me," he wheezed.

Her sister didn't move, so Caroline stepped over to the couch and said, "Come on." She took her hand and pulled her up, surprised at her feathery lightness.

The pallbearers rolled the casket over to the door that led to the chapel, and all of them started down the aisle behind it, the preacher and their mother on one side, she and Ella on the other.

The chapel was nearly empty. Mr. Wayne and Mr. Burns from the dollar store chain were there, as well as a black woman who worked with her mother and was called Smokey, though that wasn't her name. The former postmaster was there, as was the other old man she used to see around the library before they banned her for stealing books. Three or four men she'd glimpsed on streets downtown, nearly always dressed in overalls, though today they wore suits. Local farmers, she figured, probably from her dad's delivery routes. William Barkley was there but not his father. His failure to attend might have had something to do with the lawsuit Barkley Petroleum expected—correctly, it would turn out—to be filed against the company. The presence of these few people did not surprise Caroline, nor did the absence of others.

What did surprise her was the sight of Coach Raleigh and, just ahead of him in the next pew, Mrs. Taggart. She thought she saw the coach's face turning pink as she passed. Mrs. Taggart clutched a white handkerchief.

The oration lacked both direction and inspiration, as it became clear at the outset that the minister did not know their father from Adam or, for that matter, Eve. He apparently thought he worked at a filling station, which led him to rhapsodize about "the absolute centrality of gas pump attendants in a vehicular culture like ours." At one point, he speculated that it would not be long before he met up with the deceased in the great beyond, since he himself was now ninety-four years old. He hadn't missed being a Confederate by all that much.

Once or twice, Caroline glanced past her nearly comatose sister at their mom. She looked straight ahead, her eyes as clear as Ella's were cloudy. It was as if she were preparing to confront their collective future head-on. Come October, when Ella was a senior and Caroline a junior, she would miss the first house payment, and by January would fall behind on their tuition. Due to the intervention of an anonymous benefactor, they would both be allowed to finish the year, meaning that Ella would graduate from Loring Academy, though Caroline would not. Ella's senior year would be spent in grim silence except when she opened her mouth to sing at vocal competitions or in the back yard, where in good weather she went to practice scales. She would spend hours studying for the ACT and would test at the top.

Some months later, when Ella started school at the east coast college that had awarded her a voice scholarship, Caroline would be living in Pine Bluff, Arkansas, with their mother and Mr. Burns, the regional manager of United Dollar Store, where she would work after school and on the weekends. Big changes lay ahead. A year and a half from the day of her father's funeral, she'd be back on the road, like the afternoon her mom put her out of the car and told her to find her way home.

•

At the graveside service, the minister got their father's name wrong, referring to him as Allen rather than Alton. After a three-gun salute, a navy bugler played "Taps," and then an honor guard bent before their mother and, on behalf of the president and the congress and the joint chiefs of staff and all the other unnamed citizens of the greatest country on earth, presented her with a neatly folded flag that resembled a tricorn hat. The preacher said another prayer, concluding—bizarrely, Caroline thought—with a request for their father to tell his own dearly departed wife that he'd be seeing her again soon, probably a little later this year or early the next. The few folks who'd made it over from the funeral home wasted no time leaving. Except for Mrs. Taggart, who was still sitting in her Cadillac, sipping from a flask, when Caroline and her mother and sister drove away.

THE SUMMER OF '76. THE BICENTENNIAL. The big goodbye.

Ella is alone at home, though it will not be home much longer. Mr. Burns, whom her mother plans to marry, has directed Mr. Wayne to hire Caroline part-time, so she's prowling the aisles, charged with keeping an eye on potential shoplifters. Every day she returns with a few pilfered items: a deodorant stick, a pair of tweezers, an emery board.

They've sold a lot of their stuff. What they haven't sold has been boxed up. The boxes are stacked in the living room, in the kitchen, in her parents' bedroom. There are boxes in hers and Caroline's room, too, but they only contain Caroline's possessions. Her own things were shipped to Massachusetts last week. Mr. Burns paid the bill.

Mr. Burns is a stubby man, a couple of inches shorter than their mom. His fingers are short and plump. They remind her of Vienna sausages. Not the real ones, which she hasn't yet seen and doesn't even know about, but the ones that come in a can. Her father used to eat those with Saltine crackers. She ate them too. He told her they were good and she believed him.

There is nothing Mr. Burns could tell her that she would believe. He's told her he loves her mother, and she doesn't believe that. When she asked her sister if she believed him, Caroline shrugged and said, "Whatever." Mr. Burns has told her Ouachita Baptist University, which also offered her a scholarship, is just as good as the Berklee College of Music, and she doesn't believe that. He's told her he probably makes more money overseeing all the United Dollar Stores in the ArkLaMiss than she will ever make singing or teaching others to sing, and while she doubts that this is necessarily a lie, she doesn't believe he knows enough to offer an informed opinion. He's told her he hates for her to head off up north, where the winters are so bad and the folks are so rude, and she doesn't believe that for even a fraction of a second. It's just what he thinks he's supposed to say if he wants to keep their mother leaning his way.

She doesn't believe he needs to say that. Their mother has nowhere else to lean. Mr. Wayne, being married, is not an option. Mr. Burns, twice divorced, is.

It has gotten harder and harder to talk to her mother, and for her it was never easy to begin with. *Bifurcated*: another of Mrs. Batch's words. Theirs was a bifurcated household. Caroline talked to their mom, Ella talked to their dad. Now he's gone, about to be replaced by Mr. Burns, who'd make a perfect upper-class villain in a western.

These are the thoughts she's been thinking when she steps into the kitchen, where a thick string dangles from the ceiling. For most of her life, she wouldn't have been able to reach that string even if she'd stood on a kitchen chair, as she's about to now, but that didn't matter, because until today she had no interest in the attic. Her dad claimed it was nasty up there, and she believed him and, as it turns out, he was telling the God's-honest-truth.

The ceiling opens, the ladder unfolds, and she puts her foot on the bottom rung. When she reaches the top, a blast of hot air hits her in the face. Outside it's in the mid-nineties, and up here it must be a hundred-and-thirty-or -forty degrees. The flashlight beam reveals spider-webbed rafters, a staved churn that she recalls watching her grandmother churn butter in years ago, several crumbling cardboard boxes, an old suitcase that looks like it's made out of alligator skin and might fall apart if you touched it. Everything, including the planks and joists, is covered by a thick layer of dust. There's a point at which dust turns into dirt, and the attic has long since passed it.

In her hand that isn't holding the flashlight, there's a fifth of Four Roses. It came two days ago, in a large brown package with her name on it and no return address. Taped to the bottle was a note. *I am so sorry about what happened last year and everything that didn't happen since. Don't hate me, please. Good luck in Boston. Maybe one day we'll be friends again?*

She hoists her legs into the stifling attic, intending to hide the bottle. Not because she thinks her mother would confiscate it, or that Caroline might steal it or ask to drink it with her. She just doesn't want anybody to know she has it. She plans to take it with her to Boston and drink it there. With the house so empty, it could too easily be discovered.

She crawls some distance from the ladder, intending to prop the bottle against the wall behind the churn. That's when she spots the lockbox. It's on the other side of the churn, where it would have remained hidden from view if all she'd done was stick her head into the attic and look around. It's almost perfectly square, about two feet tall, gunmetal gray.

On her knees she stares at it for a long time. If it's not locked, she decides, she won't bother to look inside, reasoning that whatever might be in there must not be important. If it is locked, she's going to bash it open, smash it to bits if she has to. She has no way of knowing that this is a decision she will replay off and on for the remainder of her life, rarely going more than a couple of days without returning to the attic, where she's a seventeen-year-old girl in the grips of her own curiosity.

There's different kinds of knowing, their grandmother used to say. *Some of them's a lot worse than others.*

Her hand reaches out to touch the lock. To her amazement, it feels cold. How could anything be so cold in such heat?

Boots 'n' Flannel

THE RESTAURANT STOOD AT THE corner of Newbury Street and Mass Ave. Nominally a steakhouse, it sold at least as much fish as beef and had high-backed booths evidently intended to resemble those in English pubs. It claimed to offer the coldest beer in town, as well as some of the cheapest, in part to offset the overpriced and mostly lackluster food. During the years Ella worked there, it was the favorite haunt of the novelist Richard Yates, whom she served two or three times a week. For a while he half-heartedly hit on her, paying her raspy compliments, asking her to say things *like y'all come back now* so he could get the dialogue right if he ever wrote a classic Southern charmer into one of his books. A slope-shouldered, gray-haired man with big sad eyes, who even when drunk somehow always managed to seem elegant, he wore dark Brooks Brothers blazers and neatly knotted ties and generally dined alone. One evening he brought her a hardcover copy of *Liars in Love*, signed

to Ella with admiration
your friend,
Dick Yates

Years later, when she read his obituary in the *Globe*, she was stunned to learn that at his death he was only sixty-six. He already seemed much older back when she waited on him.

For her, working at the restaurant was problematic but not because of Yates. Berklee was a stone's throw away, and while faculty from the music school didn't often dine there, she would sometimes see a couple of them, always male, sitting at the bar having after-class drinks. If any of them recognized her, they didn't let on. Why would they? She didn't act like she knew them either.

But she couldn't stop herself from eavesdropping on their conversations. One evening a man she didn't know—mid-forties, red hair, a scruffy beard that didn't quite match, a trombone case propped against the railing—was chatting with a member of the percussion faculty, a jazz drummer who'd played with major figures like Anthony Braxton, Archie Shepp, Mal Waldron. "It's been going on a little while," the trombonist said, then tipped a glass of whiskey back and took a good-sized swallow. "I told Mike about it."

"He see a problem?"

"Hell no. I see more of a problem than he does."

"Yeah?"

"Yeah. I told him given the situation, her not quite eighteen and so on, I'd rest easier if he conducted her performance review and gave her the grade. You know what he said?"

"What?"

"He said, 'I got a better idea, Richie. Why don't *I* fuck her and *you* grade her?'"

The drummer laughed so hard he spilled suds on the other guy's trombone case. Walking home past midnight, she promised herself that first thing the next morning she'd start looking for another job. It's hard to get going, though, if you manage only a few hours of broken sleep, and during that particular summer she was having a rare spell of sleep troubles. She rented a tiny studio in the basement of a brownstone, at a time when Back Bay was between its last elegant period and its next. Directly across Marlborough stood a halfway house, and somebody was always screaming in the middle of the night, and she couldn't close her window without suffocating. Add the fact that this entire part of Boston was undergoing renovation, with construction crews hammering and banging from eight AM on, and rest was all but impossible. When she woke the following day, her resolve had deserted her.

By then, she was used to letting things slide. She'd left school without a degree, the result of no specific decision. One day she didn't go to her classes, the next day she did, the day after that she didn't, and so on until she missed two straight weeks and never again set foot in any of Berklee's facilities, not even years later when singers she admired performed there. It didn't take her long to learn that nearly everybody else in the voice department had more talent than she did, not to mention two or three times as much ambition or determination—whatever name you wanted to give to whatever she lacked. Other concerns figured in, too, and at the time she didn't know the name for them either.

She hadn't talked to her sister for more than two years. She didn't even know where she was. The last time they spoke, Caroline called collect from a pay phone that she said was in Beaumont, Texas. But a few weeks later, when Ella received the bill, it said the call had been placed from Gilroy, California. This made no sense to her, since Caroline had gotten in touch to ask if she could wire her two hundred dollars, which Ella proceeded to do, sending it to the Western Union office in Beaumont. When she finally inquired, nobody there could tell her anything except that the money had been claimed the same day she sent it, by a woman who must have convinced the clerk on duty that she was Caroline Cole, otherwise the funds would not have been released.

She often weathered nightmares in which they were together again in high school, and the basic plot was always the same: she committed some monstrous act of betrayal, shaming her sister in front of the assembled student body, revealing her to be a thief, reporting her to the principal for cheating, removing her clothes from the locker room so that she had to hide there all night naked. Sometimes she woke drenched in perspiration, with the most visceral certainty that like their father Caroline was dead. She met her end in various ways, dying in a car wreck, leaping off the Golden Gate, raped and murdered by Albert DeSalvo or Charles Manson or Ted Bundy, shot by the police while attempting to rob a convenience store, disappearing into the desert where her mutilated corpse was found months later.

She hadn't talked to her mother for a long time, either, though they did exchange the occasional perfunctory letter or postcard. She and Tommy Burns had taken in a mongrel as well as two stray cats, and the mongrel was fond of one cat but not the other. Then the cat that the dog liked got run over. Tommy Burns suffered a heart attack. Her mother was now working two jobs: cashiering at United Dollar Store, pulling waitress shifts a few evenings a week at a truckstop on the road to Little Rock. *Looks like we ended up in the same "profession,"* her latest note said. *I wasn't hoping better for myself, but I hoped better for you.* She never asked why Ella quit school a year away from graduation, and Ella never told her. She did ask, several times, if she'd heard from her sister, and she always had to say no. The other question she posed, if only once, was couched as a P.S., after she'd closed "Love, Momma."

Is there no one in your life?

•

On Tuesday, her evening off, she agreed to meet a friend in front of Trinity Church. They did this pretty often, especially in the summers. Sometimes they went for Cherrystone clams at the Union Oyster House, at other times they made sandwiches and ate them in front of the bandstand on the Esplanade, once or twice they went to Fenway. Several years older than Ella, a tallish brunette whose wrinkles were starting to show, Liz worked in the beauty salon at the Fairmont Copley Plaza. She was the only other Southerner in Boston that Ella knew. True, there had been a handful at Berklee, but when she quit she lost touch with them. Most of them never learned her name anyway.

As usual, Liz showed up late, hurrying across the square, her skirt swishing in the breeze, sunlight glinting off the bracelets she wore on each wrist. "I just did a page boy," she said, "on the most awful woman who ever lived."

"What was so bad about her?"

"Well, to start with, she no sooner sits down than she starts to complain that the chair's too narrow."

"Is it?"

"If your butt's as broad as Texas, it definitely is. Hers would've spilled over into New Mexico and Louisiana. Soon as I tell her I'm sorry, she looks up at me and says, 'You're surrey? My God. Where did you come from?' Now, I'm not about to say Monteagle, Tennessee, to somebody like that. I told her I grew up in Quincy—"

"Quincy? And you expected her to believe you? With your accent?"

"—and that when I was a child, I caught a mysterious virus, which a world-famous audiologist at MGH said did irreversible damage to my Eustachian tubes, so that I can't really hear what I sound like or what others sound like either. 'For instance,' I said, 'to me, you sound a lot like Granny Clampett on the *Beverly Hillbillies*. But since we're in Boston, I know you couldn't possibly be a hillbilly, and of course you don't look like one. Hillbillies are usually scrawny.'"

"What did she say to that?"

"Not one more word did the old bitch squawk."

"Yeah? Well, what kind of tip did you get?"

"*Nada*. But in this case, it was worth the sacrifice."

They got on the Green Line, then changed at Park. Twenty minutes later they emerged from the subway into Central Square. The odor of pot hung in the air. The Red Sox broadcast seemed to be coming from windows on both sides of Mass Ave, and you could hear four or five different kinds of music issuing from the bars that lined the street: reggae over here, metal over there.

"Which way's north?" Liz asked.

"You're joking, right?"

"In Cambridge I don't even know which way's up."

Ella pointed. "North's that way."

Though it ran counter to what she would have expected before she came here, country music and bluegrass were big in Boston in the summer of '83 and would only get bigger in the years ahead. A guy Liz knew from back home was in town this weekend, playing pedal steel in a honkytonk band, and they were performing at the Boots 'n' Flannel Lounge, about halfway between Central and Harvard.

Something had been bothering Ella on the T, and as they made their way toward the venue, dodging drunks, street preachers, panhandlers and the largest assembly of Hare Krishnas this side of the Ganges, she said, "That story you told me back there about the woman who sneered at your accent? Was it true?"

Liz didn't break stride. She was a complicated person. She'd bought a bus ticket to Boston after falling in love with a businessman she'd met in Nashville, at the luxury hotel where she worked as a cocktail waitress. She knew he was married, that he had no plans to leave his wife, yet she decided that since she wanted out of Tennessee anyway, she'd follow him and see how long it lasted. It didn't last long, but she said she had no regrets. She'd been making good money for several years, saved a lot, and when she socked away enough was going to open her own restaurant in one of the heavily Irish working class suburbs. She believed a good southern cook could clean up. Sooner or later, she maintained, almost anybody would get tired of cabbage, roast beef and lamb stew. Even the Irish. "The story about my customer," she said now, "was mostly true."

"So which parts weren't?"

"I gave myself snappier dialogue. Or to put it another way, I had myself say what I would've said if I could just think a little bit faster. Why are you asking? She really was pretty awful."

She'd asked the question because the anecdote didn't quite sound right: Liz prized her tips too much to risk alienating her clients, no matter how rude or offensive they might be. The only people who'd ever really hurt Ella were those who lied with silken ease. Her sister. Her father. Kim Taggart. She feared glib liars, whether the lie was large or small, whether love was involved or no love at all. Even if you didn't buy the lie, you always had to wonder about the motive behind it. "No reason," she said, "other than simple curiosity."

The Boots 'n' Flannel was up ahead, identifiable not only by the sign jutting over the sidewalk but also because a bunch of guys were milling around out front puffing cigarettes or sipping from cans of Schlitz and Blue Ribbon, and nearly all of them wore shitkickers and sported tattoos. She even saw a John Deere cap. Save for the loud talk of "cahs" and "bahs," this could have been a Mississippi roadhouse on any Friday or Saturday night.

The lounge was packed and noisy, but shortly before the music started, they found stools at the L-shaped bar with a view of the stage. Liz ordered a gin and tonic, and she asked for a Diet Coke. She hadn't touched alcohol since her last year at Berklee.

The band mostly performed covers of such country warhorses as "Cold, Cold Heart" and "The Wild Side of Life," along with a handful of forgettable originals. They sang and played well, though. The pedal steel drew loud applause after every quavering solo.

When they took a break, Ella promised to hold onto Liz's place while she went backstage to visit. The guy on the other side of the vacated stool, who'd been there when they came in, looked at her and said, "So what do you think?"

"About the music?"

"Yeah." He had reddish Brillo pad hair and was probably in his mid-thirties. A pen and an open notebook lay in front of him next to a half-empty beer mug, the top page of the notebook covered in jottings.

She gave them a thumbs down.

He laughed. "That's about what I think," he said. "Understand, they're all accomplished musicians, except for the drummer, who might be happier wielding a meat clever. Good vocals too. But so far, their own songs aren't doing it for me. You'll hear people in the business complain that there are no new ideas in Nashville. The truth is there are no ideas in Nashville, period. The ideas absconded for California, Muscle Shoals or Boston."

"You sound like you've got a professional interest."

"As a matter of fact, I do." He pulled a card from his shirt pocket and slid it down the bar.

> Martin Summers
> Yankee Southern Records
> 1 Rockland Street
> Cedar Park, Massachusetts 02213
> (781) 436-4389

"Yankee Southern? Isn't that, like, a little—"

"Disjunctive?"

"I don't know that I'd put it that way, exactly."

He laughed. "Of course you wouldn't. Because, unless I'm sadly mistaken, you're a Southerner, as is your recently departed friend of the band. And Southerners are unfailingly polite. Except, of course, when you all shoot one another."

"You mean like the Winter Hill gang and the South Boston mafia?"

"Touché. But they're criminals. Whereas down south, don't you mostly shoot close friends and family members?"

"It wouldn't be so difficult," she said, "for me to take offense."

He smiled. "Except that you strike me as a good judge of character, so you'll know I'm just joking."

"So what sorts of records does Yankee Southern make?"

"We take music that comes from the South and sell it up north. Kind of like slavery in reverse. Hence, the name of our label. Country, bluegrass, acoustic blues, zydeco, rockabilly." He said he and his partner founded the company five years ago but that they'd actually hatched the idea when they were still students at the Berklee College of Music.

"You went to Berklee?" she said. "When'd you graduate?"

"I didn't. I quit. So'd my partner. I left in '70, he lasted into '71."

"Which department?"

"Strings."

"I went to Berklee. In Voice. I didn't graduate either."

"Why'd you quit?"

She hesitated too long for her own taste, if not his. "I just realized I wasn't cut out for it."

"When I quit," he said, "I lied to myself about the reason. Told myself, 'These people are not about music. They're about the music business.'" He laughed. "Now look: I'm on the business side of music. The truth was everybody there could play better than I did. Well, maybe the guy's that's my partner might've been worse. But just marginally."

"Did you finish school somewhere else?"

"B.S. in Accounting at Merrimack College. What about you?"

"Not yet. But I hope to one day. Right now I'm just waitressing."

"Hey, we all gotta eat."

The band emerged from the break room, followed by Liz. Apparently, a seat near the stage had opened up. She mouthed *Okay if I sit here?* Ella nodded, though she wasn't happy. She suspected Liz might be more than just friends with the guy on pedal steel and that after sitting through three hours in a crowded bar listening to music she could take or leave, she might have to ride the T to Back Bay alone. She couldn't just walk out now, either, because Liz had left her purse behind.

"Looks like you've been deserted," Martin Summers said. "Mind if I move over?" Rather than simply handing her the purse and sliding onto the vacant barstool, he waited for a response.

"No," she said, "of course not." She lifted the handbag and hung it on her knee.

The second set was better than the first, the originals a little more striking. She saw Summers taking note of several titles that he must have liked. As the show drew to a close, the lead singer said, "We've got a special guest who's agreed to help us out on our last couple of numbers. Y'all know her a lot better than we do, so I don't think she really needs an introduction."

To loud applause and raucous shouts, a woman in the front row rose and stepped onto the stage. She was about Ella's age and height, with short sandy hair. She wore glasses, and under one arm carried a violin case. She pulled the instrument out, turned sideways to the audience, bowed it two or three times, adjusted one of the tuners. Satisfied, she stepped up to the mic, nodded at the guitarist, then played the first few notes of a tune Ella recognized instantly. Her father loved it, especially after visiting the smoke house or the barn and taking a few swigs from a hidden bottle. She saw him walking across the yard toward the house that stood near an orchard that wasn't really an orchard. His face ruddy, his eyes alight. The screen door slapped shut, the kitchen door creaked open, heavy footsteps moved through the hall. In the room next to the one she shared with her sister, he fitted the 78 onto the spindle. He had things on his mind that no one fathomed. He couldn't play, he couldn't sing, he had no means to express them. They were locked away in a metal box directly above the bed where she and her sister slept. All her father could do was listen to the music.

The woman played beautifully, with a thick rich tone that made the instrument sound more like a viola. After the intro the band modulated, just as Ella expected, and the fiddle player tucked the instrument under her arm and began to sing the opening lines of the Bob Wills classic "Faded Love."

As I look at the letters that you wrote to me
It's you that I am thinking of

A powerful contralto, she delayed hitting the octave by a beat. Her phrasing consistently surprised. She sang the entire second verse without a single stop except at the end of the final line. Even if you'd heard the song a hundred times, a thousand times, you'd never heard it like that. An untrained voice bleeding raw emotion. She took the tune out with another fiddle solo. The applause that followed was all but deafening.

When her throat felt less constricted, Ella leaned closer to the record producer. "Forget about the band," she said. "She's the one you ought to sign."

In the mirror behind the bar, over the rowed-up bottles, she saw him smile. "Oh, I've had a relationship with her for years," he said.

"Really? What's her name?"

"Maeve . . . Maeve Summers."

"She's your wife?"

He caught the bartender's eye and pointed at his empty mug. Then he turned to Ella. "Actually," he said, "she's my sister. Seven years younger and twenty times more gifted. She got most of the musical talent in the family and nearly all the intellect too. She's working on her doctorate at Harvard, writing a dissertation on Emily Dickinson."

The bartender stood a fresh beer before him and swept away the dirty mug.

"Speaking of names," Martin Summers said, "mind if I ask yours?"

THAT FALL, THE FIRST SNOW FELL ON Halloween, accompanied by gale-force winds that resulted in a white-out right around the time she finished work. The snow was heavy, wet stuff, and since the trees still had a great many of their leaves, several of them came down, including the majestic old elm that stood directly in front of her building and was now blocking the entrance. She didn't know any of the other residents' names, just the superintendent's, so even though she was already covered in snow and shivering, she had to slog to a pay phone on Newbury in hopes that the super would answer and unlock the back door. She let his number ring fifteen times, but he never picked up.

Liz didn't live that far away, but in late August she'd gotten involved with a city councilman she met at The Last Hurrah, the bar at the Omni Parker. He was married, but his wife didn't seem to mind if he spent an evening each week with Liz—at least that was what he told her—and Ella knew their tryst night was Monday. She literally had nowhere to go, as she couldn't afford any of the nearby hotels. She sat down on the floor of the phone booth, hoping the storm would pass, but it continued for another couple of hours. Fortunately, nobody disturbed her. Hardly anyone was fool enough to walk the streets that night.

When the storm finally let up, she decided to go back home and see if maybe she couldn't get close enough to the basement window to break it and crawl inside. But first, she had to shove open the door of the phone booth, which took some doing since it was blocked by about a foot of snow. Turning onto Marlborough, she could see that a crew from the

Department of Public Works had been dispatched to deal with the tree, several men in orange suits and head-lit helmets grinding away with their chainsaws. The front steps were already clear. The superintendent stood there jawing with the foreman, sipping coffee from a metallic mug, looking dry and well-rested. She ignored his cheerful hello.

That was how the fall went, the period she would come to think of as her absolute nadir, worse even than the year her father died. Back then, she could at least try to convince herself that things might get better, that she might make her way to college and a good life somewhere else, someplace exciting like Nashville or Boston. But Boston turned into the odor of fried fish, small tips from a sad novelist, a night spent soaked and shivering in a Back Bay phone booth.

●

The previous two years, she and Liz had gotten together for Thanksgiving, but this time her friend slipped off to Barbados with the married guy, who told his wife he was on a trade mission. That Thursday Ella slept until noon. It wasn't good sleep but the broken kind, in which you think you're awake even though you aren't. She finally rolled over, glanced at the clock and swung her legs out of bed but couldn't force herself to stand. She sat there for ten or fifteen minutes, maybe more, so long that she was afraid to look at the clock again. She'd been fearing a day like this, when her legs would feel like stones. She desperately wanted to talk to her sister, and she thought of calling various cities around the country to see if directory assistance had a listing for Caroline Cole. She already knew from trying once that you couldn't initiate a nation-wide directory assistance search for a particular name. You had to specify a place at twenty-five cents a shot.

She'd never be sure how much time passed before she got in the shower. She hoped the hot spray would revive her, but it only made her want to go back to bed. Finally, she turned the dial to cold, and within seconds the icy water cleared her brain. She understood with brutal clarity that she had to put some clothes on and get out of this basement cave.

There was a lot of sunshine that afternoon. A brisk breeze sent brittle leaves skittering along Comm Ave, and people were out walking their dogs or pushing prams. She made four circuits of the Public Garden, drawing the chilly air deep into her lungs, then exhaling at least some of her despondency. For a while she sat on a bench, watching a young father teaching his sons to throw spirals with a miniature football. In the evening she went to see *Terms of Endearment* but fell asleep before the end. Probably just as well since she and Liz planned to see it the following week.

She had Friday off from work, which left her with another long day and night to muddle through, and her experience of the previous morning repeated itself. This time, it was after one when she forced herself out of bed. She didn't even bother with hot water, just turned it immediately to cold. She left the apartment at a quarter past two.

The day, once again, was beautiful, a little cooler than the one before, and she enjoyed the crisp air. For an hour or more she strolled along the Esplanade. She thought of renting a bike and riding it to Mount Auburn Cemetery and back but decided not to waste the money, electing instead to walk across the Longfellow Bridge into Cambridge. She wandered around the MIT campus for a while, but the sight of couples meandering hand in hand, or frat boys playing touch football or hurling frisbees, began to make her feel like the interloper she knew herself to be. As dusk fell she set off up Mass Ave.

Later, she wouldn't recall the instant when she realized where she was headed. One moment she was browsing a third or fourth cluttered used book store, the next she was walking through the door at the Boots 'n' Flannel. It was after eight when she got there. A poster on the wall advertised the evening's entertainment: Acoustic Bluesman Mississippi Matt Crown. All the barstools and most of the tables were already taken. She waited her turn, ordering a Diet Coke and, since she'd had no lunch, a burger and fries.

She carried the glass to a small table in the corner, as far away from both the bar and the stage as one could get. While waiting for her burger, she sipped the Diet Coke, keeping her head down as if she had something to be ashamed of. She felt like where she was at this point in her life—twenty-five years old, no college degree, one friend to her name and that one friend off in Barbados with someone else's husband—was embarrassing.

Mississippi Matt Crown took the stage with a silver resonator so shiny that the light glinting off it made her blink. Without preamble, he placed the instrument on his left knee, as if it were a classical guitar. He tore into "Travelin' Riverside Blues," playing like Robert Johnson but singing like a white guy from Brookline.

She enjoyed the burger, not so much because it was good but because she consumed it to the sound of music, in a room full of other people. When Mississippi Matt took a break, she looked up to find one of those people standing beside her table. "Mind if I join you?" Martin Summers said, the notebook tucked under one arm.

"No," she said. "Please do."

He set his beer down and pulled out the other chair.

The last time she'd been here, when he asked for her name, she assumed he would call her but he didn't. In the meantime, she'd gone to a couple of record stores and seen some Yankee Southern LPs by performers she'd never heard of with him listed as producer. She searched for something by his sister but didn't find anything. Presumably music was nothing more than a hobby for her, despite her obvious talent.

He asked what she'd been up to the last few months. She shrugged and said, "What I'm always up to. Serving T-bones and battered cod."

"That's right. You work at the Newbury Steakhouse, don't you?"

She tried to recall if she'd told him where she worked. She didn't think so. "Yeah."

"Where's your Tennessee friend? Lynn, was it?"

"Liz. She's in Barbados with a guy she's seeing."

He said the name of the city councilman, followed by a question mark.

She was only mildly surprised. "What makes you say so?"

"I've seen them having drinks at The Last Hurrah. I don't think she saw me and most likely wouldn't have recognized me if she did. She was pretty wrapped up in him. I've had some dealings with the guy. I'm afraid she's not his first extracurricular. And I'm sorry to say she probably won't be the last."

"I'm not sure that'll come as a shock to her. She's pretty world-wise."

He took a sip of his beer. "What about you? You seem pretty world-wise too."

"Me? I'm an innocent."

"I don't think so."

"Does it strike you," she said, "that this conversation has grown serious very fast?"

"Yes, it does. But, see, music has that effect on people. Even as played by Mississippi Matt Kagle."

"The sign says 'Mississippi Matt Crown.'"

"His real name's Matthew Kagle. He's from Hackensack, New Jersey, and he's getting a master's in public policy at the Kennedy School."

"Does everybody who goes to Harvard end up playing here?"

"Seems that way, doesn't it?"

Mississippi Matt returned to the stage, and they listened to the second set in silence. The notebook remained closed. Clearly, the performer was not destined to grace the front of a Yankee Southern LP.

The music ended around midnight. There was no denying she'd enjoyed Martin's company, though neither of them had said a word for the last hour. Just having someone beside her was relaxing. She didn't feel like a freak or a loser and wasn't afraid to meet the gaze of another person.

"How about a nightcap?" he asked.

"Here?"

"Hell no."

He led her across the street to a small Italian restaurant with a well-stocked bar. Two couples were still eating dinner, though there was no one at the bar itself. The host, who seemed to know Martin, gave them a table near the window with a view of Mass Ave.

"You don't drink alcohol, do you?" he asked.

"I haven't for a few years."

"Is it religious—if you don't mind my question?"

"If you thought I did mind, would that stop you from posing it?"

He chuckled. "Probably. But it wouldn't stop me from wondering."

"Well, it hasn't got anything to do with religion," she said as a waiter approached. "Actually, I think I'll have a glass of chianti."

He ordered a Bushmills on the rocks. When the waiter left, he took a deep breath, exaggerating the effort. "Well . . . drumroll, please . . . I'm divorced. That's my secret."

"I think I knew that."

"Yeah?"

"Yeah. Though I don't think I realized I knew it until now, if that makes any sense."

"Makes all the sense in the world to me." The waiter brought their drinks, Martin said "Cheers," and they clicked glasses. Then he asked, "So why'd you *really* leave Berklee?"

What would it indicate if she knew, as she seemed to, that this particular question was coming? Some strange type of chemistry that couldn't be predicted or broken down into its various elements? Or controlled? "I really left Berklee," she said, "because I realized that I just wasn't that talented. Or that driven either."

She would always believe that if he'd responded, she would've stopped right there. A simple "And?" was all it would've taken. But he didn't say "And?" He didn't say anything, nor did he smile wryly. He just sat there.

"And," she finally said, "there was one other thing."

You didn't call professors "Professor" at the Berklee College of Music. You just called them by their first names or sometimes even their nicknames. Bob. Ramón. Tooty. Jack. He would know this. So she said a name. It meant nothing to him, which didn't surprise her. There was a lot of turnover, musicians dropped in, got two or three years' worth of paydays, then went back to the lives they'd had before. The man whose name she'd spoken, the last she heard, was on the west coast, working for Disney, doing something related to film music, God knows what. He'd be in his forties now.

Slim, prematurely gray, with ice blue intelligent eyes. A devotee of Sondheim, Bernstein, Cole Porter. Admirer and close friend of Randall Thompson. He must have come from money, he had a nice apartment in a nice block on a nice street near the BSO. Why he'd leave a flat like that to work for Disney, she said, was anybody's guess. The place was truly elegant, the only sign of disorder his record collection. Some of the LPs didn't have sleeves, they were just piled up on one another, and they lay everywhere: on his dining room table, on top of his books, on the floor.

This whisky is a Speyside, he said, handing her a glass that contained a good two inches. She'd been invited there to discuss her diction. In her performance class, despite her best efforts, he'd detected a tendency to slur vowels. In jazz and blues, he'd informed her, that might be tolerated or even desired. But in musical theater, the audience needs to understand the words. A plot point might be missed. If he could, he said, he'd like to help her.

She wasn't faring well in his class—this she knew. He would soon be involved in her performance review. The serious one. The one that everybody said was make or break.

He moved a stack of records off the leather loveseat and gestured at it. Smoothing her skirt, she took her place beside him. She'd worn the nicest one she had, a pleated midi that she bought at a used clothing store in the South End.

He asked her lots of questions about herself: where was she from again, what was musical education like at her high school, did she attend class with blacks or was it one of those places he'd read about—what were they called? Segregation academies, right?

Two more inches of Speyside malt. Easy on the peat, lavish with spice.

Was the color line as hard and fast as they said? He'd been set to go down there once—Summer of '64, his last year at Julliard, but then Chaney, Goodman and Schwerner happened, and there's no way to sugar coat this, he said, I simply chickened out. I liked being alive. I still do. Don't you?

Yes, she said, of course she did. She heard herself grow garrulous, beginning to relate a story, something she hoped would make him laugh. A car stopped near their house, she said. Summer of '64. She would have been six, getting ready to attend first grade. Smoke billowed up from the engine, they could see it. A guy got out. He raised the hood and stood there gazing down and shaking his head. Then he walked toward their house. You stay here, her father told her before opening the door.

Her dad went down the road with that stranger, who looked and sounded different and was probably about the age her present host would have been in the summer of Chaney, Goodman and Schwerner, whom she didn't even know about back then. She watched through the window while her father put his head under the hood and did something, and then he came back and went around to the pump house and she watched him fill a bucket from the hydrant.

One last drink? her host interrupted. She must have nodded. After all, he wanted to help her.

So anyhow, her father carried the bucket to the car and poured the water in, and then the guy got behind the wheel and the car started and her father put the hood back down and the stranger drove away. And when her father returned, she asked him where the young man was from, and he said he's one of those damn COFO workers from up north. Arizona.

She knew she was making a fool of herself, she just wasn't sure why. She didn't love school. Actually, she didn't even like it. She was there because she had nowhere else to go. And of course, her instructor missed the point of the story. He thought her father didn't know where Arizona was, but in fact it didn't matter to her dad that Arizona was in the west. In the Chaney, Goodman and Schwerner summer, if you lived in Mississippi, there was the South and there was the rest. And the rest was called the North.

Her professor—whose facial expression never changed—got down to business, loosing a cascade of terminology, speaking about breaks, those sudden tonal shifts between the chest and the head voice; about her tendency to over-breathe before attempting to project; about the importance of diaphragmatic control in the placement of notes and vowels. He rose from the loveseat and requested she do the same.

"The next thing I know," she tells Martin Summers, "he's standing behind me, his right hand pressing my diaphragm. Then his left hand comes around my shoulder and touches my neck, right where a doctor checks to see if your lymph nodes are swollen. That's about what it felt like too, as if I were being examined."

Martin stirs his drink with the swizzle stick but maintains eye contact. "You don't have to continue," he says, "if you'd rather not."

"And you don't have to hear it," she says, "if that's what you'd prefer."

"It isn't."

She says she could feel his breath on the nape of her neck. Both of his hands remained where they were. How long they stood there silently, she can't say. It could have been a few seconds. It could have been a couple of minutes.

"Then I hear him speaking, his voice muffled by my hair. 'Somewhere between here,' he says, exerting a little more pressure on my diaphragm, 'and right here'—more pressure on my throat—'something's getting lost. But the real problem,' he says, 'is somewhere else.' He takes his hand off my neck and pats me on the head, as if I were a golden retriever. 'It's in here,' he says. 'You sing without passion. If I were to guess, I'd say it's because you've never felt any.'"

"Jesus Christ," Martin says.

She takes a sip of her wine. It tastes good. Tart and crisp. She likes wine. She's missed it. She's missed so many things these last few years. "So he spun me around," she says, "and I was so drunk and dizzy that I might've fallen down if he hadn't held me upright. Then he walked me into his bedroom. And he taught me what passion doesn't feel like."

For just an instant Martin Summers bows his head. Before long, she will learn that while he last attended mass during middle school, he still harbors certain religious feelings. When he hears that someone is sick, or that they've been hurt, or that they're grieving, or hungry, or lonely, he always drops his head and says a silent prayer. In later years he will do the same thing after disasters strike: when the Twin Towers fall, when Hurricane Sandy ravages Atlantic City and a tsunami lays waste to Zanzibar. He doesn't want anybody to notice, so he never shuts his eyes, and his lips never move. After she finally figures out what he's up to, she will ask him exactly how much he can say, even silently, in the second or two that passes. He will admit that it's a single word, addressed to some force he doesn't even know if he believes in: *Please*.

"Of course," she says now, "this is probably a whole lot more than you wanted to know when you invited me over here for a nightcap."

"No, it's not. Though I wish it hadn't happened."

"I never gave him a chance to fail me on my performance review.

If I'd gone through with it, I probably would've deserved failure. But I wasn't about to let him do it."

"You didn't think of reporting *him?*"

She drains her glass. "No. He would've just said it was consensual. And in the least important way, maybe it was."

He finishes his Bushmills. "I think I need another one. What about you?"

"I don't need one. But I'll have one."

He catches the waiter's attention and raises two fingers. Then he looks at her and says, "My car's parked in a garage a couple of blocks away. After this next round, could I drive you home?"

She's only felt this bold one time before, and that was nine years ago on the balcony at Kim Taggart's. "Whose home?" she asks. "Yours? Or mine?"

WHEN CAROLINE, WHO WAS THEN known as Carin, looked out the kitchen window, the Tule fog was so thick she couldn't see across the street. In one sense, no great loss. The place Julio rented in this small San Joaquin Valley farm town stood opposite a junkyard, which offered a less than entrancing view of rusting cars and trucks. Unfortunately, the fog also kept her from seeing if the cat was still there.

A calico with green eyes, it had two black ears. One side of its face was black too, but the other was orange, and its nose and cheeks formed a perfectly inverted white V. It had first shown up last week, perched on the roof of a two-toned Camaro that got towed in a couple of months ago. The car looked like an eighteen-wheeler had smashed it: shattered windshield, crinkled hood, the driver's side caved-in, the entire frame listing. Julio said he doubted whoever was in the automobile had survived such a bad wreck. He knew what he was talking about, too, because before he got the job at the liquor store and went back to school, he'd worked full-time in a body shop.

Every morning since the cat first appeared, she'd seen it atop the Camaro, sometimes sitting, more often lying. Sometimes it was there when she got back from work, sometimes not. Yesterday, she'd filled a plastic bowl with milk, shoved it under the tension wire and tried to coax the stray. It watched with interest but didn't budge. When she returned around dusk, it was gone, the bowl empty. She couldn't help but wonder if the folks the poor thing belonged to had died in that car. She'd heard about cats and dogs traveling hundreds of miles to find owners who'd lost or abandoned them.

She opened the refrigerator, poured a little milk in the bowl, pressed the button on the grimy Mr. Coffee, then went to wake Julio.

He groaned and, using the sleeve of the flannel shirt he'd gone to bed in, wiped sleep from his eyes. The Valley, he'd remarked the other day, was experiencing the coldest January he could recall, snow flurries as far south as Visalia. He said he guessed that wouldn't impress somebody like her who'd grown up in the Midwest.

She'd fed him only a limited number of lies, the main one being the childhood she invented for herself in Hannibal, Missouri. No use in pretending that if she'd known how much she'd come to care about him, she would have told him the truth. Lying—once a means of entertaining herself—had become a necessity. Shortly after she finished the Paloma he'd bought her at Sancho's Cantina, he said, "You don't sound like a Valley girl. Where are you from?"

In a matter of moments, she conjured an entire biography that was at least more solidly rooted in the factual than any of those she'd served up in similar instances over the past five or six years. Gone was the highly-rated private school down south. Gone were the mother who graduated from Duke and wrote poetry, the father who, though among the most successful corporate attorneys in Memphis or Birmingham, Baton Rouge or Atlanta, had abandoned the family when Carin was in junior high. Gone was the older brother who died at Khe Sanh. Her dad drove a milk truck, she said, until he lost his left eye in a fight at the VFW. Her mom worked at K Mart, and her sister waited tables at a truckstop. As for how she got from Hannibal to Central California, well, that was a long but not especially dramatic story. She hitchhiked.

Yawning, Julio swung his legs out of bed. He was the shortest guy she'd ever been with, 5'8" or, at most, 5'9". Objectively, she would have to admit he was also the least physically attractive. Several years older than her, he was still a month shy of thirty yet had quite a few gray strands in his closely cropped hair and even more gray chest hairs. He was soft in the belly and biceps where all the others had been hard. But he was soft inside too. And the others had not been—though unlike Julio, every single one of them made a great first impression.

"What time is it?" he asked now.

"A quarter past seven."

He grinned. "Day-um," he said, poking gentle fun at her accent.

She'd accounted for it by explaining that her father had grown up in the Arkansas Delta, brought his pronunciation north and passed some of it on to her. Every lie she told seemed to necessitate at least one more. Lies were not like roads. They seldom dead-ended. "Damn indeed," she said. "If you don't hurry, you'll miss your Civics class."

"Civ's not at eight. That's Psych. Civ's at nine."

He had a certain look in his eye, and a glance at his underwear confirmed her suspicion. "Nope," she said. "You're too close to your associate degree to start missing class. Go eat your Wheaties and down a cup of joe. *Amor* can wait."

He reached for her, and she let him pull her into bed. They hadn't made love for three days. For them, a long break.

"In Psych," he whispered before starting to plaster her with inartful kisses, "I got a real solid B. We'll have to finish up in time for me to make Civ."

He left at 8:40, running for the truck with his plastic go-cup in one hand, his backpack in the other, his hair still wet from the shower. The community college was in a slightly larger town twelve miles away, and as long as some deputy didn't catch him speeding he ought to get there before class started. The sheriff's department cut nobody any slack if they looked Mexican, even if like Julio they'd been born in the US. It was one of the things he dealt with that she'd been clueless about before she came to California. The Golden State had taught her plenty.

•

By the time she left the house, enough fog had burned away for her to see the cat. It sat on the roof of the Camaro, body parallel to the street, its head turned to the side so that it appeared to be looking right at her.

She locked the front door, waited for a pickup to pass, then carried the bowl of milk over to the fence. "Hey," she said, "do you belong to anybody?"

The green eyes didn't blink. They did briefly rotate downward, or so it seemed to her, as if the cat understood what was in the bowl and was not unhappy to see it.

She squatted and shoved it under the fence. Then she stood and pressed her face against the cold chain links. "You're a cutie," she said. "I wouldn't be opposed to taking you in. I've always wanted a cat." She pointed across the road. "We live over there. I kind of got taken in myself. It's not always so bad. There's a lot to be said for a warm bed and a cuddle. Check you later, baby."

The McDonald's was a mile from the house, near the 99 overpass. Its proximity to the freeway guaranteed a fair percentage of customers who were just passing through. The town itself was a destination for nearly no one except migrant laborers, and even they had no reason to come here during winter. Dead except for the Sun-Maid Raisins plant, a handful of stores and bars and churches, this was a good place to disappear.

She'd landed here a little more than a year ago when a trucker let her out. She'd climbed into his cab on the outskirts of Fresno, where she spent several months working in the City College cafeteria. She had a staff ID there granting her access to the library. It wasn't a very good library—in fact, it was pathetic—but you could request titles from other schools, and when necessary she did. Her reading was no longer ill-informed and indiscriminate. She knew what she was asking for and why.

As jobs went, the one at the cafeteria was far better than most she'd had. She was allowed to move around, sometimes working the serving line, sometimes washing dishes, sometimes sponging off tables or mopping the floor. The pay was not quite atrocious, nobody ever yelled at her, and she could take classes for free in the evenings, something she fully intended to do if she lasted into the spring semester. But one day she was overcome by the premonition that she'd better move on, that if she remained much longer trouble would find her just as it finally had in Gilroy.

By rights, the job at McDonald's should have been deadening. But customers talked to her about anything and everything: the potholes on 99, the latest pileup on the Grapevine, the air in LA, the absence of snow melt from the Sierras, the woman whose body had been found on

Pescadero Beach, the five-year-old who'd been abducted in Antioch, the closing of the Golden Gate due to high winds; the Russians, the Contras, the Rams and the Raiders, the Stones, U2, Mötley Crue, Jodie Foster, Debra Winger, Meg Ryan, *Octopussy*. Her boss was always reminding her and the others to act interested, even as they hurried people along. She didn't need to act. She was fascinated by the things they said, how much they revealed of themselves to someone they might never see again, the gestures they used, the way their mouths moved.

This morning, she went in the bathroom and washed her hands, then punched the clock and checked to see that her nametag was pinned to her blouse beneath the image of the golden arches. For the first half of her shift she worked the counter, making it through the lunchtime rush without letting the line grow too long. She saw a few regulars, mostly people from the Sun-Maid plant who treated themselves to McDonalds once or twice a week, but the rest were strangers.

After her break she took over for a co-worker at the drive-through. Nobody liked working that position, but everybody had to do it four or five times a week, and the manager made it less onerous by limiting them to two-and-a-half hours per stretch. She'd made it about halfway through her stint when a powder blue F-100 pickup pulled to the window. She hadn't noticed anything unusual when its driver placed the order: a double Whopper with cheese, large fries, Diet Coke. She wasn't even sure if the voice on the intercom belonged to a male or a female.

She grabbed the sack and drink from her friend Maricela, then slid the window open to accept payment and hand over the order.

Often, over the next couple of decades, she would try to imagine how she must have looked to the driver in the instant when she recognized him. Did her eyes grow large like Tweety's at the sight of Sylvester the Cat? Her cheeks slacken and her mouth loll open? Thank God, she thought, that he couldn't know how much it cost her not to hurl the order out the window and run.

The thing was, he did know. Sooner or later, everybody who loved him, or thought they did, either ran away when they caught sight of him or summoned enough moxie to master the urge. Among the latter, she was otherwise singular. All the others he'd easily forgotten. Her, he couldn't chase from his mind. It was not just her wild red hair, nor the scary intelligence that lit her eyes, nor how she clamped those eyes closed when, straddling him, she arched her back and turned her face toward the ceiling and the orgasm tore through her. Nor was it the maddening kindness she showed street folks in the Haight, giving every panhandler a quarter when he knew she didn't have more than three dollars in her purse, having riffled through it and taken ten. He'd done shit he couldn't afford to because of her. They'd called security on him when he barged into the cafeteria in Fresno—a guy he knew said he'd seen her there. Guys he knew were always claiming they'd seen her somewhere. One of them claimed he'd seen her here.

"It's me, it's me," he said. "It's Ernest T. Bass."

It was not Ernest T. Bass, whose lines she used to hear him quote on the long, lazy afternoons they'd spent together more than five years ago in a glass A-frame with a view of Lake Tahoe. The place had cable—oh, it had everything. She recalled the wine rack filled with expensive vintages, the liquor cabinet stocked with rare single malts, the freezer full of steaks an inch-and-a-half thick, the copies of *The New Yorker* and *Harper's* that you could find in every room. On the floor they lay watching syndicated sit-coms. *Andy Griffith. My Three Sons. Bewitched.* From time to time he switched off the TV, or turned down the sound, and they took another hit.

He said he was an actor and a model, that he hadn't landed any film roles yet but had done underwear ads for Macy's, Merwin's, J.C. Penny. She might also have seen him, he said, in the Sears Roebuck catalogue. He wore a suit in that photo. The hottest blue polyester outfit that ever existed. One hand in his pants pocket, the other in the air, like he was gesturing while speaking to a civic group. "The Kiwanis Club," he chuckled. "That's what the photographer told me. 'Act like you're talking to the Kiwanis Club of Cleveland Heights.'"

"Why Cleveland Heights?" she asked as he began to trace rings around her nipple.

"Hell if I know. Maybe he was born in Ohio."

A point in his favor: you could name almost any town of decent size, and odds were he could tell you what state it was in and reel off several facts, including plenty of minutiae. In retrospect, that should have given her pause, since it was the kind of thing she could have done herself. But back then she lacked a "pause" button.

She didn't remember when they got to the house on the shore of Lake Tahoe. First they were in a car heading for Sacramento after a weekend at a studio apartment in the Mission District—he said it belonged to a friend—then they were driving over a mountain pass, very high late at night, and he was saying something about the Donners, how they froze and ate one another in the snow. It wasn't snowing that night, it was summer, all the windows were open but she was cold anyway. She asked him to close them, and he did. She leaned against the roof post and drifted off again and woke up in the A-frame, which he also said belonged to a friend. It would be a couple of days before she discovered the broken lock on the side door. She didn't mention it. She'd recovered enough of her wits to be scared but not scared enough to slip through that door and disappear.

He reached out, grazed her hand with his palm, and took first the Diet Coke and then the sack of food. His touch, which used to electrify her, now had a very different effect. She shivered.

"I'm afraid I'll have to ask you to put these on my tab," he said. "I've suffered some reverses."

Maricela had just stepped over to the counter, where she was jawing with her boyfriend, who appeared every day at the same time.

"What are you doing here?" Caroline asked.

"Guess you got tired of picking garlic?"

"I wasn't picking it. I was packing it."

"Not much difference, just one vowel."

"Please." She hated the whine she heard in her voice. "Please. Leave me alone."

"You get off at six like yesterday?"

She swallowed hard but didn't answer.

"In other words, yes," he said. "So I'll tell you what, hon. Meet me behind your friendly local Save Mart. And just a word of advice. Don't think of bringing your boyfriend, or your best friend, or a borrowed Rottweiler, or this little town's version of Barney Fife. Because you know that could cause me trouble, and anything that causes me trouble's pretty much guaranteed to do it to you too. And we don't want that, do we, angel? Both of us have already had plenty." Those clear blue irises she once found so beguiling seemed to see something behind her that suggested it was time to leave. "Be there," he said, then pulled away from the window.

She felt a hand on her shoulder. "Carin," Maricela said, "is everything okay?"

If she wasn't careful she'd start sobbing and babbling stuff she couldn't afford to tell her or anyone else. "Sure," she said. "Everything's just fine. That stupid guy was trying to pick me up. But fortunately, I'm not susceptible to pretty-faced losers."

THE SAVE MART STOOD AT THE far end of Main Street, only a couple of blocks past the liquor store where Julio worked. As luck would have it, he was pulling a shift this evening, so in order to avoid being seen by him, she walked over to Third, then turned onto Kern and approached the grocery from the rear. On the way she passed a pay phone and thought once again of calling her sister. But shame, and the need to keep her whereabouts unknown, prevented her.

She saw Tom before he saw her. He was sitting in the almost empty lot, about twenty or thirty feet from the loading dock, parked at an angle, presumably so he could study her as she walked the half block or so from Main. She knew his profile very well, having woken up beside him every day for six months. He always slept on his back, and since she slept mostly on her right side, the first thing she saw when she opened her eyes was his left cheek and jaw, the same as today. His hair had been longer back then and black. Now it was salt-and-pepper. He needed a shave.

The window was open only a couple of inches, and she had on gum-soled shoes, but he must have heard footsteps. He turned in her direction, then rolled the glass down farther. "Get in," he said pleasantly.

"I don't want to."

"Why?"

"You know why."

"Actually, I don't."

She noticed something that had escaped her attention at the drive-through: two of his front teeth were chipped, one quite badly. "Well, you *should* know. It's not my fault if you don't."

"You'd never guess what I did last night."

"I'm sure I wouldn't."

"So I'll tell you. I bought a bottle of wine from your boyfriend. Julio, right? Or is it Jose? Anyway, I bought the cheapest thing they had in the store, some kind of off-brand cabernet. I must have stood there and shot the shit with him for ten or fifteen minutes. Turns out he grew up in Paso Robles. When he was fourteen he started picking grapes at Covino Vineyards. To this day, he's partial to their Zinfandel and tried his hardest to sell me some. You know what that suggests to me?"

A response could only reveal her fear and, perhaps more importantly, her exhaustion. She wasn't tired of work. She was tired of thinking about him, of wondering if he'd find her again. She thought about this off and on all day, she dreamed about it at night, and now it had happened.

"To me, that suggests he's not exactly Cesar Chavez. If I'd been out there picking rich people's grapes for peanuts when I was a kid, I wouldn't be so eager to put money in their pockets later on. I'd be looking to take some out."

"You'd be looking to take money out of their pockets whether you'd picked their grapes or not."

"*Thieves Like Us*," he said. "Ever see that movie? It's set in Mississippi."

She'd never told him she came from Mississippi or that she'd been born Caroline Cole. Back when they were together, he'd found an old driver's license in some of her things—this was why whatever foolish girl he'd been with a couple of years ago could pick up money in her name at the Western Union in Beaumont, Texas. She'd been stupid to hold onto the license and hadn't known what went with it until she was summoned to the phone at the garlic plant. He said he was desperate, that if she'd help him then, he'd never bother her again. She hadn't believed him. She left Gilroy the following day and ended up in Fresno. Then she left Fresno and ended up here. She should have gone much farther.

As if he'd read her mind, he said, "You know, hon, California's not that big. People think it is, but they're wrong. Here we are together again.

Get in."

"No."

One thumb idly tapped the steering wheel. "I need a little help," he said.

"What kind of help?"

"I could use some cash."

"What'd you buy that bottle of wine with last night?"

He shook his head. "Oh, Carin."

"Oh, Carin, what?"

"I could've just taken it, right? I was in there late, maybe half an hour before closing. Probably no more than three or four cars went by the whole time I was talking to him." The wrong kind of smile began to play on his lips. "I could've taken a whole lot more than that bottle. Couldn't I?"

She struggled to keep her voice even. "There's a surveillance camera."

"I know. But whoever decided where to put it must not be a security specialist. It's mounted in a corner up front, so the only thing it catches when you walk in's your back."

"You still have to get out."

"There's a rear entrance. And if somebody did do something nefarious, that person could just step around the counter and walk out the back door."

"They keep a .38 under the register," she lied, her pulse starting to pound.

"That's useful info. Little bit smaller caliber weapon than I might've chosen. Depending on somebody's body mass, it might not cause enough blood loss to stop 'em from doing whatever they wanted. Assuming they intended to do something other than make a lawful purchase, that is."

Her right leg was starting to quiver. But he wouldn't notice it. Surely, he wouldn't. "If you need money," she said, "you've come to the wrong place. You might've noticed I work at McDonald's?"

"Of course, I noticed that. I notice all kinds of things, hon. I think I probably notice more than you do, since you didn't notice me when I drove by your place this morning. I had my eye on you from the moment you walked out the front door till you stepped under those golden arches.

I saw you leave the bowl of milk or whatever it was for that junkyard cat."

On her way to work, she'd stopped at the B of A and withdrawn her portion of the utilities along with an extra forty dollars because they'd planned dinner in Bakersfield on Saturday night and intended to see a movie. Julio had never asked her to help with the rent; when guilt finally led her to broach the subject, he said he'd continue to handle it but that if they ever made it "official" they could just merge their finances. What he didn't know—and she felt bad about not confessing it—was that for somebody who almost always worked minimum wage, she'd saved a surprising amount. In Fresno, she babysat for the cafeteria manager on the side, and cleaned houses, too, and she babysat for her current boss as well. She had over a thousand dollars socked away. And Tom had watched her visit the ATM. "I hate you," she said. "I really do."

"You're not the first."

"And won't be the last either." Keeping her eyes on him, she reached into her purse, unzipped the pocket where she'd placed the wad of twenties and pulled it out. She tossed the bills into the pickup, to make sure his hand didn't touch hers.

He shook his head, as if her behavior was both puzzling and hurtful. "How much is that?"

"A hundred and forty fucking dollars. Basically, a week's wages, you son of a bitch."

A lot of women had called him that, and even worse. Yet he'd never called any of them a cunt, or a slut, or a whore because, at least when they were with him, he preferred to think they weren't. He never even raised his voice to them. The other thing he'd never done was hit them, or get rough with them in bed. Eventually, all of them came to fear him, though why this was so he both did and did not understand. They liked to get high with him, they liked to fuck him, and they liked how he looked beside them. Six-foot-three, a strong chin, rippling abs, and the kind of eyes—according to his momma—that made Sinatra rich. They hadn't made him rich. Apparently he was like the off-brand jeans his grandma used to buy him when he was growing up: great-looking at the outset, but they never quite fit and after a certain number of wash cycles they began to unravel. It was all so unfair, and when he thought about it, which was not infrequently, it made him mad. It made him do some things he sometimes wished he hadn't.

"A hundred and forty bucks won't last too long," he said, "even with me sleeping in this old truck. I mean, don't misunderstand, I'm grateful. But it won't take me past Albuquerque, and I kinda need a big change of scenery. I'm thinking Tampa-St. Pete."

He watched, with interest, as she realized where this was all heading. She was less predictable than any of the others. She never became truly submissive, not even when she was scared, and she was plenty scared now.

"Go fuck yourself," she said. She set off toward Main Street.

She might not have been predictable, but he was. He did exactly what she figured he would when she took the first step, switching on the ignition and beginning to creep along behind her.

This town was seldom troubled by traffic at six-thirty on a weeknight, since nearly everybody was with their families or significant others, sitting down and sipping beer after a long day at the raisin plant, or getting ready to eat dinner. He could slowly follow her all the way home, if she went home, and there wouldn't be anybody to stop him from doing whatever he chose to: an overgrown lot flanked their house on one side, an empty rental on the other. The junkyard would be deserted except perhaps for the stray cat. She could go to the liquor store—he probably wouldn't follow her inside—but she couldn't stay there until closing without telling Julio what was up. By the time she reached Main Street, she realized she really had only one choice.

When she spun on the truck, it halted. She walked to the passenger side, and he leaned over to open the door. She shook her head. He stared at her for a moment, his face impassive, then rolled down the glass.

"I have five hundred dollars in the bank," she said. "If I give it to you, will you leave me alone?"

"Sure. No problem. I hate to be in this situation, but—"

"Just shut the fuck up. You know where the bank is. You can stay close enough to keep an eye on me. I'm sure you don't trust me any more than I trust you, and you don't have any fucking reason to. When I get to the ATM, you park in front of the florist shop. Leave the engine running—you won't be there long. If you climb out of this truck, so help me God, I'll scream my head off. The stores are closed, but there are rental apartments above every goddamn one." She didn't wait to hear if he accepted the offer or not, just set off for the B of A.

He did as instructed, parking down the street from the bank and leaving the engine running. She withdrew the cash, put her card away and walked back to the truck.

"I bet you had at least a thousand," he said. "Maybe two thousand."

"Bet all you want to." Again, she flung the bills at him.

He let them flutter past his face.

"Now it's my turn to watch you," she said. "I'm going to watch your taillights until they disappear onto 99. Then I'm going to the police station, which I can get to in about ninety seconds if I run—and I will run—and tell the cops a stranger in a green Ford Galaxy tried to abduct me. They'll take me home and have somebody watch the house the rest of the evening."

He didn't bother to conceal his fascination. He'd met his match—they both knew it. The difference was that this meant one thing to her and something else to him.

"Check you later, baby," he said, then backed into the street.

DOWNTOWN CEDAR PARK, THE NORTH Shore community where Martin had grown up and lived for all but the few years he attended college, consisted of two blocks of shops. It seemed as if every second or third business made use of the town's name: Cedar Park Drugs, Cedar Park Hardware. The latter, directly across Main Street from the seafood restaurant where they were sipping their drinks while waiting for a table, had snow shovels, trashcans and wheelbarrows piled up behind the plate glass window. The clutter reminded her of the hardware back in Loring, where her father hunkered in the plumbing section, hiding from the woman he loved.

"You've again got that look in your eye," Martin said.

"What look?"

"The one that tells me you're someplace besides here."

They were scrunched shoulder to shoulder in the alcove that housed the bar. This restaurant, which he claimed was the only good one in town, did not take reservations. You just appeared, gave them your name, ordered drinks and bided your time. He didn't need to give them his name, though. The woman at the hostess stand simply smiled, said "Hiyuh, Mahty" and made a note on her list. Everybody knew him.

The snow, limited earlier to flurries, was beginning to fall harder. Getting back into the city could become a problem, but this didn't trouble her as much as it might have a month ago. The reasons were too complex to parse just yet. "I'm here," she said.

"Your body is. But where's your mind?" He shut his eyes for a second or two, then opened them and snapped his fingers. "I know! It's in Mississippi. You're either thinking about high water everywhere or going down to the crossroads and doing a deal with the devil." He was smiling—that open, guileless smile that suggested he'd be easy to hurt, that it had happened to him on numerous occasions and he was one of those who, for some reason, did an inadequate job of protecting himself. "How about it?" he said. "Is yo' daddy right? Or is yo' daddy wrong?"

He had a good ear, he knew immediately that his tone was off. "I'm so sorry," he said. "That was in bad taste." He stirred the ice in his watery Bushmills. "Sometimes I'm a bit of a dolt."

"Sometimes we all are."

A waitress nudged her way through the clustered bodies and told them their table was ready. They grabbed their drinks and followed her to a booth at the rear of the restaurant, beneath a massive mounted swordfish. Before handing over the menus, she listed the evening's specials, concluding with something called Panko Parmesan Haddock. After checking to see if they had any questions, she promised to return in a few minutes.

"What about it?" he asked. "Their stuffed lobster's killer."

"I might as well be honest and admit I don't like what one has to do to the lobster before eating it. What else is good?"

"Everything. At one time or another, I've eaten it all. The Gloucester Sole's pretty fabulous. They wrap it around a crab cake."

In the end, she chose stuffed shrimp, and he picked the fisherman's platter. They ordered a bottle of sauvignon blanc and, when it came, he raised his glass. "To whatever," he proposed.

"To *whatever*? That's a vague sort of precision."

He'd become accomplished at the art of the rueful smile. He didn't know what it looked like, but he knew when it was happening, and it was happening now. How he'd gotten good at it remained a mystery to him. It used to annoy his wife. As did so much else.

Rather than respond to her observation, he said, "Back before Cedar Park turned into a bedroom community, this place used to be pretty different."

"How so?"

"It smelled different, it looked different. They served about five things, four of which were fried. You never saw anybody in here with a tie on, but it wasn't uncommon to encounter one of the guys who'd caught the fish on your plate. You might see him and his wife celebrating a birthday or anniversary, often with some other men from the boats and their wives. Lots of wind-burned faces, loud voices, raised mugs. It was pretty downscale. Things started changing around the time my dad suffered his first stroke. He closed his law practice after that, which was just as well. He'd probably never had a client who didn't live in this town or an adjoining one. He was on the Board of Aldermen for something like thirty-five years. For him, Cedar Park, Massachusetts, was the center of the universe." He paused and gazed into his wine glass, as if embarrassed at divulging so much.

The night he drove her home from the restaurant in Cambridge, he'd stayed at her place. She was the one who suggested it, and she wasn't sure she would do it until he pulled up in front of her brownstone, perfectly willing to tell her good night and let her out. She opened the door, even placed one foot on the pavement. "Would you like to come in?"

"I would."

He parked in front of a hydrant, the only available space. When she pointed out that his car would almost certainly get towed, he said, "I'll worry about that when it happens."

Nobody except Liz had been inside her place in the three and a half years she'd lived there. She realized, as they descended the basement stairs, that it was a worse mess than usual, due to her Thanksgiving malaise. Sticking the key in the lock, she said, "I'm afraid—"

"I'm afraid too."

"Jesus."

"What?"

She still hadn't turned the key. "All I meant to say was that I'm afraid my place looks like a hurricane hit it."

He laughed. "Well, I guess my fears are larger. And more existential. If you've changed your mind, I'd understand. Just say so."

"Jesus," she said again, then unlocked the door and switched on the lights.

Clothes lay scattered on the floor: a fleece jacket she'd owned since high school, a Red Sox tee shirt she'd bought at Fenway, a winter boot missing a heel, a pair of faded Levi's all but reduced to a thread collection. At least, she reflected, no empty liquor bottles stood on the counter. They would have completed the portrait of squalor and despair. "I'm afraid I don't have anything to drink here. I mean, except for water and coffee and some Diet Coke."

"Diet Coke's fine."

"Aren't you worried it might keep you awake?"

"Not really. I kind of like being awake."

"Did anyone ever tell you that you're an odd man?"

"Been hearing it for most of my adult life. Before that, they told me I was a strange little boy."

The studio was freezing. She turned up the thermostat, then opened the small refrigerator, pulled a can out, popped the tab and handed it to him. They sat down on the loveseat, the only real piece of furniture she had except for the nearby bed and a rickety table barely big enough for one person to eat at. If her circumstances appalled him, he did a good job of concealing it. "So why did people think you were a strange little boy?" she asked.

"The usual reason. I did strange things."

"Strange how? You mean like, say, torturing the neighbor's cat? That kind of thing?"

He laughed. "There was no neighbor's cat. Properly speaking, there were no neighbors. The house I grew up in's on top of a hill, at least a hundred yards from the next home."

"Somehow, that fails to subdue my concern."

"For instance, there was this clear-channel station up in Maine that broadcast country music all night. I fell in love with the sound of a pedal steel, and I discovered that if you wrapped an ordinary pocket comb in a sheet of notebook paper, put it against your lips and whined through it, you'd get the same kind of vibrato."

"Well, that is weird. But not cat-killing weird."

"In high school, I paid my sister, who was around nine at the time, to learn to play the fiddle."

"I'd say that was money well-spent."

"My folks didn't think so. They thought I was encouraging her to become as frivolous as me. My dad wanted me to be a lawyer, and my mother wanted me to be a doctor, and all I wanted was to lie on my back and play electric guitar like Mike Bloomfield. You know who he was?"

"I'm afraid not."

"Super Session? With Al Kooper and Stephen Stills?"

"Sorry. I'm drawing a blank."

After that, a couple of minutes passed in which neither of them could come up with anything else to say, though both of them were thinking as hard as they could. He felt that as badly as he wanted to stay, he really owed it to her to go home because, after all, he'd maneuvered her into having a couple of drinks, which she clearly wasn't used to, and the alcohol had probably clouded her judgment. How different was he, she might wake up thinking, from her voice instructor? As for her, she wished she had one more glass of wine, or maybe even two, so that she could find the courage to say she wanted him to spend the night there, that she dreaded waking up alone and feeling like she'd felt the last couple of days.

He looked at his watch, and his mouth started to move. She reached out, locked her fingers around the stainless steel expansion band and pulled the timepiece right off his wrist. "Tissot," she said, examining its austerely elegant face. "Those are supposed to be good."

He sat looking at the pale strip of skin where the band had been. Until then, he'd never noticed how white it was. He wore the watch all the time except when taking a shower. That suddenly seemed like a bizarre thing to do, since he had so many empty hours to fill however he could. "Why did you do that?" he asked.

"Because I'm training to be a jewel thief?"

Her bed wasn't really large enough for two people, but two people slept there, her on her right side, the black mask covering her eyes, her face so close to the wall that her nose made contact with it a couple of times during the night; him behind her, one arm resting on her pillow, the other against his own ribcage. He slept in his underwear and tee shirt, and she did the same, having put on her Red Sox apparel when she stepped into the bathroom. She told him to use her toothbrush, and he did, noting that the bristles were much softer than his. He swished some Listermint around in his mouth.

When she woke the next morning, he'd already gotten dressed, walked over to Boylston, bought croissants, brioches and a copy of the *Globe*, which he was reading while he sipped a cup of the coffee he'd taken upon himself to brew. She watched him for a moment before he realized she was awake. He looked very much at home. He'd removed his shoes after his shopping expedition, and his legs were crossed. She saw a jagged hole in the heel of his sock.

He took care not to watch her as she climbed out of bed and shrugged on her bathrobe. They ate breakfast on the loveseat, not saying a whole lot, each of them trying to determine what, if anything, falling asleep in the same bed might mean. Finally, he sighed, picked his watch up off the floor and consulted it. "Believe it or not," he told her, "I have somewhere I need to be this afternoon. My partner and I—I think you'd like him, by the way—we're mixing this rockabilly album we'll be releasing in a few months. I'm supposed to meet him for lunch up in Lexington around one-thirty, and then we'll go on into the studio. Want to join me?"

She said she'd love to but couldn't, that she needed to be at work by three and wouldn't have time to get back if she went out there.

He bent over to put on his shoes. "Are you busy next Friday and or Saturday night?" he asked.

"I don't yet know."

"Okay."

For the second time in a few hours she laid her hand on his arm. He quit working on the shoe laces but continued to bend over them.

"I *honestly* don't know," she said. "We get our schedules for the week on Monday morning."

"In other words, you're not just brushing me off? Not yet, anyhow?"

"Can I make a couple of observations?"

He finished tying his shoes, then sat up straight. To her, his face looked plasticized, as if its structure depended on some artificial agent. He said, "Sure. Have at it."

She'd been about to jocularly note that for a man in his thirties he was more than a little insecure and that his right sock had a huge hole in it and probably ought to be retired. Instead she said, "I think I would like to see you again."

"That's only one observation. You said you wanted to make a couple. What's the other?"

"I think," she heard herself say, "that I might actually want to see you again and again."

•

Their dinner, when it came, was superb. She gave him one of her stuffed shrimp, and he passed her a couple of fried oysters. Normally, she avoided fried foods, especially fish because she smelled so much of it at work. But she had a weakness for oysters. Her dad loved them, and every now and then he'd bring home a couple of orders. Her mom didn't care for them, and neither did her sister. She told Martin about it while sipping the last of her wine.

He laid down his fork. "I didn't know you had a sister," he said.

They'd gone out to dinner three or four times by then, always on short notice. She sensed that he was being careful, and she knew she was. He hadn't stayed at her place again. She'd never even seen his. After Christmas he went three weeks without calling. It was a lonely time. She and Liz celebrated New Year's Eve together, buying First Night buttons that allowed them entry to all the events, but nothing really caught their fancy except the ice sculptures in the Common and the fireworks at Waterfront Park. The next day Liz left for ten days in Costa Rica with her city councilman. When she returned, she worked a lot of extra shifts to make up for lost pay, which left her too few hours for entertainment. The weather was terrible, snow nearly every day, and Ella again felt herself sinking into a depression too deep to be called a rut. Something needed to change. Something had to happen that hadn't happened before.

"Well, I do have a sister," she said. "And as I just acknowledged, I also have a mother and father."

"I figured as much, since everyone does."

"But until now you never asked about them."

"Something told me to wait until you worked your way around to the subject. Tell me more?"

So she told him where her mother lived and where she worked and about her marriage to Mr. Burns. She told him she hadn't heard from her sister for a couple of years and didn't know her whereabouts and had nightmares in which she discovered she was dead. And then, over the next half hour or so, she told him what happened to her father, including the part about his letters to and from Grace Pace. To his credit, Martin didn't act horrified.

But he was. His ex-wife's father had been murdered. South Boston Irish, he'd gotten part of his nose bitten off one night by somebody in a rival loansharking crew and then, after failing to heed that dramatic warning, he disappeared, his remains eventually washing ashore on Constitution Beach. Martin hadn't known any of this during his junior year at Merrimac when they began dating. He learned it following graduation, on the evening he proposed. By then, it didn't matter. Later on, it did.

"And you think," he said, "that your dad . . . that he caused the explosion on purpose?"

"No," she said, more sharply than she'd intended. "I don't think that at all."

"But the lawsuit . . ."

"People file lawsuits at the drop of a hat. And a lot more than a hat dropped there. The gas company gave Mr. Pace some kind of settlement. But there never was any admission of guilt."

"What happened to Mr. Pace after that?"

"I don't know. And I don't really care. I haven't been back to the town since I left. I don't plan to go there again."

"Well, I can understand that."

"Oh? Can you?"

He didn't like her tone. "You mean that maybe I can't because I still live in the town where I grew up, this little picture of American tranquility?"

He sat with his back to the window. A blizzard was in progress, impressive even for Massachusetts, and this would explain why, even though it was only 9:15 on a Saturday evening, the restaurant was all but empty. The bartender had been glancing at them for a good half hour, and on her most recent visit their waitress did not conceal her impatience.

"I'm sorry," Ella said. "I'm sure it's not as tranquil as it might appear. At the moment, it doesn't appear tranquil at all." She gestured toward the street. "Take a look."

He turned and glanced over his shoulder, though he didn't need to. He paid attention to the weather forecast, which was why he'd phoned her on Wednesday and asked if they could have dinner here on Saturday night rather than Friday, as originally planned, because something had come up involving an important client. What would she think, he wondered now, if she knew he'd acted in such a calculated manner, hoping she'd have no choice but to spend the night?

What would *he* think, she asked herself, if he knew that she paid attention to the weather forecast too?

SHE WAKES BENEATH A QUILT so heavy it calls to mind her father's old hunting vest loaded down with shotgun shells. Beyond the foot of the bed there's a Naugahyde couch and, behind that, a turret with bay windows, the curtains pulled back to let the sunlight in, though the day has opened gray. She hears the hum of forced air.

She's alone now, though she wasn't when she fell asleep. She replays the end of the evening: the climb up the treacherous hill, too slick for his Volvo, which stood parked at the bottom; the cognac they drank in the living room in front of the fireplace where a synthetic log flickered; the no less treacherous climb up the stairs to bed, how she quickly shed her clothes while he visited the master bath; the relief, the gratitude she saw in his eyes when he emerged to find that she would not have to be coaxed.

It was clumsy, it was messy. She felt a trace of excitement toward the end. She assured herself of that.

"Oh, Jesus, God," he whispered into the cleft of her neck. "Four miserable years. I'd wait twice as long for you. Three times even."

Are words worth less, or more, if you take a while to say them? Does the delay prove you're thoughtful? Deceitful? Opportunistic? Or just tired? "You won't have to wait anymore," she finally promised.

"Truly?"

"Truly."

She pushes back the covers and rises, remembering that the bathroom is on the far side of the bed and around the corner. Thoughtfully, he has left a robe for her on an ottoman at the foot of the four-poster. To whom might the robe have belonged? His mother, who once slept in this room? His ex-wife, who slept here too? She puts it on, knots the cinch, pads over to the bathroom and taps at the door. No one answers, so she turns the knob and pushes it open.

On the counter: a single-edged razor, a can of Barbasol aloe shaving cream, a ceramic mug containing not one but four toothbrushes in assorted colors. A neatly folded white towel lies waiting near the sink, and another hangs from a hook next to the shower. The toilet seat is raised. At some point during the night, when she found her way in here to pee, she almost fell in. She lowers it again.

When she returns to the bedroom she catches a whiff of fried bacon. It must have wafted up through the vent. She hasn't smelled it first thing in the morning for many years. Not since the last time her mother fixed her breakfast.

He has probably heard her moving around, and it seems wrong to make him come get her. She's barefooted, and though the room is warm, the floor is not. Her eye lights on a pair of furry moccasins about six sizes too large. She appropriates the house shoes, scrunching up her toes to keep them from flopping off her feet.

On the landing, she can see her reflection in the flooring. The boards have recently been waxed. He must use a cleaning service—she can't imagine Martin Summers with a mop in his hands. As she makes her way downstairs, she lets her palm glide along the banister, afraid that those Paul Bunyan-sized moccasins will slip right out from under her.

He's got on blue slacks and a powder-blue shirt with gray pinstripes, and his sleeves are rolled up. He's also wearing an apron, white, with a map of the Emerald Isle on the front, all the major cities denoted by red dots. "Good morning," he says. He turns the gas off under the skillet, then meticulously transfers the bacon, one slice at a time, to a platter covered by a paper towel. "No point in needlessly clogging our arteries," he says. "We'll just let that drain." He lifts the skillet, sets it in the sink and turns on the water. A cloud of steam billows up. "Sleep well?" he asks while rinsing his hands.

"I slept great."

"So did I."

"How much did it snow, do you think?"

He dries his hands on a dish towel. "According to the *Globe*, more than two feet."

"They were able to deliver the paper? How did they get up this hill?"

"Cedar Park does a good job of clearing the streets. The minute it begins to slack off, the plows go to work. I'm surprised you didn't hear them last night. You slept through the snow blower too."

"You already went out and used a snow blower?"

He laughs. "Not on your life. I've got a guy that does it for me."

She looks around the kitchen, which has glazed tiles on the floor and walls, open shelves, a work island with storage drawers and another sink and four stools, two on one side of the island and one at each end. The stools are covered in red plaid that matches the fabric of the armchair in the corner next to a reading lamp.

He seems to know what she's thinking. "My dad was about as successful as a small-town lawyer could be," he says. "And so was my grandfather, who's actually the one that built the house. The success gene seems not to have been passed on to me."

They eat at the work island. Three strips of bacon, scrambled eggs with scallions, toast, and strawberry jam that he says he bought last fall in Vermont. She offers to wash the dishes but he says no, that he'll deal with them later. They carry their coffee into the living room, where this time he's got a real fire going. He says he burns a couple of cords a year. "About the only similarity between me and my dad," he says, "was the love of a good fire. From about the middle of September through the end of May, we had one nearly every night. It's not so much the warmth or the aroma that appeals to me, though I like them too. It's that crackling sound. Back at Berklee, I composed an instrumental called 'Hardwood Pop.' It wasn't half bad."

"Do you still play?"

"Yeah. But mostly just for myself. Occasionally I'll do some filler stuff on one of our records. But that's rare."

"Would you play for me?"

He has no acting ability—that's something she already knew, though she wasn't aware she knew it until now. He protests that he's not very good, but he can't quite hide his pleasure at being asked. "Only if you insist," he says.

"I insist."

He gets up and comes back a few minutes later carrying a beat-up sunburst acoustic with the Gibson logo on the headstock. "Okay," he says, "don't blame me, you asked for it." He sits down beside her, places the guitar on his left knee and launches into a tune she doesn't recognize, a snappy rag in a minor key. He doesn't use a pick, just plays with his bare thumb and three fingers. He plays really well, but she accepted it as a given that he would. You don't get into Berklee if you can't.

When he stops she says, "That's beautiful. I mean it. Is it one of your own songs?"

"I was just making it up on the fly. Will you sing one for me?"

This takes her by surprise, though when she thinks about it tomorrow, she'll realize that it shouldn't have. She'll need another day or two to admit that his request made her no less less pleased than hers made him. Nobody has asked her to sing since the day she left school. Nobody cares if she has a voice or not. "Can you play 'Moon River'?"

"Badly. What's your key?"

"How about D?"

He plays a surprisingly swingy intro. She's never sung "Moon River" up tempo. But he's established the mood, and evidently he's not having a melancholy morning. She hears a teasing lilt in her voice that has never been there before. Where did it come from? The lyrics don't warrant it.

"I love your voice," he says when she's sung the last line. "It's so pure. You don't strain."

"Well, I love the way you play. Very smooth. And lots of color."

"Maybe we ought to form a duo."

"What might we call ourselves?"

"How about the Music School Drop Outs?"

"It doesn't exactly inspire."

"The Berklee Bums?"

"I don't think so."

"The Plain Old Nobodies?"

"That has a certain ring."

He suggests another song, then she suggests one, then he suggests another. Songs she hasn't sung for years or has never sung at all. Show tunes, country gospel, sunshine pop, soft rock; murder ballads, Christmas songs, the Rice-a-Roni jingle, "Bang-Shang-a-Lang," "Proud Mary." She sings "Mack the Knife," mimicking the accent of Hildegard Knef. Time passes, then more time. He throws another log on the fire, and then another and then another. He opens a bottle of cognac like the one they finished last night. The day grows darker, it begins to snow again. Objects lose line and edge. The world beyond the window falls away.

EASTER FELL ON THE 22ND of April, and they'd agreed to spend it at the home of Julio's parents, in a small town near Sacramento. As they drove north that Saturday morning, he told her his folks moved there in 1973, after they finally made enough money working for Covino Vineyards to open their café. It served only breakfast and lunch, and his dad did all the cooking while his mom handled the register. They mostly hired girls right out of high school to wait tables. His dad was scrupulous, he said, about making sure everybody who worked for him had their papers. The last thing he wanted was to get on the INS shit list. "Over there at the winery," he said, "it was never a problem. The Covino family made sure of it."

"How?"

He laughed. "How do you think?"

"They paid off the Feds?"

"Sure, they've got their price, like everybody else. But it's too high for a guy like my dad."

"What about you? Have you got a price too?"

She'd been teasing, but he took her question seriously. "There are things I'd do for money. And there are things I wouldn't do."

She looked out her window. The morning was unusually clear, so she could see the Sierras. Most days, the mountains remained invisible behind a thick curtain of smog. There was still a lot of snow up there, whereas down here in the Valley it was in the mid-80s. Julio was running the pickup's AC. In the interest of saving money, they'd agreed not to use

119

the evaporative cooler at home until the thermometer hit 90. It didn't work all that well anyway. She could stand the heat okay but worried about Querida, whose hair was long and thick. They'd finally coaxed the calico into the house and laid claim to her. For a cat who lived in junkyard, she adapted pretty quickly to domestic life, climbing into their laps at the slightest opportunity. Somebody somewhere must have loved her before.

"You think your parents'll like me?" she asked.

He took his eyes off the road for an instant, flashing her a big smile that revealed his recently filled molar. A couple of weeks ago, when the tooth began to bother him too much, he mixed some zinc oxide together with oil of cloves, creating a homemade filling that he applied himself. His dad taught him, he said. When he was growing up, his family didn't have health insurance, let alone dental. "They'll love you," he told her. "Guaranteed."

"Think so?"

He glanced in the rear-view mirror, then pulled into the left lane to pass a semi with the Albertson's logo on the side. "I know my folks. *Tienen buen gusto.*"

"They have good taste?"

He laughed. "In no time you'll be speaking Spanish like María Felíx."

"Who's that?"

"A Mexican actress my folks love. My mom loves her one way. And my dad, he loves her another."

His parents' house was a lot nicer than she expected, a neat white Tudor with gingerbread trim and a bay window through which they could see his mother peering anxiously at the street. Her face lit up when they pulled into the drive. She straightened her hair, then disappeared.

"My mom, she doesn't like the empty nest," Julio said, grabbing the sack of wine off the seat. His sister lived in Florida, near the Air Force base where her husband was stationed, and she hadn't been able to come home for six months.

Mrs. Huerta met them at the door. Roundish, with gray hair pulled back in a bun and an olive-toned complexion that perfectly matched Julio's, she began to plaster his face with kisses, then grabbed Caroline and applied a few more to her cheeks. "I'm so happy to meet you," she said. "My son, he wasted too much time describing you. He wrote three or four pages when all he needed was one word. Julio, you don't know the word *beautiful*?"

"I know it, Mom. I even know how to spell it."

His mother took her by the elbow. "You're starving," she said, in a tone that precluded objection. "You'll eat lunch now. My husband's still at the café. I told him he needs to close it on the day before Easter, but he has his rules. And what's the main one? Each and every human being's supposed to work like a burro."

She'd already had her lunch, she said, so she sat and watched while they ate. She'd fixed stuffed poblanos with chorizo filling, Julio's favorite, and a big bowl of salad. They each drank a bottle of ice-cold Chihuahua. While she ate, Caroline took in the photos that stood on the hutch in the dining room: a young Mrs. Huerta, holding an angry-looking baby wrapped in a white blanket, mouth wide open, one fist protruding, and right next to that, another, almost identical snapshot of her holding a happy-looking baby in a yellow blanket.

"Can you guess which one is Julio?" the older woman asked.

"The one that looks mad?"

"Of course! He was not calm like his sister. He had the colic. My husband, he used to put him in the carriage in the middle of the night, over there in Paso Robles, and walk him for hours, up and down this little street we lived on. The problem was, the sidewalks were buckled, and bad kids liked to shoot out the streetlights, so you couldn't see that well. Just around when he'd fall asleep, the carriage would hit one of the rough spots, and once again little Julio would pretend he's a beagle. Once you got him hollered out, he'd sleep half the day. But us, we had to stay awake and go to work. We didn't think we were living that nice of a life in those days, we were always sleepy, but now I know we were wrong. You don't see that kind of thing until you look back at far-off times. What was your growing up like?"

In later years, when she looked back at her own far-off times, she would recall how artfully this woman who used to pick grapes led up to that question. And she would recall how smoothly she glided into her lies, mixing in just the right amount of random detail, the stuff that seemingly had nothing to do with anything but progressed to something that did. How, for instance, back in Hannibal they lived near a creek that emptied into the Mississippi and the creek sometimes flooded and backed up and once they found a snake skin in the chest of drawers, and their father said it wasn't poisonous, though later on he admitted that it was. How every Friday, when their dad returned his milk truck to the dairy he drove for, he'd pick up a half-gallon of freshly made ice cream and bring it home for her and her sister.

"Was it always the same flavor?" Mrs. Heurta asked.

"Always. Black Walnut."

How each year Santa left their presents around the tree for them to find when they woke. Then one year her older sister heard that St. Nick was fictitious and told their dad. On Christmas morning the presents were right where they'd always been, along with an irate note: *Girls, next year please remind your father to get the chimney cleaned. I look like hell now and I still have to visit Texas and the West Coast.*

Laughing: "What presents did he leave you that year? I bet you remember, don't you?"

"Yes, ma'am. I got a pink tricycle with streamers on the handlebars."

How her mother tried to raise her Baptist, and her father tried to raise her Methodist, but her uncle on her father's side married an Italian woman, who of course was Catholic, and she, Carin, was always jealous around the holidays, because it seemed like her cousins ate better food and had more fun.

"Did they live in Hannibal too?"

"No ma'am, they lived in Memphis. Not Memphis, Tennessee, though. Memphis, Missouri. It's a town in Scotland County, up close to the Iowa border."

By the end of the meal, she'd set Mrs. Heurta's mind to rest. "*Mi hijo,*" she told her son, "you better be good to this young lady. *Ella es la mejor.*"

The problem was that the lies—retailed with poise because she'd done the homework she didn't do in school, studying the *Rand McNally* to learn what was where in the latest past she'd invented for herself—did not rest easy on her own mind. She thought it less and less likely that she could make a life with Julio without coming clean. But not completely clean, she could never do that. Some dirt sticks to you forever.

.

His parents knew they were living together, but they still assigned her to a separate bedroom, as Julio had warned would be the case. His father, who was even shorter than his son, with a weathered face that suggested he'd spent a good part of his life outside, led her down the hall, pausing a couple of times to comment on family photographs. Pretty much every inch of wall space was covered by framed snapshots, many of them black and white, with the deckled edges she recalled seeing in the '60s.

"This one here," he said, "that's me and my friend Esteban, taken down in the Imperial Valley the year we came north. 1944." In the photo, two young men sat on the tailgate of a pickup, both of them wearing work pants, long-sleeved shirts, broad-brimmed hats and shoes of the type her grandmother used to call brogans. The man on the left looked exactly like Julio.

"Have you ever heard of the *braceros*?" Mr. Huerta asked.

"Yes, sir. Julio told me a it was a guest workers program that started during World War II."

He laughed. "That's right. But they didn't make us feel like the kind of guest we're gonna try to make you feel like. Thirty cents a day we got for picking artichokes. We went to the field at six o'clock AM and stayed there all day. They're supposed to feed us for free, see, so when do they serve breakfast? Four, because they know some of us are so tired we'll sleep till five and they'll save on the food. I learned a whole lot about economics."

"That's how black people got treated in Mississippi when I was . . ." She corrected course. " . . . growing up in Hannibal. My dad used to read to me about it from the St. Louis paper."

"Yeah? Well, down in the Imperial they didn't need no black people. They had us."

He opened the door to the bedroom and gestured for her to enter first. The walls were purple. On one of them hung a gilt-framed high school diploma issued to Julieta Martina Huerta in 1975. A large stuffed bear reposed on the bed. It was missing one eye.

Before she could fully catalogue her surroundings, he stepped in behind her and shut the door. She turned to find him standing only a couple of feet away. "So," he said, "our Julio, he's a good boy. Been a fine son. He never caused us a problem, ever. When the other kids were getting in trouble, he was helping out. You know what I'm talking about. I'm sure you were the same kind of girl. I got a good sense for these things. I can tell. See, I know a good person when I meet one. I don't know how I got this skill, but that don't really matter. What I'm saying is with Julio you can't do wrong.

"The thing is, he never really felt like this town was his home. He grew up over on the 101. But you need a lot more money over there to open a business. We never could've done it. We never could've bought this house either." He waved his hand around the room. "He was already out of high school, see, when we made enough to do it. His sister, she don't really love the place herself, but that's okay, she graduated from here, she's got some local friends. She's happy enough when she visits. That's all that matters to us. I'm sure your mama and papa feel the same way, that you got to go back to that town in Missouri every now and then.

"What I want you to know, and the reason I closed the door for a minute, is our café's a good solid business. The local paper, it does a Best-Of list every December, and we made it six years in a row. Everybody likes Felipe and Margarita's. I like it too. I like what I do. But I don't mean to do it forever. You're a smart girl. You know what I'm saying. I can tell you got good business sense. There's something here a person can depend on."

She didn't trust her voice, feared it would break. Then it occurred to her that whatever he heard in it would at least be real, whereas nothing else she'd said since she stepped into this house that he and his wife worked so hard for was anything but a lie. "What about your daughter?" she asked. "Wouldn't she want to come back and run the café?"

"Our daughter, she's got her Air Force officer. He'll be a general one day. Or at least a colonel. That man, you ought to hear him bark *Yes, Sir!* The walls shake. Our daughter, she's set." He put his hands in his pockets. When he smiled, she saw just how many wrinkles the sun and wind had etched into the face of this small, proud man who arrived forty years ago to pick artichokes. "Who knows?" he said. "Maybe one day our little café will be called Julio and Carin's."

.

They stayed through Easter lunch, at which the table all but sagged beneath the spread his parents laid out: fish soup with lima beans; raw shrimp covered in a sauce made with cinnamon spice and pumpkin seed; cactus leaf salad; bread pudding with cheese, peanuts and raisins; fruit turnovers. She drank more wine than she normally would have. She thought she might actually be a little bit drunk.

Maybe that could account for what happened when she bid his parents goodbye. Crying was not the kind of thing she did, but that afternoon she couldn't hold back the tears. His mother let loose too, and even his dad's eyes looked damp. They begged her to come back soon. She assured them she would. Many times.

"Like I said," Julio told her as they drove away, "I know my folks. You took them by storm."

"They took me by storm too."

"They're great people. I worry a little bit about my mom. She's got really high blood pressure, and the women on her side of the family tend to die in their late fifties and early sixties. But so far, so good. Now my dad, he might live to be a hundred. My great grandpapa actually did."

By the time they reached the freeway, she was nodding off. He told her to go ahead and take a nap, that he hadn't drunk much and didn't think he'd need to be spelled, though traffic was heavy and home four hours away. She leaned against the door and shut her eyes.

While she slept she dreamed. She was in a pickup with her sister, and they were both little, and their grandma was driving, taking them somewhere they'd never been before, someplace that even she hadn't been, and it was raining and there was thunder and lightning, and the wipers didn't work. Their grandma said she couldn't see, then the windshield split open and the truck was veering toward a precipice, and she wanted her sister to hold her but she wouldn't. She was all alone at the edge of the seat, and the door gaped open and out she went. She was falling and howling but nobody heard.

"Hey," a voice said. "You okay?"

When she opened her eyes, they were traveling slowly through what looked like a small town, not on the freeway anymore. In front of them, a propane truck like the one her father had driven was creeping along, its tank painted green. She'd never seen one before that wasn't white. Why would anybody deliver propane on Easter Sunday? She rubbed her eyes. "Where are we?" she asked Julio.

"Los Banos."

"What are we doing here?"

"The traffic on 99 was horrible, so I thought I'd cut over to the 5. I guess everybody went somewhere for Easter, just like us."

"I guess so."

"Speaking of going somewhere?" he said.

"Yeah?"

"I was thinking maybe we'd treat ourselves to a little vacation. We deserve one. When my school's over, I believe I could get a few days off. I'm sure you could too. Your manager loves you. I've got more money saved than you might think."

"Sure. I'm game. You got any particular place in mind?"

"Yeah. You ever been up on the North Coast, where the big redwoods are? Up around Arcata or Crescent City?"

The last few syllables wreaked visceral havoc. A wave of nausea welled up, and for a moment she felt sure that all she'd eaten, and all she'd drunk, would come roaring out her mouth, laced with bile and stinking of death. She turned her face to the window. The Bonanza Motel and Ponderosa Restaurant slid by. "I've never been anywhere near the North Coast," she told him. "And I'm not sure I want to go there right now. I think it's a little too far."

ANOTHER MORNING IN MAY.

Julio's school year would end in a few days. The following week, he'd graduate with his associate degree—becoming the first in his family to make it beyond high school—and then they would take their brief vacation. They planned to go south, not north, spending three nights in a San Clemente Comfort Inn on El Camino Real. Supposedly the town had a long pier that jutted far out into the ocean and a beach that was five miles long. Her manager said if you walked far enough, you could get a glimpse of La Casa Pacifica, where Richard Nixon lived in palatial disgrace.

She'd just dressed for work when she heard the knock on the door. She thought it was probably Julio, that he'd forgotten something for school and come back to get it and just left his truck running.

She opened the door and there Tom stood, looking considerably better than when she'd last seen him. His hair was freshly washed, his jeans were clean. He wore a Skull & Roses T-shirt. He didn't shock her nearly as badly this time, because she suspected he would be back, that there was only one way to escape, with all the associated costs. Querida, who as always followed her to the door, took one look at him and ran for the bedroom. The cat knew trouble when she saw it.

"What do you want?" she said, her foot against the door to shove it shut if need be. She would not let him enter this house, at least not willingly. He could get inside if he chose to. He could break a window. He could break almost anything.

"A better question," he said, "is what I'll settle for. What I want's obvious, isn't it?"

"Is it?"

He gestured at his pickup, which she saw parked across the street, directly in front of the junkyard. "I want us to get in that old thing and ride. Like we used to. Have us a little fun before it's too late. One day we'll be in the ground. You can't play in that old cold clay." He snapped his fingers. "Damn," he said, "wouldn't that make a hell of a title for a country song?"

She felt strangely calm. She had always been calm once she ran out of choices. When you only have one option, the way ahead is clear. "Since I'd just as soon get in a truck with Ted Bundy," she said, "you'd better tell me what you'll settle for. That's all you might get."

"Oh, I'll get it," he said.

"What makes you so sure?"

"Well, to state the obvious? I'll get it because if need be, I'll take it. You know what your boyfriend does at night when it's his evening to close the store?"

She knew. And she'd understood that sooner or later, Tom would find out too. This moment had been inevitable since the day he located her. In the meantime, by pressing her luck and Julio's along with it, she'd experienced a little more joy while there was joy to be had. "No," she lied, "I don't."

"Well, how about I tell you." He said that after locking the front door at the liquor store, Julio lowered the security grating and locked it in place. And then he carried the canvas bag he'd slipped under his waistband down the street to the B of A, where he opened the night deposit box and dropped the bag down the chute. Then he kept right on walking and in another ten minutes he was home. "Here to cuddle up in his nice soft bed with his hot gringa."

"Really?" she said. "I wasn't aware of it. I mean, except for the last part. That I knew. And by the way? He's plenty fucking hot himself."

"Yeah? Well, that's surprising. He looks pretty milquetoast to me. Of course, I have seen him do a couple of surprising things."

Instantly, she understood what was coming. In his own way, Tom was resourceful. Why work to attain only one goal if two might be within reach? Especially if you knew you'd never get the top item on your list.

"Twice now," he said, "I've seen him stop halfway down the block, when he's out from under the streetlights, and stick his hand into his drawers like he's adjusting old John Henry, or Juan Enrique, I guess I should say. As soon as his hand turns loose of his crotch, he slips it in his pocket. I doubt he's taking a huge amount, because he probably hasn't got that much ambition. Twenty bucks here, thirty bucks there. Just enough to buy you a few drinks down at the cantina."

Julio wouldn't steal, period. "Well," she said, "I guess we all have our price, don't we?"

"I know I do. You want to know what it is right now?"

"Sure. Then you can get out of my way and let me go build a few more Big Macs."

Tonight, he said, when Julio got to that dark spot on the sidewalk, he needed to stick his hand in his drawers again. Then he needed to pull that sack free and drop it in the municipal trash can that stood right there. Then he just needed to keep on walking, careful not to look over his shoulder. He needed to walk at a normal pace until he got to this block, at which point he should break into a full-tilt sprint for the last hundred yards so he sounded stressed and winded when he reached home, where he'd pick up the phone, call 911 and tell the cops he'd been robbed by a black guy who rode up beside him on a Harley, stuck a gun in his face, called him a motherfucking spick—"put that in for good measure"—and demanded he surrender the bag, which he had no choice but to do, since he wanted to remain alive so he could continue to consume tamales.

"Easy as that," he said. "I get enough money to blow California once and for all. You get me out of your life. With any luck, you still get laid this very evening. You and old Pedro can have yourselves a fine time. Got the picture?"

"Why would I agree to this? Why would Julio?"

He grinned, exposing the chipped teeth.

•

The Fall of '78.

For the last few weeks they've been driving around the Pacific Northwest. Eugene, Coos Bay, Portland, Tacoma, Port Townsend, Seattle, Orcas Island. They've slept in a tent, they've slept in the car, they've slept in the occasional fleabag motel. Near Lincoln, Oregon, they slept in a magnificent summer home. They had no trouble getting in—he easily disarmed the alarm, which he said was a piece of cake— and spent the night in a second-floor bedroom with a view of the ocean. The next morning, when they opened the door to go downstairs and see what they could find to eat, the supposedly disabled alarm began to shriek, so they forgot about breakfast and jumped in the car. On the coast road, they met a cop headed in the opposite direction, lights flashing, siren blaring.

They drive back into northern California the last week of October. He says they're going to visit a friend he hasn't seen for a couple of years, a guy named Beamer who used to do set design for Warner Brothers. Beamer, he explains, got tired of the LA rat race, decided to go back where he came from and built himself a cabin in Mule Deer Creek. She figures he deals drugs. This tends to be the case with the "friends" they go to visit: they deal drugs, they run chop shops. One guy in Choteau, Montana—she actually liked him—was a professional rustler. She told him she didn't know people still stole livestock for a living, and he said, in what she recalled as a kind voice, "Honey, you show me anything in the world that's worth a dollar, or a pound, or a peso, or a ruble, and I'll guarantee you there's somebody that specializes in transferring the possession thereof."

Tom moves drugs for some of his friends, he moves cars for others. She doesn't know what he did for the rustler. She's learned not to ask. "Just enjoy the ride," he always says, and for a while she did. She liked seeing new places, sleeping when she was sleepy and waking when she wasn't, not having to show up when someone ordered her to perform some meaningless task. She also liked the sex, particularly when she was high. But by the last week of October she'd long since started to worry about what might come next. The rustler let it slip that he'd done a couple of years in the state penitentiary. She suspects he isn't the only one of Tom's friends who's gone to jail. As soon as they get to a good-sized town, she's decided, she will hop on a bus and disappear.

Mule Deer Creek is not a good-sized town. It's hardly a town at all, just a collection of cabins about fifteen miles off Interstate 5. The one his friend built is the nicest, or at least it looks like the nicest when they pull up in front of it that night. The problem is that it seems his friend no longer lives there, a fact that only becomes apparent after Tom raps on the door, hollers "Hey, Beamer, open the fuck up" and finds himself facing an elderly woman and an assault rifle.

A bad mood descends on him. They sleep in the car again that night and the next, him in the front seat, her in the back, and it's so cold he has to turn the engine on every couple of hours to warm them up. The next day, on 101 near McKinleyville, when she sees the golden arches and asks if they can stop for coffee and maybe some Egg McMuffins, he says, "I'm fucking sick to death of McDonald's." By then, they haven't eaten for almost twenty-four hours.

Late that afternoon they sit on a cliff above the ocean for a long time, just listening to the waves crash on the rocks below and sipping from a bottle of Christian Brothers Brandy that he bought the day before in Willits. When the level drops to a couple of inches, he turns it up and swigs the last. Then he hurls the bottle off the cliff, gets up and heads for the car. She decides to wait and see if he'll drive off and leave her. She hopes he will. She prays it. She hears him open and close the door. Yes, she begs silently. Please do it.

Instead he rolls down the window. "Get the fuck in the goddamn car!"

They drive north, back toward the Oregon state line. When she reaches over to turn on the radio, he bats her hand away. "I need quiet," he says. "I'm thinking."

"What about?"

No answer.

She peeks at the dashboard. The fuel gauge shows less than a quarter of a tank. "We don't have a whole lot of gas left," she observes.

"That's not all we don't have."

She starts to ask what else they don't have but is afraid to hear the answer. She opens the glove compartment, paws through the maps, finds the one for Northern California and unfolds it. She has only the vaguest notion what lies ahead. When they drove north before, they used I-5. She knows that the cliff they sat on was in Patrick's Point State Park. The closest town, Klamath, looks to be about twenty miles away.

Though it has a little store with a gas pump out front, they pass right through. The next town will be Crescent City. She turns the map over. According to the population data, nearly five thousand people live there. Large enough, maybe, to be served by Trailways or Greyhound.

They get there at dusk. He turns off 101, onto what she thinks must be the main drag. No bus station but two convenience stores with gas pumps, though he doesn't stop at either. The needle is moving toward empty.

"Tom, what are we going to do if we run out of gas?"

"I'll deal with it. First I want to take a little nap."

He turns onto a smaller street—according to the sign, Lighthouse Way. "Take a look out there," he says and points toward the water.

A few hundred yards away, on her right, there's a rocky island with a single tree and three small buildings. From the roof of the largest protrudes a white tower topped by a red lantern.

"That structure you're observing is Battery Point Lighthouse," he says, adopting a scholarly tone she's never heard him use before. "Back in 1964, this area was devastated by a tsunami that killed quite a few people. A wall of water, forty or fifty feet high, slammed into that little island, but the lighthouse survived. It caused major destruction in the town itself, knocking down the buildings back there on Front Street, rupturing gas lines. There were fires wherever you looked. It was a disaster of huge proportions, front-page news around the globe."

His mood has suddenly improved. Rather than settling her own jangling nerves, though, this does just the opposite. What is there to feel sanguine about? They're running out of gas, they're starving—she is anyway—and it seems they're about to reach a dead end: the road ahead stops at the water.

"How'd you happen to know that?" she asks. He's told her he grew up "all over," that because his father was in the Marines the family moved around, that he's lived in Florida, Texas, Virginia, Guam, and a host of other places.

"Oh, I've been here before," he says.

"Really? When?"

"Various times."

"Were you here during the tsunami?"

As is increasingly the case, he ignores her question. "I'm going to grab a little shut-eye. Then we'll gas up and get a bite to eat. I think we'll spend the night around Redding."

"But that's in the opposite direction."

"Sometimes, babe, it's wise to turn around."

His eyes close. Within seconds his mouth drops open, and then his breathing turns raspy, which always happens when he falls asleep sitting up. She waits a couple of minutes, then opens the door and climbs out, leaving it ajar.

Her jacket is in the back seat—she doesn't want to risk waking him—and the ocean breeze slices right through her, making her teeth chatter. Shivering, she walks over to the edge of the water, where she stands gazing toward the lighthouse. How might it have looked if you were up there in that tower, back in 1964, watching a wall of water rush toward you? You could not even dream of escaping. It would have been too late. All you'd be able to do was brace yourself and hope that the waves, when they broke, didn't wash you away along with everything else. You'd have to hold your breath and hope for the best.

She turns and looks back toward town. The bigger street where the stores are can't be more than a half-mile from here. She thinks, for some reason, of the day she jumped off Coach Raleigh's porch and ran away. It would be easy to cover the distance to the main street, easy to slip into an alley behind one of the stores and hide for a few hours, easy to hitch a ride like she did six months ago with Tom at a Chevron in Barstow, easy to find a bus station wherever the driver let her out. She'll rehash these few moments for the rest of her life, asking herself what stopped her, what kept her from seizing the chance to take off and run hard, avoiding everything that will happen next. Each time she poses the question, she will arrive at the same simple answer: she was just too fucking cold.

•

He wakes around eight-thirty. Sighing contentedly, he stretches like a big cat, then climbs out, walks over to the water's edge and turns his back. She assumes he's pissing, and it occurs to her that she hasn't done the same since late morning. Nor does she need to, which perhaps is cause for concern. It will turn out that she's developed a urinary tract infection, and while it will eventually land her in the hospital down in Fremont, she'll always be grateful for it. It will get her off the streets, hide her from view and keep her fed.

When he returns, he walks around to the trunk, raises the lid for a moment, then slams it shut.

To her surprise, he approaches the passenger side and opens her door. "Good thing I checked the spare," he says. "It's low on air. Listen . . . there's this little hole-in-the wall Mexican grocery between here and Smith River, three or four miles up the road. They make some shit-kicking burritos—best I ever ate anywhere, and I've eaten plenty. I'll pick us up a sack of those and then we'll gas up and head south. But I want you to drive. I don't want to turn the engine off again until we refill. It burns a little extra every time you start it."

"Why don't we get the gas first?"

"'Cause the fellow that operates the Mexican place closes at nine on weeknights, and in case you hadn't noticed, this is Thursday. I'm telling you, these burritos are something special."

He holds the door open, so she climbs out, walks around to the driver's side and slides behind the wheel. She turns the key. She's seldom been more grateful for anything than she is when the heater comes on. She reaches over and turns it all the way up, not requesting his permission.

He directs her back through town. As they pass the second of the gas pumps, she asks if he doesn't want to stop, and he says no, that they'll return after they pick up those burritos. They take 101 north but only stay on it for a couple of miles, during which she tries unsuccessfully to avoid looking at the gauge. It hasn't hit empty yet, but it won't be long.

He makes her turn onto a narrow country blacktop called Beaten Valley Road. "How weird," she says. "Beaten Valley?"

"There used to be some folks around here with that last name. James and Johnny Beaten. We called 'em the Beaten Boys, though there was nobody that could really beat them, since they were both about six-foot-six."

"So you lived here at some point?"

"It's just about a quarter mile ahead."

When her headlights strike the building, she can see it is as he said: a hole-in-the wall, not much longer or wider than a railroad car, with weathered siding and a rickety-looking porch. A board propped up near the door says Rigoberto's Mexican Market. The parking lot is empty except for an old pickup.

Out of habit, she starts to turn off the engine, but he slaps her hand. "No," he says. "You just sit here and let it run. I'll grab some food and we'll go back to town and gas up and head south." He opens the door, climbs out and hitches up his pants.

As soon as he's gone, she flips on the interior light, picks up the map and studies it. If they spend the night in Redding, she decides, she can surely buy a ticket as far as Sacramento and, once she gets there, figure out what to do next. She's hidden forty dollars under the sole of her right shoe. She remembers once hearing somebody say that was what black people did with their money, if they had any, when they went to the field to hoe cotton.

The instant she hears the popping, she thinks of her dad. When he went out and shot Coke cans off a fence post, his .38 sounded like that. "Oh, Jesus, God," she says. "Sweet Jesus."

•

The *Oakland Tribune* that she picked up off a bench on Saturday morning in Berkeley explained what happened, as well as the particulars of the person it happened to. His name, to her surprise, was not Rigoberto. It was Daniel. Rigoberto was his father. Daniel was eighteen, a senior at Crescent City High, a shortstop on the baseball team and, according to the article, a straight A student. He planned to enroll at the College of the Redwoods the following year, then transfer to one of the CSUs, probably Humboldt State. He wanted to teach history and coach. His father estimated whoever shot him walked away with more than five hundred dollars. There was construction going on nearby, and they'd done good business that day. They didn't have a security camera, nothing like that. Their customers were almost all local people they'd known for years. They never worried, Rigoberto said, his voice breaking, tears streaming down his cheeks. Who would do this? Nobody.

Two shots to the chest, followed by another to the head. The assailant evidently stepped behind the counter because he left bloody footprints on the floor as well as several on the porch. There were deep ruts in the parking lot, the Del Norte County sheriff said, where the driver of the escape vehicle floored the accelerator. The car that he believed was involved had later been abandoned on 101, just south of Crescent City. He said he couldn't discuss what evidence, if any, had been collected from it, nor would he name the make and model. He did, however, reveal that he thought an accomplice was involved.

If he and his deputies had paid a little more attention to the indentations in the gravel, they might have seen how, after coming within a few yards of the car that made the ruts, a set of footsteps veered off to one side, how the space between them grew much wider, because the person the footprints belonged to was suddenly running, as he chased the car that he'd recently climbed out of. If the officers had combed the roadside some three or four hundred yards from Rigoberto's Mexican Market, they might also have found a couple of slugs fired by the gunman at the fleeing automobile that had unexpectedly, and inexplicably, left him behind.

•

She peeked through the curtains until Tom climbed into his truck and pulled away from the curb. Then she went to find Querida. The calico was under the bed, but it wouldn't have been fair to say she was cowering. She looked watchful, her green eyes wary, her forepaws ready to defend herself.

"Come on out, baby. Let's get you some food."

Querida let herself be carried into the kitchen, where Caroline gave her a whole can of Puss 'n Boots, rather than half like she usually got. After eating, the cat observed her as she sat at the table, sipping a Miller Lite, trying to remain calm enough to write the note. At first the words came slowly. Then the cascade began.

She told Julio that several years ago she'd made a bad mistake. It was the kind of mistake, she said, that stopped you from ever again being who you really were and turned you into somebody else. Not that I knew, she wrote, who I really was, or was supposed to be, because I didn't. I didn't know who I was supposed to be until I met you. But I can't be that person because of who I was before.

She said she knew this wouldn't make much sense, because there were things she couldn't tell him. Not because she didn't trust him but because it would be better for him not to know. But there were a few things he had to do.

The first was to call in sick this evening. The second was to find another job as fast as he could, one that didn't require him to walk around late at night with a bag of someone else's money. The third was to take sweet care of Querida, as she knew he would. The fourth was to tell his mother and father she would have loved to be their daughter-in-law. The last, and most important, was to keep an eye out for a particularly dangerous guy, whom she went on to describe with all the detail she could muster.

There's nothing he might not do, she wrote, *to get what he wants, though what he wants changes from one minute to the next. He once tried to kill me, and if I stay here he will never, ever leave us alone. All I can do is disappear. Then he'll eventually lose interest in you. But if you see him in the meantime, call the police and lie low. Promise me. That's all I ask. That's all I care about.*

What I can't ask is that you forgive me. And please don't think I will ever forgive myself. It seems impossible that somebody my age could have already messed up so much. But I did. That's who I am and will always be. And by the way, Julio, my real name is Caroline, and I am not from Hannibal, Missouri. The day we met I'd been reading Mark Twain, a book called Roughing It *about a vagabond like me. I've been roughing it too. But it was never rough to be with you.*

Dry-eyed, she walked into the bedroom, opened the closet and grabbed the frayed orange duffel she'd been living out of when she met him. She threw most but not all of her things into it, looked around to make sure she hadn't left anything she couldn't do without, then started to close the closet. That was when his old flannel shirt caught her eye, the one he'd slept in all winter. She reached out and stroked it a couple of times. Then she picked Querida up, kissed her nose and told her goodbye. She put the cat down, hoisted the duffel onto her shoulder and slipped out the back door.

THE BENJAMIN G. HUMPHREYS BRIDGE spanned the Mississippi River between Greenville and Lake Village. During Ella's childhood, nobody called it by its real name. Everybody called it "the Greenville Bridge." Her sister once wondered aloud if, to people on the other side, it was "the Lake Village Bridge," a possibility Ella never entertained.

The bridge terrified her. For one thing, she'd heard her father say that a man was entombed in one of its concrete piers, killed during Depression-era construction. For another, it was tall and narrow, and on the dizzying ascent to its central span, you couldn't even see what lay beyond, whether there was a roadway up there or not. And then there was the matter of how she first came to cross it. Her mother and her grandparents had packed her and Caroline into her grandfather's gray Ford and were taking them someplace unnamed. When she asked where her father was, nobody answered. She was seven. She and Caroline should have been in school, and she ought to know her father's whereabouts. She'd just asked again when they began the perilous climb, and then suddenly the world fell away on either side, and she saw the wide expanse of brown rushing water and began to scream.

It turned out they were heading for her great aunt's house in Texarkana, and they would be there for several days, during which she kept hearing her mother and her grandparents and her aunt talk about something called "a court order." That sounded similar to "short order" and made her think it might involve hotdogs or hamburgers, though at her aunt's they never seemed to eat anything but chicken and gravy, or steak and gravy, or biscuits and gravy. She kept asking where her father was. Finally her mother told her that if she posed the question one more time, she'd get a whipping. She asked again, and her mother halfheartedly began to spank her, but her grandfather said to stop, so her mother quit smacking her and started to cry. A few days later, they got back in the car and crossed the river once more, this time at night, and the next morning she woke up at home. Nobody ever mentioned the trip again. She continued to fear that bridge, though, even into her teens.

She thought about this on the way to the Cape with Martin when she saw a steel arch up ahead, gleaming in the early summer sunlight. "Do we have to cross that?" she asked.

"The Sagamore Bridge? Only way to get over the canal, except for the Bourne Bridge, and that'd add quite a few extra miles to the trip. Why? You don't have acrophobia, do you?"

"Not really. Though I'll admit I'm not overly fond of high bridges."

He took his eye off the road for a moment, glancing at her. They were barely moving. It had been like that all the way from Boston, people fleeing the city on Friday afternoon, heading for the Cape. He said it was always like this and had tried to talk her into leaving on Thursday, but she told him she needed to work that night. "Do you get nervous on planes?" he asked.

She'd never been on a plane, but for some reason she didn't feel like admitting it. She'd told him nearly everything else there was to tell, except what happened to her at the Sun 'n' Sand when she was sixteen. "No."

"Of course," he said, "you've probably never been on one, have you?"

"If I hadn't and chose not to tell you, would it really be wise to press?"

"That'd depend on the nature of our relationship, wouldn't it?"

Having no good comeback, she looked out the window. They were passing a gas station with a six-foot tall ceramic ice cream cone out front, the second she'd seen since Plymouth. The top of this one was green.

"Speaking of airplanes," he said, "I was thinking that maybe after I finish up the album we're doing with that bluegrass group, you and I could take a little trip."

"Aren't we taking a little trip now?"

He laughed. "A bigger little trip. I was thinking someplace in the Caribbean. Maybe Montego Bay."

He'd been to Dublin, London and Paris, and during college he spent a semester in Florence. He didn't grow up like her, considering a visit to Jackson or Memphis a big deal. For her, the horizon was so close she could reach out and touch it. For him, practically speaking, it didn't exist. "Montego Bay's in Jamaica?"

He nodded. "On the northwest coast, a hundred and fifty miles or so from Cuba."

"I haven't got a passport."

"Why don't I pick up an application for you? You'll need two photos. There's a little studio on Main Street in Cedar Park."

It was the kind of thing he'd been doing now for several months. He offered to prepare her tax return, telling her that she was losing money by taking the easy way out and using the short form. So she let him, and the itemized deductions earned her a few hundred dollars. He offered to have a shoemaker replace the heel on her damaged boot, and she let him do that too. She let him buy her dinner again and again, and just last week she'd let him purchase her an inexpensive little acoustic guitar, which he planned to teach her to strum. He offered. She acquiesced.

"Okay," she said. "Maybe we can fill it out next weekend."

"You'll be coming up, then?"

"Sure, assuming I'm invited."

"You're always invited. I hoped that by now you understood that."

She did understand, and she thought she knew what it meant to him. She just wasn't certain what it meant to her. "I'll be working next Friday. Can you pick me up late if I ride out there on the Orange Line?"

"I've got to be in Boston that afternoon to meet a client. So why don't I just hang around town until you get off and I'll pick you up at the restaurant? If you wouldn't mind letting me borrow a key, I could go get a little work done at your place. Maybe even grab a nap."

Over the last few days, at the cost of sleep, she'd been thinking things through, and this brought her a little closer to clarity. So she reached for her purse. "Actually," she said, "I had a couple made for you." She pulled them out. "The silver one's for the main entrance. And the bronze one unlocks the door to my hovel."

•

The house was about a mile from Truro, on the bay side, just across the road from the water and hidden behind a tall hedgerow. When they pulled into the yard, two other cars were already there: a silver El Dorado that was about half a block long and a canary yellow Beetle with a Newport Folk Festival sticker on the trunk.

On the way down, he'd told her that after his grandfather died, his dad and his Aunt Tess, who didn't like to be called "Aunt," came to an agreement. She got the Cape property, he got the big house. The arrangement satisfied both of them. She'd never liked Cedar Park, and his father had never liked anywhere else.

Bare-footed, Tess answered the door. She was about sixty-five, with frizzy reddish hair rendered all the more dramatic by her plum-colored velour pants and blouse. You couldn't tell if they were pajamas, warm-ups or street clothes. She carried an empty martini glass. "Hello, hello! You must be Ella. I'm so glad you could join us. After that drive, I'm sure you're dying for a drink. How could you not be? Martin, go in there and fix this young woman a drink. Get yourself one too. And while you're at it, make me another." She handed him her glass. "You remember how I like them, right? It's been a while."

"I was here at Christmas. Four ounces of Beefeater shaken over five ice cubes for exactly six seconds."

Tess rose onto her toes and kissed him on the cheek. "He'd make such an attentive husband," she told Ella. "I don't know why what's-her-name didn't see it."

"She had no problem with the way I made drinks," Martin said. "It was everything else."

He disappeared into the kitchen, and Tess showed her into the living room, where the unmistakable odor of pot permeated the air. His sister Maeve sat on a zebra-striped futon beside another woman. She'd known Maeve would be there, because he told her on the way down. She found it odd that they'd never yet been introduced since he talked about his sister all the time. She had a bedroom at his house—technically, she still owned part of it until he finished paying her for her share—but so far she'd never been there when Ella spent the night.

The other woman was ten or maybe even fifteen years older, late thirties, early forties. She had on full-length jeans and a black long-sleeved pullover that looked nice against her tan skin. It was hard to say if she'd been born with that complexion or just recently spent a lot of time in the sun, but if she'd had to guess, Ella would have said the former. She wore her dark hair in a bowl cut, had an extremely large nose and really filled out her clothes.

"Maeve you know," Tess said, evidently assuming she must. "And this is . . . Jesus Christ, I really shouldn't smoke that stuff when I'm drinking . . . I'm sorry, I forgot your—"

"Irma," the other woman responded.

"Irma. Jesus Christ. And Irma's from Louisiana like—"

"Actually, I'm from Georgia," Irma said, rising off the couch and offering Ella her hand.

"And Ella's from . . . Just go ahead and tell me, before I pick the wrong Southern state or make one up."

"Mississippi."

"Really," Irma said. Her palm was warm and slightly damp.

Maeve didn't bother to stand, just smiled and said, "Glad to meet you, Ella. I hear great things."

Martin reappeared with a tray on which he'd placed a glass of white wine for her, the martini for his aunt and what looked like a triple whiskey for himself. Driving down, he'd told her that he loved his aunt to death, that she'd always treated him and his sister like adults even when they weren't, and that when he was around her he tended to let go.

Over the next few hours, nobody moved except to visit the bathroom or make another round of drinks. Ella even made a round herself, though Tess insisted on accompanying her, to ensure that she got her martini just right. "Next time," she said in the kitchen while Ella carefully measured the shots, "I'll trust you. By the way, it's better to err on the side of excess. That last shot didn't quite reach the rim. If a little spills onto the counter, it'll just protect the wood from bacteria."

The conversation was wide-ranging: what real estate cost on the Cape, whether Walter Mondale would choose a woman as his running mate, how to make a good fennel-apple salad, the possibility that a thinly-veiled version of Tess might appear in the Provincetown novel Norman Mailer was about to publish.

"Tell the truth, Tess," Martin said. "Have you ever jumped in the sack with Stormin' Norman?"

"Absolutely not."

"Are you one hundred percent certain?"

"Absolutely."

"Don't lie to family."

"Ninety-five percent."

At one point, Ella learned that Irma had been Maeve's professor a few years earlier when she was a Harvard undergrad. This resulted in some awkwardness when she tried to make conversation by asking what courses Irma taught there.

"I don't teach anything there anymore. I'm at the University of Rhode Island now."

"You didn't like it at Harvard?"

Irma laughed. "Not especially, but the more serious problem was that Harvard didn't like me. I got turned down for tenure. In other words canned."

"Tenure," Maeve interjected, "is a crock of shit. It allows some people to mail it in while it shuts more deserving people out." She reached over and squeezed the older woman's hand. "Irma wrote one of the best books ever published about Melville."

Irma shrugged. "The book was perceived to be passé. The department committee called it 'just another standard piece of New Criticism.'"

"If it's 'new' criticism," Ella asked, "how can it be passé?"

"Well, these days, New Criticism's considered reactionary. See, in my racket, words often don't mean what they do elsewhere. Think Great Britain, where liberal can mean conservative and a public school's private. Academia has its own lingo."

After a final round of drinks, it was decided that they'd eat dinner in

Provincetown—or P-town, as Tess called it—and this led to a discussion about which of them stood the best chance of driving there and back without drawing police attention. Tess, it seemed, had already talked her way out of two tickets in the last month. Irma got elected.

As a new guest, Ella was assigned the passenger seat in Tess's El Dorado, while Martin sat in back, flanked by his aunt and sister. The three of them passed another joint, got silly, and started telling one another stories about Uncle Cormac and Aunt Brigid, who despite hating each other nevertheless remained married for fifty-three years.

"Remember when she hurled the brick through his windshield?" Tess asked.

"Was that the time the Cedar Park police put her in the straightjacket?"

"Maeve, that's just the half of it! They put them *both* in straightjackets, because when Cormac saw them putting *her* in, he jumped one of the cops."

Over the raucous backseat laughter, Irma asked her where she was from in Mississippi.

"A small town in the Delta. Loring."

"That's about halfway between Greenwood and Greenville?"

"Yeah. Don't tell me you've been there?"

"I did some voter registration in the Delta."

"When?"

"Freedom Summer. '64. Me and three other University of Chicago grad students—all of whom, I hasten to add, were from places outside the South. After the killings in Neshoba County, the other three took off. Do you remember much about that summer?"

"I remember it very well. At the time, though, I didn't know anybody had been killed. It wasn't the kind of thing your parents told you. I never even heard about Emmett Till until college."

"That doesn't surprise me. There was a famous lynching near my hometown a couple of years before I was born, but I didn't find out about it until I left. By the way, where'd you go to school?"

"I was a voice major at Berklee. But I didn't finish. Now I just wait tables."

"Sweetheart, I've waited lots of tables in my life. I even waitressed in

Brookline for a few months after getting bounced out of Harvard. You do what you have to. Why'd you leave Berklee?"

Ella hesitated just long enough to make the other woman take her eyes off the road and look at her. "Please forget my question," Irma said. "I shouldn't have asked."

"I wouldn't mind telling you. Just maybe some other time?"

"Of course. Say no more."

They ate at a seafood place with a view of the harbor. The food was good but not especially memorable. What was memorable was the walk they took after they finished their meal.

Commercial Street was clogged by men holding hands with other men, women strolling arm in arm with other women, people who looked like men but dressed like women, or looked like women but dressed like men. She saw one person of indeterminate sex clad in a toga, with a gold Roman-style helmet that had raised squares and medallions and, on top, a red feathered comb. Garish colors predominated.

She'd seen gay and lesbian couples together in Boston and Cambridge. Invariably, she seemed to be in the company of her friend Liz when this happened, and Liz's reaction was always the same. Under her breath, she muttered a single syllable: "Yuck." Ella never responded, but each time it happened, she was reminded of an event from seventh or eighth grade involving Irwin, the same boy who some years later would stick his tongue in her mouth after the Halloween dance. News circulated that Irwin, puzzled by the meaning of a particular word, asked a high school football player what the term "homo" meant, to be duly informed that it referred to "guys that play with dicks." Irwin became an object of ridicule after sharing this information with a friend, then confessing, "I'm scared I may be a homo. I mean, I play with my dick sometimes. I thought everybody did." About ninety-nine percent of the people she knew growing up—basically everybody but her sister—casually tossed around words like "homo" and "queer." Even Kim did it. "You know I'm not a homo, don't you?" she'd whispered as they fell asleep at the Sun 'n' Sand before Brad Moss showed up as though to help her prove it.

Irma and Maeve strolled ahead of them, talking in lowered voices.

A couple of times Maeve reached for Irma's hand and gave it a quick squeeze, and Irma reciprocated but never initiated contact herself. Tess kept up a running stream of banter and, every thirty or forty steps, seemed to encounter somebody she'd known for years. When she and her other two guests stepped into a small art gallery to see if a watercolor Tess was interested in might still be available, Ella and Martin lingered on the cobblestones. "So," he said, "what do you think?"

"About what?"

He waved his arm in an all-encompassing gesture. "P-town. The Cape. The moon and the stars."

"It's cloudy now. I can't see the moon and the stars."

"You're a very literal young woman."

"Probably because I lack imagination." For the last minute or two, she'd smelled a peculiar odor that she couldn't identify, though it was oddly familiar. Now it came to her. "Is somebody making cotton candy nearby?"

"Yes, indeed." He pointed ahead. "There's a confectioner's shop down at the end of the block. Why? You want some?"

"I think maybe I do."

He entered the gallery and said something to his sister, then came back outside.

It had gotten quite chilly, and he must have seen her shiver, because he put his arm around her and pulled her close. "In case you hadn't noticed," he said as they walked toward the confectioner's, "my sister and Irma are a couple."

"I noticed."

"And?"

For much of the day something had been bothering her, something she could not quite put her finger on or issue a name to. Now she knew. She'd been feeling as if she were under observation, the goal of which must have been to determine whether she could rise to the level of sophistication of the people around her. "*And* I don't know why you apparently felt you couldn't tell me."

"I don't know why I didn't either."

When they got to the sweet shop, she reached for the doorknob, but his hand closed around hers. "Wait a minute," he said. "Please?"

She let go of the knob. "What?"

"I should have told you."

"It's not a case of should or shouldn't. It's a question of why you didn't."

"I just wasn't sure how you'd react."

"Obviously." She opened the door and stepped inside.

The cotton candy machine had been cleaned and shut down. No one else was in the shop except for the woman behind the counter, who was wiping her hands on her apron and about to close. She didn't look pleased to see new customers.

Glass-fronted display cases stood on both sides of the register, containing several rows of chocolates: salted caramel fudge straws, Italian espresso truffles, coconut snowballs. Ella had half a mind to ask for a Hershey Bar to witness the effect on Martin. "I'd like a buttercream bonbon," she said.

"Just one?"

"Unless *he* wants something." She felt him there beside her, puzzled and wounded, just as she'd intended. He operated from a favorable position, occupying the high ground like the Union army at Gettysburg. The fact that he was quite possibly the kindest, most gentle person she'd ever met and that he was in love with her did not absolve him of his inherited advantages.

"Let's have five of the bonbons," he said. "And maybe five of those lavender chocolate truffles."

The woman finished bagging them and started to ring them up.

"Damn it." He thumped the counter with his thumb. "I've tried my hardest, but I can't talk myself out of a chocolate-covered peanut butter truffle. I guess I just got a taste for a Reese's Cup tonight."

"I think I'd like one of those too," Ella said.

"Make it five," he told the woman.

The dispute was resolved that easily, without further discussion, and at the time this seemed all but miraculous. In her own family, a conflict that began before her birth continued until the day her father died. For the most part it simmered, only occasionally boiling over, as it must have when her mother and grandparents absconded with her and Caroline via the Greenville Bridge.

Outside, the others were waiting. As they all returned to Tess's El Dorado, they passed the bag of chocolates among themselves, occasionally smacking their lips. Tess had purchased the watercolor, frame and all, and it was wrapped in brown paper and tucked beneath her nephew's arm.

When they got to her car, she unlocked the trunk, and Martin carefully laid her package on the mat, then asked how much the watercolor set her back.

"If I told you, you'd just warn me that if I keep indulging my every whim, I'll be penniless before I turn seventy."

"Because you will be."

"What if I don't make it to seventy? Think of all the pleasure I would've denied myself."

"Tess," Maeve said, "have you ever denied yourself even *one* pleasure?"

"No, dear, and I don't intend to start tonight. Radically altering life-long patterns of behavior is what sends so many old people downhill. The next thing you know, you're riding a runaway train. Incontinence, loss of bowel control, senility. There was an article about it just last month in the *Atlantic*."

When they got home, Tess proposed a final drink, but everybody else wanted to go to bed, so she poured herself a glass of wine and told them good night. Ella and Martin had been given a large room on the second floor with a private bath. Sitting down to untie his shoes, he said his parents used to sleep in this room when they visited and that tomorrow morning they'd have a great view of the water. "Or at least we'll have a great view of the fog. Maybe we'll head down to the beach and take a walk before breakfast? Tess, as you might suspect, is not exactly an early riser."

"Sure," she said, "that sounds good."

"You want the bathroom first?"

She sat down on the side of the bed and yawned. "You can have it."

"Thanks." He pulled off everything but his briefs, threw on his bathrobe, stepped into the small bathroom and closed the door.

While he brushed his teeth, he thought about what he'd say when he went back out. He believed he needed to say something. By and large, his father had been a silent man around the house. And a silent man—one of those who made you read the map of his face, trying to glean what might have caused the deepening of that line beneath his left eye, the all but invisible pinkish tinting of his forehead—was the very thing he'd resolved not to turn into. True, it was to his own detriment that in his marriage he voiced nearly every thought he entertained, every fear he'd ever felt. He told his ex-wife he was scared, for instance, of her uncle Jimmy, who'd done two stints at MCI Shirley and been mentioned numerous times in the *Globe* in connection with organized crime. That's a hell of a thing to say to your wife—even though, shortly after their divorce, her uncle did kill a guy and get sentenced to life in prison. He also told her he loathed himself for bailing out of Berklee, that he'd been too quick to give up, that he'd just gotten tired of the look he saw on his dad's face every time he came home excited about something else he'd learned in guitar class, how he'd never forget the sour expression terms like "mixolydian mode" could provoke. He talked her out of every last ounce of respect she might have retained for him.

He hadn't told Ella about his sister and Irma for the worst of all reasons: he was scared she'd disapprove. She came from the Bible Belt, but if he was honest the main thing he knew about the South was that it produced ninety percent of the music he loved. Except for a few layovers in the Atlanta airport, one failed business trip to Nashville and a spring break at Pompano Beach, he'd never been below D.C. The time he saw her Tennessee friend with the married city councilman at The Last Hurrah, though, he heard Liz say she bet the bartender was a fag.

He looked at himself in the mirror. I guess I was thinking that if you disapproved, it wouldn't matter once you met her, because you'd like her, he was going to say when he went back into the bedroom. I should have trusted you to begin with. It's just that my sister's always been my best friend, and I was scared what it might mean if you disapproved and then couldn't get past it. It would have meant I had to choose between her and you. And I would've chosen you.

He composed himself, then opened the bathroom door and

discovered that at least for tonight he'd been relieved of the need to make his little speech. She was fast asleep.

"YOU GOT YOUR COTTON CANDY after all," he said. "We're walking through it."

Flog blanketed the beach just as he'd predicted the night before, and though the thermometer propped on the kitchen windowsill said it was fifty-five degrees, down here it felt more like forty. Fortunately, she'd put on the pair of cords she brought along, as well as the Red Sox windbreaker she borrowed from Liz.

She said, "You know, I never even liked cotton candy. I don't know why I thought I needed it. The truffles were many times better."

He reached for her hand and she let him take it. Together, they skirted a large piece of driftwood.

"If you ask me," he said, "the word 'need' is open to interpretation."

"You could say the same thing about lots of words, don't you think?"

"No doubt. My mom, for instance, used to say that I used the world 'need' when what I really meant was 'want.' It seemed like I always had a runny nose growing up, and every time I felt the faintest hint of nasal drip, I'd start hollering, 'Kleenex! Kleenex! I needa!'" He laughed. "She never let it go, always said, 'What you mean is you want one. You don't need one. You need food, you need water, you need a place to sleep, you need good health. A Kleenex would be useful, it would be nice, but you don't need it. You just want it.'"

"I guess that seems a little rigid to me. Maybe because I remember too many kids in elementary school—always boys, I'm afraid—who never even bothered to wipe their noses, let alone blow them." She shuddered.

"I can think of one in particular. He was called Scooter, and from first until fourth grade it looked like he had Karo Syrup trickling toward his chin. Trust me, that kid needed a Kleenex."

"In fourth grade he learned to blow his nose?"

"No. In fourth grade, his family moved to Yazoo City, and we never had to look at him again."

Up ahead lay a massive pile of kelp. When they reached it, he let go of her hand, bent over and pulled loose a few strands, which he examined for a moment before tossing them back on the pile. "Sugar kelp," he said. "It's a crying shame nobody hereabouts realizes what a potential gold mine this is. They've been cultivating it in Asia for centuries. In the '40s, the Japanese got really inventive, stretching underwater nets between bamboo poles to catch seaweed spore, and then they'd transfer them to a river where the minerals in the water would make the seaweed grow a lot faster."

"What could be made out of kelp?"

"In Japan it's used in soups, salad, sushi, all kinds of things. It's really just about making do with what's available. They're better at that in Asia than we are."

"I guess so. Down where I'm from they used to grow a lot of soybeans. I once asked my father what good a bean was that you couldn't eat. I had a plastic soda cup in my hand at the time, and I remember being shocked when he told me soybeans had probably been used to make it."

"Not to mention tofu."

Rather than take her hand again, he locked arms with her like courtly men used to in black and white movies. She found it excessively formal, especially since they were walking along a beach and had sand all over their sandals. "I'd love to see where you come from," he said. "I've thought about it a lot."

"I wouldn't mind for you to see it. I just don't want to see it again myself."

"You never miss it?"

"Never." She said it on principle, though she knew it wasn't true. She did sometimes miss the sense of certainty she'd taken for granted for most of the time she lived at home. Somebody else made enough money to place food on the table. Back then, she lived hand-to-mouth only in the sense that she used her hand to put that food into her mouth. Between the day she dropped out of Berklee and the night she let Martin take her across Mass Ave for a drink, she'd begun each morning knowing that if she didn't work she couldn't eat. It was just that simple. It didn't matter whether she felt like going to work or not, it didn't matter if she got sick, or if she grew sad or lonely. She was in the position now that her father and mother had been in. Except, thank God, she had no kids to look after.

A few words left his mouth, spoken in such a flat tone that at first she thought she'd imagined it. Then she looked at him and noticed that he was staring into the distance, though nothing was in front of them except a few hundred yards of deserted beach.

She freed her arm. "What?" she said. "What did you say?"

He stopped walking and faced her. "I said," he replied, "that I want to marry you."

"You *want* to marry me?"

Despite the brisk breeze, beads of perspiration appeared on his cheeks. His face was flushed. "That's what I said."

Just like that, he'd surrendered his advantages. The high ground was hers. Should she choose, she could mow him down. She gave some thought to it. She'd never been in this position before except on that turnrow with Irwin. She might never be in it again. "It isn't something you just *say*."

"Well, maybe not. Probably not. But I just did."

"You sound like you didn't even know you were going to do it."

"Oh, I knew. What I didn't know was when. The moment just seemed right. I mean, the beach, the ocean, what we talked about last night. You don't sound too happy about it, though. I guess you aren't, are you?"

"Because you don't just tell somebody you want to marry her. You're supposed to ask."

He bent over, pulled off one of his sandals, then knelt and clasped it to his heart. "Will you marry me?" he asked. "Please? I mean it. I'd really love it if you would. Don't say no, even if no's what you're thinking. If you need time, you can have all you want."

Trembling, whether due to joy, anger, shock, fear, or all of them together, she grabbed the sandal from his hand, then spun toward the bay and hurled it as far as she could. Together they watched it crash into the water and disappear. Within a few seconds, it bobbed into view again to rock languidly on the surface.

"Birkenstocks have cork footbeds," he observed. "That makes them unusually buoyant."

•

They found Tess at the kitchen table, drinking a Bloody Mary and reading the *New York Times*. "Ron and Nancy just threw a party they called 'the Congressional Seafood Festival' on the White House lawn," she informed them. "It says they had Mississippi farm-raised catfish flown in to compete with New England lobsters and Pacific Northwest salmon." She looked at Ella. "Your family doesn't raise catfish, do they?"

"No, ma'am."

"Oddly enough, however," Martin said, "we *were* just discussing farming. Along with kelp and runny noses."

"Kelp and runny noses? Why in the world would you be talking about either of those?"

"Because they helped me work my away around to proposing."

"Proposing? Proposing what?"

"Marriage."

"To Ella?"

He nodded.

Tess laid the paper down. "Ella, whatever did you say? Don't keep me in suspense. My heart can't stand it."

"I said yes."

"Oh, my. Good Heavens." Tess lifted her glass and downed the rest of the Bloody Mary. With a glint in her eye, she rose and wrapped her arms around Ella and kissed her on the cheek. "Welcome to the family," she said. "Jesus Christ. We've seen a little bit of everything. Gangsters. Lawyers. Accountants. Record producers. Fiddle players. Now we've got ourselves an honest-to-God Southern belle. Martin, make me a double-double martini. Then go wake your sister and Irma. I'm about to throw a party that'll put those trashy Reagans' bash to shame."

CAROLINE GOT OFF THE BUS in Tulsa at a quarter before midnight on the 4th of July. They'd suffered a breakdown that afternoon on the outskirts of Ponca City and had to wait, sweltering, while a mechanic was summoned. He showed up drunk and without the necessary parts. So they waited some more, until finally, as dark fell, a sober mechanic arrived. She took turns helping the driver hold a flashlight so the mechanic could see what he was doing.

The bus station snackbar was closed and she'd had nothing to eat since morning. She'd been considering taking a 5:30 bus to Little Rock, then calling her mother to see if she might be willing to drive up from Pine Bluff and get her and let her stay there for a couple of days. She hadn't told her she was coming, hadn't been in touch at all for eighteen months. Always, in the back of her mind, was the awareness that because Tom had found that old driver's license, he knew what town she'd grown up in. If he went there looking for her, as she was convinced he eventually would, it would take him about fifteen minutes to find out that her mother had married another man and moved to Pine Bluff. So maybe it was just as well that she'd missed that Little Rock bus. Mr. Burns had never made her feel welcome there anyway.

She'd spent the previous night in the Denver bus station, she was dirty and smelly and couldn't afford to waste money on a motel. Scanning the departure board, she saw there was a bus to St. Louis in thirteen minutes. Without thinking too much, she walked over, bought a ticket and climbed aboard. It was cool inside, and the instant the driver pulled out she fell asleep.

She kept traveling east, putting distance between herself and California. For a few weeks, she worked at a Ramada Inn in Clarksville, Tennessee, cleaning rooms and sleeping in an efficiency apartment that belonged to the guy who managed the hotel. The pay was terrible, but the manager was nice enough. Sometimes, on the weekend, when he and his wife went to Nashville to see a movie or hear somebody at the Grand Ole Opry, they hired her to babysit their kids, who knew her as Caro. One evening in late August, when she was missing Julio so badly she felt like she'd die if she didn't call him, she went to a local dive, drank way too much and spent the night in a Motel 6 with an airman from Fort Campbell. When she woke, he was still asleep, but in the bright morning light, she could not ignore what she apparently had chosen to overlook the previous evening: he'd told her she was his girl now, that every time he got leave they'd be together, she was unlike anybody he'd ever met, goddamit! She slipped out the door, walked across town to the Ramada, got her things from the efficiency and hitched a ride with a trucker who took her all the way to Virginia.

A waitress at the greasy spoon where the driver let her out told her that Virginia Tech was only a few miles away in Blacksburg and that she'd heard they were looking for custodial workers. This possibility didn't pan out, but she got hired at a strange little ice cream parlor/sandwich shop near the university, operated by an enormous guy named Briley who also owned a vintage clothing store around the corner and walked back and forth between the two businesses bare-footed. What made the establishment so odd was that it had no air conditioning, so she and all the other employees would be standing there soaked in sweat, scooping out Double Dutch Fudge and trying to concoct a chocolate sundae and ring it up before the whole thing melted. None of the sandwiches had meat in them. They served things like goat cheese and honey on bruschetta, humus and veggies on whole grain, scrambled chickpea and spinach pitas. Given the runny ice cream and the unusual sandwich concoctions, the only reason it was wildly popular, she figured, was the huge outdoor balcony attached to the second floor. Bird shit occasionally splattered the rickety picnic tables, and the roof sometimes leaked. But from about eleven AM until closing, you could seldom find a free spot.

The first few days in town, she lived in a cheap motel out on South Main, where the carpets smelled of mildew and it took hours for the shower to drain; if you stayed in the stall for more than two or three minutes, it would overflow, which was probably why the carpet stank. Rundown as it was, it nevertheless consumed over half of what she earned working for Briley. Then she saw an ad for a room in a private home belonging to a couple who worked for Tech. It said only female applicants would be considered and that the owners would not tolerate drinking or other licentious behavior. They sounded sanctimonious but safe, so she placed a call and was invited over the same night.

The house stood about four blocks from campus, on a street where nice cars sat parked in the driveways and there were lots of trees. The woman was a secretary in the Department of Mechanical Engineering, a plump lady of about fifty, with a patch of psoriasis on her left cheek that would never go away. Something was wrong with her hip, too, so that when she walked it looked almost as if it were attached by a hinge and had to swing to catch up with the rest of her. The man was most likely a couple of years older, and his thick beard made Caroline, who'd told them she went by Caro, wonder if he might be Mennonite, though that proved not to be the case.

While his wife went to get her a glass of lemonade, he told her he was the chief purchasing agent for Food Services. "Basically," he said, "if you eat it on-campus, I bought it. But you want a little advice?"

"Yes, sir."

He laughed. "Don't ever eat on-campus."

"I won't," she assured him. "I'm not a student."

The room for rent was on the second floor, with a full-sized bed and a window that overlooked a shady back yard. The rent they proposed was so low it stunned her, and she immediately said she would take it. They exchanged a glance, and then Mrs. Carlton said, "Great. You can pay at the end of each week, if you'd like, rather than at the beginning. Would that help?"

"Yes, ma'am. Thank you."

Mr. Carlton picked her up the next morning at the motel, and she moved in before going to work. She could tell he was surprised that she had so few belongings, just as she'd been surprised the previous night when they didn't ask more questions about where she'd come from and what she was doing in Blacksburg. Their demeanor caused her to keep her lies to the absolute minimum. She told them she was from Tennessee, that she'd lost both of her parents in an accident and just decided she needed to move on. She planned to study acting, she said, and hoped eventually to move to New York City.

The sandwich shop wasn't open for breakfast, so she never had to show up until 10:30. Since the Carltons left for work before eight, on weekday mornings she usually had the house to herself, and the bookshelves in the den were an immediate draw. Whereas she never saw Mrs. Carlton read much of anything except the Bible, her Sunday school tracts and the *Roanoke Times*, her husband's taste was a lot more interesting. He seemed always to be reading one novel or another, which began to make sense one day after she peeked into the room he called his office and saw the framed degree that hung on the wall: a B.A. in English and history, earned in 1953 at Emory & Henry. He owned several hundred hardcover copies of books like *The Optimist's Daughter*, *Revolutionary Road*, *The Last Picture Show*, *Wise Blood*, *The Executioner's Song*, and one that spoke to her more insistently than any other, Edna's O'Brien's *The Country Girls*. As soon as she heard the couple drive away, she made herself a cup of coffee, then pulled a book off the shelf and read for a couple of hours.

In later years, she thought of these mornings as her graduate school. Sometimes, she disappeared into the books, forgetting that she was in Blacksburg, Virginia, in a house that wasn't hers, that she'd ever set foot in the state of California, where she'd loved someone and left him and, before that, had sat behind the wheel of a car while nearby a young man lost his life. Those were the books she liked. At other times she read something that hurt so much she felt as if she would suffocate, that if she didn't immediately stop reading, she'd never draw her next breath. Those were the books she hated. But they were also the ones she loved.

•

Until close to the end, the months she spent in Blacksburg were a quiet and solitary time, exactly the respite she needed. Aside from the Carltons, the only person she really got to know was the heavy-set brunette who worked the counter at the post office, and the only reason it happened was that Briley asked her to drop a package off there one day on her way home from work. Just as she placed the package on the counter, a tremendous boom rattled the walls, reminding her of the Sunday morning when the New Madrid fault shifted and an earthquake struck the Mississippi Delta, cracking their front doorsteps.

"Was that an earthquake?" she asked the clerk.

The woman set the package on the scale. "Not hardly, hon. Most likely a planned explosion over at the Radford Arsenal. You must not be from around here. They make propellants and explosives for the military over there, so you get used to this happening once or twice a month. 'Course, every now and then, it's not planned. My daddy worked at the arsenal and got killed in an explosion just a couple of months before he would've retired."

Evidently, something showed on Caroline's face.

"What's the matter?" the clerk asked.

The post office was empty except for them. "It's just . . . well, my father died in an explosion too. Back in 1975."

"I'll be damned," the woman said. "That's the year after my daddy died. October 16th, 1974, a Wednesday, around eleven in the morning. That was the longest, saddest day of my life." She glanced at the wall clock. "Listen, I get off in ten minutes. Want to go drink a beer? It's on me. Seems like we might have a good bit in common."

She started to mention her landlords' ban on drinking, then thought what the hell. They wouldn't see her. They'd probably never been to a bar in their lives.

They went to a place out on South Main, not too far from the cheesy motel she'd stayed in. It had a concrete floor, a jukebox that played nothing but country music, and exactly one beer on tap: PBR, at seventy-five cents a mug. The bartender wore overalls and, when he saw her companion, said something that sounded like "Whatcheeont, Deena? Two biguns?"

"Two'll do just fine to start, Slate."

The older woman paid for their beers, and they carried them over to a rickety table plastered with Virginia Tech Hokie decals. On the jukebox somebody was singing a song about how he didn't care if he was the first guy you kissed as long as he was the last.

"So," Deena said, "our daddies both got blown sky-high. How'd it happen to yours?"

She told the entire truth, or at least as much of it as she knew, except for the part about it happening in Mississippi, since she'd already told the Carltons she grew up in Tennessee. When she finished, Deena said, "You think he was screwing around with the other woman?"

"I'm not sure. I think he loved her, though. At least . . ."

"At least what?"

"I hope he did. Because he never loved my mom. And he never loved me. He loved my sister, though."

Deena said her own daddy was a sweet man, good to her and her brother, good to her momma too. "But a daddy like mine," she said, "he can represent a great big old mixed blessing."

"How do you figure that?"

Deena took a couple of big swallows from her mug. Her knuckles were red and rough-looking. Riding to the bar in her pickup, Caroline had noticed what you couldn't see in the post office, due to the fact that she stood behind a counter: she had a pretty prominent belly. It didn't look soft, though. It looked hard. So did her face. Her nicest feature was her eyes. They were a darker, deeper brown than her hair, and she had long lashes that curled just a bit. "You get a daddy as considerate as mine was," she said, "and you grow up thinking that's how men are."

She'd been married once. Her husband was an absolute nightmare. An insurance agent over in Radford, thirty when she was nineteen, he used to eat supper at the diner where she worked after she graduated from high school. He'd always flirt a little and leave her a nice tip. One night, he also left a sealed envelope with her name on it. Inside, she found a note telling her that though she might not know it, he was really shy, and that given their age difference he was scared she'd be offended or repulsed if he asked her out. But if he was wrong about that, he said, maybe she could just put an X on this note and lay it down on the table the next night when he came in to eat.

"If somebody left *you* that kind of note," Deena asked her, "how would you react?"

"Now? Or when I was nineteen?"

"Honey, I think maybe you and me were supposed to be friends."

Both her parents loved him, Deena said. And truthfully, he was nice about ninety-five percent of the time. "Thing is, this company he worked for—it was based in Richmond—he never could sell enough policies to keep 'em satisfied. They'd have these quarterly meetings, and his boss'd chew him out, and he'd come home with a bottle of Jim Beam and when he'd drained it, he'd start wanting me to do things with him that I just plain do not believe in. Understand, now, I'm not a puritan—I like a wild time as much as the next girl. Anyhow, he'd played sports in high school and was fairly strong, especially when he'd had him some Beam, and he meant to do those things or be damned. I'm not exactly a little woman, and you can bet I put up a fight, but I lost every time. He was careful where he bruised me, figuring as long as folks couldn't see it on the street, nobody'd ever know, because I wouldn't tell."

"How could he be sure of that?"

"He knew I'd be worried that if I told, my daddy'd shoot him full of holes and have to spend the rest of his life in jail. And he was right. That was exactly what my daddy would've done."

"So how'd you get rid of him?"

"It was actually real simple, though it took me a few years to figure it out. I *told* him that I'd told."

"You *told* him that you'd told?"

"Yeah. But I hadn't."

"And what happened?"

"He left town within about fifteen minutes, and neither me nor anybody else there ever laid eyes on him again. Once I knew he was gone for good, I *did* tell my daddy, and he went to see this judge that he sometimes sold firewood to, and the court granted me a divorce on the grounds of abandonment. And I've stayed abandoned ever since."

"You never wish you could be with somebody?"

Deena laughed, then rolled her eyes toward the bartender, who was pouring a shot of whiskey for another customer. "Honey, I've been with a number of somebodies. I'm with 'em when I want to be, and I'm not when I don't."

"I mean be with someone permanently."

The lines around Deena's mouth deepened. "The six years I spent married," she said, "felt like fifty forevers. I got me a nice trailer out near Price's Fork now, and a nice garden to go with it. I got a dog named Deena Two. I just call her 'Two' for short. I got pretty much every record Dolly Parton, Loretta Lynn, and Tammy Wynette ever recorded. I'm a good cook, and I feed myself well, though I may eat a little too much. When I want companionship, I can get it, though the day'll probably come when I can't. My guess is that by then, I won't want it anyway. I'm not saying that's for everybody. Works well for me, though. What about you?"

Maybe it was the country music playing on the jukebox, the voice of a singer who sounded familiar, though she didn't know his name. She felt sure he was the one who sang a song her father played so often one summer that it drove her half-crazy and made her consider laying the record on the windowsill in hopes the vinyl would warp. The only thing that prevented her was the certainty he'd place the blame where it was due. The tune was about being on the run with only the highway for a home.

The possibility, no matter how faint, that she was on the verge of confessing to a total stranger horrified her. "I guess I've had a few bad experiences," she said.

"Of course you have, baby. Unless my eyes deceive me, you're a woman. Show me one who hasn't had 'em."

"I met one guy I really loved, though."

Deena crossed her arms. "He was married?"

"No. He wasn't."

"So what happened?"

She lifted her mug, drained it and set it down too hard. "I screwed him over. I screwed him over so bad."

The sight of a woman trying not to cry had always intrigued Deena

McAllister. What good would crying do? You'd just lose a little body fluid and make yourself look vulnerable, so that if one of the many sons of bitches walking the streets happened to see you, he'd think *Ah ha! I been needing a doormat, and yonder she is.* Sometimes—like right now—it made Deena wonder if something might actually be wrong with *her*, whether she might be missing a gene or a chromosome or whatever it was that so often evoked such a different response in others. When her husband hit her, she didn't cry, she just she hit him back, and though she always ended up on the losing end, it seemed like the times when he risked taking a swing at her got farther and farther apart, up until the day she figured out how to make him run off.

She downed the last of her own beer, picked up the girl's mug and carried it over to the bar. "Two more," she told Slate. She leaned closer. "Throw a shot of Jack into the one on your left. But do it under the counter. My new friend over there needs some pain medication."

Slate made no inquiries. He probably would have done pretty much anything she asked, as long as it didn't lead to incarceration.

She sat there with the girl for a couple of hours, during which the bar filled up with guys who'd just gotten off work. She bought her four more spiked PBRs and eventually heard all about her boyfriend, whose name was Juan through about the end of the third mug, then turned into Julio. The girl's reasons for leaving him didn't make a whole lot of sense, even considering that she was still young and young people did senseless things. There was something she wasn't saying, and Deena suspected if she knew her long enough, she'd learn what it was. Working the counter at the PO, she saw a lot of young women, NOVA's mostly—girls from Northern Virginia—who'd been raised in places like McLean and Falls Church, had plasticized faces and wore clothes that cost more than she could earn in a month. It stood to reason that a decent percentage of them were miserable, too, but she never felt a moment's sympathy for them. This one was different. Her sorrow had real depth. When she finally put her head in her hands and disgorged a few silent sobs, you could tell she'd had plenty of practice.

"You know what we oughta do?" Deena asked over the chatter that never failed to get loud when all the guys in the bar began to realize just how bad they didn't want to go home. "We oughta get something to eat."

"I think I might be too drunk."

"Baby, from where I sit, I'd say you're too drunk not to."

She took her to Wendy's and bought her a double cheeseburger, and a big cup of coffee, and with impressive speed the girl's eyes lost that glassy look. "You've been really good to me," she said. "I think I needed company."

"I think you did," Deena said. "Sometimes we all do. Now, I'm fixing to ask you something. And it's okay to lie to me if you think you need to, though I don't believe you do. Agreed?"

She never had to pose the question. "My name's not exactly Caro," the girl said.

"Not exactly?"

"It's Caroline."

Deena began to laugh. She laughed so hard she almost tipped over her Diet Coke, and she laughed so long that Caroline began to regret she'd told her the truth. She'd started to trust her, which might be a mistake.

When the other woman's belly quit jiggling and her shoulders stopped shaking, Caroline said, "Okay. What's so funny?"

Deena reached over and patted her hand. "Honey, I'm not the kind of person that puts a pricetag on everything. But for the sake of argument, let's say I was. Getting that extra syllable out of you cost me eight or nine dollars."

•

When her new acquaintance dropped her in the Carltons' driveway, it was almost ten-thirty. She assumed they'd be asleep. Unfortunately, Mr. Carlton was sitting in the easy chair in his office reading a book, and she had no choice but to pass him on her way to the stairs. She hoped she didn't look drunk.

Her hopes were dashed when he glanced up, cocked his head and, she thought, sniffed the air. Could he smell beer from ten feet away? Jesus Christ. She knew what was coming. He'd make her move out.

Instead of ripping into her, he smiled. "What you been up to?"

"I went out with a friend."

"Good. I've been worried about you. All work, no play. You're too young for that."

The way he was looking at her made her feel like she needed to respond. Maybe he wanted to gauge how much she'd imbibed before he decided whether to send her packing. "What're you reading?" she asked.

He held the book up, showing her the title. *The Witches of Eastwick.* "Have you ever read anything by Updike?"

"No, sir."

"The reason I ask is, I know you're a reader."

She couldn't help it: she dropped her head. "I'm sorry. I should have asked if it was okay to read your books. I won't bother them again."

"Are you joking? I'm thrilled you've been reading my books. I haven't had anybody to talk . . . Well, basically, I haven't had anybody to talk to about books since I graduated from college." He laughed. "These days, I spend most of my time haggling with salesmen over the cost of twenty-pound turkey rolls. You can read whatever you want to. I can't recommend this one, though. It's not his best. If you want to read something by Updike—and you really ought to—I'd probably start with *Rabbit, Run.* There's a copy in the den."

"I'll do that. Thank you."

"My pleasure."

She pretended to stifle a yawn. "I guess I'd better head off to bed."

"Be careful on the stairs. You look a little tipsy."

"Yes, sir. I'm afraid I am."

He chuckled, then reached under his chair, pulled out a small glass with about an inch of amber liquid in it and, before taking a sip, told her to sleep well.

FALL IN SOUTHWEST VIRGINIA WAS the prettiest she'd ever seen. One October Saturday, the Carltons took her for a ride on the Blue Ridge Parkway, where the colors were so bright and varied it seemed like an alternate reality. She would have loved to stop and take a walk, and she probably would have asked if they could do it were it not for the realization that even walking through the house was difficult for Mrs. Carlton. From the backseat Caroline noticed how often her husband reached across the transmission hump to give his wife's hand a little squeeze.

As Thanksgiving approached, they apologized for not inviting her to holiday dinner. Mrs. Carlton's parents were both still alive and living in Fredericksburg, and they'd been driving over there for several years to spend a few days with them and the family of Mrs. Carlton's sister. This worked out fine, because Deena had invited her to dinner, and that was where she preferred to go, though turning down an offer from the Carltons would have felt wrong. They'd begun to treat her like family.

Deena's trailer, which she'd been to a couple of times before, stood parked on a hill above the New River. "Now the New River," Deena told her that afternoon, as she got ready to pop the turkey in the oven, "is anything but new. There's some folks that say it may be one of the oldest in the world. I went to hear a bunch of geologists talk about it once at Tech. They got some method of taking samples from the rocks in the riverbed and figuring out how long they've been there, and we're talking a few hundred million years. There's a song about the river, too, called

'The New River Train.' And that train still runs. We'll hear it tonight around the time we sit down to eat. It's not a passenger train anymore, though. Just hauls stuff like coal and lumber."

While the turkey roasted, they sat in a pair of overstuffed armchairs, drinking beer, listening to music and talking, Deena gently poking her dog once or twice to stop her from snoring. The TV was on, the Cowboys playing the Eagles with the sound turned off. Caroline had no interest in the football game, and it was apparent that Deena didn't either. She never even looked in that direction. On both of Caroline's previous visits, the TV had also remained on but stayed silent, and it was hard not to wonder if in fact she ever turned it off. She finally risked asking why she left it on if she wasn't watching.

The question seemed to startle Deena. "I don't know," she said. She began to peel the sweaty label off her longneck Bud. "My folks always kept theirs on, and more often than not it was silent. I hadn't really thought about it. You want me to turn it off?"

"No, I was just curious. I didn't mean to make you uncomfortable."

Deena's cheeks pinkened. "Who says you made me uncomfortable?"

"Nobody. It's just that when you're a little ill at ease—which I'll be the first to admit doesn't seem to happen very often—you start peeling the label off your beer. Assuming one's handy, of course. Like the time we were at that country music place in Roanoke, when Slate came in with his wife and the two of you made eye contact? You went to work on the label then, too, pulling off tiny strips and rolling them up into little balls."

As if it were incriminating evidence, Deena leaned over and stood the beer on the coffee table. "What else have you noticed about me?" she asked. "Actually, just tell me one thing. I don't think I want to know more than that."

"Well, both times when I was here before, I noticed that nearly every time you pass that window over there, you glance at that big cluster of lights on the far side of the river. Mr. Carlton told me it's the Radford Arsenal."

Deena shook her head. "Damn, girl," she said. "Now you *are* making me uncomfortable."

"Don't be. You've noticed plenty about me."

"How you figure that?"

Caroline laughed. "I noticed you noticing."

"Oh, bullshit."

"I'm serious."

"For example?"

"Well, for example, when I drank too much the first time we went out together, I slipped and called the guy I was in love with by his real name. You noticed that—your head tilted to one side, and your tongue began to probe your jaw. And by the way, I know you told Slate to throw some whiskey in my PBR. I was glad you did it. I needed it, and it improved the taste. It made me feel like you gave a damn about me, too, even though I was just a total stranger. That was really nice."

Deena shook her head, then stood, grabbed her beer, switched the television off and went to check on the turkey. When she returned, she'd poured the Bud into a mug with an inscription on the side.

God is Great

Beer is Good

People are Batshit Crazy

She sat back down and crossed her legs, something Caroline had never seen her do before. "Okay, baby," she said, "time to 'fess up. Who is it you're running from? I want to know in case I ever see 'em coming."

Caroline wondered, as she had so many times before, what exactly went on inside people's heads when they made decisions. It had something to do with synapses, she understood, and she'd looked the word up in more sources than one. A neurotransmitter fired impulses from one nerve cell to another across this mysterious little junction. Lives changed, nations crumbled. But since nerve cells were part of the body, just like hair and toenails, did this consign morality to the realm of physiology?

"The family that gave me a ride across the Mojave," she said, "they'd picked me up in Needles. Nice people. The guy was actually from Virginia like you, though he said they'd been living in Scranton, Pennsylvania, the last few years. The woman was from Poland. An immigrant. They also had a baby, who was strapped into the backseat of this green Ford Pinto. They were moving to Northridge. He'd had some kind of temporary faculty position in Scranton but had just been hired permanently at a university near L.A. I was surprised when they picked me up—I think his wife felt sorry for me. She was in the front seat, but she tried to talk to me, and her English was quite good. She'd tramped around Europe to make money that she could carry back to Poland and exchange on the black market. She mentioned working at an ice cream parlor in Berlin and being a bartender in one of the London suburbs. I liked them. I think they would have probably let me ride with them all the way to L.A. They didn't seem eager to get rid of me, even though that car was full of their stuff and they really didn't have the room. I was squished in there next to the baby. They had like six or seven packages of Pampers in that car and a bunch of stuff on the roof rack.

"The thing was, their air conditioner didn't work—he said they were going to get it fixed in the fall, when he drew his first paycheck. Do you know how hot it gets in the desert in May? I couldn't believe it. In Needles, it had been in the high nineties, but halfway across the Mojave it was a hundred and thirteen or fourteen. He said we wouldn't have been able to use the AC anyway, because the car would've overheated. It actually got kind of scary, but they'd bought two gallons of water at a 7Eleven and we passed them around. The baby started screaming her head off. I felt awful for her and tried to distract her, but nothing helped. I was never happier, I don't think, than when we started seeing signs for Barstow.

"They stopped to gas up at a Chevron. The woman said she'd stay with the baby so her husband and I could go to the bathrooms, and then he could watch her while she went. They just seemed to assume that I'd continue on with them. But when I left the bathroom, I slipped around behind the station, peeping around the corner where I could see both of them looking around for me. Finally, the guy glanced at his watch and said something to his wife, and they got back in their car and drove off.

"It was one of those stations where they have drinks and a few food items inside and a couple of booths where you can eat whatever you bought. So I went in there and got myself a thirty-two ounce bottle of water and a couple of Twinkies and sat down in one of the booths and drank and ate as slowly as I could. Because, of course, it was cool in there. I sat watching the pumps until I saw this fairly good-looking guy in his mid-to-late twenties climb out of a red Falcon and start gassing up.

"I threw my stuff in the trashcan and went outside, and the heat almost knocked me down. Underneath his car, though, I could see a little puddle forming. Run-off from the AC. So I walked over and asked for a ride. He took a good look at me but didn't answer, just finished filling his tank. Then he put the nozzle back on the pump, screwed the cap back on the tank and told me to get in the car. I'll go to my grave wishing the AC had been working in that family's Pinto."

DECEMBER 14TH WOULD HAVE BEEN her father's birthday. She didn't think about the date's significance until afterwards. As she approached the sandwich shop that Friday morning, all she had on her mind was the show she and Deena planned to attend that evening. Dolly Parton would be performing at the Roanoke Civic Center. Caroline wasn't a huge fan of her music, but Deena was and that mattered.

She and the older woman had been seeing a lot of each other. It was nice to have a close female friend, she'd never had one before. She'd finally told her what no one else knew. If Deena was shocked, she concealed it well. She said Caroline hadn't done anything evil, she'd just done something stupid, going along for the ride. Maybe the law wouldn't see it that way, maybe they *would* have called her an accomplice, but in her own heart she had to know she'd just been a spectator. If she hadn't been behind the wheel when it happened, some other unwitting girl would have been. Some days Caroline almost managed to convince herself her friend was right. Other days she couldn't even come close. Her conscience was a harsher judge than Deena.

That crisp mountain morning, Tech students poured out of nearby dorms in their maroon and orange hoodies. A Saint Bernard waited before the sandwich shop, hitched to a parking meter. He belonged to Briley, who sometimes asked her to walk him. She leaned over and patted the dog's head.

Business was nearly always brisk on Fridays but even more so that week. Later, she would learn that exams had concluded the previous day and many of the students had slept through breakfast and were having lunch with friends before saying goodbye and returning home for the holidays. As always everybody sought space on the balcony, protected from the chill by patio heaters.

She was working the register and by one-thirty, when her break rolled around, she'd rung up about eighty sandwiches, probably an equal number of smoothies and thirty or forty salads. She sat in the kitchen to eat her own lunch, then went to the bathroom. She was in there on the toilet when she heard a loud crack followed by a tremendous impact, as if an artillery shell had smashed to earth nearby. The building shook and toilet water splashed onto her thighs.

She assumed it was another planned explosion at the arsenal. Then she began to hear the shrieks and moans that seemed to be coming from just beyond the bathroom wall. Quickly, she dried herself with paper towels, straightened her clothes, washed her hands and opened the door.

Pandemonium prevailed. She saw a Tech coed sitting on the floor in front of the register, her back against the counter, hands over her ears as if to mask the sound of her own screams. Others had left food on their tables and run outside. Through the front window, she saw Briley, his face ashen as he shoved people out of his way, then disappeared around the corner.

One of the other counter workers pressed the phone to her ear. Tears streaked her face.

"What happened?" Caroline asked.

"The balcony collapsed!"

Caroline ran through the kitchen and out the rear door. When she rounded the corner of the building and emerged into the narrow alley that the deck used to overlook, she saw a dazed guy climbing from one of the two green dumpsters that stood beneath the balcony, blood streaming from his face and neck. The dumpsters had broken the falls of several students, but the receptacles were full of glass that inflicted shrapnel-like wounds. Most of the thirty-odd patrons, as well as the busboy who'd been collecting dishes when the balcony caved in, had simply fallen onto the strip of asphalt between Wiley's and the next-door book store. One of them, a junior from Arlington who'd die before they got her to the hospital, was impaled on a splintered 2x4. Others lay pinned beneath picnic tables, broken joists, overturned space heaters. Caroline, who'd never been assigned to work the deck, hadn't asked herself what powered the space heaters, assuming they were electric. On Sunday, she would learn from the *Washington Post* that in all likelihood they played a role in the collapse, as each one weighed around 150 pounds. She would also learn they ran off propane and that even though they came equipped with tip switches, it was all but miraculous none of them exploded.

Fire trucks, police cars and ambulances were already arriving. She spent the next half hour bringing water and coffee to emergency personnel through the back entrance. The news van must have pulled up on one of her trips inside. It was parked behind the shop, a blue logo emblazoned on the rear quarter panel: *WDBJ 7*. Next to the number, the all-seeing eye of its affiliated network. The instant she stepped into the alley, a woman stuck a microphone in her face. Why did she look familiar? Deena's TV. She would see her there again tonight, though she'd only see herself in the shorter segment that was going to run on the *CBS Evening News* with Dan Rather.

"Today, in Blacksburg, Virginia," Rather would inform millions, "an outdoor deck attached to the second floor of a popular sandwich shop collapsed, killing one person and injuring more than twenty-five others. Caro Cole, a cashier, was in the bathroom when she heard a loud noise."

Cut to Caroline, dumpsters visible behind her, flashing lights on the other side of those, firemen and police officers sifting through the debris. "When I got out here, I saw a big pile of boards and picnic tables. People were bleeding and screaming."

The voice of the female reporter. "Were there problems with the deck before?"

Caroline again. "I don't know. But I don't think so."

Back to a stone-faced Rather. "Several of the injured remain in critical condition in area hospitals."

Immune to Deena's entreaties, she left town the next morning.

WHEN HER PHONE RINGS, ELLA is taping shut the last of five boxes. They contain everything she owns. She drops the Scotch tape and lifts the receiver. Earlier, Martin warned her it might be midnight before he picks her up, as he and his partner are trying to finish mixing several tracks before knocking off. Studio time is cheapest close to Christmas.

"Els?"

She last heard her sister's voice the previous Friday on the ten o'clock news after her mother called to alert her. Directory assistance in Blacksburg, Virginia, yielded no phone number for Caro Cole or Caroline Cole, so she tried to reach the place where her sister works but she kept getting a busy signal, as if someone had left the phone off the hook. She spent much of Saturday and Sunday talking to representatives of various law enforcement agencies: the Blacksburg Police, the Montgomery County Sheriff's Department, the Virginia State Police. They couldn't tell her anything except that since her sister had not been accused of a crime she was of no interest to them, unless of course Ella chose to report her missing. Martin suggested she file the report, but so far she hasn't. He acted strange when she told him what happened. She can't blame him, given what she knows of his ex-wife's family. He has to be wondering if every woman he falls in love with will come attached to disaster.

"Caro," she says. "Caro freaking Cole."

"I guess you saw the news, huh?"

"Jesus. How could you do this to us? I've been having nightmares for years. I thought you might be dead. How *could* you do this?" Her hands are shaking, and if an open liquor bottle were nearby, she would drink whatever it contained. "Momma's beside herself," she says. "Have you called her?"

"Not yet."

"Well, you better. Just as soon as we hang up. Where in God's name are you?"

The truth is that Caroline doesn't exactly know. Somewhere in New Jersey, in a phone booth at a bus station that smells of urine. Several people are asleep on benches, and one old man who reminds her of Redd Foxx from *Sanford and Son* is propped up near the door drinking from a paper bag, his eyes glassy, unfocused. She's heard people speaking in some kind of patois. Outside, a snowstorm is over-performing. You can't even see across the street. The woman at the counter told her that nobody will be going anywhere anytime soon.

"Something-Orange, New Jersey," she says. "East Orange, West Orange, South Orange . . . I'm not sure."

"What are you doing there?"

On the last bus, riding beside a woman who could have been any age between forty and sixty but looked closer to the latter and fell asleep with her mouth open, spit trickling down her chin, Caroline decided to ask if she could come live with Ella, at least for a little while. She'd never told Tom she had a sister, so maybe he'd never find out. She'd get a job—any job, something stable, maybe even waitressing at the steakhouse, if that's still where her sister works—and try to reconstitute herself. Otherwise, she's going to end up like her seatmate. Or worse. "I was thinking," she says, "that I'd come visit you. That maybe we'd spend Christmas together? You like Boston, don't you? I mean you must, since you've stayed there all these years."

The silence at the other end lasts long enough for Caroline to know that she needs to fill it, that if she doesn't, her sister will have to and it will provide one more reason to wonder if her own life has become unlivable. She searches for words but finds none.

"Sure," her sister finally says. "Sure . . . of course. But . . . well . . . here's the thing, baby."

Caroline can't recall either of them ever once employing such a term of endearment. Whatever they are to each other cannot be captured by *baby*.

"I'm actually about to get married. And the wedding . . . well, it's going to be on Christmas Eve down on the Cape. Cape Cod, I mean. And Martin . . . Martin Summers, that's my fiancé, he's a record producer who's also a CPA . . . he has this aunt who lives down there in a pretty big house, and it was her idea. Her name . . . it's . . . her name is Tess."

Across the lobby, Redd Foxx chuckles, takes another swallow from the paper bag, then slowly slides to the floor.

"I think you'd like her. Tess, that is. She's old but energetic. She's got a lot of colorful friends too. Like that writer, the naked and dead guy . . . the one who wrote the book that you got caught . . . the library book, you know? Norman Mailer. I met him. At Tess's. He's kind of awful, actually. But listen, sure, I'll tell Martin and he'll talk to Tess. Are you. . .Do you have a place to stay tonight? I mean, I'm worried about you. Are you okay?"

The voice of the operator, nasal and bored, comes on the line. "Please deposit a dollar fifty for another five minutes."

Ella says, "Can you reverse the charges and make this call collect?"

But it's already too late. Her sister has hung up.

A Whole Other World

IN JULY OF 1986, IN THE Cedar Park hospital, she gave birth to their first daughter, whom they named Hayley after Martin's mother. A second daughter, Alexandra, followed nineteen months later, and they quickly began to call her Lexa, though both of them had sworn they would stick to her full name. Hayley got her mother's blonde hair. Lexa's was chestnut-colored rather than red like Martin's. At various times, from middle school through high school, she would dye it. During one period, if only for a couple of weeks, it was purple.

A quiet baby, Hayley smiled a lot, and like her mother she seldom had trouble sleeping. Lexa, on the other hand, was born with a hiatal hernia, which led to esophageal reflux, and over the first year or so she seldom slept more than a couple of hours at a time. Ella and Martin lost a lot of sleep then too; she occasionally became irritable, but he never seemed to. Pete, his partner in the record company, who came equipped with a towering temper as well as a couple of other problematic traits, dubbed him "Merry Martin." Ella called him that when she was especially happy with him, which in those days was frequently the case.

Both of them considered it important that they do things together as a family. His folks hadn't, mostly because his father was so wrapped up in his law practice and his role as a civic leader. Hers hadn't, because her parents' marriage, as far back as she could recall, was all but devoid of affection. They'd never gone on family vacations, and lack of money was not the only reason: her parents wouldn't have been able to stand being together in a car for more than a few hours. She and Martin and the girls drove all over New England—the Maine Coast, the White Mountains, the Green Mountains, the Berkshires—and congregated at Tess's each June with Irma and Maeve to spend a week or ten days enjoying the Cape. They drove all the way to California, into the Pacific Northwest and back, and most years they also took a trip outside the country: Paris, London, Rome. One year, the Grand Caymans.

For Ella, the best of times. She felt at home where she lived. She knew the big green house on the hill as well as she'd ever known the one where she grew up, which was not even one-tenth as large. She knew the little town six miles north of Boston in ways she'd never known Loring, Mississippi, and she liked it many times more. She'd become friends with various locals who attended high school with Martin, and she'd grown exceptionally fond of Tess, talking to her on the phone almost daily. She remained close to her old friend Liz, too, though during the Clinton years their political differences occasionally led to heated conversations, in which Liz parroted whatever opinions she heard from the likes of Rush Limbaugh. She'd finally achieved her dream and opened a successful Southern-style restaurant in Wakefield, the next town over, and sometimes walked her dog all the way to Ella's so they could have a drink together on the balcony.

"One day," she liked to say a little too frequently, "I'll have a house like this myself. Maybe I'll marry one just like you did."

Difficult to do, Ella often thought but never said, when every guy you get involved with already has a wife.

Hayley and Lexa knew her as Aunt Liz. They had Aunt Liz, Aunt Maeve, Aunt Irma and Aunt Tess, though following family tradition they never called Tess "Aunt" to her face. They were on a first-name basis with most of their parents' other non-familial friends. Every Thanksgiving, when Pete threw his big holiday bash, Ella drove them into Brookline four or five hours before dinner, so they could help him and his wife peel potatoes. Traditions, they learned, were to be adhered to and treasured.

They got along well. Each of them had her own bedroom, but up through middle school they took turns "sleeping over," as they put it, and even after that they would often spend two or three hours in one or the other's room chattering away. Hayley was without question the more consistently focused. She never made anything less than an A. She knew early on that she wanted to be an art historian and work at either Boston's MFA or the Isabella Stewart Gardner Museum, and she single-mindedly prepared herself for such a future. Lexa's attentions turned in various directions. Once, after they spotted a school of porpoises off the Cape, she informed everyone she was going to study marine biology. That lasted until she made a C- on her fourth-grade science project, at which time she decided that like her father she would become a record producer. The problem was that she had no more than passing interest in music. So one morning as the four of them were eating breakfast, when she was all of eleven years old, she cleared her throat and announced, "I've thought a lot about this, and I believe it's just plain *unhealthy* to decide too soon what you want to be. I'll figure it out when I have more life experience. I might be around, like, *forty* or something."

Satisfying times for Ella, when what she did with her days and nights made sense and what she didn't do made sense too. Mostly what she did was concentrate on her daughters, reading to them when they were little, Tove Jansson's *Finn Family Moomintroll* series their favorite as well as hers and the primary reason that in '94 they nixed a trip to Mexico, opting instead for Finland, so they could visit Moominworld. She fed them filling breakfasts and inventive dinners, she took them to ballet lessons, to karate lessons, took them ice skating, roller skating, took them to family concerts at the Boston Symphony. She took an interest in what went on at school, twice serving as president of the Cedar Park PTA. She did everything she wished someone had been willing and able to do for her.

She possessed not only the will but, thanks to Martin and Pete, the means. Yankee Southern Records, hatched one night in 1975 after the pair drank ten or twelve pints of Narragansett at the Boots 'n' Flannel, was hardly breaking even when she met Martin. That it had lasted till then was due to the success of his accounting firm and the fact that Pete married the daughter of a big Boston developer. Over the next decade, though, as the interest in American roots music burgeoned, so did their fortunes. They won their first Grammy in 1987. A slew of others followed. By the end of the '90s they owned the most successful roots record company in the world.

Easy times for everyone at 1 Rockland Street, so different from the straightened circumstances in which she had been raised. She did everything she could to ensure that her own marriage bore no resemblance to her parents' and that her daughters' childhoods bore little if any to hers and that of her poor lost sister, whom nobody had heard from since the night she called Ella from New Jersey.

She'd never told anyone, not even Martin, the whole truth about that final conversation. The truth was that she feared her sister would ruin her wedding, that she'd do or say something embarrassing and that Tess and Irma and Maeve and all of Martin's friends who were becoming her friends would know it and start wondering what sort of familial dysfunction he was inflicting on himself the second time around: first gangsters, now white trash? It didn't matter that she overcame her fear and issued Caroline the grudging invitation. What mattered was that her sister heard the hesitation in her voice and understood its source. Rather than slam the phone down in whatever shabby, smelly bus station she was calling from, she quietly placed it in the cradle. Such an emphatic sound, that silence.

Every now and then, when the girls were at school and Martin was at work, those dark thoughts intruded. If the weather was nice, she could usually banish them by going for a long walk, enjoying the natural beauty of the place she'd come to call home, so different from the only other one she'd known. If the weather was bad, she could usually build a fire and put on some quiet music or lose herself in a good book. In other instances—and fortunately, these were rare—nothing could chase them away but two or three glasses of wine and the blurring of time.

HER MOTHER WAS NOT LOST.

She lived in Pine Bluff with Tommy Burns until his death in 1993. On multiple occasions, Ella and Martin planned to take the girls to meet their grandmother and her husband, but something always seemed to go wrong before they could get down there. In June of '89, when Lexa was still a baby, they bought tickets and booked a hotel, but the day before they were to fly to Little Rock, Tommy Burns suffered his second heart attack. He was ill for a long time. They planned another trip for Christmas of the following year, but Saddam invaded Kuwait, the Bush administration began rattling its sabers, there was talk of bomb threats, and they decided to wait until things settled down. The next attempt was undone by chickenpox, which both girls contracted simultaneously.

When her mother called with the news that Mr. Burns was gone, she seemed more relieved than anything else. "Well," she said, "that's that. At least he's not just having to lay there and stare at the ceiling anymore." The last few years, Ella knew, had been a slog. She and Martin had begun sending her a check each month after the setback in '89, and while she protested the first few times, she never let them go uncashed. She couldn't afford to. They were living off disability and the pittance she earned at the truckstop.

As luck would have it, her call about his death came in the middle of January when Martin was in California with Pete at a music industry trade show. The thought of taking the girls out of school, or in Lexa's case pre-school, and flying to Arkansas for the funeral without him, seeing her mother for the first time in all these years, finding her living in poverty, made her gaze with longing toward the dining room where the wine rack stood. If only she'd answered one of the cordless phones. Instead, because she'd been in the kitchen, she grabbed the wall phone. The cord was long. But not that long.

"When's the funeral?" she asked. "I'll book our flights as soon as we hang up."

"You don't need to worry about that, hon."

"We want to be there."

"Yes, I know. But the thing is . . . well, honey, the thing is, Tommy actually died three days ago. We buried him this morning. Or I did anyway. Me and two or three others that remembered him from when he was still able to work."

"Oh, Momma." Everything she hadn't done bore down on her. She could have gone to Arkansas by herself at any time—Martin wouldn't have objected—but she never wanted to. Not solely because she disliked Mr. Burns, or because she dreaded seeing her mom with another man. She just didn't want to be alone when she confronted the past that her mother represented. She preferred to face it, if she had to, with everyone who made the present dissimilar. "Why didn't you let me know?"

"Honestly, Ella?" June Cole said. "I think . . . well, I think my girls already attended one funeral too many. And I know for damn solid certain I sure have. The next one I go to'll be my own."

•

That evening, Martin called her mother from Anaheim, and though he said it took him close to an hour, he persuaded her to fly to Boston. Ella purchased the ticket, arranging for her to land at Logan twenty minutes after his returning flight. Unfortunately, he was delayed by more than an hour, so she was sitting there alone, nervously sipping coffee, when her mother walked off the plane. She didn't like being photographed and never sent pictures of herself, so Ella had been wondering how dramatic the change in her appearance might be. She recognized her luggage before she recognized the woman holding it:

the old strapped-leather suitcase that once belonged to her father. She must've used it as a carry-on.

"Maybe tell me hello or something?" her mother said. Fifty-eight years old, she looked closer to seventy: iron-gray hair, leathery face, faded Wranglers, blue-and-white checked blouse and a thin white windbreaker with colored stripes on the chest and shoulders. She was going to freeze before they reached the car, which was parked on the upper deck.

Ella stood, and June set the suitcase down and they hugged. Her mother had never been a smoker, but she smelled like cigarettes, though you couldn't smoke on planes anymore. "Where's Martin?" she asked. "I thought he was supposed to get here before I did?"

"His flight was delayed in Orange County. He should be here by two-thirty. Are you hungry?"

"They gave us some little something on the plane. One of those . . . I don't know how to say it. One of those quarter moon-shaped sandwiches."

"A croissant?"

"Yeah. It wasn't bad. Had ham and cheese in it, and they gave us a bag of chips."

"Would you like a drink?"

"I wouldn't mind a Coke."

"Let's go get you one. There's a bar directly across from Martin's assigned gate."

Her mother ordered the Coke. She asked for a glass of Chardonnay.

It seemed there was nothing to say. But something would have to be said, and so she asked the cause of Mr. Burns's death.

Her mother shrugged. "Officially, it was heart failure."

"Officially?"

"Yeah. In reality, I think he just lost interest. I think that's what most folks die from. I saw a fellow die once at the truckstop. I was waiting on him. I don't know who he drove for, I never asked, but he came through Pine Bluff once or twice a month, and it didn't matter what time he sat down, whether it was eight in the morning, two in the afternoon or midnight, he always asked for the same thing: a cup of coffee, a glass of milk, scrambled eggs, bacon and hashbrowns. The night he died, he'd drunk his milk, cleaned his plate and finished his coffee, and told me 'Miss June, that sure was fine.' He looked like he was fixing to say something else. Instead he just kind of smiled—like 'what are you gonna do?'—and leaned against the wall and died. Didn't look like there was a thing in the world wrong with him."

Their waiter brought the Coke and the Chardonnay. Ella drank a third of the wine in one swallow.

Her mother took note. "Don't be shy," she said.

"Shy? About what?"

"Enjoying your wine."

"I'm not."

"I can see that, hon. I was being ironic."

"Ah."

They talked about the girls for a while, then they talked about Boston. Ella said she was going to take her to all the sights: the Old North Church, Faneuil Hall, the State House. She started to add the Granary Burying Ground to the list but was afraid it might prompt another anecdote about death.

"Is that pond still here?" her mother asked. "The one where the hermit went and lived by himself in the cabin?"

"Walden? Of course."

"You don't think I could rent the place, do you?"

"Rent it?"

"I was making a joke."

She'd seldom been happier to see Martin. When he stepped off the plane, she downed the rest of the Chardonnay, consulted the check, laid a twenty on the table and said, "There he is. Let's go."

Her mother left her Coke untouched.

•

Despite the inauspicious beginning, the ten-day visit was a good one, and for that Ella would always be grateful. The major reason it went so well was Martin. The moment he walked off the plane, he began to manage the situation. On their way out, he stopped near one of the sports apparel shops you can find in any major airport.

"June," he asked, "how do you feel about the Boston Celtics?"

"The Boston who?"

"The NBA team. Professional basketball."

"Oh, I don't know. I don't pay much attention to athletics except Razorback football. I used to watch some of that with Tommy."

"So is football your favorite sport?"

"That's the only one I know anything about. Why?"

"Hold on." He stepped into the shop, and they watched while he spoke to a salesclerk, then gestured at her mother and came out, a moment later, carrying a thickly insulated New England Patriots jacket. "Put this on," he told her.

"Why?"

"Because it's about twelve degrees outside, and I think we'll have a much better visit if we can spend it with you at our house rather than MGH. Coming from the South, you can't possibly be acclimated to this kind of weather, and that windbreaker's not going to give you enough protection. I don't intend to let my mother-in-law get sick the first time she comes to visit."

Her mom didn't protest, just compliantly pulled off the windbreaker and slipped on the ridiculous red, white and blue jacket with the image of Pat the Patriot on the back. Later, when Ella asked him why he hadn't suggested buying her a nice coat at one of the overpriced luxury shops they'd just passed, he said that if he'd tried to do that, she would have felt embarrassed and that even if she agreed to wear it, it would set the wrong tone. They'd buy her a nice coat, he said, when the time was right.

For the first couple of hours, she was shy with her granddaughters, but they were not shy with her—they didn't do shy, and they didn't do reticent—and Lexa, still not quite five years old, quickly captivated her. "Grandma," she said at dinner, "I want to thank you for sending us such a good momma."

June swallowed and patted her lips with her napkin. Martin had insisted on pouring her a glass of wine, and she'd also let him pour a second. Her face had taken on a rosy glow that Ella had never seen while growing up. "Why, you're welcome, darling. I don't know how much I had to do with that, though."

"Understand, now, I'm not saying she's perfect," Lexa continued. "There's some stuff she could work on."

"Like what, hon?"

"Well, she won't let me watch Mr. Rogers if I don't eat all my cinnamon oatmeal. And cinnamon oatmeal's okay but within limits."

"You might have a point."

Lexa glanced triumphantly at Ella, then back at her grandmother: "Could you maybe talk to her about it?"

"I'll see what I can do. I don't reckon you've ever tasted cheese grits, have you?"

"No!"

"Well, if your momma doesn't mind, I might fix y'all some one morning."

"Be my guest," Ella said, suspecting that after cheese grits, cinnamon oatmeal might be viewed in a kinder light. To her surprise, Hayley and Lexa both loved the dish, and her mother prepared grits for their breakfast, along with bacon and eggs, for the remainder of her visit.

To give her more time with her mom, Martin took the girls to school or, in Lexa's case, pre-school, then went on to work, and she and her mother picked them up. In between breakfast and three PM, they were alone together each weekday. The first morning she was there, she asked for a tour of the house, so Ella led her from room to room, first floor to third, showing her all the porches and balconies and the little climate-controlled, soundproofed room in the northeast corner of the top floor where Martin kept all his musical instruments and had a small home studio.

"How many guitars has he got?" her mother asked, taking in the instrument rack that covered an entire wall.

"I don't know. Fifteen or twenty, maybe. And there are a couple of mandolins and an electric bass and a banjo."

"How many can he play at one time?"

"Three."

"Are you serious?"

"Sort of. I once saw him fill in with a band in Cambridge where he switched back and forth between acoustic guitar, mandolin and Dobro on the same song."

He mom just shook her head. "I guess the good Lord, if He exists, knew your husband wasn't the kind to bury his talents and apportioned them accordingly."

After they made their way back downstairs, she paused in the foyer to examine the framed photos of Martin's ancestors, including Great-great Grandfather Eamon, a sour-looking man who immigrated to America with the Famine Irish in 1850.

"That one there," she said, "he looks like some of our folks. What'd he do for a living?"

"From what I know, he was a hostler."

"That's somebody that takes care of horses?"

"Yes, ma'am. There used to be a big hotel on Main Street—these days, it's a really nice gym—and I think he spent most of his life working there."

Her mom waved her hand around the entryway: at the pier table with satinwood inlay, the Victorian storage bench that Ella had never liked but left there because Martin's grandmother allegedly loved it, the Metropolitan chandelier that she'd bought herself for 2800 dollars to replace an older, more ostentatious one. "There must have been some real upward mobility," her mother said, "between the horse-handler and Martin."

"His dad and his grandfather on his father's side were both successful lawyers. I think the grandfather was the first one in the family to attend college."

Her mother sniffled. Despite the Pats' jacket, she'd caught a cold anyway, probably on the plane. "What'd his momma's people do?"

"Both his grandparents on that side worked in a shoe mill. I think that's where they met."

Her mother laughed. "So I guess there's a long tradition of intermarriage with blue-collar folks."

"Momma . . ."

June reached over and hugged her. She no longer smelled like cigarette smoke. She just smelled like her mom. "Baby, I'm as happy for you as I can be. You've got a couple of great little girls, a great husband and a great house. At least one of my two made it."

"Have you . . ."

"Heard from her?"

Ella nodded.

"No. I would have told you."

"I haven't either. I would have told you too."

Her mother sighed and pointed at the storage bench. "Is that thing something a person can actually sit on? Or is it just there for show?"

"You can sit on it. But it's not comfortable. Why don't we go into the living room?"

June followed her in there and took a seat on the couch. Martin had built a fire that morning, and the coals were still glowing, so Ella picked up a log and laid it on the grate, then sat down beside her.

"You don't remember our old fireplace, do you?" her mother asked.

"Not before it was boarded up. Did Daddy really find a dead snake in there?"

"No, hon. That snake was alive. Your daddy just said it was dead because, well, you know how your sister was about anything that crawled. It was a cottonmouth, probably four feet long. He thought it must've fallen onto the roof from that big cypress tree and then slithered down the chimney. He grabbed it with a pair of tongs, then pitched it off the porch and put a load of buckshot in it. I guess he figured if it happened once, it could happen twice. So he nailed the fireplace up. I was scared to have a fire in it anyhow, worried it'd burn the house down." She stared at the log, which had begun to smoke, then looked at Ella. "One time a fellow came asking about her in Pine Bluff," she said.

"About Caroline?"

"Yeah."

"When?"

"Not too long before she was on the television in Virginia. I was waitressing that night, but Tommy said the guy knocked on the door and told him he was a friend of hers and had lost track of her and wanted to get in touch. Tommy told him that he didn't know where she was and that I didn't know, but the guy didn't want to accept his answer. He asked if he could come in, and Tommy said no and started to close the door, but the guy stuck his hand out to shove it open. Thing is, Pine Bluff's a tough town, and Tommy never went to the door at night without first tucking his little Derringer under his belt. So he whipped it out right quick and the guy took off. You remember Smokey from the Dollar Store in Loring?"

"Yes, ma'am."

"She called me the very next morning and said a fellow had been there the day before asking for Caroline's momma and that the manager told her I was married and living in Pine Bluff with Tommy. So I guess that's how he found us. Tommy said he was a tall, fairly good-looking guy. Mid-to-late thirties. We called the police and Tommy kept an eye out for him, but he never did bother us again." Her mom fingered a tassel on one of the throw pillows. "She's still alive somewhere. I don't know how I know it, but I do. With all my heart I know it. What about you?"

Ella's heart told her something else. Her sister had always courted trouble, stealing things, telling extravagant lies, running off from school, then later on running away from her mother and Mr. Burns without telling them where she was going. Asking for money to be wired to her in Texas when she was clearly in California suggested she'd gotten herself into a different kind of trouble than she'd gotten into before. The fake names, the tragedy in Virginia, the desperation in her voice when she placed that call from New Jersey—it all suggested somebody whose luck had run out. And she'd never had much luck to begin with.

But it was clear what answer her mother wanted to hear and needed to hear and so she gave it. "I think so too," she said. "I'm sure she'll get in touch with us again one day. She might well be living it up on the Champs-Élysées."

"On the what?"

"It's a street in Paris. I just meant that she might be almost anywhere. For all we know," she said, gesturing at the bay window, trying to sound hopeful, though hope was not what she felt, "she could be right out there."

•

They did all the things she'd promised her mother they would do and a few others as well, visiting the Common and the State House and other sites in central Boston. They took a walk along Marlborough, and she pointed out the brownstone where she'd lived back in the early and mid-80s. They rode the Red Line to Cambridge, walked around the Harvard campus for a little while, then grabbed a taxi down to Central Square, so she could show her the Boots 'n' Flannel and take her to lunch at the little Italian place where she and Martin went to have drinks after the blues concert. She drove her over to Walden Pond, which was frozen solid, and they tromped through the snow to look at the replica of Thoreau's cabin. It was closed for the winter, but at least she got to see the outside.

"Still want to rent it?" Ella asked.

"Not unless they install a heat pump."

"I didn't think so."

But the subject of where her mother would live for the remainder of her life did come up. First Martin raised it with Ella, and they discussed what he had in mind, and then the night before her mom left for Arkansas, he raised it with June herself. While the girls were parked in front of the TV watching *Charlotte's Web* for perhaps the fifteenth time, he told her there was one thing they hadn't gotten around to showing her, so he and Ella led her outside into the frigid air.

When they stepped behind the garage, the motion detector turned on a pair of flood lights, revealing the staircase. "This is what I wanted to show you."

"You got you a little workshop up there?"

"Right now, I've got me a big mess up there. Hold onto the railing."

The three of them climbed the steps, Ella at the rear. She hadn't told him that she had mixed feelings about what he'd proposed. The source of her reticence was the worrisome voice which occasionally whispered that her present life was all a dream, that people like her didn't live like this. They lived hand to mouth like her mother, in a house heated by space heaters, a place colder in winter than Martin could ever imagine, where a slop bucket stood on the back porch to collect the food scraps they fed their hogs when they still had them. Where you could hear what everybody did in the bathroom and smell it too. Where you were destined to work at the dollar store or a truck stop and live off scraps yourself, and where things were never quite right between those who lived there. She hated that those associations clung to her mother, who'd always done the best she could. Even if her best was not all that good, it could have been many times worse.

Martin opened the door, then flipped on the lights.

The space was full of old furniture, old newspapers, old magazines, old paint cans, old paint brushes, old brooms, old mops, everything covered in cobwebs. "My family's as Irish as anybody this side of Gerry Adams," he told her mother. "But my grandfather and my father were both infected by a strain of Germanic sentimentality. That chest of drawers in the corner contains not only my baby clothes and my sister's, it's even got a bunch of my dad's and my aunt's. I've been looking for a good reason to clean this place up, have it fully finished with a bathroom and kitchenette. It's a lot bigger than it looks while it's filled up with all this junk. A hair over nine hundred square feet. We could add a dormer window to look out onto Rockland and then put in insulation so you wouldn't die of diesel fumes from my old Volvo. If you occasionally got sick of us, you'd still have your privacy. So what do you say, June? Sound good?"

What should it have told Ella that the first thing her mother did was glance at her? This time around, unlike the night her sister called her from New Jersey, she was ready. "Please, Momma?" she said. "It would mean so much to me and the girls. They'd have their grandmother, I'd have my mom. We could start making up for some of the lost years."

"As for me," Martin said, "I lost both of my parents when I was still in my twenties. The girls never even got to know them. You're the only grandparent they've got. It'd be great for them and great for Ella and me too. This is something we'd really like to do. What about it? Are you in?"

Ella had seen her mother cry exactly one time, and that was the day she spanked her in Texarkana for asking where her dad was. There in the garage apartment, she thought she might see it again, and she wished she would, so that she could join in. They could cry for her father and cry for her sister and maybe even produce a tear or two for Mr. Burns. But her mother's eyes remained dry, even as she said that yes, she thought she could do that, if both of them felt like she wouldn't become a burden, and both of them assured her she would not.

•

The following week, her mother called Martin at work and apologized but told him she'd thought long and hard on it, and that as much as she appreciated his and Ella's offer, and as badly as she wanted to see her grand girls again, she was just too old to make that kind of move. She said something about not liking cold weather, according to Martin, and something about not being able to understand what folks said to her up there in public places and knowing they couldn't understand her either, and something else to the effect that she didn't quite know how to break the news to her daughter. So, Martin being Martin, he told her not to worry, that he'd tell Ella himself. He also told her mother that he was still going to renovate the space above the garage and that it would be there for her if she ever changed her mind, which he fervently hoped she would do.

They never found out if she would have changed it or not. Three months later, before the renovations could begin, she suffered a massive stroke and died alone in the home she'd shared with Tommy Burns. She'd just turned fifty-nine.

EARLY MARCH OF '9I: THE BERLIN WALL for sale in tiny chunks at souvenir shops, Saddam swiftly chastened, the nation riding high, unaware that in a matter of months the economy will enter a downward spiral culminating in the defeat of a president whose approval rating at the moment is 89 percent. Caroline doesn't see the crash coming either. Her own crash came long ago and has been maintained, to one degree or another, in the interim. She's had better times and worse. She's sung for her supper, her lunch, and her breakfast, though she's only performed for the morning meal once, and that happened earlier today, after she spent the night in a luxury hotel on Newbury Street with a man she'd met in a bar. He was in Boston on business, he'd said. To prove it, he handed her a card. *Bingo*, whispered a little voice in her head. She'd landed on a stool beside a literary agent. She knew the name of the outfit he worked for, one of the big talent agencies that represented novelists, journalists, screenwriters, even actors and directors. She let him buy her three Manhattans while he consumed four big Glenlivets. Things went the way they sometimes do, except that last night he couldn't finish and they had to wait until morning. He was about her age, maybe a year or two younger, sweet, well-behaved. After breakfast, when they said goodbye outside in light snow, he kissed her cheek and told her to keep him in mind when she finished that novel they'd discussed. There was, of course, no novel, except the one she'd invented at the bar. Halfway through her spiel, she realized it would not be a bad book if she could actually write it.

She tromped back to the fleabag where she'd left her stuff, picked up her duffel and asked the stale-smelling guy at the front desk if he could call a taxi. He didn't even look at her, advising her to go outside and wave one down. Knowing that she was about to commit an act of some extravagance, she climbed into the cab and gave the driver an address. Her flight out of Logan, half the price of one from JFK, was not until nine that night. Even allowing for the need to arrive early, there were eight hours to kill and she'd decided last week how to waste them. Martin Summers, CPA and record producer, had not been hard to find. He lived in a little town named Cedar Park, a few miles from the center of Boston. She knew their home phone number but elected not to call ahead.

The driver, disinclined to converse, made sure she got the message by turning up the radio. He was listening to a sports call-in show, where guys who sounded like the hoodlums in *The Friends of Eddie Coyle* bitched about the Celtics' free-throw shooting. As he drove north on I-93, the snow began to fall harder.

When the cab left the interstate, they traversed a couple of grimy-looking neighborhoods, passing big red brick buildings in which nothing seemed to be happening, their windows boarded up, their roofs in ill condition, their parking lots empty. Shuttered mills, she assumed, having read that the area was once known as the shoe capital of the world. The houses were small and poorly maintained, with rotting front steps and peeling paint. Not the kind of place you'd expect a record producer to live, especially if he had an aunt who owned a big house on Cape Cod and was friends with Norman Mailer.

Then the color of the street signs changed from maroon to blue, and they were no longer hitting potholes, and the houses grew exponentially larger, culminating in a huge lime-colored Victorian that she could see some distance ahead. It stood on top of a steep, snow-covered hill looking like a fairytale castle, with its large bay windows, turrets and cupolas. The driver hit his blinker and waited for a break in oncoming traffic, apparently intending to turn into the street that led up the hill.

"Is that it?" she asked. "That huge green house?"

"Lady, the address you gave me was 1 Rockland Street. According to the street sign—" he pointed, and she saw the name on it "—that's Rockland. You see another house up there? I don't. So I'm guessing that's number 1. Looks to me like whoever lives there may own the whole freaking hill, if not the entire town."

In a matter of seconds, disbelief turned to anger, then to resignation, then to a heaviness in the pit of her stomach that began to expand as if it were malignant. It would remain there all the way across the Atlantic, robbing her of her appetite, so that when she landed the next day in Frankfurt she would not have had a bite to eat for more than twenty-four hours. She wouldn't eat there, either, instead stepping into a bathroom stall, where she'd put her finger down her throat, hoping to disgorge whatever was tormenting her, but nothing would come out. Whatever was down there causing all the trouble had become part of her, like her liver or gallbladder. She already knew that unlike those organs, it couldn't be removed by any surgeon, no matter how skilled he or she might be.

She told the driver she'd changed her mind and asked him to take her straight to the airport. He shook his head as if at the craziness of her request, then wheeled into Rockland.

"No place for me to turn the fuck around," he said, "except in their goddamn driveway."

He drove up the hill, then pulled into the drive. Before he backed out and headed for the interstate, Caroline saw a small face pressed to the window, a little blonde-haired girl who looked exactly like her sister, circa 1964.

•

With the college transcript she'd forged while a member of the custodial staff at Fairleigh Dickinson University, in Madison, New Jersey, and the TESOL certificate she had studied hard for and earned, she got a job teaching English at an adult education school in Budapest. Eastern Europe was the new Wild West, the place to go if you wanted to do a makeover. She kept that job for nearly two years, sharing a decrepit, post-Communist flat with two other women, both Americans, one from Portland, Oregon, the other from Harbor Springs, Michigan. Her roommates were several years younger, mid-twenties, and every bit as lost as she was, though neither of them appeared to know it. Both fancied themselves singers and regularly performed on open mic night in bars frequented by other Americans who'd ended up there to eke out a living explaining the difference between transitive and intransitive verbs to would-be entrepreneurs while deluding themselves with visions of grandeur.

She and the other two women lived on busy Bela Bartok Street, and the sound of vehicular traffic and trams ruined many a night's sleep. Also, Caroline frequently suffered nightmares. She often saw herself waiting in the parking lot outside Rigoberto's Mexican Market, where sometimes Tom managed to jump in before she screeched away, or hit her when he fired at the fleeing car. She saw him standing over her as she bled to death, shaking his head and saying *Why'd you ruin everything?* In a different dream, it was Julio who found her bleeding, and told her in the most soothing tones not to worry, that he'd make sure she was decently buried. She dreamed about the lime-colored mansion on the hill north of Boston, and one time it was bittersweet, her sister opening the door and walking out to the taxi with the little girl, telling her to come in and get warm. Another time, Ella jerked the child away from the window, then stepped out onto the snow-covered deck and started yelling for her to get the hell away. *Don't bring your poison here.*

She had to contend with crawling creatures. The roommate from Michigan was a pig, leaving filthy dishes in the sink. Dirty Styrofoam containers, recently full of goulash, lined the kitchen counter. Fearless roaches ruled. One night, after she'd been living there for eighteen months, she turned down the covers to find an entire brood. That was when she lost it and started screaming at the top of her voice and went and banged on her roommate's door. A guy was in there with her, a different American than the one she'd brought home the previous night. Her roommate didn't act scared, but the guy did, his eyes wide with fright, his face almost white.

"Clean the kitchen! Now, goddamn it! This place is like a scene out of the fucking *Metamorphosis*!"

"The fucking *meta* what? Get a grip on yourself, you insufferable bitch!" Her roommate tried to slam the door in her face, but Caroline pushed back so hard that the girl lost her balance and sprawled onto the floor. "Jesus," she said. "You're fucking dangerous."

"Oh, if only you knew how dangerous I can be. Get up and clean the kitchen."

Word had it that this particular roommate came from General Motors money, and her behavior had always reflected a sense of entitlement, the feeling that unlike Caroline and the girl from Portland, she didn't really have to be there. Nevertheless, after Caroline knocked her down, she turned docile, putting on her bathrobe and tidying up, enlisting the help of the guy she'd been in bed with, whom Caroline never saw again. She and the roommate never became friends, but the night before Caroline left Hungary for good, the two of them and the one from Oregon had a few beers, and both of the others wished her well, whether they meant it or not.

Over the next several years she taught at language schools in Prague, Brno and Bratislava, and the drill was the same as in Budapest: she worked five or six days a week, sometimes even seven, and periodically her boss handed her an envelope containing her wages, always in cash, everything off the record. Sooner or later, nearly all of them started trying to screw her out of money she'd earned, and when that happened she moved on. While each of the cities she worked in had its own distinct character and she picked up Czech and Slovak much more easily than Hungarian, the context of her personal life remained the same. She could just as easily have been in one place as another. She shared rundown flats with other native English speakers, most of them piecing together an existence from teaching while assuring themselves that their present situation was temporary, that they were really painters, poets, musicians, novelists or playwrights. She prided herself on avoiding that kind of self-deception, having long ago concluded that real writers possessed some quality she lacked. But in Bratislava she did buy a cheap laptop and began making notes about stories that might be one day be worth telling. It gave her something to do that wasn't strictly related to putting food on the table.

From time to time she brought a man home, though she avoided those sorts of entanglements with other Americans, and Brits too, restricting herself to the local fare. Most though not all of her lovers were married, and while several of them fell in love with her, the others just wanted what she did, which was little more than the equivalent of a good cold beer on a hot humid day. She quenched the thirst, then forgot about it until she felt thirsty again. Objectively, she knew this was no way to live. Unfortunately, she was getting all she deserved.

Her biological clock kept perfect time, never missed a beat. One day she woke up, looked in the mirror, and a forty-year-old woman looked back.

EVENTUALLY, SHE HEARD ABOUT AN English language institute in Warsaw run by a Canadian who was paying better than anybody else and was reportedly a decent person to work for. She emailed him her resumé, and he responded promptly, asking for a photocopy of her transcript and TESOL certificate, along with references from two previous employers. A couple of weeks later, he wrote back and offered her a job for almost double what she made in Bratislava.

Her new boss, Alastair, was probably a few years younger than her, slim, square-chinned, blue-eyed, with bronze wire-rims. What he had neglected to tell her until she got to Warsaw and went to meet him in a surprisingly well-kept building right in the center of town, just off Three Crosses Square, was that unlike the other people she'd worked for, he didn't pay under the table. She'd require a work visa, which he'd help her to get. Every three months she'd need to cross the border.

"I know it's a nuisance," he said, "but I'm in this for the long haul, and they make me do the same thing. You'll have to pay local taxes, too, but they're not high, and Poland has a tax treaty with the U.S. So whatever you pay here will offset what you pay back home." He studied her across his desk, the top of which was bare except for a phone, the contract she'd just signed and a picture of him standing beside a small boy who wore a white tee shirt with the Polish eagle on the chest in red and was holding a soccer ball. She'd been able to tell the moment she walked in that she was several years older than Alastair expected. He hadn't asked for a photocopy of her passport, and the forged college transcript she'd sent him listed her graduation date as May of 1989. "If you haven't been paying taxes back home," he said, "that's none of my business."

She rented a room from a woman in her early seventies named Klara, who'd spent more than thirty years in the Chicago suburbs, working as a receptionist in a real estate office, then returning to Poland after the death of her American husband. The flat was tiny. Her landlady slept in the living room so she could watch TV all night if she chose, but she was considerate and kept the sound turned down. A big-boned woman with a bawdy sense of humor, she once told Caroline that she could bring guests home anytime she wanted. "But I just ask one little thing."

"What's that?"

"Pick a guy that's got a grandfather in good condition, and tell him to invite *dziadek* along to entertain me. I can still put my heels in the air. You might be surprised."

Caroline didn't think she'd blushed, but evidently she had.

"Look at you," Klara said. "Red as a beet. What you think old women do with their feet? Just stand on 'em and stare at 'em? Mostly, that *is* what we do, and you'll be it doing one day too. But what's wrong with having dreams?"

Warsaw was a boom town, Klara told her. That's why she'd come back here a few years ago and sunk everything she had into this shabby flat. From their windows on the fourteenth floor they could see huge office towers under construction. "Central Warsaw, it's got some of the highest property values in the world. All these companies running in here to turn a profit. One day, if I live long enough, somebody like Mitsubishi or Apple's gonna want the land this hulk stands on, and me and my neighbors'll cash in. After the War, if you told me the city's ever gonna look like this, or be worth anything to anybody, I'd say you was crazy. Just a pile of rubble's all that was left."

Their building, which always smelled of fried meat, stood a short distance north of the main railway station and not all that far from the area that had once been the Ghetto. She took a walk there her first weekend in the city. It was now just an ordinary residential neighborhood, nearly all traces of the suffering that occurred there erased. One of the books she'd read in the Loring Public Library before they banned her was Leon Uris's novel *Mila 18*, about the extermination of the Ghetto. She found ulicja Miła—ironically, "Nice Street"—where the last of the Jewish resistance fighters were murdered. The house that once stood on that ground was gone, though a mound had been built to honor those who died in its basement.

One evening, not long after she started her new job, she and Klara were sitting on the couch, sipping sherry, when the older woman said she had something to show her. She rose, walked over to the large dresser where the TV stood, opened a drawer and pulled out what at first looked like a rag but was actually the armband she'd worn during the 1944 Warsaw Uprising. "I was fifteen years old," she said. "It identified me as a medical aid worker."

When she handed over the frayed piece of material, Caroline saw it bore brownish stains.

"That's the blood of a boy who died in my arms. Right in the middle of Marszałkowska, no more than a ten-minute walk from here. He couldn't have been over seventeen or eighteen. Had on the uniform of the AK, what we called the Home Army, but honest to God, I don't think he needed to shave, his cheeks were so smooth. He'd been hit by machine gun fire. Probably had enough lead in his poor body to make a toy soldier."

Caroline didn't want to keep holding the soiled fabric, but her fingers seemed unwilling to let go of it, almost as if they were stuck.

"Don't misunderstand me," Klara said. "By then, a body itself was no big deal. See, the streets had been full of 'em for years. You'd be going down the sidewalk and there'd be one or two left as reminders, and at first we might maybe glance at 'em, to see if it was anybody we knew, but even if it was we'd just keep right on walking. After a while we wouldn't stop to look. But this was different. Because he was alive and then he wasn't. And I didn't just see him die, I felt it too, how everything that made him who he was left him all at once."

"Do you have nightmares about it?"

"No. I don't have nightmares."

"Never?"

"No."

Caroline turned the armband over in her hands, then watched as her fingertips began stroking the bloodstains. She couldn't stop them. "Do you think it's because you did everything you could to help him?"

"That don't have anything to do with it. Back then, our entire life was a nightmare. You didn't know if you were dreaming or if what you saw was real. These days, when everything's pretty quiet, I sleep like a boulder. I'm just a big old thing that don't move."

The conversation had taken a turn Caroline didn't relish, but she intuited that she was in the presence of somebody who knew more about living, and more about dying, too, than she ever would. While her fingers continued kneading the fabric, she asked, "Are you scared of death?"

"Not a bit. And it's not because I believe I'll go to heaven and see my husband again or any of that clerical hash. It's also not because I don't have nothing to answer for. I got a *lot*. I got stuff that if I told you about it, you'd shake your head and say, 'Good Lord, what a hussy!'" She cackled. "I just wish I had me a little more. But seriously? I'm the only one I answer to. And when I'm not around to answer to?" She shrugged. "So what? The world'll go right along. This one'll be screwing that one's wife, and that one'll be breaking into this one's house and pilfering through his cabinets, and the one over there, he'll be peddling the notion that he's the medicine to cure everybody's woe, the only one that can save 'em. Things run in cycles, and one day they'll cycle on without me. And you, if you live another thirty or forty years, you'll see a great war like I did. Just imagine how much more there's gonna be to knock down." She gestured out the window at a still unfinished tower with the DaimlerChrysler logo on the side. "Last time around, the tallest thing in town was a church spire."

That night Caroline drank too much sherry and then a couple of shots of vodka, and when she finally excused herself and went to her room, she dreamed about a dead boy. He didn't die in the middle of a Warsaw street, he died behind the counter of a grocery store. But he was not Mexican, and the grocery was not in California, it was in the hot dusty Delta, and the dead boy was not even a boy, he was a grown man. And she, Caroline Cole, the bad sister, the one who'd been nobody's idea of a Christmas tree angel, the sister who talked mean and thought mean, who lied and cheated and stole, who would eventually run away and disappear from the eyes of everyone who knew her, including her mother and her sister and the man who'd had no better sense than to gift her his love, Caroline Cole who went by so many names, at so many different times, in an effort to escape from herself: she had a gun in her hand. And she saw that the body on the floor belonged to her father. "I did it," her dream-self said. "You never loved me, not for a second. Now just take a good look at how I've unloved you."

Her dad did as commanded. He sat up and with intense curiosity looked down at the gaping hole in his chest. Then he put his hand into the cavity and began to grope around, searching for what wasn't there.

IN WARSAW, HISTORY ASSAULTED HER each day, plaques all over town announcing that on such and such a date X number of people were murdered on this or that spot. The city routinely and matter-of-factly demystified death. In Polish, when you want to say somebody is dead, you simply say "*On nie żyje.*" He doesn't live. It puts a different spin on things.

Yet she found the city strangely enticing, it made her want to stroll its streets each Saturday and Sunday when she didn't have to go to work, to wander through its alleys, sometimes even step inside an apartment house she had no right to enter—if, as was occasionally the case, she happened to notice a door left ajar. The broad avenues, vast parks and restored palaces like Belweder and the Royal Castle might conjure the relative grandeur of the Interbellum period, but once you ventured beyond the Old Town into the more far-flung parts of the city, you were in the world of the *bloki:* enormous pre-fabs that went up in the '70s, concrete warrens where people were packed together like sardines. There had been a few of these blocks in the other cities where she'd lived, but until now she'd never felt compelled to go inside. She saw plenty of hallways and stairwells where the walls were crumbling, the lighting fixtures missing. The doors to residents' flats often displayed four or five different locks, one above another, to discourage burglars. People played their TVs louder than she'd ever heard anywhere else, and when they talked on the phone, they tended to holler, as if every conversation were a crisis and at any minute the connection might be lost. Oddly, the *bloki* reminded her of the house where she grew up, which, though tiny and surrounded by cotton fields that stretched to the horizon, nonetheless always felt claustrophobic, at least to her, because you could never say a word, or take a step, or sneeze, or look thoughtful without the other people who lived there knowing it.

Her weekends were solitary, a time when she took care to see no one she knew, usually not going back home until late, so that if Klara were still awake, she could say she was worn out from giving private lessons. On the weekends, she allowed herself to be alone with the strangeness that she knew was spreading inside her. People on the street seemed caught up in alien pursuits. She lost interest in the kind of coupling she'd engaged in for years. When she felt the necessity for physical release, she took care of it herself. Gradually, even that need began to recede, leaving her at peace.

•

Weekdays were a completely different matter. They began early, with a six AM class taken by students who had to be at work before eight, and that first autumn she established a routine that she maintained each fall during all the years she lived there, walking to the Institute while it was still dark, the air brisk and sometimes biting. Once she got beyond the massive Palace of Culture and Science, she turned onto Jerozolimskie, where to the music of clanging trams she passed one beautifully reconstructed Nineteenth-Century building after another, occasionally stepping over the outstretched legs of sleeping drunks. None of them ever threatened her—they didn't even wake up. At the Institute, she sometimes had a cup of tea with Alastair, who usually arrived before everyone else. His Polish wife had divorced him, leaving him for a much younger cinematographer, and his main reason for staying in the country—"Other," he said, "than the fact that I'd lose my mind if I had to return to New Brunswick"— was his desire to remain close to his son. He got Marek each weekend, which for the most part saved Caroline the trouble of fending off her boss. Almost immediately, he'd taken an interest in her. She knew it, it flattered some part of her, but she had nothing left to give.

After that first class, there was a big gap to fill before the next, which began at noon. Rather than return to Klara's and take a nap, she either went for a walk in the lovely, sprawling Łazienki Park, sometimes lingering near a pond filled with golden carp, or carried her laptop to an elegant old café on Nowy Swiat where photos of famous patrons like Ignacy Paderewski, Henryk Sienkiewicz and Józef Piłsudski decorated the walls. For only a few złoty, she bought a cup of coffee, then unzipped the new leather bag she'd splurged on after her first payday and pulled out her laptop.

The first time she did it, it was because she'd had an idea for a story about a woman like Klara, who'd lived for decades in America, then returned to the city where she'd been raised. She had recently read an interview with the great Irish writer William Trevor, in which he talked about his method. Before starting a story or novel, he made a list of all the characters who would be involved and before he ever began the narrative, he wrote page after page of facts about each of them, stopping only when he could think of no more facts to record. Big things like when and where they'd been born, whether they were Catholic, Protestant or Atheist, or just weren't sure. Whether or not they'd ever seen another person die or watched one being born. Smaller things too: what they ate for breakfast, whether they were right- or left-handed. Whether or not they'd had pets as a child. Could they draw? Did they play an instrument, could they carry a tune? Had they ever flown in an airplane?

She planned to list all the characters who'd appear in the story based on the life of Klara and then write down every fact she could think of about each of them. There would of course be the protagonist—Hanna, she'd decided to call her—plus her American husband, along with the young soldier who'd died in her arms. She'd have to have parents and so on. Caroline hoped that this would finally help her write something. So far, her notes for story ideas had never become more than notes. Somehow, she always found a reason not sit down and see if she could do it. Maybe because the likely answer filled her with dread.

She turned on the laptop. As she waited for it to boot, she suddenly recalled that the woman who taught French back at Loring Academy was named Hanna Walton. Her classroom was right across the hall from

Mrs. Batch's. She had a degree from Trinity University in San Antonio, Texas, which was unusual since nearly all of the teachers had gone to Delta State or Ole Miss or one of the other state schools. Though she was only about thirty-five, she had silvery-white hair. People seldom remarked on that. People seldom talked about her at all, or wondered what she was doing at Loring Academy, since she didn't live in Loring but nearly thirty miles away in Cleveland. She wasn't unpleasant, but she wasn't especially pleasant either, and she never seemed to laugh, though she didn't look sad.

Caroline hadn't taken French, but Mrs. Walton knew her name. She discovered that one day when she was leaving school early, having talked her way past Coach Raleigh. When she stepped into the parking lot, she saw Mrs. Walton coming toward her carrying a thermos, which she'd apparently left in her car. "Hi, Caroline," she said without pausing or, Caroline thought later, even really looking at her. Before she could answer, Mrs. Walton stepped inside.

That was more than twenty-five years ago. She'd be in her sixties now, not that much younger than Klara. Was that why Caroline had chosen the name Hanna? It couldn't be. She hadn't thought about her since she moved with her mother to Tommy Burns's house in Pine Bluff. Why would she remember her this morning?

The laptop screen lit up. She'd never know how long she stared at it. Definitely long enough for her screensaver, Leonardo's *Vitruvian Man*, to appear. She studied the eight-limbed creature: the rippling abs, the hairy scrotum, the droopy foreskin.

In the café, the voices faded. She ceased to hear silver spoons tapping the sides of porcelain teacups, the espresso machine hissing steam, the pages of *Gazeta Wyborcza* crinkling as someone read the news.

•

Anna Weston sometimes felt as if her husband David were equipped with four sets of limbs. The bed in their tiny house, in their small Mississippi Delta town where she taught French at an all-white private school, was hardly big enough for two normal-sized people, and only one of them qualified as normal-sized.

At 6'4", he stood nearly a foot taller than Anna, and when he rolled over, his long arms and legs seemed to trap her in a vise. The AC, a window unit, was in the kitchen, and even though they left the door open, the temperature in their bedroom rarely dropped below eighty until after the first of November. On many nights she lay there unable to move, feeling as if she might suffocate.

The prose gushed out as though it had been waiting to find its way onto the page for twenty years, or twenty-five, or even more: a story about a woman who didn't belong where she was, one who might have been fine elsewhere or might not have been fine anywhere at all. It revolved around racism, lust and boredom. The French teacher felt terrible about working at such a place, and while she admired her husband and felt comfortable with him, her marriage no longer offered much joy.

What surprised Caroline, even as the words tumbled out, was that the characters quit behaving the way she thought they would and should. She'd put a coach in the story, and he was supposed to be the antagonist, a man nobody liked, who ached to be alone with the French teacher even though he initially despised her for acting superior—she named him Hilton Kiley—and yet Caroline kept coming up with touches that made it impossible for her and, more importantly, the French teacher herself to hate him. For instance, as a child he'd been dogged by the rumor that his parents, ignorant sharecroppers, named him for the Hilton hotel chain. He knew it wasn't true. *"Boy," his father said when his son asked about it, "you think me and your momma's gonna call you after a place where we couldn't even afford to walk through the door?"*

She wrote and she wrote and she wrote and she wrote until there was suddenly no need to write more. After finishing the final paragraph, which concluded about halfway down the screen, she sat staring at the large white space that confronted her. That evening, when she read over what she'd written, she'd realize that she'd used too many linking verbs, that the story shifted perspectives much faster than she saw in most of the contemporary work she read and that while it seemed to promise that something romantic would develop between Hilton Kiley and Anna Weston, all that happened was the forging of an unlikely friendship, one that helped each of them get through their otherwise unsatisfying days. But it was, Jesus Christ, an actual story, and it kept surprising her.

Nothing went the way she thought it would when she wrote the first words. She'd written 6,845 of them. Twenty pages. About half a page for each year she'd been alive.

In the café, though, the only numbers that mattered were the ones she happened to notice in the upper-right corner of the screen. It was 11:33 AM, she hadn't even asked for the check, and her next class was supposed to start in twenty-seven minutes. She'd sat there for three and a half hours and could probably only make it on time if she managed to find a taxi. Before shutting down the laptop, she quickly jumped back to the first page. The story needed a title. So she added the first thing that popped into her mind.

The Academy

•

Due to reasons that eluded her, for nearly a decade she'd hung on to the business card she'd been given by the man she slept with all those years ago in Boston. Her laptop was too old and slow for the internet, but the main office at the English language institute had access, and she discovered that not only was the guy at the same agency, he was now listed among the handful of "senior agents." There was no email address for him, though, and it said he didn't accept unsolicited queries. When she perused the list of writers he represented, she could see why. He probably had all he could handle and was probably also filthy rich. Still, she had nothing to lose. So after revising "The Academy" twenty-three times, deepening the characters and taking care of all the other problems she could find, she printed a copy and wrote him a letter on the institute's stationary, reminding him that they'd had "drinks" in Boston back in 1991 and that he told her to get in touch if she ever wanted him to look at her work. She couldn't recall which name she used that night, but since she doubted he'd remember the evening itself, much less who she claimed to be, she signed it Karo Kohl, which was what she went by here. Alastair and the office staff knew her real name, but she'd altered the spelling for practical purposes. The initial "c" in Polish is pronounced like an "s," and an "e" at the end of a word is always pronounced "uh," and she didn't want to be known as "Saro Soluh." She put the letter and the story in a large envelope, carried it to the local post office and mailed it off to New York.

She thought it might derail her if he never wrote back—and when he hadn't after six months, she understood he wasn't going to—but a few times each week she continued to take her laptop to the café and write. Sometimes it went better than others. She quit on the story about a woman like Klara, realizing that no matter how much research she did, she couldn't evoke Warsaw under German occupation. She also quit on a story about two women living in a roach-infested Budapest flat. On the other hand, she wrote a long one she believed was pretty good about a working-class Chicano traveling outside the U.S. for the first time, coming to Poland to meet his female pen pal back when the country was still under communist control. They fell in love, but she couldn't leave and he couldn't stay, and the narrative concluded with the two characters saying goodbye in the Warsaw airport, certain they'd never hear each other's voice again, let alone see each other, since neither of them knew, as the reader would, that walls were about to fall and borders become porous, that technology would soon make the world contract, that what seemed impossible in that moment was not destined to remain so.

Even when she gave up on a story, she valued the time she spent writing it. The world beyond the window always disappeared, and the only truth that mattered was the one she put on the page. Things rarely ended well in those pages, but she always felt lighter when she finished, as if with each word she wrote she'd shed a fraction of the weight that had been riding her into the ground.

ONE AUTUMN MORNING, ELLA DROPPED the girls off at Roosevelt Middle School, then drove home, parked the car in the driveway and started to go back inside. But it was such a nice day—cool, crisp, a little overcast, a hint of frost—that she decided to go for a walk. She nearly always took one with Martin in late afternoon, but two in one day wouldn't hurt anything. She had the time.

A faint breeze rustled leaves turned gold, red, burnt orange. The odor of wood smoke hung in the air. She descended Rockland and walked for two blocks along the busy street that connected Cedar Park with the towns to the east and west, then turned onto another street that wound up into the Highlands. The homes there were stately Victorians as nice as their own, lots of Queen Annes, hipped or gabled roofs, plenty of towers and turrets. Quite a few Volvos out front, several Lexus sedans or SUVs, the occasional Mercedes like the one Martin had parked in their driveway on her last birthday, a ridiculously oversized pink bow affixed to the sunroof.

At one time or another, she'd been inside many of these houses: for parties or dinners, fundraisers for the Cedar Park PTA, the North Shore Animal Shelter, or the Massachusetts Democratic Party. She walked past one where, a couple of years ago, she'd been introduced to Senator Edward Kennedy. It belonged to a gay couple, both surgeons and high school classmates of Martin, nice people she didn't know all that well but could stop and chat with if she met them down on Main Street.

Ted, as their hosts called him, stood and talked to her beside the fireplace for a few minutes. When he learned where she was from, he told her a funny story about his first encounter with Mississippi's arch racist senator James Eastland. He said Eastland was head of the senate judiciary committee, that he was a freshman senator, and that the older man told him to come by his office one morning to discuss subcommittee assignments. "He's got two bottles standing on his desk and beside them two glasses," Kennedy said. "'Bourbon or Scotch?'" he asks me. I knew better than to drink bourbon with Jim Eastland, so I chose the Scotch, and he poured me a triple. He says, 'Well, you all have lots of Italians up there in Massachusetts, don't you, so I guess you'll want to be on the Immigration subcommittee.' I told him I'd really appreciate that, so he looks at me and says, 'Drink that down and it's yours.' So down went the Scotch, and he pours me another triple. 'Now you Kennedys are always interested in the Negroes, aren't you,' he says, 'so I guess you'll also want to be on the Civil Rights subcommittee. I said I would, and he says 'Drink that down and you've got it.' Then he pours me another one and offers me the Constitution subcommittee, and the deal's the same. It wouldn't be accurate to say that I walked out of his office. I was staggering drunk, and when I got to *my* office, there were three or four constituents with appointments to see me. I'm lucky I ever got re-elected."

Encounters like that one no longer seemed unusual. She and Martin had once hosted a fundraiser for the Boston Symphony. She'd sat at dinner tables with Sejii Ozawa, Yo-Yo Ma, Wynton Marsalis, Alison Krauss, Anita Hill, John Kerry. So what if she occasionally felt like an imposter, a person with no tangible accomplishments beyond being a good wife and mother. Nobody treated her like she didn't belong. She was married to the best person she'd ever known, and his home was her home. She was healthy, he was, their girls were. They had plenty, they had more than enough for many others. For a long time now, life had been absurdly easy. But on days like today when the perfection on display seemed a little unreal, she sometimes wondered what would happen if she ever ran into trouble again. Would she rise to meet the challenge? Or would she just surrender and remain in bed?

TOWARD THE END OF HAYLEY'S seventh-grade year, the middle school principal sent Ella and Martin an email one evening recommending that she skip eighth grade and enter high school. The email came right before dinner. Ella didn't like the idea—in fact, she hated it—but when she and Martin discussed it, she had difficulty explaining why. They waited until the girls were asleep to talk about it, and he suggested they use his sound-proofed music room, since it was too chilly to go outside and they didn't want to risk one of the girls getting out of bed to use the bathroom and overhearing the conversation. Later, it would occur to Ella that the location played a major role in determining the outcome. As best she could recall, she hadn't set foot in that room since the day she showed it to her mother. In retrospect, she would wish it had taken place anywhere but there. Even the pantry would have been preferable.

As if she were a guest, he gestured at the frayed love seat sandwiched between three or four microphone stands and a couple of Fender amps. He seated himself directly in front of her on his guitar stool. He was wearing khaki pants and a long-sleeved red shirt that she wasn't crazy about, and the shirt was starting to look tight. He wasn't overweight, at least not yet, but his and Pete's success had led to much busier lives, and he never went to the gym anymore. Lately, when they went for a walk, he grew winded climbing back up Rockland. For most of their time together, she hadn't thought much about their age difference, but sometimes now she did.

"Let me guess," he said. "You think the principal's idea is a bad one."

"You know me very well."

He smiled. "I believe," he said, "that I know you better than you know yourself."

For some reason, the remark nettled her. Why, she couldn't say. They'd had a perfectly nice evening, sipping pre-dinner cognacs in the living room and listening to Abby Lincoln while the girls prepared dinner, which they now did one night each week. The suggestion that they share the cooking had been theirs—they said they wanted to give their mother a break. Such fine girls, such good sisters. Everybody said so, and everybody was right.

"Well," she said, "I suspect I also know you better than you know yourself."

"I don't doubt that for a second." He studied her for a moment. "I didn't mean it as a criticism."

"I didn't think you did," she said, though she couldn't say how she thought he did mean it, or what there was in the remark that bothered her.

"I love knowing you so well, being able to anticipate what you might be thinking or feeling," he continued. "It's the people who can't do that who end up in dire straits. That hasn't happened to us, and it's never going to."

Who can say with certainty, at any given time, that they might not end up encountering some bumps down the road? she wondered. You can only say that when everything's over, the final period in place. And the final period was not in place yet. She hoped it wouldn't be for a long time.

"I think," he said, "that the more interesting question is *why* you don't like his idea. Is it because you believe Hayley's not yet capable of doing high-school-level work?"

Hayley, she suspected, could probably do college-level work right now if she needed to. "Of course it isn't."

"Or that later on she'll feel like she got robbed of a year of her childhood?"

"Not that either."

"Is it because you're afraid *you'll* be robbed of it?"

He'd said it with a facial expression that connoted sympathy, compassion, understanding. And maybe a measure of pity.

"It might be. Yes, actually, I think that's it. I'm guilty, Your Honor," she said. "Send me to MCI Shirley."

"Shirley's a men's prison," he said, then laughed. "I'd have to sentence you to Framingham."

She couldn't look out the window—he'd covered it with an acoustic panel—so she looked instead at her hands. "Make a joke of it," she said. "Merry, merry Martin."

"Jesus, Ella. You're the one who turned it into a joke. Or at least that's how it seemed to me. I was just responding in kind. I didn't mean to annoy you."

"I didn't say you annoyed me," she said, though she was annoyed and she knew that he knew it. In some sense she liked that he knew it, but in another she didn't. Things were getting confused, at least for her.

He leaned over and laid his hand on her knee. "You're upset. I wasn't trying to make light of your worries."

"Why do we have to rush her?" she asked. "If she starts high school next year, she'll barely be seventeen when she leaves for college."

"You know she has her heart set on Tufts, right? And that she'll almost certainly get accepted there?"

"Yes, but so what?"

"It's five miles away. How much leaving would that involve? When you went to college, you traveled fifteen hundred miles."

He should have known better than to invoke her college experience. For one thing, he only knew the worst part of it. But the rest of it was bad too, beginning with the exhausting bus trip that took nearly forty-eight hours, then her getting lost between South Station and the housing office at the college, so that she arrived after the doors were locked and might well have had to spend her first night in Boston on the streets but for a security guard who took mercy on her and called somebody who showed up and let her into her assigned room but treated her like a complete idiot. And this was only the start. "Yes," she said, "my time at Berklee went really well for me, didn't it?"

He sighed, then rose from the stool and sat down beside her. Rather than look at him, she let her eyes travel around the room. In addition to all the instruments and recording equipment, she noticed numerous cups and glasses, which explained why so many seemed to be missing. She'd asked both girls if by any chance they'd taken them to their rooms or dropped a few and broken them, and they said no, so until that moment it remained a mystery. He'd been spending more and more time in this room, a couple of hours every night, sometimes coming up here even before the girls went to bed and staying until after she went to bed, then inadvertently waking her when he finally lay down.

Well, the girls were too old now to be read to, and too old to be played to and sung to, like she and Martin did when they were little. She never put her voice to musical use anymore. She didn't even hum along with whatever was on the radio when she was driving. She'd never really thought about any of this until that evening.

"What do you do in here at night?" she asked. "Besides drinking whatever goes into all these cups and glasses."

That stung him. It was as if she thought he might be engaging in some shady activity, like watching porn or having phone sex. The cups usually contained tea, or occasionally decaf coffee, with a lump or two of sugar. The glasses were usually filled with an inch or two of brandy. Harmless indulgences that he was not ashamed of. The question of what he did besides drinking out of the cups and glasses, however, *was* problematic. He'd been intending to discuss it with her, but now that she'd brought it up, he found himself feeling both irked and embarrassed. Maybe even a little angry, though he'd never gotten angry at her before, or if he had he couldn't recall it. He seldom got angry at anybody except his partner, and he stayed mad at Pete most of the time, though nobody knew it: not Pete, not Ella.

He gestured at the instrument cases rowed up against the wall. "The things inside those cases have strings on them, and when you press down on the string with your left hand and pick it with your right, it makes a sound, which is called music. So what I'm doing in here is making the sound of music. Julie Andrews would approve whether you do or not."

For a moment, neither of them said a word. They were equally shocked at the tone of the conversation, and they were equally unprepared. Both of them immediately thought *I should apologize and stop this right now.* They both understood that all it would take was a single word. It might even take less than a word. She could have leaned close to him and laid her head on his shoulder, or he could have leaned close to her and pulled her head against his chest, and what they'd said and how they'd said it would cease to matter.

Instead, they chose not to address it. He didn't tell her that over the last few years he'd begun to regret not having pursued his own music, that he thought some of the artists he and Pete had made famous weren't necessarily doing work that was more original than he could have created, that he'd been writing songs and recording them up here, playing all the instruments and relying on some of the new software programs to create percussion when it was called for. He didn't tell her that while he'd conceived most of the numbers as instrumentals, he'd also written several with lyrics, and that when he got the instrumentation just right, he planned to ask her to do the vocals. He knew her voice very well, had written the tunes in particular keys with her in mind.

She didn't tell him that the number of days when she felt unaccountably fearful had been increasing, or that she dreamed more and more often about her sister and her mother and her father, as well as what happened to her in Jackson and at her instructor's apartment, or that the advent of the internet had led her to spend more and more time online trying to locate her sister. She didn't tell him that she'd called people named Caroline Cole all over the country, as well as a few in Canada and the U.K. and Ireland, even one poor woman in Bunnythorpe, New Zealand, whom she woke at 4:30 in the morning after miscalculating the time difference. She didn't tell him that she'd begun to worry more and more about his health, that she'd quit preparing his favorite dish, Moroccan lamb stew, because it was so high in saturated fat.

He said, "I think we ought to tell Hayley what the principal said and see how she feels."

She said, "All right." She got up off the couch, walked over to the far corner where she'd spotted an empty cardboard box and started collecting cups and glasses. When she'd gathered them all, she carried them downstairs.

HER SECOND YEAR IN WARSAW: Caroline had just taught the final class of summer session and was looking forward to a few free days when Alastair stopped her in the hallway and asked if she could step into his office. She thought he intended to reprimand her for something, though she could not imagine what it might be. He'd given her a substantial raise at the end of the spring session and told her she was probably the single best teacher he'd ever hired.

He closed the door, sat down behind his desk and said, "I've got a little problem."

His eyes, she noticed, were red-rimmed. He looked like a man who'd lain awake the night before. "What kind of problem?" she asked.

"Well, in one sense, a happy kind. Last night I found out that from now on my son Marek will be living with me."

"That's wonderful," she said. "I mean, you told me he was the main reason you decided to stay in Poland after . . . well, after your divorce."

"Don't misunderstand. I'm really glad. It just comes as sudden news. My ex called me last night to inform me that she and her cinematographer are relocating to California in a few days. I suspect she's known it for quite a while. She says they sat Marek down and asked him who he'd rather live with, and he said me."

"That's wonderful too. I'm sure you're a great dad."

"I'm not saying I am. But I love the kid more than anything. And I think that for Katarzyna, he's become a nuisance. Not because of anything bad he did, understand. It's just that she wants a different life, and I guess a lot of doors have opened in Hollywood for her film guy." He mentioned the name of a woman he'd started dating, a flutist in the Warsaw Philharmonic. Caroline had only met her once and was not taken with her; people around the Institute considered her a flake. "She and I were supposed to leave next weekend for two weeks on a fjord in Norway. She's not too pleased at the thought that I might have to cancel."

"I see."

"Look," he said, "I hate to ask. I'm sure you have plans for the break. But is there any chance . . ." His voice trailed off. He was clearly more comfortable being asked for favors than requesting one. She'd heard he sometimes loaned money to teachers when they faced financial distress, and word was that he didn't always get it back.

She'd been thinking of going to a pension in Zakopane for ten or twelve days, just holing up and writing and taking some hikes in the Tatras, which Klara told her were among the prettiest mountains anywhere. Not as high as the Alps, maybe, but in their own way just as striking. Fortunately, she hadn't yet booked her stay. "Would you like me to take care of him while you're gone?" she asked.

"Could you possibly? I'd pay you really well. You can pretty much name your price."

She told him that he could decide what to pay her, and they agreed that she'd move into his place on the following Saturday, by which time Marek would already have been handed over.

Those first few days she developed a bond with the youngster that was going to last a long time. She'd become quite proficient in Polish, and he'd been speaking both languages all his life, so they had no trouble communicating. He read a lot, and both of them typically spent their mornings doing that, and then they usually went for a walk in Łazienki Park, followed by a restaurant dinner in early afternoon, as he was used to the traditional Polish meal schedule. She'd warned Alastair that she couldn't cook worth a damn, and he told her to feed the kid and herself someplace nice every day and keep the receipts. Sometimes, after they ate dinner, she took him to a movie, and at other times they went to the Old Town and strolled around among the tourists, many of whom were

American. Occasionally, when she heard English being spoken in an American accent, she caught herself glancing over her shoulder to make certain the last person she wanted to see in the whole world was not among them. She felt a little ridiculous doing that, but the fear had never quite been banished, and she doubted it ever would be.

She and Marek engaged in some memorable conversations on those afternoons together. One day, at a sidewalk café near the Royal Castle, he asked her why she wasn't married.

"Well," she said, "I loved somebody a long time ago, but it didn't work out."

"Did he cheat on you?"

She laughed. "How old are you?"

"I'm almost eight."

"In other words, you're seven."

"Yes, but my teachers told my parents I'm *nad wiek rozwinięty*. Do you know what this means?"

"Precocious."

"Yes. So did he cheat on you?"

"No."

"Did you cheat on him?"

"Nobody cheated on anybody," she said. "It just didn't work out. Sometimes things don't."

He took a sip of his *lemoniada*. "Why not marry my father?" he asked.

"Your father's a great guy. But he's my boss, and business and pleasure are best kept apart."

"Who was the person you once loved?"

"Another great guy."

"In the U.S.?"

"Yes. In California."

"Is that where you're from?"

"Sort of."

"That's where my mother has gone."

"I heard."

"Is it nice there?"

"Some parts are, some aren't. Like Poland. Like most places."

"Have you been to a lot of places?"

"A few. What about you?"

"I've been to Krakow and Wrocław and Gdansk. And to Sofia, though I was little and don't remember it."

"Those are nice cities."

"You've been there too?"

She nodded. "All of them but Sofia."

"Would you like to have a child yourself one day?" he asked.

That led to some lip-chewing. Julio would have been a great dad. And while she might be deluding herself, she believed she would have made a decent mom. "I might like to have a child," she finally said. "But only on one condition."

"What condition?"

"I'd want one very much like you." She finished her coffee and glanced at her watch. "I think," she said, "that it's time to head home."

•

Half-an-hour later, they were walking south on Marszałkowska when they saw a large crowd congregating outside the MPIK Super Store, people staring raptly at a big LCD screen on the other side of the display window. "*O Boże!*" they heard an older woman say, both hands clamped to her forehead.

In an American accent: "Jesus Christ. Oh, Jesus, no!"

Marek grabbed her hand. "Pani Karo, what is happening?"

On the screen she saw the Manhattan skyline, the Empire State Building standing tall in the foreground, behind it black smoke belching from one of the World Trade Center towers. While they stood there, an airplane, gray and fleeting, entered from the right, then disappeared inside the other tower. An instant later, a fireball erupted.

An older man was standing beside her. He wore a gray suit and a maroon tie and did not look overly exercised. In Polish she asked him what was happening.

With clinical detachment he shrugged and said, "*Wojna w Ameryce.*" War in America.

Marek wrapped his arms around her. "Pani Karo," he said, "I'm scared. My mother is in America."

She hugged him tightly and began to stroke his hair. "I know," she said. "But it's a really big country, honey. You have no idea. You can't even imagine unless you've been there. It's just really, really big. I've seen almost all of it, and your mother's far, far away from those towers. It's almost as far from there to where she is as it is from there to here. Don't worry, honey. It's a whole other world."

A LOT OF THINGS CHANGED in Poland that fall, even though it was far from where the action seemed to be. She started seeing more soldiers on the streets, as well as in the main train station, all of them armed with carbines or assault rifles. There were many fewer tourists, owing to the paranoia sweeping the U.S. and Europe. In October, when the ground war began in Afghanistan, Poland sent troops, and two or three times, in the vicinity of Warsaw Centralna, policemen asked to see her documents. She supposed she looked suspicious.

Autumn was unusually cold, as a series of Baltic storms raked the country, bringing with them snow and ice. One day in early December, she had trouble getting to work. Klara had coughed all night, and though she tried to be quiet, Caroline heard her through the wall and at one point got up and knocked on the living room door to see if she needed help. Klara said she was fine but not to enter the room, because she didn't want to pass on whatever it was. So she barely slept and made the mistake of trying to walk to work rather than waiting for a tram, thinking a brisk stroll in sub-zero temperatures would surely wake her up. It did, but not far from Three Crosses Square she stepped on a patch of black ice, and the next thing she knew she was flat on her back. At first, she thought she might have broken her hip, but she managed to get to her feet and limp the rest of the way to the institute. In the bathroom, she could see the skin was already turning purple. By evening, she'd have a hell of a bruise.

After teaching her first class, she lay down on the small couch in

Alastair's private office. He brought her a cup of tea laced with vodka, then turned the light out and left so she could sleep. He really would have made a wonderful husband for someone, but the someone wouldn't be her, and she doubted it would be the flutist. Though she was supposed to be in a committed relationship with Alastair, Caroline had seen her having a drink with another guy in the bar at the Holiday Inn. Locals seldom went there, and the only reason she happened to spot them was that she used the lobby as a shortcut to Klara's. She almost said something to him about it but decided it was none of her business and might send the wrong signal.

She woke before noon, ate her sandwich and limped down the hall to teach her next couple of classes. About halfway through the second of those, in which they were working on intonation, she wrote a question on the chalkboard in English. "Where do you live?" It was important, she told her students, most of whom were in their twenties or thirties, to remember that whereas in Polish the voice falls at the end of a question, in English it usually rises. "So in Polish, you say '*GDZIE mieszkasz?*' But in English you say 'Where do you *LIVE?*'"

Someone knocked on the door, then opened it. It was the school secretary. "I'm sorry to interrupt," she said, "but can you give everyone a short break? I need you to come down to the office." In the hallway, the secretary told her that she'd received a call from the U.S. and the woman on the other end said it was extremely important.

Her chest tightened as she wondered who it could possibly be. The only person she could think of was Ella. Had she somehow gone to the trouble to locate her here, a third of the way around the world?

No, she had not. When she said hello, a female voice said, "Hold for Mr. Entzminger."

It was the literary agent, Jared Entzminger. "Long time," he said, "no see. No hear from either. Speaking of which, what time is it there? About half past four?"

"Yes," she said.

"Probably getting dark, I suspect?"

"Oh, it got dark nearly an hour ago."

"Cold as the bejesus, too, isn't it?"

"Below zero Fahrenheit. Or at least it was the last time I was outside. But that was several hours ago. So right now, I don't know. But let's just say it's not warm."

"How long have you been in Poland?"

"About a year and a half. But I've been in Eastern Europe since . . . well, for a good while. I worked in several other countries first."

"I think you were heading in that direction when we met, weren't you."

"Yes. I left the next day. Or the next night, anyway."

"Well, listen, about that," he said, then paused. "Back then, I was single. I honestly can't remember if we discussed each other's marital status or not. I guess that doesn't speak well of us, does it?"

It didn't, and they hadn't, because it was clear from the first sip that it didn't matter to either of them. They'd do what they'd do. "No," she said, "I don't think we did. I take it you're married now?"

"For eight years. We've got a six year-old-son. He keeps us busy. What about you?"

"I stay busy too."

"I meant are you married."

"Not at the moment."

Gamely, he forged ahead. "My wife's actually a writer herself. YA. I'm not her agent, through. She's repped by one of our rivals."

"That must be interesting."

"I'll say."

She heard a creaking sound, as if he were shifting around in a desk chair. She imagined him rising, walking over to a window, glancing down forty stories at cars and people moving along Fifth Avenue Avenue or Park Avenue or whatever fancy avenue his agency was located on. She couldn't remember.

"So, listen, Karo," he said. "This is kind of an awkward phone call for me to be making. For one thing, I know you sent us your work more than a year ago. It lay around a long time before I saw it, and then I was away for a while due to a family matter, and then Nine-Eleven hit us like a hurricane, and we're just now approaching some semblance of normalcy. And then, well, due to our encounter in Boston, I feel a little sheepish.

And I'll admit that for that reason, I almost didn't make this phone call. I came in to work today thinking I wouldn't."

As if it had finally dawned on the secretary that privacy was called for, she discretely stepped out of the office and closed the door. Her departure allowed Caroline to go ahead and let loose. How dare he condescend like that, just so he could continue to feel like a nice guy for placing a phone call to some loser he'd banged years ago in a hotel room. "So why *did* you make the phone call?" she asked. "I haven't fucked anybody in a long time and don't plan to. I'm old now. You probably wouldn't even recognize me."

"Wow," he said. "Wow. Whew."

For her, Trans-Atlantic phone silence was something new. While she waited to see if he'd disconnect, she sat down in the secretary's chair. Jesus, her hip hurt.

"This story you sent me," he said, "I'm not going to be able to sell it to a commercial magazine. To begin with, it's a little rushed, especially the ending. And furthermore, the whole segregation academy thing's going to make it seem dated to a lot of people, though I checked and I guess some of those schools still exist."

"Sorry I wasted your time."

"You didn't waste my time, Karo. Please don't make this so hard. I like your writing. A lot. You've got an unusual voice and a way of turning your characters and their situations inside out. And all the stuff you do with shifting perspective? I wouldn't expect to like that, but I do. It's radical in a good way, as if the only conventions that matter to you are the ones you make up. I still remember what you told me about the novel you were working on years ago. Just the way you described it sitting there in the bar. People I meet are always telling me bullshit about novels they're writing or going to write, but I forget it the moment I'm out of their company. Even when they talk about it, you can tell it'll never be worth a damn, if in fact they really are writing it or planning to. Were you?"

On the far side of the square, beyond St. Alexander's Church, was one of the new luxury hotels. They were springing up all over central Warsaw now, and that one had a nice bar in the lobby, a clean minimalist layout, nothing gilded or tacky in there. It might have been nice to sit beside him at a corner table and conduct this conversation over a drink or two. She dreaded returning to Klara's in the cold and listening to her cough again all night. "No," she said, "I wasn't actually writing it. But I think I can. And I've written ten or eleven more stories if you'd be willing to look at them."

"Send me all of them. What I'd like to do with this one is have my assistant start submitting it to literary magazines. But what I'd really love is for you to get to work on that novel."

"Jared," she said, wishing she didn't sound so tentative, "you wouldn't bullshit me, would you?"

"Not about this. I'm in a pretty cold-blooded business, and I've become cold-blooded myself. I sell books all the time that I don't necessarily think are that great. I sell them because they'll sell. But I need to represent work that feels fresh and different too. The story you sent me does. If the next stuff doesn't, it won't hurt me in the slightest to tell you. I do it all the time."

He gave her his email address, asked for hers, then told her that as soon as he got off the phone, he'd send her a DHL number and that she could mail the rest of her stories to him on the agency's dollar. He said he'd be in touch when he had news to report, though he didn't intend to send her each and every rejection—of which, he warned, there would probably be quite a few. In the meantime, he reiterated, he hoped she'd get to work on the novel. When she had a hundred or so pages, he'd like to read them.

After they said goodbye, she went back and finished her class, then left work. She intended to walk to the closest tram stop and go home, but if anything the cold was even more brutal than it had been that morning, and the bar across the square looked warm and inviting. So she limped over there, sat down alone at a corner table and drank a silent toast to what might never be but at least seemed closer than before.

She sent him the rest of her stories but didn't hear from him or anybody else at the agency again until mid-April, when she checked her email at work one morning and found a message from his assistant informing her that while "The Academy" was still looking for a home, her story "Julio and Janina" had been accepted by *Harper's*.

License to Lie

AS MARTIN HAD PREDICTED, Hayley got accepted by the college of her choice, along with all the others she applied to except Williams, which she hadn't been that impressed by anyhow. It was all the way out in Western Mass, and when they visited she met too many pretentious people. Nevertheless, the day she walked into the kitchen and found the thin, business-sized envelope lying on the work island, she was unable to disguise her disbelief. She'd already received nine BFEs— Big Fat Envelopes, in the parlance of the highly motivated—and had already committed to Tufts. She didn't even bother to open the one from Williams, just turned and headed for her room, taking two stairs at a time. Lexa started after her, but Ella said to leave her alone. Her first brush with failure seemed unlikely to be her last, but in a day or two she'd recovered her equilibrium. As Martin observed, "You can be seventeen years old or seventeen years young." Maybe, unlike her mother, she would prove to be the latter. Ella could only hope so.

When they pulled up outside her freshman dorm the Saturday before Labor Day, a bubbly move-in assistant materialized with a large canvas ready-to-roll cart. She helped Ella and Hayley load it with clothes, laptop, books and Bose, and while Martin parked the car, they checked in, picked up keys and took an elevator to the third floor. The door to the room was open, so the assistant left them alone with Hayley's new roommate, whom she'd been in contact with for several weeks. Her name was Candace, she came from Council Bluffs, Iowa, and planned to study Cognitive and Brain Sciences. She and Hayley hugged each other, and then Candace hugged Ella too. She said she felt like she already knew the Summers family—apparently, Hayley had written lengthy bios and sent numerous photos—and that she was glad her roommate was local, because even though she'd only been away for eighteen hours, she really, really missed her mom. She looked like she might cry, so Ella told her that as soon as they got a break from orientation, she should come to their place for dinner. She remembered all too vividly her first days at Berklee, as well as many of those that followed.

Martin soon appeared and welcomed Candace to Massachusetts. While Ella helped with the unpacking, he adjusted the height of Hayley's bed, helped her attach a couple of posters to the wall and hooked up the Bose. "Don't let her inflict too much Britney Spears on you," he told Candace.

"Oh, Dad," Hayley said. "Britney's last-century."

When there was nothing left to do, they told both girls goodbye, gave Hayley a hug and walked out. Neither of them said a word on the way to the car, nor did they speak while driving back up 93. She was afraid that if she said anything, she would cry, and she didn't want to. Life, she assured herself, would not necessarily be worse now, just different. Still, if she'd been given the choice, she would have chosen to go back in time and live the last seventeen years all over again. Not because she would do anything differently, but because they were the best times she'd ever known. With a family of her own, she had a chance to do things right, and she believed they had done them pretty well.

It would have surprised her to know that he harbored similar feelings: after all, he had his work. People's careers depended on whether he said yes or no to a project and whether, having said yes, he pulled every string he could on their behalf. His was not a purely private life. True, she knew in a general sort of way that the music business was changing. But she didn't know how radical the change was, how Napster and the demise of independent record stores and the bankruptcy some months ago of once-mighty Tower Records were rapidly demonetizing the industry where he and Pete built their reputations. She didn't know that Martin's merriness was now powered by Zoloft, or that he was taking Lisinopril for high blood pressure, or that the blue pills he took so they could make love weren't working very well anymore, or that sometimes, in an urge for some kind of gratification, he dropped by Stop & Shop on the way home from work and bought a can of Beer Nuts and sat there and devoured them in the parking lot. He hadn't told her any of these things because he didn't want to worry her. Despite his determination never to turn into his father, it seemed to be happening, and he felt all but powerless to stop the transformation. He looked more and more like his dad had looked in his mid-fifties, and he was aware that it took greater and greater effort to maintain a sunny disposition around his wife and daughters. If you'd told him he could turn the clock back seventeen years, he would have seized the opportunity. Let's do it all over again, he would have said. Let's do it as many times as we can.

That evening, Lexa was with a friend and her family at Lake Winnipesaukee, so they had the house to themselves. He'd grilled enormous steaks the night before, and a good pound or so was left; since neither of them was especially hungry, they agreed they'd use it to make a salad. Around five, he went down to the basement and came back carrying a dusty bottle, which he brushed off before handing it to her.

She picked her reading classes up off the coffee table, put them on and held the bottle out at arm's length so she could read the label. "Chateau Margaux. It's a 1986, her birth year! Where did you get this?"

He turned and stepped into the dining room; she heard him open a drawer and pull out the corkscrew. He came back a moment later carrying the corkscrew and a couple of glasses. "A better question is when I got it," he said, standing the glasses on the table. "The answer is a couple of days after she was born, at Beacon Hill Wines. Believe me, I wouldn't be buying it now."

"Expensive?"

He took it from her, wrapped his hand around the foil and twisted it off, then stood the bottle on the table, worked the corkscrew in and removed the cork. "For what it'd cost today, I could probably buy a nice birth-year D-28." He lifted the bottle and sniffed. "Jesus, God, this smells good."

"Maybe we should've waited until we could drink it with her?"

"Nope. This is just for us. For her we're buying a Tufts education at thirty grand a year." He poured wine into their glasses, then sat down beside her. "To Hayley," he said. "And, damn it, to us too."

They clicked glasses, and each took a swallow.

"My Lord," he said, "that's so freaking good."

It was, though she couldn't really taste a huge difference between it and what they normally drank for ten or twelve dollars a bottle. For the first time in many years, she thought of Irwin Majori, the boy who'd given her that first taste of wine on the turnrow in the fall of 1974, then plastered his lips to hers.

She must've smiled, because he said, "I love seeing the pleasure on your face. I was scared that tonight I'd see nothing but tears."

"Well, I was afraid I might see some tears on yours too."

"You didn't need to fear that."

"No?"

"Nope. I cut loose in the garage first thing this morning and then I had another little fit in the bathroom as soon as we got back. Where'd you do your crying?"

"Right here."

"When?"

"When you were in the bathroom doing yours."

"Really?"

She reached over and ran her hand through his hair, which was growing thinner and thinner. The other night, as he got ready for bed, the light hit the top of his head just right, and she realized a bald spot was developing. He'd turn fifty-four in November. She couldn't imagine her life without him. Except for that one unpleasant encounter in his music room, which remained in the back of her mind and, she suspected, in his too, their marriage had been all she could ask for. If something was missing, she couldn't identify it, or had at least chosen not to. "No," she said. "I lied. I didn't actually cry. But all day I felt like it."

He chuckled. "I bet that's the first time you ever lied to me, isn't it?"

There are lies, she thought, and there are lies. Certainly, there were things she hadn't told him. For instance, she'd never told him what happened in Jackson at the Sun 'n' Sand. Though it wasn't quite ancient history when she met him, by now it had been ancient history for a long time, and she'd seen no reason to bring it up, even though she thought about it almost daily for reasons she did and did not understand. She also hadn't told him that a couple of years ago, at one of the big Thanksgiving parties Pete and his wife threw, she'd emerged from the bathroom late in the evening to find Pete standing there holding probably the sixth or seventh glass of whiskey he'd poured himself over the last few hours and that when he leaned toward her and placed his hand on her shoulder and she saw the look in his eyes, she said a single word—"Don't—and he didn't. She also hadn't told him that Pete called her the following Monday, shortly after Martin left for work, and asked her if she'd mentioned the incident and she said no and that she never would if it never happened again, which it never did. "I can't think of any other time I lied to you," she said. "I guess you're right."

"I lied to you once," he replied.

At first, she thought he was joking, so she started to float a joke of her own. Then she noticed that his left knee was moving rhythmically like it would if he were getting ready to attempt a daunting guitar solo, one that he wasn't quite certain he could pull off. One that demanded real virtuosity.

"Remember," he said, "when I flew down to Memphis searching for that old acoustic bluesman in the spring of '99?"

"Vaguely. Why?"

"You remember I told you it took three days before I learned for sure that he was dead?"

"Sort of. Yes, I guess so."

"That was a lie. I found him right after I got there. In the cemetery next to a black church."

Now, after all this time, he was going to tell her he'd done something tawdry, that the one person she'd always trusted had done the kind of thing her dad wanted to do, and might actually have succeeded in doing, with Grace Pace. She'd never been more surprised in her life. She guessed she was about to learn he'd banged some barmaid at the Peabody Hotel. Maybe that was why they never made love anymore. Maybe he'd learned to satisfy that sort of need elsewhere.

Instead, he confessed that with two-and-a-half days to kill before his return flight, he decided to drive down into the Delta and visit her hometown. "You may or may not recall this," he said, "but before we went to Arkansas for your mom's funeral I suggested that afterward we drive across the river so the girls and I could see where you grew up. And you said no."

"Because I didn't want to go there," she said. She felt a sudden urge, which she knew must be resisted, to drink all the wine in her glass.

"But *I* wanted to go," he said. "I wanted to go really badly. And when I found out the bluesman was dead, I thought What the hell."

He proceeded to tell her how he checked into a motel on Highway 82, then drove over to Loring Academy, parked in the teachers' lot and walked right in. In the hallway where they displayed photos of all the graduating classes, he found hers. She was standing in the front row, in her cap and gown, looking just as much like Hayley as he expected, though it still gave him a jolt. How he went over to the cemetery and found her father's grave. How he visited the library where her sister got caught stealing the book. He scrounged through bound copies of the town paper, located the article announcing her win in the state-wide vocal competition. He found the articles, too, about how her father and Grace died in the explosion, how Grady Pace brought a lawsuit against Barkley Petroleum.

Then he strolled over to the courthouse, went through county records and located the address of the house where she'd grown up. "Route 2, Box 79," he said. "A pickup stood parked in the yard alongside an old car with flat tires. I knocked on the door but nobody answered. Either they weren't home or they just didn't feel like being bothered."

He stayed in town for forty-eight hours. He liked walking the streets where she'd been young, trying to imagine what things looked like back then, trying to imagine her walking those streets herself. He found the former dollar store. It was empty, like so many other buildings on Main Street, quite a few of them boarded up. He walked beside the green bayou and saw what he thought was a nutria.

"I could see how it might once have been a pretty town, though objectively it wasn't anymore. But to me, it still was. If it weren't for that town, I wouldn't have you. Or Hayley. Or Lexa."

In his love for her, he'd found the will to deceive. There was no distance he might not travel for her, nor was there anything he couldn't conceal. Her knowledge of his deceit was something new. And with it came a certain thrill.

As if he understood the moment's import, he picked his glass up and drained it.

"How much of a birth-year D-28 did you just drink?" she asked.

"Oh, probably the peghead and half of the neck and fretboard."

"Well, here goes the rest of the neck and fretboard," she said and tossed it back.

It had been a long time since she gave him more than a peck on the cheek, but she planted a serious kiss on him then, followed by another and another, a whole garden of kisses: sunflowers and peonies, tulips and roses. He pulled her close, squeezed her so hard her shoulder bones cracked, then pushed her back onto the couch, her head against the throw pillow as he struggled with his buckle.

•

Later, they poured the remainder of the Chateau Margaux into their glasses and finished it off. He pulled his pants on, then went to the dining room and returned with an ordinary bottle of wine that tasted just as good as the expensive one, and they drank it too, dinner long since forgotten. They talked about some of the trips they'd taken together with the girls, they told funny stories about Tess and money, about Tess and gin, about Liz and married men. They opened a bottle of Champagne Cognac.

Around ten, he disappeared for a few moments, then came back and popped a CD into the stereo. At first, she wasn't really listening, but then she was. He'd done things like this before, bringing in a new recording by an unknown artist that might or might not ever see the light of day and asking her what she thought. This one was hard-core Americana, plenty of lonesome sounding slide guitar, a touch of dissonance here and there, lots of sevenths, ninths and thirteenths. The third or fourth tune really grabbed her attention: in three-quarter time, it was hauntingly spare, nothing but an acoustic guitar, a Dobro and a bass and the occasional sound of a croaking frog or chirping cricket.

"I like this a lot," she said. "Who is it? You're not about to tell me you guys signed Bill Frisell, are you?"

He laughed and shook his head. "Not quite," he said. "It's actually a guy nobody's ever heard of or ever will, just a regular kind of joe, and it's strictly a homemade recording. He wrote all the tunes and played all the instruments, produced and engineered it himself. I happen to know that this tune we're listening to was conceived and written in a Quality Inn, in Loring, Mississippi, around one in the morning, in late April of 1999. The title of it's 'Waltz for a Girl from Your Town.'"

How could either of them have known that that particular Saturday night, perhaps the finest they'd spent alone together, was as good as things between the two of them would ever get, that they were already on their way down?

THE MUSIC BUSINESS KEPT GETTING worse. That was one thing, and not a small thing, but it didn't threaten their family's security. Martin had never closed his accounting firm, had instead long ago turned over the day-to-day operations to a younger CPA with a law degree, and she'd actually expanded, providing tax services to countless individuals and small businesses up and down the North Shore. Financially, Martin and Ella would not suffer.

But personally, Martin was struggling. While Yankee Southern's backlist remained a root music treasure trove, they released fewer and fewer new titles, and he felt less and less engaged. They lost a few of their longtime artists after their agents had a final falling out with Pete—never with Martin—and it seemed he and Pete had at least one contretemps per week. They'd been disagreeing with each other since playing together in an electric blues band their freshman year at Berklee, and it was nearly always Martin who made the overture that allowed them to patch things up. Now he was starting to think that he was too old to waste his time trying to reason with a wall, no matter how much affection he might still feel for the wall. A couple of times, he developed a violent headache following a dispute. It would have helped if he'd had someone to talk to about it, but he kept the dissatisfaction to himself.

Tess, a constant in his life for as long as he could remember, was in a nursing home in Stoughton. The last time he and Ella visited, she didn't recognize either of them. Another constant, his sister, was now thousands of miles away: when Irma retired from the University of Rhode Island, she and Maeve pooled their resources and moved to Puerto Vallarta. With luck, he might see her every couple of years. The other thing he'd always been able to count on, at least since 1955, when his parents gave him a ukulele for Christmas, was playing music. Even that had fallen into neglect. For most of his life, he'd played for at least an hour or two each day, but recently he sometimes went two or three days in a row without touching an instrument. His playing, he knew, would still have sounded good to all but the most discerning ears, two of which were attached to his own head.

From Ella, for no reason he could assign a name to, he sensed a turning-away. She wasn't having an affair—about this he felt certain. It wasn't the kind of thing she would do any more than he would have. There wasn't that much outward change. At dinner parties, she was still her old charming self. She still liked listening to good music, enjoyed reading good books about composers and performers, was attentive to Lexa her last couple of high school years without seeming to hover. She stayed in touch with Liz, and he'd still sometimes come home to find them sitting on the balcony enjoying a glass of wine, laughing and talking, he supposed, about Liz's latest flame.

He'd noticed, in the incremental manner in which couples everywhere notice things they would have preferred not to register, that they were going through a good bit more wine and liquor. He drank more than he used to, but his intake had remained steady for many years, so he knew he was not the one depleting their stock. He didn't think Lexa was doing it either. She drank with her friends just like he had at her age, and there were times when she'd ask him or Ella if she could have a beer or a glass of wine, and they always said yes. So that left only Ella. He never came home and found her drunk or thick-tongued, which was in some ways more disturbing than if he had.

Too much time went by before he began to have further inklings. That he came to them due to technological mishap said more about the state of their marriage than he wished to admit, though admit it he eventually would, if only to himself. One day, after an honest-to-God shouting match with Pete—his partner wanted to sign a singer songwriter whose talents, in Martin's estimation, were mediocre at best, which led him to suspect Pete either wanted to sleep with her or already had—he left work in the middle of the day, went home and saw that Ella's car was gone. He made himself a big cup of coffee, then sat down at the desk in his study and turned on his laptop to write Pete an email and tell him just how insufferable he'd become. Evidently, though he was not aware of it, his hand was shaking, and when he grabbed the cup to take another big swig and fortify himself, it slipped from his hand. Twelve ounces of Major Dickason's cascaded onto his PowerBook.

"Son of a bitch!" he cried. He grabbed the laptop, wiped the keyboard off, then carried it to the kitchen, stood it in a big roasting pan and covered the keyboard in rice. Then he stormed into the nearby alcove where Ella kept her laptop and paid their monthly bills. To his surprise, she'd set a password. He hadn't set a password on his home computer. Why had she? Later, he would try to analyze his actions, to determine if what he did next was the result of his determination to send his partner an email right then or if it was instead evidence of suspicions that he was not aware he'd entertained. He typed in 1Rockland. That didn't work. Neither did Ella1958, Hayley1986, Lexa1988 or Martin 1949. Bootsnflannel1983—no dice. He was about to give up when sheer desperation made him try one more time. Two highways intersected in her hometown. So he typed 49Loring82. Blue wallpaper appeared, the toolbar at the bottom.

He opened Safari to go to his webmail. But he couldn't quite prevent himself from clicking the "History" tab. What he found was that twice in the last week she'd launched searches for "Caroline Cole." The previous Sunday alone, she'd clicked on eighteen different results. He closed the browser, located her Documents folder, found a file labeled CC and opened it. She'd compiled an extensive list of people with her sister's name, nearly seven hundred in total, along with information about each. Sometimes the info included birthdates, sometimes addresses and/or phone numbers. Several were marked D. Quite a few were marked CNF. Many more were marked NH, but neither the addresses nor phone numbers indicated they lived in New Hampshire. He finally figured out the abbreviations. D: Deceased. CNF: Could Not Find. NH: Not Her. He was still staring at the screen when he heard a car pull into the driveway.

He clicked "Shut Down," jumped up and hurried back to the kitchen and was standing there making himself another cup of coffee when she walked in carrying a Stop & Shop sack. "I didn't expect to find you here so early," she said. "Everything okay?"

"Sure. More or less."

She stood the sack on the work island, then pulled off the black leather jacket he'd always loved to see her wear because it seemed to accentuate her blondness. She draped it over the back of a stool, then noticed the roasting pan on the counter near the sink. "Why's the laptop in it?" she asked, stepping over to take a closer look. "And my God, why's it full of rice?"

"I accidently spilled coffee all over the keyboard."

"Accidentally? Well, I wouldn't have thought you did it on purpose. Do you think you can save it?"

"I hope so." He waited for her to say he could use hers if he needed to. But she didn't. What she did instead was glance over her shoulder at the alcove, where he noticed what she could not have failed to notice herself: he'd neglected to reposition her chair, which now stood at an angle a couple of feet from her desk. He thought sure she'd ask if he'd used it, or tried to, but she didn't.

Instead, she walked back over to the work island and began to pull items from her shopping bag. "Since you're here," she said, "any chance you could pick Lexa up from school? I would've gone straight there, but I bought some Ben and Jerry's and wanted to get it in the fridge. We're having a boneless leg of lamb stuffed with spinach and goat cheese, and a little extra prep time would help. I was planning to use that pan, but I think it'll fit into the smaller one."

"Sure. No problem. I'm glad we're having that particular dish. It's been a while."

"The lamb looked too good to pass up. So did the Ben and Jerry's." She glanced at the wall clock. "You might want to get going. She hates having to wait."

He never told her what he'd done, and she never asked if he'd done it. But one evening a couple of weeks later, when he came home past midnight after attending a performance by one of their artists at Club Passim, he again switched on her computer and typed in *49Loring82*.

She'd changed her password, which meant he couldn't even turn off the machine without doing a force quit, which of course she would be informed of the next time she turned it on. So he didn't bother. He quietly pushed the chair back under her desk and went to bed. She never said a word about what had happened, and neither did he. As had become their hardened habit, they kept their concerns to themselves.

LEXA WENT TO COLLEGE ALL the way across the country at UC Santa Cruz. Her grades were good but not stellar, and she probably would have gotten rejected by the same schools where her sister was accepted. That might have accounted for her decision to apply only to large state universities in the western US. She had her choice of several, and they took her to visit three of them on spring break. They started with the University of Washington, but it rained nonstop when they were in Seattle, and she decided against the school before they left town. She liked the University of Oregon and Eugene a good bit better. But when they got to Santa Cruz and she saw Boardwalk Beach and smelled all the pot in the air around campus and downtown, Ella realized the deal was sealed. She wasn't wild about the idea—actually, she hated it—but she resigned herself to it. It was Lexa's life. She hoped the decision would be the right one.

In late August they took her to Logan and put her on a plane to San Jose, where they'd arranged to have a limo pick her up. On the drive back, they were again silent just as they'd been after leaving Hayley in Somerville. But otherwise the day bore no resemblance to that earlier one. When they got home, Ella told Martin she was going back to bed and asked him not to wake her—she'd gotten up at three AM to make breakfast—but instead of going to their bedroom, she went to one of their two guest rooms, where she'd left a bottle of wine the night before. She removed the cork and poured herself a glass, thinking she'd have just one and then try to sleep. The problem was that she didn't really feel all that tired. If anything she felt a little bit wired. She'd drunk four cups of black coffee before they left home, whereas she normally had only one or at most two. The first glass of wine didn't accomplish much of anything except to make her feel worse than she had before she drank it. The second began to anesthetize her a bit, and with the anesthesia came a degree of clarity. Her days, once so full, were going to be long and empty if she didn't find some way to fill them. No more getting up early to feed the girls, no more driving them to and from school, no more PTA meetings, no more long phone chats with Tess, no more, no more, no more. Something was happening to Martin, too, something that sometimes left him silent and brooding. She didn't know the source of it. Of course, how could she, since she hadn't asked? And why didn't she ask? Lack of interest? Or had something happened to both of them to preclude that kind of interest?

Finding the answers, if they were to be found, seemed to depend on her having another glass of wine and then one more after that, but when the bottle was finally empty, she still had not found the answers. All she'd done was forget the questions.

•

A few days later, on her forty-seventh birthday, Hurricane Katrina roared ashore. When she got downstairs that morning, Martin was already gone. On the counter he'd left her a note, reminding her they had a seven PM reservation in Boston at *Un Coq Rouge*, so she'd need to be ready to leave no later than six. *And by the way*, he wrote, *your home state's taking quite a beating and so is New Orleans. You might want to turn on the TV*. He'd left coffee for her in the stainless-steel carafe; she poured herself a cup, grabbed a carton of yoghurt and walked into the family room.

Along with the rest of the country and much of the world, she watched as levees and flood walls were breached and water began to inundate New Orleans, sweeping people away in the Lower Ninth Ward, leaving others stranded on rooftops. That afternoon she watched the hurricane blow a hole in the roof of the Super Dome, saw water cascading into the darkened structure, scores of tired, terrified people, nearly all of them black, huddling together, hoping to stay dry, then just hoping not to die. Commentators were comparing Katrina to Hurricane Camille, suggesting it might exceed even the fury of that epic storm.

She was a week shy of her twelfth birthday when Camille smashed into the Mississippi Gulf Coast. A Sunday night in late August. They lived 250 miles from Gulfport, where the storm was predicted to make landfall around midnight. The wind had picked up by the time they ate supper, but their father said he wasn't concerned, hurricanes never did much damage this far inland, except for one he remembered from when he was a boy. He said, "That sucker chugged on up the Mississippi, and because we were on the dirty side, it leveled a slew of trees, knocked down some power lines, blew off some roofs." He tossed around a few technical terms—"right front quadrant," "additive effect," "atmospheric flow"—but told them not to worry, they'd fare just fine. That kind of thing only happened every hundred years or two.

By the time their mother turned out the overhead in hers and Caroline's bedroom, the wind had grown much louder, both of the big pecan trees in their front yard swaying and sighing, the branches of the cypress tree out back brushing the roof. Nevertheless, in a few seconds she was fast asleep.

Sometime later she felt a hand shaking her shoulder. "Ella? Ella? Please let me in. I'm scared."

Through the dark, she saw the pale face of her sister, poised at the top of the ladder. Something was wrong, it had to be, the little lamp that stayed lit all night had gone out, and the wind did not sound like any she'd ever heard before. This wind had voice and presence. The panes rattled, the floorboards creaked.

She scrunched up against the wall to let her sister climb in beside her. "Don't worry," she said, though she was now officially worried herself. "Daddy said it's not dangerous. He said we'll be just fine."

"I don't trust Daddy," Caroline whispered, laying her head on the pillow next to Ella's.

"Do you trust me?"

"Yes, I do."

"Then I'm telling you too."

She put her arm around her sister and began to stroke her back, and in half-an-hour Caroline was asleep. For the first time in her life Ella remained awake to see dawn, by which point the winds had died down. One of the pecan trees, they would discover, had fallen onto a power line, their mailbox was gone, and the cypress tree had raked ten or twelve shingles off their roof. Practically speaking, Gulfport and Biloxi no longer existed. Hundreds of people were dead.

She thought about that evening off and on all afternoon, as the flood waters in New Orleans continued to rise. She wondered if Caroline was alive somewhere in the world seeing the same images that she was seeing and whether, if she was, she would remember that night in 1970, when her older sister knew what to do, and what to say, and provided the comfort she sought.

•

At her birthday dinner, they drank too much. *Un Croq Rouge*, their favorite restaurant, was close enough to the Financial District to draw bankers and brokerage types for post-work drinks, and it was filled with them that night, everybody standing around glancing every few seconds at the flat screen TVs mounted above all four sides of the elegant lozenge-shaped bar. Their table was not yet ready when they arrived, so they ordered drinks—a Black Bush neat for him, a vodka martini for her—and took them to one of the raised bar tables. She started to tell him about her recollections of Hurricane Camille, how her sister had woken her in the middle of the night, how the pecan tree had fallen, but he kept glancing at the TV, as if he were a lot more interested in the current disaster than the one in her past, so she stopped talking to see if he would notice, but he didn't. She saw his lips form the word *Please* as he stared at images of people straddling roof ridges or, in one case, a tree limb.

She finished her drink and waved at a waiter, and when the waiter came over Martin quickly finished his, too, and they both ordered another.

He glanced over his shoulder at a nearby table, where two guys in suits were talking with animation, occasionally pausing to toss some bar tidbits into their mouths. "You hear what they're saying?"

"No," she said. "No more than you heard what I was just saying."

"I'm sorry?" he said.

"Never mind. What are they saying?"

"How happy they are that the Dow, NASDAQ and S&P all posted gains today." He pointed at the closest flat screen. "It's as if none of that suffering up there even happened. I just don't understand it."

"I don't either."

"But then look at us," he said.

"What about us?"

He paid their untouched dish of mixed nuts clinical attention. "I don't know. I just . . ."

"You just what?"

"I guess I just need that other drink."

They got the other drinks, which they ended up carrying to their table in the dining room. They each had another one there, too, and then they ordered a bottle of Bordeaux with their food. During dinner, he mentioned getting a text from Lexa, who said she was having "a blast." She told him she'd received a different one saying "Cali's so freaking with-it!" She asked if he'd heard from Hayley in the last couple of days, and he said no, and she said she hadn't either. "And what about Liz?" he asked. She said not since last week. He asked if she was still seeing Richard or Robert or Raymond or whatever the guy's name was. "No," she said, "his wife found out, and that was the end of that." Instead of dessert, she ordered a glass of port, and he requested another Black Bush.

At least they had the presence of mind to know that neither of them was sober enough to drive home. He called a taxi, which meant that since they'd taken her car into town, she would have to come back and get it the following day.

When she went downstairs the next morning, it was already past ten and he'd long since left. She recalled his saying that he and Pete had agreed to a conference call with Sony Music Group, the third or fourth conglomerate to express an interest in acquiring Yankee Southern.

Neither of them wanted to sell, she gathered, though apparently for different reasons.

He'd put away his dishes, left some coffee in the thermos on the work island, along with that morning's copy of the *Globe*. She climbed onto a stool, poured herself a cup, then glanced at the front page, where she saw a photo of a middle-aged white man paddling a boat filled with black kids. The caption said "Orleans Parish public defender Bradley J. Moss helps rescue stranded children in the Lower Ninth Ward."

In the man's flaccid features, she saw no trace of the Brad Moss she used to know, the one who walked toward her thirty years ago in that room at the Sun 'n' Sand, bouncing his penis off the palm of his hand. She told herself it could not possibly be him. She needed Brad Moss to remain frozen in time, consigned to the place she'd assigned him in 1975. She also told herself to throw the newspaper into recycling, to carry her coffee outside, to sit on the porch or one of the balconies, enjoying the fresh air and sunshine while she thought about something cheerful: apple picking with the girls and Martin, riding the big Ferris wheel in Paris with the girls while Martin waited below to take their photo, feeding the ducks with the girls in the Public Garden, feeding the birds with the girls on St. Stephen's Green, eating gelato with her family in via Dante Alighieri. Happy times that could be no more.

She grabbed the paper, intending to run it through the shredder she fed bills into after she paid them. The problem was that the shredder was in the alcove, next to the desk where her laptop waited impassively to do whatever she commanded just as it had so many times before when she conducted her regular searches for Caroline.

In only a few moments, she'd identified the members of his family: Kimberly Faye Moss, 47, of New Orleans; Nanci Lynn Moss, 24, (also known as Nanci Lynn Prideaux), listed at the same New Orleans address as her parents, as well as another one in Gretna, Louisiana, where she most likely lived with her husband; Robert Francis Moss, 22, still listed at his parents' home; and Frederick Steven Moss, 20, listed at his parents', too, but also at Harvard Yard Mail Center/Cambridge, MA 02138. They had probably helped him move into his dorm a couple of years ago, just as she and Martin were moving Hayley in two miles away at Tufts.

They didn't know she was so close by. But then they probably didn't even remember her. Why would they?

She pushed herself away from the desk, got up and walked outside. It was as hot and sultry a day as she'd ever experienced north of Boston. It felt like the Delta, where the heavy air wrapped itself around you as if it meant to pull you down. She went back inside.

The coffee was now cold and it tasted sour. She poured it into the sink, ground some more Peet's and put it in the coffee maker and pressed the button. She knew she ought to eat something—some yoghurt or toast, anything to soak up a little of last night's alcohol. She took out a Dannon, peeled off the foil, forced down a few spoonfuls. Then she poured herself some fresh coffee, took a step or two toward the living room, then turned and carried the coffee to her desk.

It had never occurred to her, because until now she'd never thought about it, that a paper as small as the *Loring Weekly Times* might be online. But it was, and it had been since January of 2000. It provided a search function but only for articles published since it went online. She all but lost interest when she figured that out. Still, the urge to type in a name or two was hard to resist. An inquiry for "Kim Taggart" produced no results, probably because she hadn't lived there for many years. Ella couldn't recall her father's real first name, so she tried "Tag Taggart." Up popped an article from the summer of 2001.

It detailed the trial, conviction and sentencing of a once-prominent local attorney, whose wife, it developed, had divorced him in 1993. He'd been living alone in their Loring home, the article said, for the previous eight years. His ex-, presently Mrs. Louise Ferragamo, of Fairhope, Alabama, refused to comment when reached by the Weekly Times, as did his daughter, Mrs. Kimberly Moss, of New Orleans. He'd been convicted on multiple counts of sexual assault against minors, committed over a period of nearly forty years. The first to bring charges, a forty-eight-year-old black man who'd mown the Taggarts' lawn back in the late '60s, was pictured on the front page, next to the photo of Mr. Taggart being escorted from the courthouse by two uniformed officers.

She followed the evidence backwards, from the beginning of his trial through his arrest in October of 2000. After the initial accusation, several other black men came forward, most of them between the ages of eighteen and forty-three, though the oldest was fifty-four and had been assaulted by Mr. Taggart in 1956, when he was nine and Mr. Taggart was twenty-four. "He's been at this," the district attorney told the jury in his summation, "since Dwight Eisenhower was in the White House. Right under our noses. How did he get away with it? Well, if children are always the most vulnerable among us—and we all know they are—he picked on the most vulnerable of the most vulnerable. He did it secure in the belief that because of who he was, a white man with money and prestige and long-standing ties throughout the community, he would never be called to account. Ladies and gentlemen of the jury, it's within your power today to prove him wrong."

She could still see his face as he sat at the end of the table in their house on the bayou, his back to the brightly-lit Christmas float. She recalled how he rose and politely excused himself, saying he needed to go to his office, even though it was Friday night, because he was working on an urgent case. She recalled, too, how as soon as he walked out, his wife rose and collected her wine bottle and the corkscrew and went upstairs to complete the process of drinking herself under.

Get up, she told herself. Turn this thing off and walk away. Call a taxi, go to Boston, get your car.

Instead she typed in other names—names of people she hadn't thought of in years. The majority of them eventually showed up, a handful in obituaries, a few in connection with crimes, but most of them in captions under the kinds of photos the paper had always run plenty of: the officers of the Rotary Club, the officers of the Lions Club, the members of the Neighborhood Beautification Society, the Loring Rebels Booster Club, the Friends of the Library. In one photo, the mayor—African American, to her surprise—was about to cut the ribbon at the opening of a new barbecue place. The owner, whom she would never have recognized but for the caption, was none other than Irwin Majori, who kissed her on the turnrow, who earlier than that had been ridiculed and humiliated after confessing he played with his own cock. He looked as if he weighed three hundred pounds now, his face pumpkin-round.

She lost track of time. She opened a bottle of wine. She went back to her desk and searched some more.

She didn't empty the bottle, and she felt very good about that. Though it still had at least another glass in it, she poured that down the drain, then carried the bottle to the garage and placed it in recycling, careful to rearrange the contents of the big blue container so that the bottle slipped all the way to the bottom. She went back inside and brushed her teeth. The day had passed more easily than most of the days since Lexa flew away. She'd filled the time. She lay down on the couch to take a short nap so she could get up and be ready when Martin got home. She intended to prepare something nice for dinner, a pasta dish he'd always loved, with anchovies and broccoli rabe.

The problem was that she was still asleep when he came home. She woke to find him standing over her. Something was stuck to his sweater, just above his belt. Peanut skins, it looked like. "Where's the car?" he asked.

"What car?"

"Your car."

"Oh, my God." She sat up, not even bothering to look at her watch. She could tell from the angle of the sun that it was past five. "I forgot to go get it," she said.

"Well, what the hell. It's only a Mercedes. I mean, everybody's got one, right?"

"Are you guys going to sell the company?"

"Everybody's got a Mercedes, right?"

"What do you want me to say?"

His face was not exactly red, but it was definitely pink. "I want you to say 'I wasted my day. I did absolutely nothing worth doing, and I did it for eight hours.'"

"It wasn't eight hours. I didn't get up until ten."

"That's even worse." He whipped his cell phone out, then started to scroll through his contacts but realized he couldn't read them without his glasses. So he whipped those out, stuck them on his nose and went back to scrolling.

"What are you doing?" she asked.

"Calling a taxi to take me to get your goddamn car."

She got up off the couch. "Let it wait. I'll fix us a good dinner."

"The fucking garage costs thirty-eight dollars a day. I'd rather give it to the Red Cross. There are people down there where you come from buried under a bunch of rubble, starving and dying. But you don't remember that place anymore." He waved his hand around the room. "The only place you know is this one."

That was when she lost it. "I've spent the whole goddamn day remembering that place. You don't even know what I remember."

"Because you don't tell me."

"I tried to tell you yesterday, but you were more interested in the stockbrokers."

"You tried to tell me about your sister. You think I don't know how she haunts you? How she haunts me, even though I never met her? How she's haunted us? What'd you really say to her in that final, fatal phone call? Tell her to go jump off a cliff?"

He didn't wait to hear if she'd told her to jump off a cliff, or jump in the ocean, or go fly a kite. He went back outside and called a taxi, and a few minutes later he climbed in and hadn't returned by the time she went to bed.

THE POLISH WORD *PARAPETÓWKA* MEANS "windowsill party." It's the bash you throw for friends when you move into your new home, the theory being that your guests will stand their drinks on the windowsill because, having bought the apartment, you will not be able to afford furniture. Though Caroline had plenty of furniture, she called the gathering that anyway, and coincidentally she held hers on an evening when much of the world was reeling from the financial crisis. A few days earlier, Lehman Brothers had filed for bankruptcy, and people who used to complain about Poland's strict banking laws were starting to breathe a little easier, realizing that those same laws might protect them from the chaos spreading elsewhere.

The two-bedroom apartment was the nicest place she'd ever lived, and she owned it free and clear. On the third floor of an architecturally striking building from the early 2000s, not far from the Institute where she now served as associate director, the flat was in move-in condition when she took possession. But she had new tile installed in the kitchen and bathroom, replaced all the appliances, had the floors in the living room and bedrooms refinished and the whole flat repainted. Though she didn't consider herself a particularly domestic person, or an acquisitive one either, she spent many evenings at Ikea choosing furniture, buying bedclothes, kitchen utensils, bookcases. She didn't need costly things, but she wanted to find them aesthetically pleasing. The one fairly expensive item she bought was a Bose Wave Music System. The only outlet in the entire country where you could purchase one was in Galeria Mokotów, on the outskirts of the city.

The day she went to pick it up, Alastair's son Marek, whom she'd continued to babysit until he was too old to require oversight, volunteered to accompany her. In the back seat of the taxi on the way to buy the Bose, he told her about school, the teachers he liked, the ones he didn't, the courses he wished they didn't make you take. Though only fourteen now, he was nearly two meters tall.

When he paused, she asked, "And what about girls?"

"No."

"No, what?"

"No, there are no girls."

"Not in the whole school?"

His complexion, naturally fair, grew noticeably darker. "That's not what I meant. They exist. There are actually more of them than there are of us. It's just . . . I don't know any I like. They all seem so wrapped up in themselves. I hear them talking. They talk about clothes. Who's wearing what, who's not. They bore me. They do." He cracked his knuckles. "They are not much like you."

She took mercy on him and changed the subject, telling him about her recent trip to Halle. Because of her visa status, she still had to cross the border every three months, and she always did it on the weekend and had spent a fair amount of time in Germany, especially eastern cities like Dresden, Leipzig, and Berlin. She treated herself to weekends in other places too: Amsterdam, Vienna, Dublin, London. Where she hadn't been for the past seventeen years was the U.S. She often thought she might never go there again.

Alastair paid her well, which was one reason she could afford to travel and buy an apartment. The other reason was that she'd earned a nice advance for her first book, a collection of short stories, several of which initially appeared in mass circulation magazines, though the mighty *New Yorker* continued to reject her. The book got good reviews and attracted the attention of publishers in Germany, the Netherlands, the U.K., and Poland. It also led to a much larger advance for her novel-in-progress.

The only serious difference she'd ever had with Jared, her agent, involved the question of publicity for her collection and any subsequent books she might be lucky enough to publish. In an email, she told him that she did not want her photo to appear on book jackets and that her bio should say no more than what appeared in magazines: "Karo Kohl is an American writer who lives in Poland."

He wrote her back a single line. *Are you joking? With your looks?*

The exchange led to a phone call, which she made from her bedroom at Klara's. As a measure of her new status, his assistant put her straight through.

"First of all," she said as soon as he told her hello, "I don't look like you remember."

"And secondly," he said, "I shouldn't have said what I did. It was sexist. I'm really sorry."

"I know you are. You were probably sorry about three seconds after you hit send."

"More like two. What's this about, Karo? Your publisher's going to ask me, I suspect, so I need to know." He chuckled—but it was a nervous chuckle. "Are you on the lam, or what?"

A magnificent lie came to her all at once, like lies used to when the truth was inconvenient, as the truth mostly was and sometimes continued to be. Her father had been a famous novelist, she could say, with whom she'd never gotten along. Which was why as a teenager she'd run away from home and changed her name. She would not divulge his identity, nor where he had lived, nor the name of his publisher. You would know him, though, she would say, and so will everybody who decides to review my book. And things being what they are, one of two outcomes is likely, each of them problematic. The first possibility is that I'd get better treatment because of my lineage. The second is that I'd get worse. I want to be treated like the nobody I've been for most of my life. Let my work stand on its on if it can. If it can't, so be it.

Why she couldn't lie to him, she wouldn't have been able to say. But when she thought about it later, it would seem pretty simple. She liked him. He was in a business, and until the collection sold he'd never made much money off her, yet he'd stood by her because he cared about her work. Truth be told, he probably even cared about her. "Yes," she said.

"Yes, what?"

"Yes. I'm on the lam."

Silence. Then: "Are you serious?"

"I'm afraid so."

He didn't launch another joke. Consternation was running riot in an office on Park Avenue. "Okay," he said after the lengthiest of pauses. "Go ahead. Give it to me straight, Karo. No fiction."

Just like that, she told him, just as she'd told Deena in Blacksburg, Virginia, almost twenty-five years ago. It took only a few sentences: "It was the fall of '78. I was eighteen years old. I'd fallen in with a guy. We were in Northern California. I waited in the car outside a little store. Out in the middle of nowhere. Late at night. He said he was going to buy burritos. The best burritos ever. So he went in. And then I heard gunshots. And I drove away as fast as I could. He shot at me, too, but he missed. So here I am. And there you are. And now you know. Don't you wish you hadn't asked? The boy he killed played shortstop. He wanted to teach history and coach baseball."

For a long time, he didn't say a word. She assumed she'd just lost her agent and, probably, her book contract too, and whatever future the contract might have secured her.

"Let's draw some lines here," he finally said. "First things first. Do you need help, Karo?"

A decade or so down the road, in fiercer times than those, when people began to dismiss the work of writers whose personal character had been found wanting, cancelling their books before they even appeared, as if the words on the page mattered much less than the background of the person who'd written them, or as if they didn't matter at all, she'd recall his response, which by then would have been considered quaint by many, if not most, of his colleagues. By then, certain sorts of people in need of help would be left to their just deserts. Forgiveness was anti-woke.

Her throat tightened. "What sort of help?"

"Legal representation. Because it sounds to me like you were a witness and a potential victim but not an accomplice. I take it you never contacted the police?"

"No. I was too cowardly."

"Cowardice is not a crime. Do you know whatever became of this . . . of the guy in question? Have you ever done an internet search for him?"

Until a few years earlier, the answer would have been no. But she'd eventually had to buy a new laptop, which of course was internet-ready, and one night curiosity got the best of her, keeping her on various search engines until four AM. In July of 1985, according to an article from the *Washington Post*, a man with Tom's first and last names was identified as the suspect in the robbery of a branch bank in Roanoke, Virginia, thirty-five miles from where she'd been living when she got caught by the TV reporter after the balcony at the ice cream-and-sandwich shop caved in. His age at the time—thirty-two—would have been about right. The article said he had prior convictions in Florida, Ohio, and Montana. But he'd never been apprehended for that crime. She'd found the name in connection with other reported crimes too. Sometimes the age matched, at other times it didn't. His first name was common, his last name too. A couple of people with his name had gone to jail. They might have been him, they might not have been. She never looked anymore. He might be dead, he might not be. She always assumed he wasn't. She also assumed that if he wasn't, he might find her one day, though probably not if she stayed here and kept her head down. "I searched," she said, "but didn't find anything conclusive. His name's pretty common."

"Did he ever get connected to the crime in California?"

"Not as far as I can tell."

"There's a way to find out, you know."

"I don't want to. Whatever the answer is, it wouldn't bring back the person he shot, it wouldn't relieve me of my own guilt, and it wouldn't make me want my face on the cover of a book." Neither would it alter the fact that her mother died without knowing where she was, or that she had not seen her sister for going on thirty years. She knew Ella was still rich, though, still living in the big green house. You could find out all sorts of things online. You could find hundreds if not thousands of Caroline Coles, in places all over the world. But she was not one of them, and she meant to keep it that way.

More silence. "All right," Jared Entzminger said. "I'll express your wishes to your publisher, Karo. I gotta tell you ahead of time, I don't know for one hundred percent certain how it'll play. I hope it'll be okay. Several of them have been burned lately by writers pretending to be somebody they aren't, though that mostly involves memoirs. Fiction gives you license to lie, but only within certain limitations."

In the end, her publisher raised no objections. Instead, the publicist assigned to her—who, on the phone, sounded like she was around twenty years old—seemed to relish the mystery surrounding her identity. "We could get some extra mileage out of this," she enthused. "There's just the right amount of intrigue. Who is she, what does she look like, that sort of thing. Also, what American writer in her right mind chooses to live someplace like Poland? Don't get me wrong, I'm not anti-Polish or anything like that, though I guess my great grandmother died over there in some kind of ghetto or something. It's just that Warsaw's not exactly Paris. Know what I mean?"

Yes, she said, she believed she did.

•

She hired a catering company to deliver food for her *parapetówka*, and she bought enough whisky, vodka, wine and champagne to keep everybody drunk for a week. Her flat looked great. She had some nice wall art, including a framed poster of her American book cover, and her floors were freshly waxed and smelling faintly of linseed oil, her furniture comfortable and inviting. She tried but failed to suppress a sense of pride. Somehow, after so many mistakes, so much wasted time, so many lonely nights in bus stations, hostels, cheap motels and rented rooms, she had her own home.

Her guests included Marek, Alastair and the flutist, six or seven people from work, a couple of Warsaw writers, her Polish editor and his wife, and Klara. Her former landlady, who'd be dead in six months from breast cancer and was probably already concealing her illness, kept everybody laughing with her risqué jokes, a couple of which made Alastair playfully clamp his hands over Marek's ears, to his son's unfeigned outrage.

"Do you seriously think," the poor boy asked, "that I don't know what adults do with one another at night in bed? Get real, for God's sake!"

"I don't do anything with anybody," Klara said, then drained her wine glass. "But it's not for lack of trying." She winked at her red-faced prey. "What about you, Marcin? You do something with somebody after sunset?"

"Marek! My name is Marek!"

"I bet the young women cling to you like wallpaper, don't they? I know I would. Ooh la la!"

At that point, he stormed into the bathroom and stayed there for a long time. When he emerged, he made straight for the balcony. By then, everybody but Caroline had drunk too much to take note. She followed him out and slid the glass door closed.

He was standing at the railing with his back to her. Below, a motorcycle roared past. "Such noise," he said, "it would drive me crazy."

She stepped over to stand beside him. "It would have driven me crazy too. That's why I had soundproof windows installed."

"I don't mean the noise out here." With his thumb, he gestured over his shoulder. "I mean in there. That old woman. She's awful."

"Actually, she's lovely. She was my first Polish friend."

"Why does she talk all the time about sex? Doesn't she realize how old she is?"

"She knows exactly how old she is, Marek. I imagine she talks about sex because she misses it."

She was looking at him, but he wouldn't look at her. He stared across the street at the Carrefour Express, prompting her to glance in that direction. At this hour, the store was closed and dimly lit. A drunk had gone to sleep with his back against the door, on his head a leather cap with ear flaps. It made him look like Baron von Richthofen.

"She had her chance," Marek said.

"Her chance to do what?"

The first tear moved swiftly down his cheek, then dangled from the tip of his chin, taking a comically long time to drop over the railing. Others followed in rapid succession. "She had her chance," he said, "to fuck. It's somebody else's turn now."

Until that moment, caught up as she was in the excitement of having her own place and being treated like a person of substance, she hadn't given that much consideration to what he must be going through. It had a name, of course. Puberty. Thus, the sea of pimples on his forehead. "Fucking," she said, "is not really a zero sum game. Her not getting to do it doesn't enable someone else."

Even though he'd just dropped an F bomb himself, she could see it unnerved him when she did. But once he'd processed it, he became emboldened and spun around to face her. "Would you fuck me?" he asked. "You could just show me how, and then I'd leave you alone."

If he left her alone after she fucked him, he'd be the first male who ever did so, and she came within a second or two of telling him that. Instead, she reached out and laid her hand on his forearm. He jumped as if struck by a cattle prod. "You're a nice young man," she said. "My youngest friend in the entire country. I'm forty-eight years old, nearly forty-nine—almost old enough to be your grandmother. When you wake up in the morning and think about what you just said to me, you're going to be scared and embarrassed and, I can all but assure you, revolted too. So when that happens, I want you to tell yourself that I thought it was sweet. Then I want you to totally wipe this moment off your mental hard drive. It didn't happen, okay? You didn't ask, I didn't say what I just said, and you don't need to blush the next time we're in close proximity. In fact, I'll be mad if you do, so work on getting control of your blood vessels. Now go back inside before anybody wonders what we're doing out here. I'll be there shortly."

She didn't need to tell him again. After he left, she remained at the railing, thinking over what had just occurred, wondering if she'd inadvertently done something to bring it on, whether she'd handled it well or poorly. Better that he'd said it to her, she supposed, than to the flutist, whom she'd always found a little histrionic. Caroline loved the kid and she wasn't sure anyone else did except his father.

Before returning to her gathering, she saw that the sleeping drunk had attracted company. A stray cat was sniffing at his feet. From the balcony, it looked like a calico. She stood there for a long time, staring at it, recalling the junkyard across the street from Julio's place, the mangled Camaro, the chain-link fence, how she'd used milk and sweet words to lure Querida into the house so she could adopt her, then how she'd left her and him and a large part of herself behind.

•

By two-thirty AM, all except Klara were on their last legs, but nobody had left. A couple of bottles of champagne remained, so Alastair lifted a glass, struck it once or twice with the side of a spoon, then announced, "Even though tomorrow's Saturday, some of us who toil for our daily bread had probably better get some sleep, else we'll be no good come Monday. I suggest each of us say a few words about our talented friend, then toast her and go home. I'll start by telling you that the Institute is what it is today because not only is she a great and inspiring teacher, she's also a first-rate administrator. For instance, some of you may recall that once upon a time, our hallways were painted a slimy shade of green. One day, she walked into my office and said, 'Alastair, as a boy in New Brunswick, did you ever drink too much Gatorade? I'm asking because these walls look like what happens after somebody does that.'"

Everybody except his son laughed. Marek couldn't even muster a half-hearted smile.

"She helped me re-design everything, making it a lot nicer place to teach and learn. And when you look around at these new digs of hers, you have to appreciate her taste. I know I do. I appreciate everything about her."

Klara followed, with a thoroughly fictional anecdote about how, after Caroline moved in with her, men began to hang around the entrance to her building, even asking Klara out to dinner in hopes of gaining an intro to her tenant. After that, Caroline's co-workers and the literary people chimed in. Soon the only one left was Marek.

"Son?" his father said. "Want to say a few words?" He poured a tiny amount of champagne into a glass and handed it to him.

At first, when he appeared to be tongue-tied, she feared Marek might confess what he'd said outside. Sexual confusion could make you do all sorts of things. It had certainly done that to her.

Eventually, he forced his lips to move. "I would like to say that Karo . . . I would like to tell everyone that Karo was once my babysitter. But," he added fiercely, "she never treated me like a baby. Or like some dumb little kid. She just treated me like a person. So I propose a toast to my first American friend, my babysitter, my educator. *Na zdrowie*, goddamn it!"

He turned the flute up, chugged its contents, then held the glass out and stared at his father. Alastair's notions of who his son was, or might become, seemed to be changing before their eyes. He poured the remaining bubbly into Marek's flute, then watched along with the rest of them while he downed it.

SHE'D OUTFITTED HER SECOND BEDROOM, the smaller one that overlooked a courtyard, to serve as her study, buying herself a nice desk and, because she often wrote for seven or eight hours at a stretch and was beginning to have neck and back pain, an ergonomic chair that adjusted to her changing posture. Other than the desk and chair and her laptop and printer, the only items in the room were a few hundred books, a couple of wall hangings, a small daybed and the Bose. She couldn't listen to vocals while she wrote, but she often listened to chamber music. Dvorak, she discovered, provided especially good company.

Her assumption, when she moved in, was that now writing would be a lot easier. She'd previously written primarily in cafes or, when the weather was nice, on a bench in Łazienki Park. She had the ability to shut out the sounds of car horns and coffee grinders, but every now and then something or someone would disrupt her concentration. She'd developed a rabid dread of encountering friends when she was trying to work. The more people she came to know, the more often that happened. She never tried to write at the Institute. People always knew when she was there, and no matter how tentative the knock on the door, she found it all but impossible not to get up and open it.

By the middle of December, after living in the new flat for more than three months, she was forced to admit that her writing was in a bad place. She'd had what she thought was eighty-two solid pages of the novel when she moved in. Since then, she'd thrown away nearly as many new pages. Three times she started her third chapter. Three times she failed. Then she began to worry over the pages she'd previously felt good about. When she read them with a cold eye, the narrative texture seemed thin. You could see the characters, and you could even see what they saw. But you couldn't hear what they heard or smell what they smelled. You couldn't feel the air making contact with their skin. There wasn't much interiority either.

Rather than go buy a Christmas tree, as she'd promised herself she would this first year in her new home, she spent five consecutive nights going back over the opening pages and inserting details and ruminative passages. Instead of becoming more vivid the prose grew puffy, those first eighty-two pages morphing into ninety-eight. When she read the whole thing from the front on the evening of the 22nd, she realized she'd created a large, leaden mess. The next morning, though it was the last day of class and the Institute's Christmas party was scheduled for that evening, she called in sick.

She'd promised to spend Christmas Eve with her Polish editor and his wife and a couple of their friends, but she phoned late that morning and claimed to have food poisoning, and by the time she talked his wife out of bringing her ginger tea and rice, she felt fairly certain that her friend knew she was being lied to. She couldn't help it. She just didn't want to face anybody. In particular, she did not want to face herself. But about that she had no choice.

For too much of her life, she'd let others define her. To her father, she was a troublemaker. To her mother, a chore. To her sister, an embarrassment. To the people of her hometown, the bad sister. To Tom, a great fuck. To her Michigan roommate, an insufferable bitch. At one time or another, she'd bought into each of those identities, and even now it would be all too easy to fall back into any one of them or into all of them together. The only identity she'd chosen for herself was that of a writer. She'd become one by doing. Should she quit doing it—or quit doing it well—she couldn't imagine very many tomorrows. She wasn't writing for money, though it was nice to have. She was writing, or trying to, for her life.

She spent a sleepless Christmas Eve, finally dropping off around five AM, then waking again at eight. Most of Christmas day she sat in the living room in her pajamas, listening to bells toll and sipping from a bottle of Cardhu left over from her *parapatówka*. Every two or three hours she glanced at her cell. The calls were starting to accumulate.

One of the Polish novelists she'd become friends with had told her to try to ignore her reviews, whether they were good or bad. To the extent that she could, she had. But her publishers were always sending them to her, and while she mostly looked at the last couple of lines, where the thumbs up or thumbs down was usually given, she didn't delete the emails. On Christmas night, her head abuzz from too much Scotch and too little food, she began to go back through them, in an effort to determine what people seemed to like about her earlier work. A reviewer for the *Guardian* wrote that "unlike so many American writers, whose worlds—and, for that matter, their interests—seem narrowly subscribed, Kohl is at least as much at home in Budapest as in Bakersfield, always providing the few sharp details that suggest others that are not actually present on the page. She convincingly inhabits the minds of a young Chicano laboring in a California vineyard; an elderly Polish immigrant who answers the phone all day for a suburban real estate firm somewhere in the Midwest, then returns to her apartment craving sleep, only to suffer nightmares about her wartime experiences in Łódź; the driver of a Pine Bluff, Arkansas, propane truck who spends his days making deliveries on rural backroads while pining for his lost love; a married Hungarian taxi driver hopelessly in love with the British Pakistani who gives him English lessons; a Ukrainian violinist with conservatory training who waits tables at night in a Berlin bistro after busking all day to earn the hard currency she sends her ailing mother. The author seldom cues the strings to wheedle emotion from her readers. She has the confidence to let us reach our own judgments about her characters, secure in the belief that their experiences, if vividly realized, will earn our empathy when empathy is called for, our scorn should their actions warrant."

The praise was not what stayed with her. What did was a single phrase that kept coming back to her as clocks around town struck midnight: "the few sharp details that suggest others that are not actually present on the page."

She'd once stepped off the S-Bahn at Berlin's Zoologischer Garten, seen a tiny woman standing nearby playing "Czardasz," the violin case at her feet filled with Euros. She watched her, she walked over and put five Euros in the case, then seated herself at a nearby café and spent some more time observing her. It was spring, the woman wore a white blouse with a bright yellow sweater that needed de-pilling, a wispy blue skirt with a pattern of white hearts, oddly old-fashioned brown leather shoes with frayed laces. She played for hours, mixing gypsy melodies with "The Kreutzer Sonata," Bach's "Partita," "Sweet Georgia Brown," "Orange Blossom Special." The smile, as if pasted there, never left her face. When she finally stopped, she withdrew a thin white towel from her skirt pocket, knelt down and, balancing the violin on her knee, removed all the coins and notes from the case and tucked them into her blouse. Then, as if it were an infant, she laid the violin in the case, placed the thin towel on top of it, snapped the case shut. Carrying it under her arm, she walked toward the station entrance, her head down, no bounce in her step. Caroline resisted the urge to follow her. She knew all she wanted to. The rest she could invent.

Her problem, she suspected, was that to write a novel making use of multiple settings, she was going to need to know most of them in a much deeper way than she needed to know Berlin to set a story there. Otherwise there would be no reverberations beneath the surface of the narration. No counterpoint to the melody.

For reasons of her own, she'd started her novel in a small town in northern Tennessee, up next to the Kentucky line. She didn't call it Clarksville, but that's what it was in her mind. Not Clarksville in the year 2008, but Clarksville as she remembered it from the mid 1980s. The town had a medium-sized state university. A large military base was close by. There was a significant black population, but whites vastly outnumbered them, and the racism was muted. There was no all-white private school. People got along as best they could. The history of their ancestors, as she depicted it, was fairly generic. Some of them fought in the Second World War and came home heroes. Some of them fought in Korea or Vietnam and came home losers. Nobody had an unusual job. They worked at the Western Auto, or they farmed, but the crops they grew were never mentioned, because she didn't know what crops they grew. Her teenaged main character, a girl named Jade who had no siblings and no close friends, not unreasonably found the town bland and boring and wanted to get away the instant she could. So one day she hitchhiked to St. Louis, where she worked for a while in a diner probably inspired—though Caroline hadn't realized it until now and was mortified when she did—by the sit-com *Happy Days*, since one of the guys Jade regularly served wore a leather jacket like the Fonz, rode a motorcycle and, though he played the tough, was sweet to her, always leaving good tips. When he asked her if she'd like to ride his Harley with him all the way to California and back, she agreed. That was where the second chapter ended.

Not everything that could be wrong with a work of contemporary realism was wrong with her pages. The words were spelled correctly, the commas and quotation marks were where they belonged, her subjects and verbs saw eye to eye. But the characters existed to do the author's bidding, their responses were nearly always predictable, and setting exerted no real pressure on their lives. There was no urgency in the telling.

A calmness settled over her. She pulled some three-day-old Razowiec out of the bread box, covered it in farmer's cheese and laid on a couple of slices of lox, carried it to the couch and ate it while looking out the window as snowflakes the size of gnats drifted down. She'd seldom had a more satisfying meal. She washed her plate, put it away and crawled into bed.

While she slept, the flakes grew more numerous and when she got up at a quarter past nine, they had already covered the old, dirty snow with a pristine layer. She made a pot of coffee, carried a cup of it to her study, sat down and deleted every word of her novel. Then she started over.

THE PROBLEM WAS NOT THAT they never had any more good times after Lexa left home. They had quite a few, taking another trip to Europe, attending the Grammys where a record he and Pete co-produced won Best Bluegrass Album, throwing a party for Hayley when she landed her dream job as an assistant curator of American Decorative Arts and Sculpture at the MFA. The problem was that the good times were fewer and fewer and that the bad times, when they experienced them, grew more and more bitter.

On the morning of May 4, 2009, they had a terrible argument. It started, like so many of them had those last few years, over seemingly nothing. While he sat on one of the stools at the kitchen work island looking at the *Globe*, she pulled a container of yoghurt from the refrigerator and carried it over to the armchair in the corner, where she'd begun to eat breakfast. As she stuck a spoon in the yoghurt, she asked if he'd upgraded their seats to first-class. In a couple of weeks, they were supposed to fly to California for Lexa's graduation. She'd recently been accepted to law school at UCLA.

The previous fall, on their flight home from Europe, he'd experienced what he himself acknowledged was an excruciating pain in his right calf. She insisted he go see his doctor, and the doctor immediately dispatched him to the hospital for an ultrasound, which detected a small blood clot in his peroneal artery. Telling her about it afterwards, he said the doctor considered it no huge concern like it would have been if it had appeared in one of the larger veins above the knee. He was put on a course of blood thinners, warned not to cross his legs and prohibited from flying. Three months later, a second ultrasound detected no clot, a blood test confirmed that it had already dissolved, and the doctor said he could fly whenever he needed to but that it would be smart to wear compression socks and get up and move around the cabin as much as possible, especially on longer flights. The doctor also said that since he could afford it, he ought to buy extra room, which Martin made the uncharacteristic mistake of telling her. What the doctor didn't know was that even though he'd earned a significant amount of money producing records, her husband remained at heart an accountant. Generous to a fault with family, friends and the artists whose careers he supported, often despite a notable lack of gratitude on their part, he hated spending money on himself.

He acted as if he hadn't heard her question about upgraded seats. The expression on his face never changed. Idly, he lifted his cup, took a sip of coffee, then set the cup down and turned the page.

"Did you *hear* me?" she asked, a little more sharply than she intended.

"I may have."

He refused to look her full in the face and experience the bewilderment he often felt when their gazes met, but out of the corner of his left eye he could see just enough to know she was staring at him, that her coffee cup had paused halfway to her mouth, that the off-handed response had achieved the desired effect. In moments like this he hardly knew himself. He loved her more than anybody or anything. Why had it become so hard to show it? He'd die for her if need be. He sometimes felt as if he already had.

"You *may* have?" she said.

"Yeah. Or maybe not. I don't know. See, most people walking around out there think hearing's just an automatic response to wave propagation. But sound engineers know that's not true. It's also an event," he said, starting to improvise. "An event of a perceptual and sensory nature. Yeah, plenty of strictly mechanical stuff happens in the cochlea, where frequency resolution occurs. But then nerve impulses get transmitted from the inner ear to the brain. And once that happens? All bets are off."

"All bets are *off*?"

"Yeah, that's right. Because the brain's where things like prejudice and predisposition come into play. In other words, what a person *expects* to hear affects what he thinks he *does* hear. He may hear it but not know he heard it, because he didn't want to hear it. Or he may think he heard it, because he was hoping to hear it, when in fact he didn't hear it. There's some really interesting stuff on this in the *Journal of Psychoacoustics*."

She sat her coffee cup down on the floor.

"For instance," he said, "I definitely heard that. Very percussive."

She jerked her phone out of her bathrobe and began to tap furiously at the screen.

"I hear that too."

"There's no such fucking thing," she said a moment later.

"What fucking thing?"

"There's no such *thing* as the *Journal of Psychoacoustics*."

"Well, there should be, and it's a shame there isn't. So maybe I'll start it up and make myself the editor and publisher. After all, it'd be cheaper and a lot more useful to start a journal of psychoacoustics than to fly two people to California and back first-class."

Something her therapist had helped her learn about herself was that she was angry because she chose to be. Until she chose not to be, she'd remain that way. Another thing she'd understood was that her anger was not really directed at Martin—why would it be?—but at herself. It's just that he nearly always happened to be nearby when she needed to unleash it. And he was nearby now. Right there across the room, on one of those stools that used to be covered in red flannel but was presently upholstered in black leather, just like the chair she sat in. They'd redone everything in the kitchen a decade ago. They'd redone everything in the house at one time or another. Whatever she asked for she got. So why not first-class seats to California, since the added room might keep another blood clot from forming and taking his life and leaving her alone like her father left her mother alone when he got himself blown up with Grace Pace. The nerve of him. The nerve of them both.

"If you want to let your stinginess kill you," she said, rising, "be my guest. You've loaned money to half the folks from Tennessee and North

Carolina who can plink the theme song from *Deliverance* on the banjo, which is probably half the folks in both states, and the next thing you know they're recording for somebody else and when you want to go hear them play with Alison Krauss, you have to buy a ticket and can't get backstage, and when you have a few drinks afterwards and start feeling hurt and send them a text, they blame it on Alison's fame. The truth is they don't want to see you. Why? Because they still owe you money. And not knowing you any better than they do, they think you might actually ask for it."

She knew she ought to walk out or, better yet, apologize and step over and wrap her arms around him and tell him she loved him, which would not have been untrue. But she just couldn't do it. She needed to fight someone, since she didn't know how to fight herself and win.

He joined the combat with greater gusto than the norm, his pulse beginning to pound in his ears as if Keith Moon had taken up residence somewhere in his cranium and was bashing those double bass drums. He said some things that he'd often thought but never believed, not even now when he was saying them. He said, "Funny you should mention money, since I guess that's what you married me for. That and a lack of better options." He said, "I bet you concocted the story about that sleazy instructor at Berklee, just trying to play on my sympathy." He said, "You've got a lot of Elvis in you. Both of you wanted to rise. He made it to Graceland and you made it to Cedar Park."

About halfway through his monologue, he seemed to have dismounted the stool. Though both feet were firmly planted on the floor, he felt as if he lacked anchor, as if he were floating above the scene, looking down at the two of them, seeing the unsightly bald spot on the crown of his own head, the few gray strands in her otherwise still golden hair. He didn't know whether she dyed it or not. He'd never asked. Furthermore, he'd never wondered, because it had never mattered since he loved her. Even now he loved her, though a few seconds ago he'd hated her. Love was funny like that, how quickly it could turn to its opposite and back again.

Who he hated now was himself for telling her what he'd just told her. "Listen," he said, "I'm sorry. I shouldn't have said any of that. Most of it isn't true."

He took a weightless step toward her, but she put her hands up. "A lot of it isn't. But some of it might be. I don't even know for sure, and that's an awful thing to confess. I'm so sorry, Martin. I truly am. You deserved better."

She cinched her robe more tightly and walked out of the kitchen. That was how it ended.

SHE DRESSED, GOT IN THE CAR and headed over to Route 1, thinking maybe she'd run up to Gloucester or Rockport and eat lunch someplace with a view of the water. Approaching Danvers, she began to reminisce about a fall long ago, when the girls were still little, remembering how the four of them had gone to a nearby orchard to pick apples. After they filled their sacks, they ate bad barbecue and onion blossoms, and then while she sat and watched, he led the girls off to pet some smelly goats. Autumn was beautiful, winter just a trial she'd learned to endure. If she suffered the occasional dream about her missing sister, or sometimes woke in an icy sweat, thinking she was back in that stifling attic, confronting that lockbox, begging herself not to open it, to let the unknown remain unknown, it seemed a small price to pay for the security and certainty that pervaded her days.

Absorbed by these thoughts, she missed the exit to Route 128. Rather than try to get off and head back, she decided to eat lunch in Newburyport, a town she'd always liked and often wished she could live in. When she got there, she parked in a lot near the Firehouse Center for the Arts, thinking that after lunch she'd go for a walk along the waterfront, see how she was feeling about what she'd said and what he'd said and try to determine what ought to happen next. Maybe it was time to make changes. The question was what changes? Rent an apartment in Cambridge? Go back to school? Open a yoga studio? Write poetry? She almost pulled her cell out to see if he'd called her—she bet he had—but dissuaded herself.

She found a small café and ordered a salad and a glass of white wine. The wine came, and she waited until her server walked away, then downed it. It was cold and crisp, a Sancerre. When her server returned with someone else's food, she caught her attention and pointed at the glass. It didn't take too long for her to finish it either, and she gestured for a third, which she drank more slowly, since it would be her last. Then her food arrived, and she thought What the hell? "I'd like one more," she said. "It's been a long they . . . a long day, I mean."

"It's okay," her server said. "I've had a few long theys myself. I think I might be having one now."

She ate her salad and drank the wine, talked herself out of a fifth glass, asked for the check and left a large tip.

She walked along the waterfront as far as she could go and was rewarded with a view of Plum Island. After sitting down on a bench, she zipped up the fleece she'd had the presence of mind to come equipped with. The wind was brisk today, redolent of sea rot, a smell that she found appealing, along with nearly everything else that came from the ocean. Until she met Martin, she'd never even seen the Gulf of Mexico. She'd seen so many sights for the first time with him, and there was so much to be said for that.

She wondered how he'd respond if she told him she wanted the two of them to move here. Just pick up and start over a little farther north. Pretend today had not happened and see if they couldn't sink in to quiet domesticity. There was a lot to be said for that too. Just live a settled life with a best friend in a pretty town near the water. Four glasses of Sancerre assured her she could do it, that he could as well and might want to.

She pulled her phone out of her bag, and sure enough she'd missed two calls from him, the first about half an hour ago, the second two or three minutes later. He hadn't left a message either time. Maybe he'd pocket-dialed her. Or maybe, and this struck her as more likely, he'd tried to summon the right words but failed. She thought of calling him, but rejected the notion, realizing that her voice would probably sound thick and he'd correctly surmise she'd been drinking. They'd waited this long. They could have the conversation when she got back home.

She retraced her steps to the Market Square, went into Starbucks and bought a latte, which she carried the short distance to her car. Traffic was heavy on Route 1, and she briefly considered cutting over to I-95 but decided not to. If there was one commodity she always seemed to have too much of these days, it was time. She should have done more with herself. He'd once asked her to do harmony vocals on a folksinger's album, assuring her that her voice would meld perfectly with the artist's, that her timbre would provide a nice contrast with his gravelly baritone, but she'd declined, assuming he was just being kind. And maybe he was, but she still could have tried. She wasn't without talent. She'd gotten into Berklee on her own. They didn't give scholarships to people from tiny high schools in Mississippi because they felt sorry for them. She'd had something. She must have.

When she reached Cedar Park, it was a few minutes before three, and she got caught in a long line of cars near the high school. If she'd cut over to I-95 like she considered, she would have driven into town from the opposite direction and missed all the traffic. Had she done that, she almost certainly would have gotten home fifteen or twenty minutes sooner, maybe even twenty-five. Whether twenty-five minutes would have made a difference, no one could say. The consensus was probably not. Most likely she would still have been too late. The only person who could have made a difference was Martin himself. When he began to feel the warning signs, like shortness of breath or tightness in his chest, he should have called 911. Instead he called her.

A Really Nice Place

SHE SOLD MARTIN'S SHARE OF the record company to Pete, since she had no idea how to run it and suspected that if she did have, she'd immediately come into conflict with him, just as Martin so often did. She feared, too, that with his partner out of the picture, Pete might go back to hitting on her, and she didn't want to subject herself to that. She'd often suspected, without having been told as much by her late husband, that Pete's libido was one reason they had trouble holding onto their most successful female artists. She also suspected that absent Martin's influence, he'd destroy Yankee Southern in no time.

Pete and his wife and most of Martin's other old friends who'd become her friends probably thought she was doing as well as could be expected. She went to parties and dinner engagements when invited, and she seemed to be invited six or seven times a month. She still saw Liz for drinks and idle chitchat, though on several occasions she'd had to remind her that she did not want to be matched up with some guy. She regularly visited Tess in the extended living facility, even though Tess was in her own world and the facility was the most disheartening place she'd ever set foot in.

She also took in kittens for North Shore Feline Rescue until they could be permanently placed. Generally, she accepted an entire litter at a time. In a couple of instances, she had two litters simultaneously, with as many as thirteen kittens under her roof. She kept each litter in different rooms and spent a lot of time feeding and caring for her charges, cleaning up after them, holding and petting them. They loved it when she wore her fleece bathrobe, probably because the material reminded them of their mothers, and she sometimes sat for hours while two or three of them lay in her lap kneading the fabric. She cooed and sang to them and always felt a sense of loss when someone came along to adopt the last of a litter. But she resisted the urge to keep a couple herself, because she felt more useful serving as a surrogate mother to many. It kept her from going completely mad.

She'd never told anyone what happened at breakfast the day Martin died, not even her therapist. Sometimes she experienced her culpability so deeply that she felt as if her chest would split in two. That she'd behaved so callously toward him seemed unthinkable. And yet there it was: she had done something both inexcusable and inexplicable. And she had not done it just once. She'd done it many times, over many years, and it was always rooted in her own dissatisfaction with herself. When she tried to think of anything he'd ever done wrong beyond making the occasional cutting statement after she'd pushed him beyond his limits, she couldn't come up with a single misdeed. His fatal flaw was that he loved her too much.

On evenings when the guilt exceeded her capacity to withstand it, she knocked herself out with sleeping pills, booze or sometimes both. If anything, she felt even greater remorse upon waking, realizing that if she took one too many pills combined with one too many drinks, her daughters would have lost not one parent but two and would assume the second one left them of her own volition. She was going to have to keep drawing one breath after another until her body gave out.

She thought constantly of her sister's predication: *Someday trouble's gonna smack you right upside your pretty blonde head.* It had smacked her now, and it kept on smacking her, every hour of every day, as long as she remained awake, and when she fell asleep it smacked her some more. The second part of the prediction had come true too: she needed her sister. But her sister could not be found.

•

After Martin's death, every time one of Liz's relationships ended, she would badger Ella to take a trip with her. "Come on, baby," she'd say.

"Let's just go away and be *girls* for a few days." She'd never told Ella exactly how old she was, but she had to be nearing sixty. She didn't look it, though. And she certainly didn't act it.

Martin once observed that their friendship would not have been possible anywhere but Boston, and that was probably true. Back in the '80s, when the city was a lot more insular than now and considered Southern origins a pathological condition, it seemed natural to band together. But Liz had never read a book in her life, nor voted for a Democrat, and the main things on her mind most days seemed to be men and money. Once, a few years ago, she'd cheerfully told Ella about ordering ninety-five-dollar martinis at the Oak Room on an evening out with a financial type who worked with Mitt Romney at Bain Capital. "It took a whole team of guys to serve them," she said. "I drank three of 'em, but I didn't feel bad because he was chugging single malt at a hundred and fifty bucks a shot." She said the bar tab alone was more than 1300 dollars. She also said she made sure later that he considered his money well spent.

As different as they were, though, Liz had always been a loyal friend, kind to their daughters when they were growing up and eager to do anything she could for Ella and Martin. Every time they went on a trip, she collected their mail, watered their plants and kept an eye on things. Ella knew she was worried about her. Liz was probably the only one who hadn't been fooled by her efforts to show the world a bright face.

One November afternoon some eighteen months after Martin's funeral, she appeared at the kitchen door with her latest Black Lab, a clumsy but vivacious three-year old named Sadie. She rang the doorbell but Ella didn't answer. She couldn't. She was on the other side of the kitchen, in the black leather chair where she'd instigated the final argument of her marriage. She'd been there since morning. She'd only managed to sleep a couple of hours the previous night and had drunk three cups of black coffee, thinking they'd give her a lift, that she'd call Hayley and ask if they could have dinner together that evening. All the coffee accomplished was to make her nauseated, so she stepped into the half bath and threw up. Then she brushed her teeth, walked over to the refrigerator, pulled a bottle of Gray Goose from the freezer and poured a couple of ounces into a water glass. When she finished that drink, she had another slightly larger drink and then an even larger one after that.

Pressing her face to the window, Liz saw her sprawled out in the chair, her head lolled to one side, chin resting on her shoulder, her mouth open wide. On the floor beside the chair lay an empty bottle. Liz shrieked—she'd been fearing this—and it frightened Sadie so badly that she began to bark as only an agitated Lab can. While her owner fumbled through her backpack, searching for the house key that she'd had for years and begun to carry constantly the last few months, the dog threw herself at the window. Miraculously, given that she weighed around eighty-five pounds, the glass didn't shatter. But the noise roused Ella from her stupor. She didn't exactly sit up, but she did raise her head, and by the time she opened her eyes, Liz was already inside, moving toward her. The dog tore the leash from her hand, bounded across the floor, hurled herself at Ella and frantically licked her face.

"Jesus," she cried, as Liz pulled the dog off her, "what's going on?"

Liz whacked Sadie on her hindquarters and told her to shut up. Then she snatched up the empty bottle and brandished it at Ella. "What's going on is you were lying there blotto. Goddamn, girl, did you drink this whole thing?"

"It was only about a third full."

Liz stood the bottle on the kitchen island, then grabbed her by the hand and said, "Get up."

When she stood, nothing dramatic happened. The room didn't spin, her stomach didn't revolt. Her relationship to the objects in the kitchen remained unaltered. The refrigerator was right where it should be, as was the work island with the four black stools arrayed around it. The toaster stood on the counter to the left of the sink just as it had for years. But she experienced the strangest feeling that someone else had been here before Liz showed up, that they'd observed her as she drank herself senseless. "I feel like somebody's been watching me," she said, fully aware how bizarre the claim would sound.

"*I* was watching you. I saw you through the window."

"I don't mean you. I mean . . . I just have this odd feeling that somebody else was here. In this room."

"People always have an odd feeling after getting shit-faced. It's called a hangover. But if you mean Martin's ghost, baby, I guarantee you he wasn't happy to see you splayed out like a rag doll."

She led Ella into the living room and made her sit on the couch. Then she went back to the kitchen, brewed some mint tea and returned with the steaming mug. "Think you can keep this down?"

"Probably."

Liz seated herself in Martin's old armchair, and Sadie lay down beside her and promptly began to snore. The rescue had apparently worn her out.

"How often does this happen, Ella?"

"Not that often."

"I don't believe you."

"Maybe every few weeks. Look, I'm sorry. I know it gave you a scare."

"I've been thinking," Liz said, "of calling the girls."

"Oh, Jesus, Liz, how could you?"

"I couldn't. So far."

"Hayley works about sixty hours a week at the museum, and Lexa's up to her ears in tort law. God. I'd rather die than have you do that."

"Well, baby, you keep doing stuff like this, you'll get your wish. I'll be calling them to tell 'em their momma's gone to Glory."

For a while, neither of them said anything. Ella sipped her tea, Liz slipped off her sneakers and drew her feet up under her. "I want you to go with me somewhere," she said.

"I don't think I'm up to it."

"I don't care. I want you to do it anyway. I've always wanted to see Rome, but I don't want to see it on my own. You've been there before and would make the perfect guide."

She and Martin had taken the girls there in the summer of '92, renting an apartment near the Pantheon for ten days before moving on to Florence, Milan and Venice. Easily the most rewarding of all their foreign vacations. "Liz, really, I'm going to be fine. I just don't want to hop on a plane and fly to Italy right now."

"That's too bad, baby. You've got no idea what an insistent bitch I can be, and you have delivered yourself unto me. Either we go to Rome together, or I'll stage an intervention, call the girls and tell them how I found you. I snapped a photo of you with my phone, by the way. You were all pitched over and drooling. I made sure to get the empty bottle in the picture too."

"You didn't."

"Well, there's one way to find out, isn't there? Now, are you going to Rome with me or not?"

AFTER AN UNEVENTFUL FLIGHT, they landed at Fiumicino around dawn on a chilly December morning and took a taxi to the city. On the way in, Liz grew animated when she spotted the dome of St. Peter's. First it was on the right, then it was on the left, then it was on the right again. Ella suspected that their driver, a garrulous woman whose English was good enough to keep up a steady stream of banter with Liz, might not have chosen the most direct route. She didn't give a damn about that right now or much of anything else. She just wanted to go to bed. Unlike Liz, who snoozed most of the way across the Atlantic, she hadn't even dozed. And to think that Martin used to marvel at her ability to fall asleep anywhere, anytime.

Their room at the Grand Palatino Hotel was, of course, not ready when they got there. So they left their luggage at the desk and walked the streets for a while, her companion oohing and aahing at the sight of the Colosseum and the Forum. When they parked themselves at a café, Liz ordered a cappuccino and Ella asked for a Peroni.

"Beer at ten AM?" Liz said.

"It's a soporific."

"A sop of what?"

"It's a sedative. I plan to be asleep about ninety seconds after I get our room key."

"Not me. I don't want to waste a minute. I'm going to check out the Spanish Steps."

The waiter brought their orders. As soon as he departed, she said, "I thought the reason I had to accompany you was that you needed me to act as your guide."

"That was just a selling point. The reason I needed you with me is I wanted to go to Rome, and I was scared for you to be at home alone."

"I've been alone a lot in my life."

Liz stirred her cappuccino. "With all due respect? In your case 'being alone' meant one thing eighteen months ago. It means something else now."

She didn't bother to argue. What her friend said was true, and she was actually glad she'd made the trip. It was nice to be out on the streets among people speaking various languages, everybody taking their time rather than hurrying along with their heads down as they stared at their phones. Even though this was not tourist season, Rome was plenty busy, lots of color and motion.

They returned to the hotel around eleven to learn that their room had been ready for the past hour. They unpacked, and Liz stepped into the bathroom to freshen up and make herself look nice. When she came out, Ella had drawn the curtains and fallen asleep.

•

She woke around one PM, not knowing where she was. Then she sat up and remembered. Liz had not come back yet, and she smelled like an airplane cabin, an odor she'd always found particularly repulsive. So she showered and washed her hair, and by the time she dried it, it was 1:45. Still no Liz. She sent her a text, telling her she'd decided to go for a walk, then get a bite to eat. *Text me if you want to meet up.*

She'd always had a good sense of direction, so she set off toward the Pantheon. She was looking for the building where she and her family stayed in '92.

Without much trouble she found the right street: Via della Pigna. Narrow, not much more than a couple hundred meters long and paved with gray cobblestones. Hayley had objected that she didn't want to live on a street named for pigs. Martin laughed, then told her the Italian word pigna meant "pine cones." "That makes no sense," she said. "There are no pine cones on this street. It doesn't even have any trees." Lexa said, "Yeah, but it doesn't have any pigs either." Martin laughed and told her that the pigs might be inside, waiting for them in their apartment.

She located the building and looked up at the second-floor windows. They'd had some nice times up there. Each of them took turns reading the girls to sleep. Sometimes he told them stories about a magic bear named Bixby who worked for AT&T and traveled all over the globe spreading the gospel for American telecommunications. Bixby seemed to go wherever they went. The previous year they'd just missed him in London. The year before that, one of the desk clerks at the Grand Cayman resort where they were staying told the girls that Bixby had been there, too, that he'd left the previous evening after installing a new phone system. When Ella discreetly asked Martin how he'd come up with a magic bear named Bixby who worked for the phone company, he said he thought he'd dreamed the bear up one night when he was drunk. That seemed unlikely, though, because back then he didn't drink very much unless they went to visit Tess.

Such nice untroubled times. Darkened only occasionally, as when she thought about how her father died, or how her sister disappeared, or what happened in her instructor's apartment near the BSO. Lighter times than these. Times when travel seemed transcendent. Like you could leave the soiled parts of yourself behind.

She checked her phone. No reply from Liz. So she stopped at a café and had a glass of wine. Then she wandered the streets a bit longer, heading in the general direction of the Grand Palatino, thinking once or twice that she recognized a trattoria where the four of them had eaten way back when. Soon the smells of food made her realize that she hadn't had a meal since the flight attendants served her dinner. At least sixteen hours ago.

She found a restaurant a short distance from the hotel and went in. The bartender, a tall woman with a rugged face, snapped her fingers at a chubby waiter who wore black pants, a white shirt and black bowtie and somehow managed to look both harried and jovial. He led her down a narrow hall into the main dining room, where there was a single unoccupied table. After pulling a chair out for her, he asked her name.

"Ella," she said.

"Mrs. Ella, what I'm gonna do for you is I'm gonna get a wine list and a menu. You never been here before?"

"I've been to Rome. But not to this restaurant. At least I don't think I have."

"If you had, you'd remember it. If I'm lyin', I'm dyin.'"

She felt a smile forming. "Where'd you pick up that expression?"

"You like it, huh? Make the lady feel at home in Rome! So I tell you how I learned. One time, not so long ago, an American man and woman come in here, and every time I pass their table, that's what the man's saying to his wife. If I'm lyin', I'm dyin.' And his wife she don't say nothing back. But because I got what we call *sesto senso* . . . You know what that means?"

"Sixth sense?"

"You speak fine Italian. That's right. I got six senses, and the extra one tells me she don't believe a word what he's saying. So next time I'm going by their table, he says it one more time—If I'm lyin', I'm dyin'—and his wife she looks up at me and in a loud voice she says, 'Waiter, call the doctor! My husband he's very ill!'"

She laughed for the first time in months.

"You like that, huh? I like it too. Now, Mrs. Ella, I'm gonna bring you that wine list and that menu and you gonna tell me what you want to eat and drink."

She ordered the Bucatini Amatriciana and a glass of Pinot Nero. While waiting for her wine, she looked around the room. Mounted on each wall, at eye-level, was a wide ledge loaded with wine bottles three or four deep. The walls themselves were covered with graffiti. People had signed their names, written adages in different languages—she saw a couple of inscriptions in Cyrillic—and drawn all sorts of images, several of which looked like the work of real artists. Directly across from her, above a table where another woman sat by herself eating, was a framed, signed photo of the actor Robert DeNiro. She squinted, trying to see what he'd written besides his name, but from that distance she couldn't make it out.

The waiter returned with her wine and told her to enjoy it. He'd filled the glass to the rim. She'd promised herself she would sip it, but the promise didn't hold. As soon as he left her table, the sense of being in Rome again but without Martin and the girls all but overwhelmed her. She took her phone out, thinking she'd log on to the *Boston Globe* website and read the news, but she discovered she'd missed a text from Liz.

> *ran into this cool guy from racine wisconsin he invited me to dinner hell he invited me to wisconsin and baby im hanging for a while may not be back til late don't be mad you know ole lizzies got a honky tonk heart!!!!*

She had only herself to blame. Yes, she knew ole Lizzie, and ole Lizzie was reverting to form. How easy it must be for all the Lizs. She'd gotten dumped by more men than Ella could count, yet if she suffered when it happened, nobody saw the evidence. She'd be up and at 'em again the next evening. Go, girl, go.

The text led to several swift swallows, and when the waiter re-appeared she signaled for another. He wasted no time bringing it, and once again he'd poured a bucket of wine into that glass. *Sesto senso*. No doubt he could recognize a reasonably well-off lonely American woman when he saw one. He might even intuit that despite the wedding ring she still wore, she was now permanently by herself. Jettisoned or widowed. For his purposes, it would not make any difference. She'd laughed at his lines. She might or might not know that in Italy the tip was built into the cost of her meal, that almost no one who understood the customs of the country would leave more than ten percent. Or, better yet, she might know it but not care. Laughter and wine, such perfect anesthetics. Give the woman what she wants. Give her all she craves. She finished it and asked for yet another, and this time his face betrayed a trace of concern. Not for her, surely. The next glass contained a little bit less than the first two.

Such an old, old story, the disappearance of her wine, the gradual blurring of lines. The restaurant was beginning to empty out. When the waiter brought her food, he pretended to be in a rush, leaving before she could ask for another glass. She tried to feel affronted. She still had a swallow left, why should he assume she'd request more? Who did he think he was? Who did he think she was? A deprived woman trying to drown her sorrows when what she probably ought to do was wobble over to the Tiber and drown herself instead? Join the ancient dead?

Swallowing a mouthful of pasta, she saw that the woman at the table beneath the picture of DeNiro was still there, Bob smiling down upon her. Until now she'd just been part of the background, less noticeable than the striking graffiti. Her plate was gone, but a half-full glass still stood before her. It looked like urine but was probably chardonnay. How old she was would have been hard to say. Fifty? Fifty-five? She wore a black blouse, over that a black jacket. Leather, most likely, though polyurethane could not be ruled out. Shoulder-length hair so black it looked blue. Big eyes. Long black lashes. Dark complexion. Lots of lipstick. Her hands rested on the table. They looked older than her face. She didn't paint her nails.

She was staring at Ella. Her head cocked slightly. Something in her eyes. Sympathy? Familiarity? Sisterhood? She lifted her glass and took a swallow. Then set it back down. Ella did the same. Now hers was all gone.

She was the first to look away, turning toward the narrow passage that the waiter had led her through however long ago that was. He stood there, arms crossed, his affability having abandoned him.

Abandoned her.

Abandoned them.

She gestured for the check. He attempted a smile but failed, nodded and disappeared down the hallway. He'd get his nap before the dinner shift.

She allowed herself a glance at the other woman. Again their gazes met, again she looked away.

A moment later the waiter returned and handed over the check. She studied it until the numbers coalesced. She withdrew a fifty € bill and, when he reached into his pocket to make change, shook her head. He nodded and said, "*Gracia.*"

Best I can do, Mrs. Ella. So sad for you.

She needed to pee, but she rose and walked out.

Quarter till five, already dark. While she was inside, soft rain had begun to fall. She had no umbrella, but she didn't care. The cobblestoned street was narrow, the stones slick and glistening beneath the streetlamps. To get back to the hotel she'd have to walk downhill. She didn't care about that either. If she fell she fell.

She couldn't decide what to do, whether to return to the room or look for a bar. How long since she'd been to a bar by herself? She couldn't even remember. Pre-Martin, most likely. What she did instead of reaching a decision was stand there between a couple of parked cars, her back to the restaurant. Directly across the street was a small art gallery. Through the windows on either side of the door she could see paintings that rested on easels. Blobs of color. Beneath her ribcage on the right side, a dull pain made itself known. She thought perhaps she'd felt it once or twice before, maybe on the afternoon Liz found her passed-out in the kitchen. She didn't care about that either.

"I plain *do* not fucking care," she heard herself say, and in that moment it occurred to her that over the last few years she'd started to sound like her sister, or at least like her sister sounded thirty or thirty-five years ago, back when she was certifiably alive and getting in trouble.

Behind her a voice said, "What you don't fucking care about?"

She thought of the lockbox. What would have changed if she'd never opened it? Her father would still be dead. Folks would still think what they wanted to. Folks always have, and they always will, even the ancients did. If she hadn't opened it, she might have maintained her delusions a little more easily, but probably not. The rest of her life would still have happened, pretty much just as it did, and she'd know nearly everything she knew right now. And she still wouldn't know everything that she didn't.

She closed her eyes, caught a hint of fragrance, dropped her hand to her side, and felt another hand envelop it. Warm and alive.

•

The other woman drives fast, either by habit or because she does not want the wine to wear off. Her fear that it might, if she's entertained such fears, is not unreasonable. Ella's head is beginning to clear. It is not lost on her that she was drunk at the Sun 'n' Sand and drunk at the home of her instructor. For all she knows, a similar experience could be waiting for her at the woman's apartment, or something even worse. She doesn't think so, but there's no way to know. There's nothing between the two of them but the transmission hump and the gear shift and everything that has yet to be said. They don't even know each other's names. Across the Tiber they go, into Trastevere. The American University slides by on their right.

Her ex-husband, the woman finally volunteers, breaking a silence that has lasted a few moments too long, was a conductor. Not exactly Riccardo Muti but not bad. To him, Ennio Morricone was Ennio, Sergio Leone was Sergio. Does Ella know those names?

"Yes."

Both of them, the other woman tells her, grew up nearby: Ennio "over here," Sergio "over there." Does she know the American Frederic Rzewski?

"Not personally."

"He once lived in this street. My husband he didn't like him. Musica Elettronica Viva? Just noise, he said. Always he argued with his friend Severino Gazzelloni. How he could play with a pianist like Rzewski who make such sounds on purpose?"

"Does your ex-husband still conduct?"

She swerves to avoid a pothole. "He died." A glance at Ella. "Your husband too?"

"Yes."

"When?"

"Last year."

"How long you were married?"

"Twenty-five years. And you?"

"Thirteen. I was nineteen when I met him. He was almost forty. All his life he lived in Rome. I come from Piacenza. You know where that is?"

She and Martin and the girls stopped there for lunch in '92. With her meal, she ordered red wine, not knowing it would be the fizzy kind served cold. "In the north?"

The driver nods. "Between Bologna and Milan. A nice town, but he never thought so. For him it was too small."

"Do you have children?"

"No. You do, I think."

"What makes you say so?"

"*Sesto senso.*"

"Is that something every Italian is born with?"

The other woman laughs. "I heard the waiter. Two weeks ago, maybe three, he told another American woman the same story. He has four or five that he tells again and again. But I do think you have children. Why, I don't know." To Ella's horror, she briefly lets go of the wheel to wave both hands at the inexplicable nature of her perception. "Just a feeling."

"I have two."

"Boys or girls?"

"Girls. Both grown now."

"Like us. We are grown now too. We can do whatever we want. Ride a broom to the moon. Fall asleep on the street." A sideways glance. "Your girls don't watch you tonight. And nobody watches me ever."

They turn onto a smaller street. The cars suggest a certain affluence. She sees a couple of newish BMWs, a Mercedes, a Lexus.

"Home," the other woman says, pulling into a parking spot. She shuts off the engine, and they climb out, and Ella follows her into a building that looks old on the outside but new on the inside: lots of metallic surfaces, the floor, the ceiling, the elevator door. It makes an industrial impression. She can imagine bicycle parts being fabricated here. Lawnmower blades. Gardening tools.

In the lift, a Schindler according to the logo beneath the keypad, the woman punches the highest number. 6. From the street the building didn't seem that tall. The door closes, the elevator rises, but she barely feels its motion. In no time the door reopens.

They walk a short distance down a hallway too brightly lit for this moment in Rome. The other woman—that's how Ella continues to think of her, because as odd as it might seem, they *still* have not exchanged names—unlocks her flat.

The instant she turns the light on, the mystery of her identity is solved. On the wall, there's a framed page from *La Repubblica*. Sabato

26 Gennaio 1985. Ella can't decipher the entire headline, but she knows it's a review of Rossini's *La Donna Del Lago*, accompanied by a photo: the other woman decades younger, dressed in bridal white. Elena in the production, perhaps the greatest role ever written for a soprano and one of the most demanding. According to the caption beneath the photo, she's Brigida in real life. Brigida Terracina.

"That's you?" Ella says, though the answer is obvious.

"For one night. Who you used to be?"

"I never really found out."

The remark, which escaped before she could stop herself, is allowed to linger too long for her taste. So, as if this were her home rather than Brigida Terracina's, she turns and steps under an arch and into the next room, where she runs her palm over the wall until she feels a light switch. She flips it on and takes in her surroundings. Gleaming wood floor, no rugs. Hundreds of record albums in shelves along one wall, books along the opposite one, in a corner a large potted fig tree. Perpendicular to each other, two sofas, black leather. A glass-topped coffee table with copies of *L'Espresso* and *Il Manifesto*.

Brigida walks over to a sideboard, lifts a decanter and pours two large doses of amber liquid into the glasses that were conveniently waiting on either side of it. "Cognac," she says, handing her one. "What music do you like?"

"Most kinds. Play whatever you want to play. Or, actually, maybe ..."

"Yes?"

"A recording of yourself?"

"I was never recorded."

"I guess ..."

"Yes?"

"That seems unlikely." She points at the framed review, still visible through the arch. "I mean, if you were good enough ..."

Brigida laughs. "How nice that you don't read Italian."

"Why?"

"I was *doppie*. I don't know what is the English word. It means I was not supposed to be Elena that night."

"You were the understudy?"

"Yes. The understudy. The real Elena got too sick to sing. Bad fish poisoning. What *La Repubblica* says is that good enough is what I was not. It says I am terrible. A joke. They say the opera house should give everybody back their money. That my husband make the conductor hire me as understudy, it would never happen if he and Pollini were not such friends."

"Pollini? Not *Maurizio* Pollini?"

When she summons memories of tonight, which she will do many times, she will recall a deepening of the nearly invisible lines at the corners of Brigida's mouth. For the first time all evening, she has induced a measure of surprise, the intimation that perhaps things are not going to go the way they usually do when Brigida brings someone home from a restaurant or bar. They are working off a different script. Ella just became the co-author.

"You know Maurizio Pollini?" her host asks.

"Not personally."

This time they both laugh.

"Yes," Brigida says. "He was conductor."

"I only know him as a pianist. I didn't realize he was also a conductor."

"He was not a very good one. My ex-husband said so, he told him many times to his face, and I think this is why Maurizio stopped doing it so much and stick to piano. Best to know where you belong."

"Who was supposed to play Elena?"

"Katia Ricciarelli."

"Jesus. You were *her* understudy?"

"Up until that night. But never again. Never again was I anybody's understudy, and never did I step onto a stage."

"It ruined your career?"

Rather than answer, Brigida says, "You are opera buff."

"No. But a long time ago, I studied voice."

"Where you studied?"

"The Berklee College of Music. In Boston."

"My God." She takes a swallow of cognac.

Something has been puzzling Ella for the past couple of moments, and she decides to go ahead and pose a question, though intuition tells her it may not be welcomed. "If the review is that bad, why do you put it there? I mean, I think if it happened to me, I would never, ever have looked at it again. I probably would've burned it. I know I wouldn't mount it on the wall so everybody who walked into my house would see it."

Brigida stands her glass on the sideboard, crosses her arms, then stares at Ella like she did in the restaurant. It's a naked gaze, both defenseless and defiant. "On my wall I put it because I am not ashamed of worst moments. Most who see it *do* read Italian. Let them read all about it, how I make a terrible fool of myself. Let them think what they think. If they worry I might stain them, make them stink, let them turn and go. Everybody designs their own fate. Katia Ricciarelli. Maurizio. You. Me. Everybody."

"Has anyone ever turned and left after reading it?"

"Never."

"I didn't think so." She unbuttons her trench coat, shrugs it off and drops it on the closest sofa. Then she raises her right heel and, aware that her motions are attracting intense scrutiny, she pulls off that shoe, then follows with the other.

"My God," Brigida says again. "Look. Just look." She sticks out her foot.

At first Ella doesn't know what she's supposed to see there. Then she notices that the other woman is wearing the exact same shoes as those she just removed, a pair of black suede Acquatalias with pointed toes. Three hundred forty-nine dollars on Newbury Street. Here, maybe less. Or maybe not.

"What size you are?" Brigida asks.

"Eight. But American sizes are different."

Brigida kicks off her right shoe, then leans over, picks Ella's up and pulls it on. It fits perfectly. "See? I am you. You are me."

It's not quite that simple, Ella thinks as the other woman steps closer, gently brushes her hair aside and strokes her cheek before delicately kissing her lips. But it turns out not to be all that complicated either.

WAITING OUTSIDE AT DAWN, trying to waive a taxi down, she hugged herself and shivered. Before packing she should have checked the Rome weather. Who would have supposed that it could be so cold? Her trench coat was too thin. No scarf. No gloves. She'd be lucky if she caught a ride before she froze. She could have used some more of the cognac they drank last night. It might have provided a bit of the warmth she was missing.

Eventually, a taxi pulled to the curb. She climbed in and told the driver to take her to the Grand Palatino. When they got there, she hurried inside. A quarter past six. She'd had no text from Liz since the one that came the previous afternoon. Odds were she did not return. Ella hoped that would be the case. It would make everything a lot easier if her friend wasn't there, if she didn't have to give her the news face-to-face.

She took the elevator—again, to the sixth floor—and walked down the hall to their room. She unlocked the door and discovered she was right. No Liz. Her bed had not been slept in. Moving as fast as she could, she threw her clothes back into the suitcase, quickly brushed her teeth, gathered up all her cosmetics and packed them. She didn't bother to shower or even wash her face. She loved how she smelled. She wanted to carry that smell across the Atlantic. Carry it all the way to the green house on the hill in Cedar Park.

Downstairs, she gave the desk clerk a credit card and told him to remove the hold they'd placed on Liz's Visa and put the entire week on her own AmEx.

"You'll be leaving us early?" he asked, running the card through his machine.

"Yes. Family emergency. My friend will stay on."

"I am so sorry. I hope it all works out."

"Everything will be fine," she said, a line she could not imagine having spoken this time yesterday morning. Yesterday seemed light years away. Materially, almost nothing had changed. When she got back home, the house would still be empty. She'd still be alone until she took in another litter of abandoned kittens. Yet everything felt different. She asked the desk clerk to call her a taxi.

On the way back to Fumicino, she sent Liz a text. *I'm going home. I hope you have a fine time with the guy from Wisconsin. Make sure you see the Pantheon and the Sistine Chapel. And don't be mad at me, Liz. I don't know exactly why I'm glad I came here, but I am. I'm grateful to you for making me.* She turned off her phone then, leaned against the door post and closed her eyes, remembering how Brigida looked an hour ago, her long dark hair spread out against the white silk pillowcase. She slept with her hands pressed together, as if in prayer.

SHE KNEW EXACTLY HOW MUCH TIME had elapsed between the morning she erased everything she'd written on her novel and started over and the moment when she wrote the final line: 1,263 days. During that entire period, she'd only taken twenty-four days off. Nearly all of those were travel days when she entered or left the country to avoid trouble for failing to cross the border as her visa stipulated. She'd worked on it in Zagreb, Sligo, Tallinn and Madrid. She'd even worked on it in Casablanca. Most of it, though, she'd written at home, in the apartment she'd come to love. She knew exactly where she'd been when she wrote each word, though to her surprise she remembered next to nothing about the artistic choices she'd made, why she'd ended a particular chapter in a particular moment, or how she knew what a character would do or say. Some things just seemed to happen of their own will.

She usually worked for two or three hours at a time and wrote about five hundred words a day. Scenes came easily, so when she was working on one of those, she might hit 750 words, or occasionally even a thousand. When she needed to say what a room looked like, or describe a landscape, she might end up with only three hundred. One rule she made for herself, and adhered to every day, was not to quit until she had a full page, which sometimes necessitated stopping to count the lines. Another rule was not to stop working on any given day until she could find nothing in what she'd written that bothered her. She couldn't tell much, if anything, from reading on the screen, so she printed everything, even when she was traveling. She bought a lightweight portable printer for that purpose and always carried a few hundred sheets of paper with her. Sometimes she printed the same page fifteen or twenty times. If she changed so much as a mark of punctuation, she'd reprint and start reading aloud from the top, listening to the rhythms. Her method was ecologically unsound, but it worked for her. When she received her next advance—if she ever got another one—she'd send money to Greenpeace.

If any of those who had tried and failed to teach her something back at Loring Academy could have witnessed her working, they would be astounded at her meticulousness. Mrs. Batch—dead now for fourteen years, according to the obituary she found online in the *Weekly Times*—hadn't even been able to make her read Jane Austen. The only person who'd ever been able to make her do anything was she herself. She'd proven the sternest taskmaster of all.

Occasionally, usually late at night, after she climbed into bed, she allowed herself to imagine the novel's possible impact on others, specifically the members of her family. If her mother were still alive, Caroline felt all but certain, she would not have wasted her time on it even if her daughter had placed it in her hand. She only read sporadically, and when she did read it was almost always a romance novel, and if you happened to see her with the book in her lap, she'd have a condescending look on her face, as if in wonder that anybody, anywhere, at any time could possibly believe in the kind of romance that led to a happy ending rather than heartache. Her sister? Far too dark for her, with her storybook life and dollhouse on the hill. If anybody in the family had the capacity to become absorbed in her book, it would have been her father. He knew a thing or two about secrecy, not to mention loss. And he did like books.

Well, none of them would ever see it. Two of them were dead, and the other one probably thought Caroline was gone as well. She'd never know otherwise. Caroline didn't need to be hidden from husbands, daughters or friends. She'd gone to great lengths to hide herself.

She read through the entire novel three more times, changing a word here, a word there.

On the morning she finally decided it was as good as she knew how to make it, she addressed an email to Jared Entzminger in New York, attached the file—121,564 words—and wrote him a brief note. *Well, here it is. Let me know what you think, whether it's ready to show my editor or not. Needless to say, I'm eager to hear your response. And by the way, thanks for all you've done for me and for being both friend and agent.*

She moved the cursor to the "Send" button and clicked.

•

After she sent the file, she took a hasty shower, dried her hair, got dressed and called a taxi. It was warm out, a nice day, and she would normally have walked to work. But she was running a bit late for a meeting with Alastair. They were having problems with a teacher, an American named Robyn. She'd been with them for almost two years, was in her mid-twenties, tall, serious and a little awkward, but during her first few terms she'd been among their most popular and successful teachers. Unlike the majority of native English speakers the Institute hired, including Caroline herself, Robyn hadn't ended up in Poland for lack of better alternatives. She'd earned a history degree at Washington University, minoring in Slavics, and had then completed a year of graduate work at the University of Chicago. She was said to be on leave from her grad program to research Poland's right-wing Law and Justice Party.

Recently, things had taken a strange turn. One day a couple of weeks ago, in the midst of her Business English class, she excused herself to go to the bathroom but never came back. Then a few days later it happened again. The students in that class were all fond of her and agreed among themselves not to mention it to anyone in the front office unless it continued. But yesterday, one of them had requested a meeting with Alastair and informed him that the previous Sunday morning, he'd seen her passed out on a bench in the Saski Gardens. Concerned for her safety, he went over and shook her awake, and when she saw him, she burst into tears and begged him not to tell Alastair or Caroline. He said he was only reporting it because he was convinced something had gone terribly wrong. He told Alastair that she was slurring her words, though he hadn't smelled any alcohol on her or seen any bottles or cans nearby.

Caroline liked her and had once gone out for a drink with her, which she sat and nursed for an hour and a half. Despite attending ritzy schools, she said didn't come from money. Her parents ran a sandwich shop in Hooks, Texas. Caroline supposed they'd have to fire her now, and she feared the task would fall to her. She'd had to let several people go for various failings, and she always hated it.

When she knocked on Alastair's door, he told her to come in and close it behind her. He'd been in a brittle mood lately. In a couple of months Marek would be leaving to begin his university studies in Gdansk. And back before Easter, the flutist he'd been dating for so long informed him that she planned to marry the orchestra's principle oboist, whom she'd known for twenty years. He kept his door closed all the time now, whereas it had previously almost always been open.

"So," she said, "what are we going to do about our friend?"

He ran his palm over his cheek. "I forgot to shave this morning," he observed.

"I wouldn't have noticed," she said, "if you hadn't mentioned it."

"I'm not surprised. I've never had the impression that you were paying particularly close attention to my appearance. Or my mood. Or my whatever."

She didn't know how to respond. And he didn't intend to give her time to figure it out.

"Our *friend*," he said, "has resigned. I got her email half an hour ago."

"Did she say why?"

"For personal reasons. Probably just to keep us from firing her. Which I did in fact plan to do."

"You mean you planned to ask me to."

"No, I was actually going to do it this time myself. I'm just sick and tired of feckless behavior." He rocked back in his desk chair and locked his hands behind his head. It was the kind of executive posture she'd never once seen him resort to in all the years she'd known him. He never wanted to look like a man who owned and ran the most successful school of its type in Eastern Europe. The armpits of his light blue shirt were badly stained. He hadn't been taking good care of himself lately, a fact of which she'd been only subliminally aware. As she neared the end of her novel, she'd been doing much of her living in her head. "Did you *truly* believe," he said, "all that business about her doing a year of grad studies at U of Chicago? And then coming here to conduct scholarly research?"

"It never occurred to me not to. Why?"

He shook his head. Then he shook it again. Then he chuckled like people do when they think something is ridiculous, or outrageous, rather than funny. She believed she knew where this might be heading. She felt sick at the thought of it. It did not pose the existential threat it once would have, but she dreaded it more than she'd dreaded anything in years. Please, she thought. Please. Not that.

"You think she minored in Slavics?" he asked. "Did you ever hear her speaking Polish?"

"I'm sure I must have at some point. Why?"

"She didn't learn her Polish in a university classroom. She learned it from a phrasebook. You spoke better Polish than she does three days after you got here."

"Well, I'd worked in Slovakia and the Czech Republic. Those languages are not that different."

"Nobody ever said you learned *your* Polish in a university classroom. You know why? Because you never were *in* a university classroom."

No point in denying what he had obviously discovered. But she would, before leaving, at least correct a misperception. "You're wrong," she said. "I was in many a university classroom. Five or six nights a week for the better part of five years. I emptied trashcans, swept and mopped the floors, cleaned the blinds and lined the desks up straight. I also erased the blackboards—but not until after reading what was on them. It didn't matter what it was, whether it was a quote from Shakespeare, the conjugation of a German verb, a list of the main points of the Yalta Conference, or a succinct explanation of the Theory of Forms. I read it. And then one day I got transferred to the Registrar's office. And that's where I forged the transcript. When did you find out?"

He sat forward in his chair and laid his hands on his desk, then studied them as if amazed to find them still attached to his arms. He looked every bit as sickened and depressed by his revelation as she was. Maybe even more so. "Two or three months after I hired you," he said.

"Something didn't seem quite right, although you were great at the job, the best teacher I'd ever employed. So I just picked up the phone one day and called Fairleigh Dickinson University, spoke to someone in the Registrar's office, faxed them the transcript and got confirmation it was bogus. They'd never had a student with your name."

That he had sat on the information all this time, promoting her to associate director, giving her access to the school's finances, making her responsible for the day-to-day business of running the Institute, even sending her to meetings with the mayor of Warsaw—none of it made sense. She said so. "I mean, I don't understand. Why did you wait until now to fire me?"

"Fire you?" he said. Again he shook his head. "You think I'm going to *fire* you? I've been unable to sleep for the past month or two, knowing you're nearly through with that book of yours and that a lot more money and fame are probably headed your way. Every day I'm scared you're going to walk in here and tell me you're moving back to the States. 'So long, buddy. It's been cool to know you.'"

She reached across the desk and laid her hand on top of his. His skin was damp. "Then what is this about, Alastair? I was wrong to lie to you. I am so sorry. And whether you believe me or not, I've often wanted to tell you the truth. But if you knew it all this time and didn't act on it and don't intend to now . . . I'm sorry. I just don't get it."

"I know you don't," he said. "I sometimes wonder how somebody who's such a fabulous writer—and rest assured, Karo, I know you are, I've read all those stories fifteen or twenty times, I bet I know them better than you do—I sometimes wonder how you could be so clueless. It boggles my simple, inartistic mind."

Once again, she didn't know what to say. She liked and respected him too much to fling any verbal bromides his way. She'd always understood that his musician friend was his second choice, and she sensed the other woman knew it too. Her behavior toward Caroline was unduly effusive. She would have made a first-rate Southerner: sugary toward those whose presence she found insufferable.

She made a clumsy joke. "Oh," she said, "you didn't fire me because of my janitorial skills. You must have noticed that back when I was still just a teacher, I never left the classroom without picking up everybody's Styrofoam cups and Prince Polo wrappers."

"Go the comedic route if you want to. I'm in love with you," he said miserably.

The urge to pull her hand away from his was not easy to resist, but she did. She managed a feeble response. "I'm a little older than you are."

"You could be twenty years older. It wouldn't matter."

"There's something cold in me, Alastair."

"Where is it hidden? Please tell me."

"Maybe cold is the wrong word."

"You're a writer. You know all the right words."

"Okay, then. The right word is 'dead.' In me, something has died."

"I don't suppose you'd care to explain?"

She withdrew her hand so that she could lean against the back of her chair and rest her shoulders. These days, probably because she spent so much time at her desk, they ached around the clock. "I finished my novel," she said. "Just emailed it to my agent this morning."

Alastair being Alastair, he summoned a smile. "Congratulations, Karo. I can't wait to read it."

She made the kind of instantaneous decision that she used to make in her youth. Back then, it had almost always been the wrong decision, and for all she knew it might be the wrong one now. She reached into her purse, pulled out her iPhone and scrolled through her sent file until she found the message to Jared Entzminger. She clicked on the attachment, then emailed it to her boss.

Dropping the phone into her purse, she said, "You won't have to wait. It just hit your inbox. Want to take me to dinner this evening and help me celebrate?"

⋅

That afternoon, a Friday, Robyn had only one class, so Caroline taught it while Alastair went through the files of rejected job applicants who either lived in the city or someplace close by. At two-fifteen, when she dismissed the students, she learned that he'd already called two candidates, the first of whom was waiting in the main office. They interviewed them back to back, conferred just long enough to see they'd both reached the same conclusion, and then Caroline stepped into her office, called the first person and offered her the job, which she accepted immediately. By then it was after five. She returned to Alastair's, where she found him standing by his Bubble Jet printing her novel.

"Disaster averted," she said. "She'll be here Monday morning to fill out her paperwork and will be ready to start that afternoon. I emailed her Robyn's syllabi. It's a shame poor Robyn went to pieces. She knew what she was doing, whether she learned it at Washington University or Folsom Prison."

He abruptly looked up. "Prison?"

"Relax. I'm making a joke."

"Ah." He chuckled. "My detective work on your own background was pretty impressive, don't you think? I bet nobody else ever caught you, did they?"

"I don't really want to answer your question. It might spoil your pleasure in reading my book."

"Oh, so it's a . . . what's the term? *Roman à clef?*"

"Just read it. Where should we have dinner?"

They agreed not to go anyplace too posh, because neither of them was dressed for that and they didn't want to return home and change. He told her he knew a nice little Italian place across the Vistula in the Praga district. It was too far to walk, so they got in his car, a Peugeot convertible, and he put down the top.

Traffic was the heaviest she'd ever seen in the city. Due to the earlier crisis and the ensuing emotional turmoil, both of them had forgotten that the Euro Cup would get underway later that evening with a game between Poland and Greece at the new National Stadium, which unfortunately was also on the east bank of the river. As they crept across the Łazinkowski Bridge behind a pickup so loaded with drunken soccer hooligans that you could hear its axles' urgent protests, she asked if he'd been to the restaurant with the flutist, and he said that he had but only once.

"Sure it won't make you despondent?"

"No. It'll probably make me euphoric. My company tonight represents a major upgrade."

"Alastair . . ."

"I absorbed your message. I'm just stating a fact, not proposing marriage." He looked at her and grinned. "Not yet anyhow."

Even after more than a decade in Warsaw, she would never have been able to find the restaurant on her own. The entrance was tucked away in a courtyard formed by three soot-encrusted Nineteenth-Century apartment buildings that had probably been joined back in the Fifties. Praga was the most rundown sector of the city, where the Red Army halted during the '44 Uprising to watch while the Germans reduced everything across the river to rubble. These days, in the midst of urban renewal, it was considered the hippest place around.

Alastair said the dining room was air conditioned, so they decided to sit inside, mostly to avoid the sound of the Euro Cup broadcast, which seemed to be coming from every direction and was bouncing off the walls in the courtyard. Inside, a pianist sat at a blond Petrov playing jazz standards. Only a few other diners were present, so they had their choice of tables and picked one in a corner, as far from the piano as they could get. The waiter brought menus and a wine list, and neither of them wasted time ordering a drink. He asked for a double Macallan neat, and she requested a vodka martini.

When their drinks came, he said, "Cheers to your novel," and they clinked glasses. He took a sip, then said, "I imagine that's a load off your mind."

She'd forgotten to ask for a twist instead of an olive. Deciding to make the best of it, she pulled the olive off her swizzle stick and ate it whole. There had been no time for lunch. "Not exactly."

"No?"

"To begin with, I'll be nervous until I hear from my agent."

"I'm sure he'll love it."

"I'm not."

"Why?"

"He hasn't seen a word of it. I got the contract on the strength of the first book and a brief outline that turned out not to be the novel I wanted to write, though I'm hoping everybody likes it so much that they don't care. Also, my first editor got fired a year ago. The new one's about thirty years old, Harvard grad, probably a trust-fund baby. So who knows?" She lifted her martini and took a sip. "Two weeks from now, I may get it flung in my face. So I'm especially glad you're not planning to fire me."

The waiter returned to see if they'd decided what to eat. They agreed to split an order of tuna carpaccio. She chose black linguini with seafood, he took the crab ravioli, and they asked for a bottle of Barbera D'Alba.

After the young man left, Alastair said, "When I first came to Poland, if anybody had told me there'd ever be any place like this in the entire country, I wouldn't have believed it."

"When was that again?"

"May of 1990."

"I never wanted to pry, but what made you come here?"

He smiled. "You just weren't interested enough to ask. I couldn't think of anything better to do with myself."

Over the next few hours, as they shared their appetizer and seafood dishes, drained the bottle of wine and then each ordered a cognac, she learned more about his distant past than she had in all the years she'd worked for him. He told her he'd grown up on the Northumberland Strait, not much more than a rock's throw from the Abegweit Passage, across which the Confederation Bridge linking New Brunswick and Prince Edward Island had yet to be built. His mother operated a grocery on the ground floor of their rambling home in the village of Melrose. Throughout his and his brother and sister's childhoods, she clung to her belief that the non-existent bridge, known then on both sides of the Strait as "The Fixed Link," would eventually bring scores of tourists right past her crossroads shop, inevitably making it flourish. As it was, she sold a little gasoline to farm families, along with a few other essentials and the occasional postcard to people who'd driven up from what was still referred as "the Boston States"—in plainer terms, New England. Their father was an officer of Canadian Rail, managing the Gordon Yard in Moncton, the largest and most important in all the Maritime Provinces. His salary kept them fed.

Alastair told her he'd had no interest in railroads or commerce or, until he reached his teens, much of anything else. Sometimes he watched television, at other times he listened to American and British rock bands. Sometimes he just sat around and stared out the window at a landscape that for much of the year he found harsh and barren. But everything changed when he graduated from the local middle school and was sent to secondary school in Moncton. "Until then," he said, "I'd never had the chance to study languages."

"I thought there would have been French speakers up there."

"Not so many where we were. My dad could speak French quite well, his job required it, but he never did it at home, and my middle school was strictly Anglophone. In Moncton, they taught French and German. The German teacher also gave private lessons in Russian, and my folks agreed to pay for them in exchange for my helping out in the store. Her name was Mrs. Rozen. Pani Gosia."

"She was Polish?"

He nodded. "She and her husband left Warsaw during that big wave of anti-Semitism the Party revved up in '68. After I took Russian from her, she taught me a good bit of Polish. I got my linguistics degree at UNB Saint John, intending to go on to graduate school and see if I could become a professor somewhere. But my dad keeled over one day at work. My brother was already married and living in Toronto, my sister was working for Data General in Boston—"

"Boston, Massachusetts?"

He snorted. "Is there some other one?"

She swirled the last few drops of her cognac. "There's definitely one in the U.K. But go on."

"So it fell to me to return home and help my mom, who began to slide downhill herself after my father died. By then, the store was doing almost no business. But I stood there behind that bloody counter for the better part of six years, ringing up bread, milk and tea. There were days, I swear, when we didn't have a single customer. For eight or nine hours, I would not see a living soul."

She could tell that even now, all these years later, when he was thousands of miles away, on the far side of the Atlantic, with a thriving business, a son he adored and a list of more recent personal setbacks, the memory could still make his face sag. It was amazing, really, how easy it was to imagine yourself behind the counter of a rural store, or see yourself lying in the bottom bunk in a small, Sheetrock-sided farmhouse, fearing your father's heavy footsteps, the discovery of your latest transgression. Not an ally in sight. Personal history has the iciest set of hands. "How'd you fashion your escape?" she asked.

He shrugged. "Fall of '89, my mom died. We sold the house. I saw Pani Gosia on the street one day in Moncton as I was leaving the solicitor's office, so we started to chat and I bought her a cup of tea. She said for 'a boy' with my skills, Eastern Europe might turn into the land of opportunity. Everybody with any initiative would need to learn English. So here I am. And here you are."

The pianist had quit playing some time ago, the other tables were all clear now and for the last several minutes the waiter had been standing in the doorway to the kitchen. Alastair looked that way and signaled. She reached for her purse. "Don't be silly," he said. "The celebration's on me." He handed the waiter his credit card, and she asked if she could at least leave the tip. "Absolutely not," he said. "When you win the Nobel, you can take me to dinner. Or better yet? You can take me to Stockholm."

•

He braked in front of her building just before midnight. Perhaps because Poland and Greece had battled to a draw, deflating what Alastair said had been unwarranted expectations about the Polish team's prospects, traffic was thin. Up ahead, on the same side of the street as her building, she could see a couple of unoccupied parking spots. He could easily have pulled into one of them, which would have made it a lot harder not to invite him in for a nightcap. She knew he wanted the invitation and if only he'd played his cards differently, she would have felt obligated to issue it. She felt certain he understood that. No other man who'd ever fallen for her would have passed up the chance. She might be fifty-two, but guys still hit on her all the time, and many of them were ten or fifteen years younger. But, Alastair being Alastair, he would have considered that taking undue advantage. There were some things the Alastairs and Julios of the world, few though they might be, just didn't do.

"Thank you for a wonderful evening," she said. "Will you call me when you've read my novel?"

"Absolutely. Though I'm not exactly Northrup Frye."

"You know who Northrup Frye was?"

"Of course. After all, *I* went to college, where we had to take Introduction to Literary Criticism—and Professor Frye, you might or might not recall, was Canadian." He glanced in his rearview mirror, then back at her. "The more interesting question, at least to me, is how you found out about him."

"How do you think?" she said. "I saw his name scrawled on a chalkboard, went to the library and looked him up. Same way I learned nearly all but the hardest of lessons." She leaned over, kissed him on the cheek and told him good night.

WHEN SHE HEARD HER BUZZER the following morning, she wondered who in the name of all that was Holy, as well as all that was not, could be trying to wake her so early. Then she saw the green numbers on her bedside clock: ten-thirteen AM. It all came flooding back.

After saying goodbye, she'd stepped into the lobby, pulled her phone out and checked her email, sure that her agent would at the very least have confirmed receipt of her novel, perhaps telling her when she might expect him to read it and respond, but her inbox was empty. His lack of communication led to a surge of anxiety, which in the elevator she unsuccessfully did her best to dismiss. Once inside her flat, she went straight to her study and sat down before her laptop.

She checked to see if any major book fairs were in progress, thinking Jared might be attending one of those, though generally, if that was the case, she received an out-of-office reply saying he was away on business and only occasionally reading his email, so if you needed immediate assistance, etc. Nothing that looked important turned up. In previous years, he'd never gone on vacation in June, it was always in July or August. That he might be visiting his parents in Kansas could not be dismissed, nor could the possibility that his wife had just undergone an emergency appendectomy, or that he'd been attending his son's high school graduation. Neither could the possibility that he'd immediately started reading the novel, realized it was not the book he'd been expecting and also that it was dreadful, that she was just a short story writer, or just a liar, or just a loser.

To distract herself, she began to aimlessly surf the internet, letting one thing lead her to another, in one of those endless, useless searches that will eventually reduce the average attention span to zero. In *Gazeta Wyborcza*, she read a two-year-old review of the restaurant they'd just been to. The review mentioned that the owner was a distant relative of Roman Polanski. That tidbit led her to a *Guardian* review of a new documentary about Polanski, which concluded that in *The Pianist*, the auteur had revisited atrocities he witnessed in childhood, when his innocence was inviolate. Whereas in crafting "surely superior" films like *Chinatown* and *Rosemary's Baby*, he'd been willing to explore the recesses of his own dark, if not demented, consciousness. Thinking about a dark, demented consciousness made her re-read the twenty-seven-year-old *Washington Post* article about the armed robber in Roanoke whose name and history matched Tom's. That in turn led her to Google "Chevron stations in Barstow," for a view of the convenience store where he'd picked her up.

Having gone down that rabbit hole, she visited Google Earth and looked at Main Street in Loring, Mississippi, advancing the arrow until she reached the store where her mother had languished so long. It was empty now and boarded up. She Googled "Route 2, Box 79" and was treated to a photo of the house where she'd spent her first sixteen years, which was even uglier than she recalled, with an overflowing trashcan on its front porch. She went to Findagrave.com and looked at her mother's headstone in Pine Bluff, then her father's back in Loring. Then, for the first time in a great while, she Googled her sister. Up came a *Boston Globe* obituary for the record producer Martin Summers. He'd been dead for more than three years. The article listed among his survivors his wife Ella Summers, 50, of Cedar Park; his daughters Hayley Summers, 23, of Arlington, and Alexandra Summers, 21, of Santa Cruz, California.

She sat staring at the picture of her brother-in-law. The caption said it had been taken in his office at Yankee Southern Records in 1999. His desk was a mess. On a shelf behind his head stood several gilded Gramophone trophies. He was leaning back in his chair, his left hand raised in elaborate gesture, his right hand on his knee. He had red hair, a little lighter than hers and a lot thinner. Late forties in the photo, she would have guessed. The photographer had captured him in the midst of a laugh. He looked like such a nice guy. A guy who would have been nice to know.

Her phone lay no more than six inches from her hand. How hard could it be to pick it up and punch 001 781 665 1255? She'd remembered that number all these years, since the day in 1991 when she called information from Madison, New Jersey, and got the number and the address of the green house north of Boston, where Martin Summers, CPA, lived with her sister and her nieces, whose existence she wouldn't know of until she saw one of them observing her through the window. Who else remembers for more than twenty years a phone number they've never called? And why was calling it now not just hard but impossible?

She rose from her chair and looked around the room: at the books, the Bose, the daybed where she'd so often lain and listened to Ravel or Debussy when her back and shoulders began to ache. Above the bed hung a Wilhelm Sansal print, *Boy Without A Face*. Aside from that, there were no images on the walls of her innermost sanctum, the place where she did what defined her and gave her life whatever meaning it had. The only pictures she retained of her family were stored in her occipital lobe. If she ran into Ella tomorrow on the sidewalk in front of her building, would she recognize her? Probably not. For many years now her sister would have had money, and it seemed likely that she and her husband and daughters would have traveled to Europe, maybe more than once. Who could say, with any degree of certainty, that they'd never walked blindly past each other on a sidewalk in Berlin, or Dublin, or Rome or Barcelona?

Feeling sick, she turned off the computer, then went and made herself a cup of herbal tea and laced it with lemon and sugar. After drinking it, she went to bed, where she rolled around for several hours. She kept seeing her parents' headstones, then envisioning the cemetery where Ella would one day lie buried beside her husband. Was it her imagination, or had she passed that cemetery in the taxi on the way back to the airport in '91? She'd never thought too much about her own death. One day, she assumed, somebody would realize they hadn't seen her for a while, so they'd come and buzz and when the buzzing went unanswered long enough, one of the security guards, perhaps accompanied by a police officer, would unlock her door.

Hearing the buzzer again, knowing it was not a dream, she swung her legs out of bed, swayed but somehow made it to the house phone and grabbed the receiver. "*Kto jest?*"

"It's me," Alastair said. "Can I come in? I haven't slept at all. I read your whole book."

In the hallway mirror, she assessed the damage: bloodshot eyes, tangled hair, lines on her face that hadn't been there last night. Her breath probably smelled like rotting grapes. "I'm a mess."

"Yeah, well, I am too. Can I please come in?"

She punched the button and held it down until she heard the lobby door close behind him. Then she stepped into the bathroom, smeared some Crest on her toothbrush and gave her mouth a quick cleaning. He could make whatever he would of the rest. Seeing her on a morning like this might be just the cold blast of reality he needed.

She hurried to the kitchen and pulled a can of Pilsner Urquell from the fridge, then went to the front door and unlocked it just as he was about to knock. His appearance made her feel marginally better about her own. He was wearing a blue tee shirt that must have been washed with something red and a pair of gray running shorts with a coffee stain on one thigh shaped like the state of Ohio. He still hadn't shaved. Whitish stubble covered his chin. Sweating badly, he stank of beer.

She offered him the Pilsner. "Want one of these?"

"No. I ran all the way from my place trying to sweat out the ones I consumed between about two AM and dawn."

"Well, it looks and smells like you succeeded. I need one. Historically, beer settles my nerves."

She walked over and sat down on her couch. The sun streaming through the window nearly blinded her, though, so she got up and moved to an armchair. Until he slipped the straps off his shoulders, she hadn't realized he'd worn a backpack.

He unzipped it and lifted out her manuscript, which he'd secured with a rubber band. To her surprise, he'd attached a bunch of yellow sticky notes to it. He dropped into the adjacent armchair and removed the rubber band.

"What in the world are you doing?" she asked.

He started to flip the pages. "There's some stuff I'd like to ask you about."

"Alastair!"

Startled, he looked up.

"Were you of the opinion that I wanted you to critique it?"

"Of course not."

"Then what are those sticky notes for?"

His lips, she realized, were trembling. He was about to cry. "Some of this . . . it happened to you, didn't it? I think maybe a lot of it did. You're Marilyn. The younger sister. I didn't even know you had a sister. There's so much about you I didn't know. You never told me."

"You never asked."

"I was afraid that if I did, you'd disappear." He looked down at the heap of pages he held with unsteady hands. Then back at her. "And now I know I was right. I can't believe you've stayed this long."

"It's my home."

"You really feel that way?"

She took a swallow of beer. God, it tasted good. "The only place I ever lived longer than Warsaw was my hometown. Or actually, not in the town itself. But three or four miles to the north."

"Was the house surrounded by cotton fields?"

"Yes."

"And your father. Did he . . ."

"Yes. But here's the thing. You can keep asking me was this real and was that real, and I can say yes or I can say no. But it's been no time since you were telling me that for years you've known I invented my own history. So why would you believe my answers now, when you already have proof that I lie?"

"Maybe because the novel feels more truthful and more revealing than anything you've ever said to me."

She could see he wished he could take it back, his face tense as he sought some way out. The thing was, his response moved her. She knew she was a liar, she'd always known she was a liar. But what are you supposed to do if conventional truth keeps leaving you in the lurch?

What she'd written *was* honest, whether it happened or not.

She took another long sip of beer, elixir of lost mornings. Then she made her second radical decision in the last twenty-four hours. "I got almost no sleep," she said. "I'm going back to bed. Want to join me?" She rose, hoping that for once, if only once, Alastair would not be Alastair.

He refused to meet her gaze. Instead, he thumbed through a few more pages of her manuscript, as if the proper response might be found on a sticky note. Finally, he looked up, his eyes filled with doubt and wonder. "I would love that, Karo. But I'm so sweaty."

"Just give yourself a quick sponge bath," she said.

THE NEXT TIME SHE WOKE, Paul McCartney was singing "Hey, Jude." She'd forgotten to silence her ringtone. She gently moved Alastair's arm and reached to decline the call, then saw the name on the screen. *Jared Entzminger*. She grabbed it, got up and ran for the door.

"Hey," she whispered before it could go to voicemail. "Hang on a second." She would have walked onto the balcony but she was naked. So she stepped into the bathroom, closed the door and locked it. Then she lowered the seat cover and sat down on the toilet. "Okay," she said. "Sorry."

"Am I calling at a bad time?"

She wondered what time it was. Probably late afternoon here, since it wasn't dark out. Morning there. "No," she said, "not at all."

"I'm sorry I didn't get back to you yesterday," he said.

Her heart was pounding. His tone did not sound promising. He'd never had to give her bad news, but this was what she'd imagined he would sound like when the day finally came, as she'd figured it eventually would. Pumpkin time, she guessed.

"The thing is, we were trying to wrap up some business, so I didn't get a chance to email you before leaving the office. And then on the train, I started reading your novel."

For some reason the phone was in her left hand. She normally held it in the other one. She was scared to attempt a transfer, almost certain she would drop it. It's just a book, she told herself. But it just wasn't. The sun didn't make her rise each day. The writing did. This morning's pleasure notwithstanding, the rest was just something to get through.

"It's not the book I expected," he said.

"I know, Jared. I should have alerted you. I'm sorry. It's just that once I got into it, I didn't want to give it up. I was scared you'd tell me to quit."

"Oh, rest assured, I don't give the slightest damn about your reasoning. And neither, I suspect, will your publisher. My wife and I are up in Rhinebeck for the weekend. I read for most of the night and just finished a little while ago. I can't talk long because she's definitively pissed at me, and we're meeting some friends for lunch. You and I'll have another conversation next week. But the bottom line is that while I hoped and believed it would be good, you never really know, especially when somebody's moving to the longer form. A lot of the time, frankly, I end up feeling like the two-book deal, which it's my job to seek, did my client a disservice. Once in a blue moon, though, everything works out perfectly. It's a great book, Karo. Congratulations. I don't think I've ever been happier for one of my writers. In fact, I know I haven't. And I'm really happy with myself for having had the good sense to recognize a special voice when I encountered it."

It was fortunate that her right hand remained free, since it had always been the stronger of the two. She braced her elbow against her bare knee, pressed her face into her palm and did her best to muffle a string of hiccup-like sobs.

He went on to say that he was thoroughly engrossed in the lives of the two main characters but wasn't completely satisfied by the resolution, which didn't bring them back together. He could be wrong about that, though, so he'd let her hash it out with her new editor, who, he told her, might be young but was scary smart and would fight for her book like a honey badger.

"Now I do have one thing to ask you," he said. "You don't have to give me an answer today, but I'll want one before sending it on over to the publisher. Karo, are you one hundred percent certain you want to describe what happens at that country store with exactly the setting and details you've used?"

"Yes," she said, "I'm one hundred percent certain."

"In that case, all systems are go. We'll send it over Monday, and I'll give a holler when I hear back."

"I appreciate that," she said. "You're still the best."

"As are you, Karo."

When she returned to the bedroom, Alastair was still asleep, his head now on her pillow instead of his own.

THE FOLLOWING FEW MONTHS WERE for her nothing less than sublime, a time she figured she could always return to as long as her mind remained strong enough to protect fond memories. To begin with, she enjoyed Alastair's company. She was not in love with him, and he knew it, but he must've decided he didn't care. They had dinner together four or five nights a week, mostly at restaurants until Marek left for the university. After that, they sometimes cooked and ate and slept at his place, other times at hers. Right before she began to feel crowded, he seemed to sense it and then would leave her alone for a few days, after which they'd go right back to sharing their evenings. She had not felt lonely during all her years by herself, and she knew that being solitary and steering clear of involvements had made it easier to get the writing done. But now that it was done, she thought, she might well have felt adrift but for him. Writing had begun to seem less urgent the moment she placed a period at the end of the final chapter. Maybe one day she'd have other stories to tell. Or maybe not.

Everything was progressing nicely leading up to the publication of her novel. Jane Lindell, her new editor, did not waste a moment letting her know she was thrilled with her manuscript, emailing her only a couple of days after receiving it. *I loved your stories*, she wrote in the first of several hundred messages, *and scene by scene this novel retains their intimacy. Yet its overall structure, as it moves from the South to the West Coast, to the East Coast, to Europe and back, is epic. I understand Jared had some reservations about the ending, but I don't. Yes, it defies expectations, but*

I didn't want everything to be neatly wrapped up. I don't think I would have believed it if you did that. She said she couldn't wait to begin editing the book.

The last remark gave Caroline pause. Her previous editor hadn't done any editing. She'd bought the collection on the strength of six stories and brief outlines of the rest, and when the whole thing was completed, she sent an email saying she loved it, and then a few months later Caroline received the copyedited manuscript from someone she'd never dealt with before. She stetted nearly all of the proposed changes and never heard a peep from either the copyeditor or anyone else there except her publicist.

When she received the edited manuscript from Jane and saw all the green ink, she poured herself a double Cardhu and sat down to look through it. Virtually every suggestion made immediate sense. For instance, she'd used the word "way" too often: "the way she did this, the way she did that." *You can vary between "how" and "way" and avoid fifty percent of the problem,* Jane wrote on the front page. *Or you can just save two words each time and say "she did this, she did that."* She pointed out that possibly because, in her youth, Caroline had sat through many a Southern sermon, she occasionally resorted to anaphora. *And that's well and good. But you also sometimes haphazardly deploy the same verb in three or four successive sentences, most likely from an otherwise laudable suspicion of ornamentation. The problem is that incidental repetition just undercuts those passages in which you resort to repetition for rhetorical effect. You can't have it both ways. Furthermore, you sometimes unnecessarily use the word "just" like I just did two sentences ago and am doing again just now.*

Working no more than three or four hours a day, she took six weeks to respond to the edit. Only rarely had Jane questioned anything other than sentence structure, word choice or choreography. They spoke almost daily. Her editor was twenty-two years her junior. If all you did was listen to her intonation, supplying the precious gestures that seemed appropriate, you might've thought you were hearing a spunky seventeen-year-old. But when you got past vocal mannerisms and listened to what she was saying, you understood that she was, as Jared claimed, scary smart, her reading both broad and deep. Once, when they were discussing a scene set on the Alexanderplatz, she was reminded of an Alfred Döblin passage and proceeded to quote a good of it from memory in German. Another time, a scene that took place in a pickup truck near where the two main characters grew up reminded her of *The Last Picture Show*, so she said "Hold on a sec," called the book up on her Kindle, then whistled. "Good catch if I do say so myself. McMurtry wrote exactly the same line of dialogue describing an encounter between Sonny and poor, unlovely Charlene Duggs. I know you didn't crib on purpose, the best writers never do. But a change, I'd say, is in order."

Every one of their conversations moved on from the edited manuscript to writers they admired: Turgenev, Woolf and Fontane. Gallant, Sontag, Kundera. It made sense that Jane would have read them. She'd majored in English at Harvard. It made little or no sense that Caroline would have, and despite their always skirting the subject of her background, she believed that her editor understood she was self-educated, respected her for it and was intrigued by it. Once or twice, she came very close to saying, "Listen, here's who I am and where I come from." But something finally happened that made her glad she hadn't done that.

Late one Friday afternoon, after a spirited debate over the serial comma, Jane said she'd better get going soon, as her father was coming to visit and was due shortly at LaGuardia.

"Where does your dad live?"

"Arcata, California. I was born out there, but he and my mom split up when I was two, and she brought me back to Yonkers where she grew up. I told my dad about your novel and actually sent him your manuscript, which he loved. He said he vaguely recalled a shooting similar to the one you describe in your book, that it got coverage in the Bay Area and LA papers. I imagine that's where you found out about it."

She'd been reclining on her living room sofa, waiting for Alastair to come collect her. They'd planned a weekend up in the Mazurian Lake District, where autumn would be at peak foliage. "Yes," she said slowly. "I read about that murder in the *Oakland Tribune*."

Jane laughed. "Your memory is *amazing*. I take it you were living out there then? You must've been."

Of course, she must have been. Where else, in 1978, long before virtually every paper in the country went digital, could she have come across an article in that particular publication? And what could she do now except present her editor with a heavily edited version of the truth? She wished to God she hadn't become so chatty, so comfortable, so trusting of someone she'd never met. She should have set that sequence somewhere else, anywhere else, like Jared wanted. She'd told him she had a reason for writing it like she did, and that was true, but now another kind of truth was hovering nearby.

Jane saved her. "Don't tell your beastly agent I pried. I just offered on another of his books, and he's a veritable highway robber. Anyhow, gotta go now, my dad can be impatient. Talk to you next week!"

Sweat was oozing from every pore. When she settled down, she phoned to see how much longer before Alastair would be there. At least another half-hour, he said. So she stepped into the shower and ran cold water all over her body, trying to wash away the sudden stench.

ON A SUNNY MONDAY MORNING, more than four years since she came home from Newburyport on the heels of their horrible argument and found Martin dead on the kitchen floor, Ella stood in that same kitchen, stroking the homeless cat she'd finally kept for herself and waiting for her taxi. Liz, who knew what was going on, would gladly have driven her into Boston and would just as gladly have waited until she finished her appointment. But Ella declined the offer. She didn't want her old friend's company. Hayley, who didn't know what was happening, could have driven her too, but she didn't want her company either. She preferred to be alone when she got the news, whatever it might be.

Cedar Park had two taxi firms, bitter rivals. One was operated by a sister-and-brother team, long-time residents of the town and former high school classmates of Martin. Both of them were nice enough people, but they were also rabid Pats' fans. Since their team had lost the conference championship the previous day to one of the Manning brothers, throwing much of New England into mourning, she knew that if she booked a ride with them, she'd have to listen to her driver bemoaning the result, analyzing costly mishaps and accusing the officials of perfidy. So she called the other outfit, which belonged to an Iranian named Gazhi. Generally, she avoided him. Contrary to the stereotype, he was staunchly, even virulently pro-American, which in his view meant pro-GOP. For once, listening to him trash the opposing party seemed the lesser evil.

She needn't have worried. On the way in, he said very little, apparently having learned from previous encounters that the two of them held opposing views on nearly everything except the exquisite properties of red saffron and golden turmeric. In the event, though, his silence left her too much time to think, and what she thought about was how, Liz's loyalty notwithstanding, she had almost no one to talk to except her cat.

After Rome, locating Brigida Terracina proved surprisingly easy. What she'd said, as they lay together in bed while Billie Holiday wistfully predicted that she'd be seeing someone in each familiar place that this heart of hers embraced, turned out to be true: she said Ella could always find her if she wanted to. The thing was that she didn't want to until many months went by, and then it was too late. Brigida, it turned out, worked in the entertainment division at Al Italia, most likely choosing the music that passengers listened to on their earbuds. The first email Ella sent went unanswered. So did the second and the third and the last. Why wouldn't they? She'd slipped out beneath the cover of darkness without even saying goodbye.

True, her daughters regularly checked in, Hayley more frequently than Lexa, but both were busy. Lives richer than hers, she hoped, lay ahead of them, and she did not want to burden them with her own concerns. Hayley was seeing another assistant curator at the MFA, a young man whom Ella had met and liked. Lexa kept her activities private, but on the phone she nearly always sounded happy. Her therapist had closed her practice, sold her brownstone and moved to Florida. Tess had passed away the previous winter. Ella hadn't been able to find a New Orleans home phone number for Kimberly Faye Moss, née Taggart, nor her husband Brad, though she did turn up a listing for Bradley J. Moss in the Orleans Parish Public Defender's office. She never called. Why would she? Nobody wanted to hear from her. Why should they?

When Gazhi stopped to drop her off at MGH, he glanced into his review mirror. Evidently, she looked as bad as she felt, if not even worse. "Mrs. Summers," he said, "I hope you are soon well."

"Thank you, Gazhi. That's very kind of you." The fifty percent tip she gave him fell woefully short of expressing her gratitude.

•

The news, such as it was, did not constitute a surprise. Cancer of the Liver, stage IV-A. It had colonized her lymph nodes but so far failed to establish a beachhead in her bones or her lungs. Without treatment, on average, she might last two or three years. With treatment she stood a "50 percent plus" chance of living as many as five. She started to ask what the "plus" really meant. Another three percent, another four? What stopped her was her sense of shame. A death sentence, no matter how far off the execution might be, was always embarrassing. Someone, most likely a medical professional, would be standing by watching as she tried and failed to draw another breath.

She scheduled an appointment for the following afternoon to discuss her options, then left the hospital. Outside, she sucked in crisp, refreshing air, the pain beneath her rib cage no better or worse than it had been for several months. She pulled her phone out to call a taxi, then thought better of it and started walking toward the Charles-MGH Transit Station.

She hadn't ridden the Red Line for years. But she found the same old mix of Harvard and MIT students and professors, nurses and lab techs from MGH who'd worked a long shift and were riding to Alewife to drive home or catch a bus, street people looking for a warm place to take a nap. Except for slightly different clothes and the fact that nearly everybody who was awake kept staring down at electronic toys, it could have been 1984. And she was every bit as lost now as back then.

She thought maybe she'd catch a film at Kendall Square Cinema, but when the train reached the Kendall-MIT stop, inertia overcame her and she remained seated. She started to get off at Central Square, too, thinking she'd see if the Italian place across Mass Ave from the Boots 'n Flannel was still there and, if it was, maybe she'd go in and have a glass of wine at the table where she and Martin conducted their first real conversation. But again, she couldn't seem to force herself to rise. Once more the doors opened and closed.

Why get off at Harvard Square? She couldn't even say when she'd last been there. Yet that was what she did, riding the escalator up in a daze, then emerging to confront the green newsstand with papers and magazines from all over the globe. She'd never learned to speak or read a foreign language. She probably couldn't even read music anymore and hadn't tried to sing for anyone other than a kitten in years. Who would have predicted this result back in Loring, Mississippi, for a Boston-bound scholarship girl? She'd wasted so much of her life. She wandered past establishments she'd either never noticed before or didn't remember: the Beat Brew Hall, the Hourly Oyster House, Parsnip, the Maharaja. J. P. Licks, coffee and ice cream. At least she knew the last of those, she and Liz used to go to the original shop in Jamaica Plain for dessert back in the mid '80s.

She crossed Plympton Street. Up ahead, on the right, stood the Harvard Book Store.

One of the many things that had changed in recent years was that she almost never finished a book, and she'd given up altogether on fiction. If a novel was any good, it depressed her. If it was not good, she lost interest. She preferred biographies, nearly all of them about musicians or composers, but most of those she didn't finish. She'd read a hundred pages, put the book aside, pick up another, and the cycle would be repeated. The only one she'd completed in the last couple of years was about Leonard Bernstein, and she wished she'd laid it down. His life ended in an alcoholic haze, the most famous conductor in the world devoured by triple tensions between who he wanted to be, who the public wanted him to be, and who he actually was, the last of which he never seemed to understand any better than she did.

She didn't intend to enter the bookstore. Instead, she'd decided to walk on down the block and have a drink at the Grafton Street Pub and Grill, where Martin and Pete used to throw dinners when one of their artists came to town. She'd always enjoyed those evenings. She knew the place was still in business, because Hayley said several friends from Tufts had thrown a Christmas bash there. She knew, too, that she was not supposed to drink now, period, that alcohol could accelerate metastasis and impede whatever method of treatment they elected. She promised herself this glass of wine would be the last, though she thought maybe she'd request an eight-ounce pour if they offered those.

Passing the bookstore, she glanced into the window, where staff members' recommendations were displayed. One of them stopped her.

STAY GONE DAYS
a novel
Karo Kohl

On the cover, against a powder-blue background, at nine, twelve, three and six o'clock, four different images appeared, all of them fading at the edges as if shot in soft-focus. A ragged farmhouse with cotton growing right up to the porch; something that looked like a country grocery at night, a single pickup parked near a pole lamp, on its tailgate a California license plate; a brightly-lit Greyhound Bus Station, snow piled knee-high and more coming down; a huge green Victorian, lots of turrets and a bay window at which you could see the face of a little girl with blonde bangs.

Beside the hardcover, propped against a book stand, a handwritten note:

Recommended by Jen
While the Washington Post calls Stay Gone Days "the first European Southern novel," this strikingly original work defies categorization. Part murder story, part love story, it is a heartbreaking tale of estranged sisters, spanning two continents and building on the accolades Kohl earned for her collection The Propane Man.
One of the best books of the year

Karo Kohl. Caro Cole.

Her right hand shot toward the window glass, smacking it so hard that inside the store several people turned their heads, as if in fear that the venerable bookshop had come under attack. Swaying, she faltered.

At that moment a young Harvard instructor was emerging with a new paperback copy of Said's *Culture and Imperialism* tucked beneath one arm. He kept loaning his personal copies to undergrads, and they kept neglecting to return them. He liked to think the books meant so much to the students that they couldn't bear to surrender them, though it was also possible that they never opened them, or cared to, and just walked off and left them at Starbucks the same day they got them. "Are you all right?" he asked, steadying her.

She looked up into the bearded face of a man half her age, one that radiated concern for those less fortunate, a group in which she knew she had just secured lifetime membership, truncated though it promised to be. "Yes," she said, "I'm sorry. I've been a little under the weather."

"Can I do anything for you?"

"No, you've already done plenty. I would've fallen. Thank you so much. I'm Ella, by the way."

His kindness never wavered, even when confronted with what he must have recognized as a need beyond name. "I'm Andrew," he said.

"Are you a professor?"

"Yes. I'm afraid I have a class to teach in a few minutes. But first, may I help you inside?"

"No," she said, "but thank you. Thank you so much, Andrew. I really appreciate it. I'll be fine."

She waited until he'd walked away, then entered the store, pulled a copy off the "Recommended" rack and carried it toward the fiction shelves at the rear of the store, where there used to be a couple of short-legged stools. The pain in her side had been superseded by a sensation even more acute, comprised of anticipation, hope and dread. She opened the book and looked at the inside back flap. It was impossible to say if she was happy or sad to find no author photo there, just a brief bio saying that Karo Kohl was an American who'd lived in Poland for many years, that she'd also written the story collection mentioned on the note in the display window, and that her work had appeared in several foreign countries. Ella turned to the front of the book, recalling that in some instances the Library of Congress Catalogue data listed the year of the author's birth, but in this case no such information was forthcoming.

She flipped to the first page and started reading. By the top of page three, she could no longer maintain a shred of doubt. The book—which was not a small one—slipped from her hand and hit the floor hard. She leaned against the closest shelf, closed her eyes and rested her head there. In her throat and ears, her pulse pounded. She'd lived fifty-five years yet had never once felt more alone. Not the morning at the Sun 'n' Sand when the woman from housekeeping found her naked in the broom closet, nor the morning after she visited her voice instructor at his home, or when she had trouble getting out of bed in her basement studio on Marlborough, or when Martin was laid to rest. On the far side of the Atlantic, her sister was alive and presumably well. But to her sister, she was dead. She'd been dead a long time.

"Ma'am?" someone said.

A man about the same age as Andrew was hovering over her, beside him a young woman. Store employees, she guessed. Maybe he was the manager. At the end of the aisle, a couple of patrons were watching, but both looked away when her eyes and theirs met. "I'm sorry," she said. "I just found out I'm pretty sick." She reached down and picked the book up. "And also, I discovered this novel was written by my sister. Who I have not heard from for twenty-nine years. Twenty-nine plus."

The young man and the young woman exchanged swift glances. "Would you like us to call you a taxi or maybe the EMTs?" the guy asked.

"No," she said, rising. She wrapped her arms around the book. "It says she wrote another one too. A collection of short stories. *The Propane Man*. Do you know if you've got it?"

"I believe so," he said, with palpable relief that she would not make more of a scene. "Just follow me."

He led her down the aisle and around the corner to the K's and pulled a small paperback off the shelf. She saw there were quotes on the back from the *New York Times*, the *New Yorker*, the *San Francisco Chronicle* and something called *Salon.com*. "I hear your sister's a fine writer," he said. "I haven't read her yet, but a couple of my colleagues really love her novel and are hoping it wins some of the big awards. Can I do anything else for you?"

"No," she said. "Thank you for helping me."

Outside, both books in a plastic bag, she wondered where to go, what to do. The most reasonable choice, returning home, then calling Liz and both of her daughters and telling them of her twin discoveries—that she was seriously ill but that her sister was alive and with any luck could be found—did not appeal to her. She started back toward the subway entrance, thinking that maybe she'd take the Red Line across the river and check into a hotel near MGH, since she'd scheduled the follow-up for the next day. She decided against that, though: she didn't want to sleep so close to the very hospital where there was a fair chance she would die. So she just kept going, past the Unitarian Universalist Church, the Old Burying Ground, Cambridge Common.

She checked into the Sheraton Commander, drawing a strange look from the desk clerk when he realized she had no luggage. After leaving the books on her bed, she took the elevator back down to the bar, where she drank two glasses of white wine and forced herself to eat part of a club sandwich. She ordered one more glass to carry with her. Thus fortified, she returned to her room.

At the bookstore she'd sensed that reading the book might exact a certain toll on her, that it could be like opening her father's lockbox. She understood, because of the image on the cover, that at some point her sister had either gazed at the house where she'd been living for the past twenty-nine years, or had at least gone to the trouble to obtain her address and take a look at the house on Google Earth. Which meant that she knew perfectly well how to find her, might have known for many years and could have done it at any time, but had chosen not to. Furthermore, the presence of the little girl's face at the window, blonde like Hayley and blonde like her, was downright eerie. She felt toyed with, stalked. It was just the sort of fucked-up thing Caroline would have done when she was fifteen or sixteen. She again recalled the strange sensation that came over her the day Liz found her passed out drunk in her kitchen—the certainty that somebody besides her friend had been observing her. In the age of the internet, you didn't have to be in close physical proximity to stalk somebody. You could stalk them from Poland if you chose.

The passages about the younger sister's relationship with her father were indeed painful to read. She recognized a few events from their childhood, nearly always altered rather than happening as she recalled. In one scene, the girls' dad ripped a book from Marilyn's hands, then spanked her and shoved her into the hallway, and she stumbled into the room she shared with her sister, trying hard not to cry. The older girl, Kelli, sat at her desk doing homework, "the flaxen-haired embodiment of duty and obedience." She didn't even ask poor Marilyn what was wrong, just kept working on her assignment. The scene diverged from the way

Ella remembered it. She knew perfectly well that she'd asked her what was wrong, why their father was mad. Jesus, it was the evening Caroline predicted that one day trouble would smack her upside her pretty blonde head, that sooner or later she'd be needed. None of that was in the scene. Instead, Kelli ignored her, continuing to scribble while her sister sat on the bed fighting tears and hoping against hope that for once, she'd be shown some concern. It didn't happen then, it didn't happen in the next twenty pages, or the next fifty, either, though all sorts of other deeply disturbing things did: Marilyn got gang-banged behind a cotton gin by four high-school football players after they lost a game, she got caught stealing a library book and she got caught stealing a rich girl's purse, she saw her father masturbating behind the barn, his eyes shut tight, his fist a blur. She peeped through the keyhole into her parents' bedroom and saw her mother propped up against the headpost, a dreamy look on her face while she caressed her own breasts, a copy of *True Story* spread open across her thighs. What she saw her parents doing did not appear to disturb the younger sister. Instead, she seemed to take a curatorial interest in the proceedings. But reading those passages resulted in a call to room service and the delivery, twenty all but insufferable moments later, of a bottle of heavily oaked Chardonnay. She instructed them to bring her the one with the highest alcohol content, not even remotely embarrassed.

The bottle proved very useful when Ella reached chapter three, which shifted suddenly to Kelli's perspective, as she and her new best friend—the richest girl in town, the same one whose purse her sister had stolen, who drove a little white BMW and lived in a big house with a perfect view of a green-tinted bayou—boarded a school bus to travel to the state capital, where a choral festival would be held.

DEPENDING WHO YOU TALKED TO, Jared Entzminger was either the most revered agent in New York or the most reviled. Within each camp—those who adored him and those who despised him—there were sub-camps. Some of the people who admired him were, reasonably enough, his writers, who invariably said the same thing: "He looks out for my interests." Some of the people who liked him were editors and publishing executives whose job it was to buy books for as little as possible. They had learned that they got straight answers from him when they asked questions like "Is she going to be contented if we publish the book and let it sink or swim on its own merits and don't lift a finger for it unless it gets the wind at its back?" Some of those who hated him were also his writers, or at least used to be. They would say "He's too cozy with editors and publishers, and the surest sign of it is how many of them like him, especially the women." Some of those who wished him slow, agonizing deaths were editors and publishing executives, who would say things like "That motherfucker fleeced me out of a million-point-two for that inspirational memoir by the blind and deaf hang glider."

The thing was, it didn't really matter to him whether he was liked by anybody but his wife, his son, his mom and dad, his sister, and a handful of close friends, most of whom lived in the same small Long Island town as he and his family did and none of whom were in any way involved in publishing. What mattered to him was doing what he thought was right. He slept extremely well nearly every night.

The writer who caused him a measure of turmoil, from time to time, was Karo Kohl. He knew agents who bedded their clients, and editors who did too, but it was something he'd never done and never would, even if he didn't have a marriage that he knew was the envy of a great many friends and colleagues. The fact that he'd slept with Karo when he was single would normally have kept him from responding when she sent him that first manuscript. But he hadn't been able to stop himself from reading it, and he could quickly see that she was a talented storyteller. Still, he started not to get back to her, figuring he could be letting himself in for trouble. What it finally came down to was that he sensed he might be her only option, that he could very well represent the one chance she'd give herself, and so he made that first phone call to Warsaw.

When her story collection was released, he received a few queries from journalists hoping he'd shed light on her identity or at least her background, but he rebuffed them all, saying that he had no information to divulge, that the author valued her privacy and was content to let her work speak for itself. The queries increased exponentially when the novel appeared, various outlets wanting to profile an American writer who would choose to live anonymously in Poland, but he fended them off with exactly the same response, though he did ask her once if she was really sure she wanted to keep turning down free publicity. In the back of his mind was the fear that one day he'd open his email to find a message from a northern California law enforcement officer. But so far that hadn't happened, and after a few months the queries stopped, though the novel continued to sell quite well.

One afternoon, when he wasn't in the best of moods after a long, contentious phone call with a film agent whom he happened to loathe, his assistant stepped into his office. She'd been with him now for eighteen months, was probably the best assistant he'd had during the nearly thirty years he'd been in the business. But lately the sight of her fresh, enthusiastic face depressed him. She had a nose for literary fiction and smart nonfiction, but she would never sell enough of either one to survive, and he dreaded the day when she figured that out. Not because he feared she'd resign and he'd have to train someone else, but because he hated to see talented young people give up their dreams. Her dream was to shepherd great books into the world.

That afternoon, her demeanor seemed off, as if she were distressed. "There's a woman calling from Boston," she said. "Her name is Ella Summers. She's asking to speak to you about Karo."

"Get her email address," he said, "then paste in my regular response and send it to her from me."

"This is different."

"Different how?"

"She's says she's Karo's sister, that her original name is Ella Cole. C-O-L-E. And that her sister's real name is Caroline Cole. And, well, I've seen the name on some of the contractual stuff, Jared."

The smart thing to do was almost always what he did. Otherwise, he would not have fared so well for so long in such an unforgiving business. The smart thing to do right now was order his assistant to tell the sister, if that's really who she was, that he'd stepped into what promised to be a lengthy meeting, that she could call back tomorrow or, better yet, next week. Then he ought to pick up the phone and call Karo and say, in some form or fashion, "What the fuck is this all about?"

But for one of the few times in his career, he didn't do the smart thing. "I'll take her call," he said. "When you leave, why don't you close my door?"

"Gladly."

He picked up the phone. "Jared Entzminger here."

To Ella, the voice on the other end sounded brisk and businesslike, pretty much how she thought somebody called an agent would sound. The last few years of Martin's life "agent" was a word he began to say with anger and, later, with resignation. "Agent" signaled the end of another relationship with an artist he'd championed and, very often, loved.

"Thank you," she said, "for taking my call, Mr. Entzminger."

"What can I do for you?"

She'd rehearsed what she planned to say. She'd written herself notes, then she'd tried to write the whole thing in the form of a monologue, then she gave up and listed bullet points, and about five minutes ago, before placing the call, she crumpled the piece of paper and threw it away. "I've been trying to reach my sister," she said. "I've tried so hard, for so many years. She used a lot of different names, and I did searches for all of them.

Caroline, Carin, I even searched for Caro Cole, but it never occurred to me she might have switched the C's to K's. I called people that I thought might be her, complete strangers, and they probably thought I was crazy, and I can see why, and maybe you do too. But I'm not. I promise I'm not. I'm from Loring, Mississippi, and I know she doesn't name it, but that's the town in the book, the one they both leave but never quite escape from. Or at least the sister based on me doesn't escape it, I guess. I don't think the other one does either, but maybe I'm wrong.

"I see that she's been written about a lot in the last few years, but nobody seems to know how to reach her or who she really is. I called her publisher this morning, but twice they put me on hold, and each time I got disconnected. I saw in the back of her book where she thanked you. So that's why I'm calling. Can you help me? Please? I'm . . . well, I'm pretty sick, and I may get well again, I really hope I do, I've got two grown daughters, but whether I do or not, I just so badly want to see her. And I want my daughters to know who their aunt is." Her voice never broke but only because she ran out of breath and finally had to stop.

For a moment she heard only silence. Then Jared Entzminger said, "Forgive me, Ms. Summers, for choosing my words carefully. I can't confirm that the writer I represent is your sister. Neither can I tell you how to reach her."

"Please . . ."

"Now, if you'll just let me finish?"

"Yes, I'm sorry. Forgive me, I . . ."

"No forgiveness is necessary. So please don't worry about that. What I wanted to say is that if you would like to send me an email, I'll see that it reaches Ms. Kohl. I'll actually do it right away. But that's as far as I can go. The rest would be up to her."

She thanked him profusely, and he gave her his email address. Her hand shook so badly from the adrenalin rushing through her body that she knew she'd have trouble reading what she'd written. So she repeated it to him twice, then thanked him again and said goodbye.

She didn't waste any time writing the email. She could have said a lot of things, many of them angry, others abjectly apologetic. But she said only the most important.

Dear Caroline,

Though you didn't put this in your book, you once told me that sooner or later trouble would smack me upside my pretty blonde head, and that when it did, I would need you. My hair is not very blonde anymore and before long it may begin to fall out. But I do need you. I need you really bad. You know where to find me, because you found me here before.

Ella

•

When Jared Entzminger got the email, it was four forty-three PM in New York. He read it three times, then hollered at his assistant—something he never did, as he was not the hollering type, except when he and his son went to watch the Jets, the Mets, the Knicks or the Rangers—to call Karo Kohl. On the double.

She appeared in his doorway. "Just checking to make sure you know it's nearly eleven PM over there," she said.

"I don't give a damn," he told her. "In fact, I freaking relish the thought of costing that woman some sleep."

IN THE LOBBY SHE WAITED for Alastair, both of her suitcases and a carry-on stacked near the door. Outside, it was still dark, but the snow had finally stopped. Minus 14 C, her phone said. When she first traveled to Europe, planning to stay for a couple of years, she'd memorized the formula and could have performed the conversion if needed. But she'd been gone so long that only the metric mattered.

Mentally, she went back through her checklist. She'd emptied her refrigerator and shut it off, cleaned and unplugged the coffee maker and other small appliances, set the radiators on low heat. In her carry-on, she had her laptop, her iPad, her chargers and convertor plugs for 110 V outlets. Reluctantly, since she despised Jeff Bezos and all he had wrought, she'd downloaded the Kindle app for iPad and purchased a few literary staples: the complete collected stories of Chekhov, Welty, Cheever, Munro and Trevor, novels by Tessa Hadley and Cólm Toibín, the collected nonfiction of Joan Didion and James Baldwin, a Susan Sontag reader. How long she might be gone was anybody's guess.

Beneath the bank of monitors on which, had he been awake, the security guard could have viewed each of the building's entrances and exits, as well as the garage and the rubbish compartment, Pan Henryk slept peacefully, his mouth open wide, revealing the gold premolar she'd seen so many times before. It used to seem strange to her that you could know the map of someone's mouth yet still feel compelled to address that person with the formal Pan or Pani. All this time he'd remained Pan Henryk, and she'd remained Pani Karo, and this now seemed perfectly normal, along with so many other Polish customs that she once found baffling: when you went to someone's home, you carried flowers but no wine; when an elderly man or woman boarded a crowded tram, you rose and gave them your seat; you let them move ahead of you in line at the grocery store; you did not feel offended when an older man bowed and kissed your hand, nor did you consider it sexist when a male of any age opened the door for you. You'd think it rude if he didn't. You might even mutter *Champstwo*!

American according to her passport, she'd become something else inside. America was a literary construct, a setting rather than a place. For a long time now, her sister had been a literary construct, too, a character rather than a person. She'd made both observations yesterday afternoon to Alastair, and he'd looked at her as if she'd just voiced support for waterboarding. She suspected he might be wondering if she viewed him as a construct.

At four AM on the dot, he pulled up in front of the building, jumped out of the car and turned up his collar. Before leaving, she stepped around the corner of Pan Henryk's desk and kissed the top of his bald head. He didn't wake, but he did smile, so maybe he was having a nice dream. And maybe she'd made it a little nicer.

The wind was both brutal and loud. "Get in," Alastair said, brusquely seizing her luggage. "All you need is to catch the flu."

On the way to the airport, he remained quiet. Radio Warsaw played Chopin, a polonaise, she believed, though it was hard to say with the sound turned down and gusts buffeting the car. She reached across the transmission hump and squeezed his knee.

He kept his eyes on the road. A plow was moving toward them, its large orange paw canted at a forty-five-degree angle, shoving snow onto the sidewalk. "Yeah," he said.

"Yeah, what, Alastair?"

"Yeah, this has been really nice."

"Wow. Past tense. So much for the fictional present."

Grimly: "'Goddamn it, Charlie. This is not literature. This is life.' Know who said that?"

"Von Humboldt Fleischer. But I think the exact line is 'All right,

Charlie. This isn't literature. This is life.' I'm impressed you read it, though. I didn't know you were into Bellow."

"I'm not, and I didn't. But last night, after about the fifth shot of Belvedere, I Googled 'literature versus life' and it was one of the first things that came up. I liked it. It's got a certain ring."

"I'll be back, Alastair."

"That's what they all say."

"Is that what your wife said when she left? Or your flutist?"

His hands, wrapped around the steering wheel, opened and closed. Not once. Not twice. But three times. "You got me there," he said. "But I still say you should've called her. Or at least written to her. 'I need you' can mean a lot of things. She might just want to be in touch via email. Or Skype. She could just want you to pray for her, for Christ's sake. You don't even know for sure that she wants to see you."

She hadn't divulged the entire content of her conversation with Jared Entzminger. He'd told her off pretty badly. He didn't see how she could diss her sister like that, he said. Just act like she was dead. After all, he had a sister, too, and when his sister was all alone and undergoing cancer treatment, having been walked out on by her no-good piece of dogshit former brother-in-law, he'd flown his ass to Topeka, Kansas, and stayed there until she was well. So that was one thing. The other? She shouldn't be surprised if those calls her sister made to the publisher set off a shit storm. She'd signed an indemnification clause, he reminded her. If the publisher got sued for libel or invasion of privacy, it could take a big bite out of her butt and also make her *persona non grata* to everybody in publishing, including the janitor. Did she know what he was saying? Did she finally fucking get it?

Yes, she assured him, she fully fucking did.

He eventually apologized for yelling at her, as she had known he would, and she apologized for putting him in a difficult position. He told her he was going to forward her sister's message, and they managed to say goodbye on much less frosty terms.

Then she read Ella's email, and a sharp pain ripped through her gut, like it used to when she got scared of the dark. It was as if, in a matter of seconds, she was back in a cramped bedroom, in that ugly little farmhouse, lying in the lower bunk, with only one person in the whole world to talk to, the sister she had not yet begun to embarrass. In her novel she'd described those times exactly as she recalled them, but the act of putting them into words allowed her to remain aloof.

Well, she had this coming. What the rest of the world recognized as reality was still out there, with a truth of its own. "I know she wants to see me," she told Alastair.

"You've had no contact with her for thirty years. How could you *possibly* know that?"

"Because," she said, "I know her."

"Fucking art," he said. He shook his head and turned up the music.

•

He insisted on accompanying her to check-in, so he parked and removed her luggage and pulled it into the departure hall, where he remained with her at the crowded Lufthansa counter until she received her boarding pass.

Silently, they walked toward security. When they reached the rear of the line, she stopped and they faced each other, and she opened her arms. For a terrible instant, she thought he would not embrace her, that she would have to fly off untouched. But he finally grabbed her and squeezed her so tightly she felt a vertebra shift. She could smell the coffee on his breath, see the moisture in his eyes.

"Will we be able to talk?" he asked.

"Daily."

"Facetime?"

"Yes. Because I'll want to see your face." She reached into her pocket, pulled out her key and handed it to him. "Look what I was about to forget."

"I thought maybe you'd decided otherwise."

"Not at all." She pressed it into his hand. "Check my place from time to time."

"Are you kidding? I'll be going there every day. I want to be where you were."

She recalled how she'd left Julio nothing but a stray cat and a note. "I love you," she heard herself say.

"Really?"

"Yes, I do." They kissed, and she watched him walk away, as nice a man as she'd ever known, and then an hour later, she gazed out the window and watched the only place that had ever really felt like home disappear beneath the clouds, the spire atop the massive Palace of Culture and Science the last thing to be obscured.

SHE LANDS AT BOSTON LOGAN mid-afternoon on the 27th of January, little more than a month shy of twenty-three years since she left the U.S. from exactly the same place. She follows the signs to Passport Control, where she waits in a snake-like line with other holders of American Passports. She recognizes three or four people who were also on the flight from Warsaw to Frankfurt and hears them conversing in Polish. Her own situation in reverse. At some point they must have left there to make a home here.

When it's her turn, she steps up to the booth. The officer is older than she is, probably around sixty, with a face that looks like it belongs in a Norman Rockwell drawing. Kind, wise, grandfatherly. He scans her passport, then looks at it, then back at her. Then he stares at a monitor for fifteen or twenty seconds. He punches a few keys on a keyboard that she can't see. Then he turns and waves at another officer who has been standing nearby: a big man, African American, mid-thirties, wire-rimmed glasses.

The younger man approaches and leans over the older man's shoulder. He points at his monitor, then shows the younger officer her passport. The second man's facial expression is slow to change, but change it does. A slight tightening of his jaw muscles. You'd have to look hard to notice it, but she is looking hard.

If it is possible to be both exhausted and wired, her current state qualifies. Keep a lid on it, she thinks. Don't be brassy, don't be bashful. Do not try to feed these guys bullshit. They are not shit-eaters.

The younger officer says, "It looks like you've been gone for quite some time," then waits for her response. She knows she needs to say something, that almost anything would be better than continuing to stand there silently, but words fail her. "Am I right about that?" he asks.

"You are," she says.

"And your passport was issued at . . ."

"The American Embassy in Warsaw."

"Looks like it's the second time you renewed there."

"I've been living outside the country since 1991."

"Purpose?"

"Work."

Without another exchange, the older man steps out of the booth, and the younger officer takes his place, the swivel-back stool creaking when he sits. "Have you ever," he asks, "resided in Charleston, South Carolina?"

"No, sir. I haven't."

"Ocala, Florida?"

"No."

"Daytona Beach?"

"Not there either."

The officer flips through her passport, front to back, back to front. "Huh," he says. He lays it down, then pushes a small notepad under the glass. Later, she will try to remember if the paper had a logo on it. It seems that it must have, but she will never be able to recall. Beside it a pen appears. A blue Bic. Of that she's sure.

"I need you to write your social on there for me, along with your middle name, your date and place of birth and your mother's maiden name."

Trying to keep her hand steady, she does as asked and pushes both the pad and the pen back under the glass.

He studies it for a moment, pushes it aside. Then he flips open her passport, holds it down with one hand and with the other stamps it so hard she flinches.

He closes it and pushes it under the glass. "Somebody else's got the exact same name as yours," he says. "First *and* middle. Different birthplace and birthdate and, of course, a different mother. And while I probably ought not to say so, it seems this other Caroline's a real bad sister. Now, welcome home, Ms. Cole. You have yourself a lovely evening."

•

She emerges from Customs to find an eager crowd waiting behind belt barriers, some waving signs. *Alex O'Leary. Jackie L. Mrs. Gupta.* After the experience at the passport booth, she badly needs a drink, her last one having been consumed somewhere over the U.K. But there appears to be no bar, just a Dunkin' Donuts and a Hudson News. Compared to European airports, this one looks dirty and outmoded, the trash receptacles overflowing.

At the information desk, they tell her that upstairs in Departures, there is a bar on this side of security, so she lugs her suitcases onto the escalator, rides it up one floor and orders a vodka Martini. They have Belvedere, one last touch of home. She resists the urge to ask for a second, puts the drink on a card, then takes the escalator back down and waits in line for a taxi.

The driver must be a Sikh, since he wears a blue dastaar. He lifts her suitcases and carry-on into the trunk, and she climbs into the back seat and tells him the address. He surprises her by being talkative. "And how was your flight?" he asks as he pulls away from the curb.

"Long," she says.

"And where did you start, if I might ask?"

"In Warsaw."

"You're Polish?"

"I don't know what I am," she says.

He glances into the rearview mirror. "For some of us," he replies, "it's hard to say. I was born in the United States, but most people assume I was not. So while I am who and what I am, I must also deal with who and what they think I am, even as I reject it."

"That makes a lot of sense," she says. She likes his eyes: dark, intelligent, inquisitive. "I was born here too. Not in Boston but down south. In Mississippi. But I've been away since 1991."

He swings into traffic, then asks, "And what brings you home now?"

The words come with surprising ease. "My sister. She's sick."

"I am sorry to hear this," he says, sounding as if he means it.

"I haven't seen her for many years. We were estranged."

"Now I am really sorry to hear that."

"Do you have siblings?"

"Yes. If I told you how many, and of what gender, you would laugh."

"Try me."

They stop at a toll both long enough for him to pass a card through a scanner. "I have no brothers. But I have seven sisters."

"Wow."

They enter a long tunnel. "All my sisters are older than me, the eldest by nearly twenty years. My father was determined to have a son. He kept having daughters, and my mother kept saying 'No more! No more!' But my father was not and is not one to accept defeat." He chuckles. "'I willed you into being,' he sometimes tells me, as if my mother was completely uninvolved."

They talk all the way up I-93 in heavy rush-hour traffic, darkness falling while the GPS on the dashboard issues directions and other drivers honk and gesture and swerve from lane to lane, searching for an advantage they will never obtain. The conversation helps her remain calm until the moment he takes an off-ramp—the same one, she assumes, that the silently sullen driver of her previous taxi must have taken in '91. They pass through an intersection, and he hangs a right, and they drive through neighborhoods that, if anything, look much worse than she recalls.

But the houses become progressively more impressive, just as they did back then, and once again the potholes disappear. He takes another turn, and then another, and they are on the street she's seen in so many memories, over so many years, in Budapest, Brno, Prague and Bratislava, in Warsaw and Dublin and Dresden, in dreams and nightmares. He halts for a break in traffic, then turns left onto Rockland, drives uphill, pulls into the same driveway where she glimpsed the little girl's face at the window. He engages the parking brake. For a moment he sits there studying the house. "Your sister," he says, before popping the trunk and climbing out, "she has a really nice place."

Four Roses

DURING THE WEEK SHE SPENDS back home that spring, Lexa, by habit not an early riser except when her job demands, finds herself crawling out of bed at seven AM so she can share coffee with her aunt, in whose face she can see how she might look in another twenty-five years if things go exceptionally well. Only a few lines, long lashes, smooth skin free of discoloration except for a small, seductive mole near one corner of her mouth. A few strands of gray near her roots, but her red hair is still long and thick. Much taller than their mom, slim without being skinny. You can tell she takes great care of herself, drinking exactly two six-ounce cups of coffee each morning, eating fruit or yoghurt for breakfast and dressing stylishly without being flashy. Even in a fleece bathrobe she looks great. It would not be misleading to say that Lexa is entranced.

The first morning, when she wanders down, jetlagged after the coast to coast flight, she's surprised to find her there. Caroline and her mother were both asleep when she got in from LA, so they have not been properly introduced, though they've spoken several times on the phone and Hayley has sent her a few pictures. She knew they shared some features. But her presence administers a shock.

"My God," she says, pausing in the archway.

Caroline lays her iPad down on the work island, slides off the stool and stands there sizing her up. "Yeah," she says, "my God's about right. I'd say I've met my doppelgänger, except technically that would mean we're nonbiologically related doubles. Whereas the truth in this case is more interesting. Give me a hug."

Lexa generally doesn't hug other women. She doesn't often hug anybody except her lovers, and from them she tends to move on, though she harbors hopes for the current one, who works at the same law firm and now lives with her. He is a great big maybe.

She takes a couple of steps toward Caroline, who says, "Actually, you don't like hugging, do you?"

That stops her. "Did my mom tell you that?"

"No."

"So what made you say so?"

"Just a vibe I picked up. It's okay."

"Were *you* that way?"

"I'm not sure. I think I may understand others better than I understand myself." Her aunt smiles, then shrugs. "But that's something I've only understood lately."

"I actually think I'd like to hug you."

"Well, then, please do."

She steps over and wraps her arms around her. She thinks Caroline smells like the duty-free section of the Zurich airport, where they sell all those great fragrances. Her aunt gives her a quick squeeze, then lets her go. "Can I get you something?" she asks. "I mean, it's your house, not mine. But I've been doing most of the cooking, so I know where everything is. Your mom said you prefer oatmeal in the morning?"

"I do, but first I'd just like some coffee."

She climbs onto the stool that belonged to her sister when they were growing up. Her aunt has taken hers.

While she pours her a cup of coffee, Caroline says, "Which of those stools was yours? I didn't take it, did I?"

"Jesus."

"In other words, yes?" She sets the cup down in front of her. "I assume you prefer your coffee black?"

"Yes, I do. This is just plain weird. Does it happen often?"

"I don't really know. Want your old stool back?"

"No, that's okay. I'll pretend to be my sister."

Caroline pours herself another cup, climbs back onto the appropriated stool, and they sit there looking at each other. Finally, Lexa says, "I read your book."

"And?"

"It's a good novel. You know a lot about different people and places." She takes a sip of coffee, then sets the cup back down. "Hayley told me not to read it."

"Well, I can't say that I blame her."

"She's not mad at you or anything. It's just that . . . well . . ."

"She may not be mad at me," her aunt says, "but she's not happy with me, either, and I can understand why. Please don't get me wrong. She's been perfectly kind. And, of course, she's very worried about your mom. And by the way?" She lifts her hand and gestures at the ceiling.

Lexa drops her voice. "I got it. Just so you know, she moves through the house very quietly. She always did."

Caroline tilts her head all but imperceptibly. It's a gesture with which her niece will quickly become familiar. It means that she's half a step ahead of you, or thinks she is. "Just so you know, I do know. She was always light on her feet."

They talk quietly about her mom's treatment. Every three weeks she undergoes an infusion. The fourth was last week, and so far she's had minimal side effects. Her hair has not fallen out, though they told her there was about a forty percent chance that it would. No signs so far of pneumonitis, either. She's itching a lot, and she's been experiencing some burning when she urinates, and she occasionally has diarrhea. But based on her conversations with the oncologist, Caroline thinks things are going quite well.

"So what was it like," Lexa asks, "the moment when you saw her again? After all this time? I've been trying to imagine it. But you know, I just kind of can't."

Later today, after Hayley has gotten off work and come by and picked her up, ostensibly to go shopping at Whole Foods but more importantly to grab a drink with her sister at a nearby Irish pub, Lexa will try to describe her aunt's reaction to the question. "I mean, she's a nice woman, and I liked her right away," she will say. "But I think she's pretty tough, even hardened. Always looks you in the eye like they teach witnesses to do in mock trial training, keeps her voice and her breathing very even, her gestures to a minimum. Probably has good blush control too. But for a minute, she just kind of lost it."

Hayley will sound skeptical. "Lost it how?"

"Dropped her head, swallowed hard, turned kind of red . . ."

"Well, she should have. I can't imagine how much grief she must have cost Mom. Disappearing like that, as if some serial killer had chopped her body up and tossed her remains in the ocean. And then what she wrote. . . My God. If somebody wrote that about a character that I knew was based on me, I think I'd die of shame."

"It's a novel."

"I don't care what it is. There's too much truth there for my taste. Though I don't believe even a third of it."

"Which two-thirds don't you believe?"

"I don't want to talk about it."

"Yeah, okay. So anyway, she sat there like that for, I don't know, at least a minute, maybe more. Also, both of her thumbs began to graze the rim of her saucer."

"Which tells us what?"

"I don't know what it tells us, Hayley. I'm just saying what I saw."

"So did she answer your question or not?"

"Eventually."

"So what did she say?"

Lexa will wrap her hands around her pint of Guinness, which by then will have stood there long enough to reach room temperature and will taste more like warm cocoa than beer. Before she takes a big swallow, she will tell her sister what their aunt said, when she was finally able to speak: "'It was easy, Lexa. She made it so goddamn easy it nearly killed me.'"

·

Back in January, after Ella sent her email to the agent Jared Entzminger, she began to look at her phone every fifteen or twenty minutes, thinking that surely Caroline would write to her. But forty-eight hours passed without a word, and then it was the weekend. She thought of calling Entzminger again on Monday, but she sensed it would be useless. He had told her what he would do, and he'd done it. He'd told he what he wouldn't do, too, and she knew he meant it.

During those few days her moods varied by the moment. Sometimes she felt she had it coming, that the deserved to be alone, scared and abandoned by the one who'd known her longest. She kept going back to the night her sister called her from the bus station in New Jersey. Had she said it was snowing there? She didn't remember. Was it snowing in Boston then? She didn't remember that either. Nor did she remember exactly what she was saying when Caroline hung up. She remembered thinking *She's going to wreck my wedding*. Just like Marilyn in the novel, Caroline would have heard the hesitancy in her voice, the fear of being embarrassed. Why should she come now when Ella hadn't wanted her to come then?

At other times, Ella was so angry at her that she wanted to hit something. When Caroline called and begged for money to be sent to Beaumont, Texas, Ella sent it, no questions asked, even though she was working her ass off just to feed herself and pay her rent, even though she appeared to have no future and was so depressed she could hardly crawl out of bed. And Caroline wasn't even in Beaumont fucking Texas, she was somewhere in California. Lies, lies and more lies. No wonder she grew up to write fiction. She lied when she was supposed to tell the truth and told the truth when she was supposed to be lying.

Of course, Ella knew she'd turned into a liar too. She'd lied to herself about herself and by extension she'd lied to the man who loved her. More recently, she'd lied to Liz about her condition, and she also lied to both daughters. She told all three of them it was Stage II, that her prognosis was great, and while Lexa accepted it at face value, Hayley didn't, nor did Liz. Both of them called her several times a day, and she took their calls, knowing that each of them had a key and could get into the house and would not hesitate to do so if they failed to hear from her. She said she was doing just fine. She didn't tell either of them she'd discovered that her sister was alive, that she'd written a book and was famous and would not answer an email.

Her first infusion was scheduled for Tuesday the 28th. Both Liz and Hayley volunteered to drive her to the hospital, but she lied and said she'd spend Monday night at The Liberty, which was just around the corner from MGH. Then she picked up the phone and called the taxi company owned by Gazhi and asked him to pick her up the following morning at nine. Gazhi was the man of the hour.

They'd told her she didn't need to do anything special to prepare, just eat normally the night before and try to get to bed early. She had almost no appetite and had been losing weight, though not a precipitate amount, just a couple of pounds over the last week. She was dying, of course, for a glass of wine, and for the past few hours she'd kept walking past the wine rack and had once actually laid her hand on the neck of a bottle and come close to pulling it out. Instead, she heated up some stir-fried tofu from the previous evening, spooned it onto a plate, poured herself a glass of water and carried it to the living room. She'd lit one of those fake logs an hour or so earlier, and it was still burning. She hadn't ordered a cord of real wood since Martin died. She didn't even know where he got the wood from, she just knew they always had it. He took care of that along with so much else.

She sat down on the couch next to Lotte, her adopted tabby. The night was clear, the long slope outside the bay window still covered in a thin layer of white that flashed when a car turned onto Rockland and started up the hill. A couple of years ago the street had been repaved and extended. No longer a dead end, it looped down the far side of the Highlands and into Wakefield. Traffic had increased, as people who lived up there tried to avoid the jam that formed near Main Street.

She thought she heard a couple of doors slam but paid them no mind, concentrating on forcing down a largish lump of tofu. She'd just forked up some more stir-fry when the cat's ears twitched and she looked toward the door. She jumped down off the couch and ran from the room just as the bell rang.

It couldn't be Liz or Hayley, as neither of them would have gone to the front door. The town was safe—nobody had ever committed an act of vandalism on their property, and the size of the house seemed to discourage canvassers—but it was dinnertime, for God's sake. She recalled, though, that a few days earlier, anticipating the incontinence they'd told her she might experience, she'd ordered a shipment of disposable under pads from Amazon. Maybe they'd arrived.

She set her plate down on the coffee table, walked over to the door and switched on the porch light. She might have cancer, and her life expectancy might be short, but she was no fool. She didn't just throw the door open. She unlocked it and opened it a crack, leaving the chain engaged. What she saw was a chin, a mouth, the end of a nose. Lexa? She was in California.

"It's me. Can I come in?"

She closed the door, leaned against the facing just long enough to compose herself to the extent that was possible, then reached out and unhooked the chain. She opened the door, stepped backwards and grabbed hold of the coat rack. It was carved from mahogany and had brass hooks and a cast-iron base with feet designed to resemble tree roots. It had been in Martin's family forever, and she'd never liked it, but it was sturdy. She held on.

Caroline stepped over the threshold but left both of her suitcases and her hand luggage on the veranda. They stood there contemplating each other: one of them tired but the picture of perfect health, tall, robust, fit; the other much shorter, pale, beginning to look as frail as she felt. In the morning, neither of them would remember who spoke first, or what she said, or who was the first to scream or what she screamed or how long the screaming lasted or, after it finally stopped, who was the first to reach for the other. What would never be in dispute was that the following morning Caroline was the first to wake. By the time Ella opened her eyes, Martin's side of the bed was empty once again, though it still bore her sister's imprint. On her way downstairs, she could smell coffee and hear Caroline in the kitchen talking on the phone. She paused on the half-landing to eavesdrop, then realized she was speaking Polish. It was just as well. Ella had never truly understood her and never would, but that morning it didn't matter.

•

Going into Boston, they both rode in the back seat, Ella behind Gazhi. A couple of times, she noticed him adjusting the rearview mirror to achieve a better view of her sister. He seemed very taken with her. While they crept down the ramp to Route 1, jammed as always that time of morning but less so than I-93 would have been, he said, "Mrs. Summers, I believe I know who your company is."

"So who am I?" Caroline said. She was looking out the window at the ugly scenery along the highway. A single sign advertised Baseball, Miniature Golf and something called Dairy Castle, with a faded red arrow pointing the way to a parking lot. Everything looked ragged, rundown. It could easily have been a Central California freeway thirty years ago. Some things in America, unlike nearly everything in Poland, did not appear to have changed all that much.

"You and Mrs. Summers," he said knowingly. "You are sisters. Am I right?"

In the backseat they exchanged glances.

"Yes," Ella said. "And my sister is a famous writer."

"Really?"

"Yes, she is. She's been published all over the world."

"Were you translated into Farsi?"

"No," Caroline said. "Though I'd love to be."

"What kind of writer are you?"

"A novelist."

"You make things up?"

Both sisters looked at each other and laughed. "I do," Caroline said.

"She always did," Ella said.

Understanding that he was not in on the joke, whatever it might be, Gazhi fell silent for the remainder of the trip.

At MGH, they went to the Cancer center and registered and then they sat in the waiting room. They'd asked if Caroline could be with her during the infusion, but the answer was no. Having read up on the procedure the night before, Caroline knew that in some instances the drug caused immediate organ failure. Her sister understood that as well: when they came to get her, she said, "I hate to say goodbye after we've just said hello."

"Goodbyes are not in order," Caroline said. She watched her and her attendant walk over to a pair of windowless doors. The nurse keyed a code in, and both of them disappeared.

In no time, a sense of heaviness descended on her. It was not just jetlag, though that surely played a role. She was thinking of all the time they'd lost. At every point during the writing of her novel, and in all the years before she wrote the novel, even before she wrote the book of stories, she knew how to reach her sister. She could have called her. She thought it likely that if she had, she would have been welcomed with the open arms that were not extended the night she phoned from the New Jersey bus station. Her sister was scared she'd ruin her wedding. And knowing her, she probably would have. When she first went downstairs this morning, she stepped into a room filled with books in dark heavy bookcases. Some of them were more than a hundred years old, but there were newer ones mixed in, including quite a few that were of interest to her and would have been of interest back in 1984. The first one she pulled off the shelf was a yellow hardcover, Richard Yates's story collection *Liars in Love*. It seemed an unlikely choice for Ella to read, so she assumed that the book had belonged to her husband. Then she opened it and saw the dedication:

> *to Ella with admiration*
> *your friend,*
>   *Dick Yates*

It did not occur to her, when she saw it, that her sister might have served Richard Yates dinner on many an evening while working at the same downscale restaurant she'd read about in Blake Bailey's biography of the writer, though ninety minutes ago at breakfast she learned that was the case. If she'd walked into the big green house and seen that book back in December of '84, it would have completed the picture of uncaring Ella, who moved in lofty circles and had to be coerced to invite her own sister to her wedding. Nothing good would have come of that.

But good things—lots of them—had come her way since the night she made that phone call from the bus station. Most, though not all of them, could be traced back to the morning in the café when she wrote that first flawed story. From then on, there had been something to do each day besides just muddling through. And it was what she wanted to protect from the reality represented by her sister.

They'd said the infusion would last about thirty minutes, that recovery might take another hour or so, unless there were complications. After two hours had gone by, she went back to registration and asked one of the desk clerks if something had gone wrong, and the woman typed her sister's name, took a look at her monitor, then said that unfortunately they had no authorization on file that would allow them to release medical information. Nothing to do but go back and sit down.

Despite her anxiety, she was asleep when they rolled her out in a wheelchair. Ella tapped her on the knee. "Hey. Wake up." Her face, when Caroline brought it into focus, seemed to have a bluish tint.

"She experienced a few chills," the attendant said. "But other than that, she came through just fine. We'd like her to remain in the chair until you get your taxi. So I can take her down if you prefer."

"Thank you," Caroline said, "but I'll do it."

She rolled her down the hall and into the elevator. In the taxi on the way home, she asked what it had been like.

"Nothing too dramatic except I don't think I've ever felt so cold in my life. I forgot that they prepare the concoction the night before, and then they freeze it and thaw it out at the last minute. It's like ice entering your veins. It's probably like . . . Well, better not go there."

Caroline reached across the seat and squeezed her gloved hand. "We're definitely not going there."

"Living in Poland, you're probably used to extreme cold?"

"I don't know that you ever get used to it. It's just that the buildings, even newish ones like mine, are built to withstand it. And I think radiators do a better job than forced air. Just my own personal bias."

"I was there once," Ella said.

"Where? In *Poland*?"

"Yes."

"When?"

"In 2008. It was the last time we went to Europe. The girls were both on their own, so we flew to Vienna, spent a few days there, rented a car and drove to Budapest and Prague, then Krakow and finally Warsaw. I remember where we stayed. The Victoria Hotel. Just a few blocks from the Royal Castle. I liked it there. I hadn't expected Warsaw to be so beautiful. We almost didn't include it on the itinerary. But Martin insisted."

Caroline felt as if a large gob of peanut butter were lodged in her throat. "Listen . . ."

"You don't need to say it. We said it all last night, right after you walked through the door."

"What exactly did we say?"

"I don't remember. But I know we said it."

"That's funny, isn't it? Because I don't remember either."

"I guess the God of our childhood," Ella said, as the driver merged into traffic, "is looking after us. It sure is a shame He didn't do such a good job of it back when we were kids."

"Well," Caroline said, "our folks *did* quit taking us to church."

•

The line draws a laugh from Lexa, her niece, as they sit across the kitchen island from each other on the first of the seven mornings when they enjoy each other's company. Caroline tells her that it made her mother laugh as well and that both of them briefly got the giggles. She tells her that they used to laugh like that when they were little. What she doesn't tell her is that later on the laughter stopped, that later on they all but quit talking.

She has been thinking about those times constantly, due to the request Ella made a week ago, which she decided to honor, though she doesn't believe it wise, nor do her sister's doctors. She would rather do almost anything in the world than what her sister asked. But that's precisely why she must.

As if she's read her mind, and maybe she has, Lexa leans toward her. "You think this trip you guys have planned is a good idea?"

"What I think doesn't really matter."

With the same urgency she must bring to judicial proceedings, her niece says, "Of course it does. She might listen to you. She won't listen to me." She looks out the window for a moment, then back at Caroline. "Actually, she never really did listen to me. She used to listen to Hayley. But now she won't do that either."

"I already told her I wasn't in favor."

"And how did she respond?"

"She didn't. And that was response enough. So I told her I'd make all the arrangements and followed through that same day."

Her niece—what a strange word to be thinking and saying—drains her cup and, before Caroline can offer to get her another, she rises and pours one herself. Then she remembers her manners and asks, "Would you like some more?"

"No, thank you. I don't need as much sleep as some, but I do need four or five hours, and if I drink another drop I won't even get that."

Lexa sets her cup on the island, then slides onto the stool. "Hayley said you left your stuff in her old room but that you're sleeping in the bed with Mom."

"Then feel free to give her an update. I lie in bed with your mom until she falls asleep, but then I move to the other room for the rest of the night. I take it your sister was bothered by it?"

"Hayley's kind of mainstream. I thought it was sweet. And I reminded her that we sometimes did it, too, even once or twice after we both went off to college. Sometimes, I think, only a sister will do."

"Sometimes," they both hear Ella say, "I feel that way too. However, daughters have their place." She wafts into the kitchen, puts her thin arms around Lexa from behind and kisses the top of her head.

It's not like Caroline needs to hit "Save" on some kind of mental keyboard. The image of her sister with her arms around her niece will last forever, or at least until death or dementia wipes it away. And she suspects that even the latter of those would have trouble destroying it, though perhaps a neurologist would say otherwise. It will remain there beside other sights she's seen, or the ones she's imagined so vividly that she might as well have seen them. While her sister talks to her daughter, she carries her cup to the sink and turns the water on full-blast, watching it splash off the stainless steel before gurgling down the drain.

A WEEK LATER, ON ONE OF THOSE Massachusetts spring mornings that seem too good to be true and usually are, Caroline, Ella and Lexa pack their roller bags into the trunk of Hayley's blue Mazda. Then the younger women climb into the front, the older ones into the rear.

"Where's your layover?" Hayley asks her sister as she's backing into Rockland.

"O'Hare."

"You couldn't get a direct flight to LA?"

"I could have, but it was a hundred and forty dollars more."

"I'm a lowly museum assistant. You're a lawyer. You can afford it."

"I am indeed a lawyer, and not a bad one, and one day I hope to own a nice three-bedroom condo on the Pacific Coast Highway in Malibu. But at the moment, I'm about 3.2 million short. So I economize. Also, long flights make me antsy. I like to get off for a little while, grab a drink, walk around." She looks over her shoulder. "Aunt Caroline, how long was your flight from Poland?"

"Warsaw to Frankfurt was just over an hour," she says. "Frankfurt-Boston was more like seven."

"I hope there wasn't a baby nearby."

Her mom says, "When you weren't much more than a baby, we flew with you to Paris."

Hayley says, "Oh, God, I had forgotten that story. That's the time she howled all the way across the ocean, right?" At the foot of the hill, she hangs a left, then asks her mom, "You remember what that French woman did?"

"I remember very well."

"What'd she do?" asks Lexa.

"She was sitting across the aisle from me," her mom says, "and since I had you in my lap, I was the first one she complained to. I told her that I couldn't help it, babies cry. So then she complained to your dad, and he was very polite and said he would try to quiet you down, and so I passed you across your sister to him. But his luck was no better. You cried even harder. So the woman complained to a flight attendant, and when that produced no results, she stood up and complained in French to the passengers at large, and then finally they found her an empty seat at the rear of the plane. But because her luggage was still in the bin above her original seat, she returned right before we landed. I carried you into the aisle, and Hayley followed, and just as your dad is about to step out, the woman starts trying to pull her suitcase from the overhead, but it's stuck. So she looks at your dad and says, 'Help me, please.' And your dad says, 'I hope that thing decapitates you. It's a shame you weren't around during the Reign of Terror.'"

The reminiscing continues all the way to Logan. If Caroline mostly listens, it's not because she feels excluded. For the past week, the four of them have dined together every evening, just them, no one else, Ella first taking a pre-dinner nap, Lexa making the drinks and setting the table, Caroline and Hayley handling the cooking. Hayley's attitude toward her aunt has finally softened.

She and Ella are flying out of terminal B, so Hayley pulls to the curb and pops the trunk. Since they will only be gone for four days, they're traveling with smaller roller bags. Caroline grabs hers and stands it on the sidewalk, then snatches up her sister's, which feels a couple pounds heavier. When they hug the younger women goodbye, she detects a glint in her sister's eye. Ella holds onto Lexa for an extra moment or two. Caroline knows Lexa usually does not come home more than once a year, and Ella must be wondering what her condition will be the next time she sees her.

Back in the car, watching their mom and their newly-found aunt disappear into the terminal, Lexa says, "I'm so glad she came." She turns to her sister. "If you ever get really sick, I'll come to you. Will you come to me?"

"Of course," Hayley says. "But I do have one condition."

"Oh yeah? And what's that?"

Hayley puts the car in drive and pulls away from the curb. She knows without looking at Lexa that her features will be arranged to convey mock outrage. But she also knows that there have been times when her sister's outrage was real. She didn't do as well in high school as Hayley, was afraid to apply to top-notch liberal arts schools, and ended up halfway across the country at the weakest of all the UCs. She changed her habits there, though, graduating summa cum laude and earning acceptance to a first-rate law school, and now she makes more money in a year than Hayley will earn in four or five. The disparity between them will keep rising. But she's happy for her sister. She fashioned her own path. "I'm not coming," she says, "unless you promise me a room with an ocean view in your 3.2 million-dollar condo. I insist on a balcony too."

•

Since they have their boarding passes and are traveling with only carry-ons, Caroline had assumed they would proceed straight to Security. Instead, Ella heads for bag-drop. It occurs to her that since her sister's bag is heavier than her own and she's in a weakened condition, she probably fears that like the obnoxious French woman in the anecdote, she might not be able to remove it from the overhead.

"We don't need to mess with bag drop," Caroline says. "I can get it if you have trouble with it. We could switch right now."

"No," Ella says. "This is what I always do. I always check my bag, and you should too."

Her laptop is in her bag, and it's got part of a short story on it that she began a week or so ago. "I never check small bags," she says.

"Well, today's a good day to start. Our connection in Atlanta's forty-three minutes, and we have to change terminals."

"I'll take my chances."

"When were you last in the Atlanta airport? It's huge."

"I've never been in the Atlanta airport. But I've flown in and out of

Frankfurt more times than I can count, not to mention Schiphol, which is in some ways even worse."

Her sister steps up to one of the automated stations and inserts a credit card. "Where in the world is Schiphol?"

"Amsterdam."

She begins entering info on the touch screen. "So why didn't you just say Amsterdam?"

"I was trying to impress you."

"I was already impressed."

Their flight is smooth and uneventful. Somewhere around Philadelphia, Ella, who has taken the aisle seat in case she has to run for the WC, falls asleep, leaving Caroline little to do but gaze out the window. Around the north end of Chesapeake Bay, the plane banks, and before too much more time has passed, she sees what she believes might be the Shenandoah Valley. She closes her own eyes then, and when she opens them they're on the descent. After a change of planes and an hour-long flight, they land at Medgar Briley Evers International. Jackson, Mississippi.

·

Inside, the airport smells like chicken fried in stale oil. The carpets are frayed, and there aren't many people to be found, most of the departure lounges all but empty. They stop by the restroom, then take the escalator down to baggage. Wanting to get out as fast as they can, they agree that Caroline will wait for Ella's bag while Ella goes to the Hertz desk, where there's currently no line, and completes the paperwork. Caroline hands over her Polish drivers' license. Ella hasn't driven since she got her diagnosis, and she feels that her eyesight is fading, a potential side effect that no one warned her about.

It takes a few minutes for the bag to arrive. While she waits, Caroline listens to the talk around her and is pleased to discover that the accents are about like she recalled, lots of thick, elongated vowels. Except for one older man in a gray business suit who has spent a lot of time on his matching hair, appearances are fairly downscale, and a lot of people are badly overweight. The day must be quite warm, because several of the women are wearing what her mom and grandmother called pedal pushers, though she long ago came to identify them as capris.

She grabs the bag, then heads for the Hertz desk where, to her dismay, Ella appears to be engaged in a dispute with the woman behind the counter, a blonde in her early thirties. "Ma'am, I'm not trying to give you a hard time," the clerk is saying when Caroline walks up. "It's just that this card—" She looks at Caroline's driver's license, then at her— "which I guess belongs to this lady, I can't read what's on it. Not a word of it. For all I know, it could be her library card. They told me I need to identify it beyond doubt."

"It's her first day on the job," Ella tells Caroline.

"It's not my first day. I started last week. And I've had several folks come through here from Mexico and I didn't have trouble authenticating their licenses."

"Maybe you studied Spanish in high school?" Ella says.

"Yes, ma'am. I did. But I was not good at it."

Caroline says, "Let me translate. *Rzeczpospolita Polska* means 'Republic of Poland.' *Prawo Jazdy* means 'Right to Drive.' Then here, you see my name—last name first, first name last—followed by my birthday and place of birth, which you'll notice is listed as USA—in fact, I was born right here in Mississippi—and then down here on the next line is the date of issue, followed by the issuing authority. *Warszawa* means 'Warsaw,' and below that is the Polish equivalent of my social security number, then the license number itself, my signature and then my Warsaw address."

The blonde acts anything but convinced. "Up there where you said your birthday is? It says eighteen, zero two, sixty. Now, as far as I know, a year hasn't got eighteen months. Not here, not in Poland, not anywhere. And then what's this letter 'B' down below everything else?"

"It just means Basic Passenger License. In other words, non-commercial."

"So it gives you the right to be a passenger in the car but not the driver."

The evaporation of her sister's patience is complete. She reaches out to snatch the documents off the counter, but Caroline gently touches her hand. She looks at the clerk, raises her eyes, then asks if they can speak in the back.

"What?" Ella says.

"Just keep an eye on the bags," she says, and the woman dutifully unlatches a gate and lets Caroline follow her behind the Hertz logo. Ella is shaking, and not because she's cold. It's the woman's pride at being ignorant that annoys her. It's a trait she recalls from childhood, from people like her uncle who lost his hand working at the cotton gin. Whenever somebody told him something he didn't already know—as, for instance, that John Quincy Adams had been the sixth President of the United States—he was likely to reply, "What good's it gonna do me to know that? What's on my mind's I got six mouths to feed. Ain't no dead president can help me do it." Everything reduced to one's own personal circumstances, at one point in time, with no willingness to look beyond. People can be like that everywhere, but each place has its own particular manifestation. In Boston, the same sort of person will at least keep it short: "Fuck if I care." Whereas down here every grievance is a Holstein. It must be milked. She's already beginning to wish they hadn't come.

Her sister and the desk clerk return, and Caroline says that all is fine, and the desk clerk apologizes, says she's sorry, she's on her third twelve-hour shift in a row, and they've got everything straight, there's no problem with Ms. Cole being the additional driver. She hands over their licenses, Ella's credit card and the rental docs, tells them to have a lovely stay here in Jackson, or wherever else they go in Mississippi, that some of the finest folks in the world live here and good eating abounds.

When they're finally outside in the sticky heat, Ella asks, "What on earth did you do to her?"

"Well, to start with, I greased her palm."

"Are you serious?" She halts in the middle of the airport exit lane, causing a taxi driver to slam the brakes.

Caroline puts an arm around her waist to urge her into the garage. "She was sending a signal."

"What kind of signal?"

"That you're an affluent woman from Massachusetts with a platinum

AmEx and she's a working-class woman from Mississippi. The tip-off was pretending she didn't know that birthdates are written with the day first and the month second in Europe just like they are in Mexico and almost everywhere else but here. Hon, don't take this the wrong way, because I know we've already had a long day, but I think maybe she felt like you'd talked down to her. Is that possible?"

"It's possible. In fact, I know I did."

"Well, you used to be a waitress. So you might remember what that feels like, right?

"I do. And I'm ashamed. I guess you probably told her I'm sick, didn't you?"

"Nope. However, as she was pocketing my twenty, I did tell her that I'm a foreign correspondent for the *Boston Globe* and that I had a good mind to do some domestic reporting about the lack of courtesy we'd encountered at the Jackson airport."

"Did she fall for it?"

"Apparently. She tried to give me back the twenty. But I insisted she hang onto it to remember me by."

They're still laughing when they climb into the rental car. Before long, they're on the interstate, and a few minutes later they're taking the ramp onto US 49 North, heading for the Delta.

.

It's mid-afternoon when they reach Yazoo City, where the road they recall traveling with their parents years ago, and the one that Ella remembers in a different context—the bus trip to Jackson, where she sat beside Kim Taggart—seems not to exist anymore. They are routed around the eastern edge of town, then they cross the Yazoo River on a much newer bridge before rolling off into the Delta proper. The temperature, according to the dashboard display, is in the mid-80s, and their windows are halfway down.

"What is all this stuff in the field?" Ella asks, gesturing toward a large parcel of land where knee-high stalks wave in the breeze like large green mosquitoes. "Cotton doesn't look like that, not even in the spring."

"They don't grow much cotton here anymore. It's corn."

"No cotton in the Delta?"

Caroline casts a glance at her sister. The most militant strain of nostalgia has infected Ella. She's seeking confirmation that things were as bad as she thought, which requires them to remain bad in exactly the same way. "People change," Caroline says. "Places do too. They mostly quit growing cotton here about twenty-five years ago. They went to farm-raised catfish in the late '80s and early '90s, but after a while the black people doing nearly all the work formed a union and Jessie Jackson's Rainbow Coalition staged a national boycott of Delta-raised catfish, and before long the bottom fell out of that. So they went to corn, hoping the ethanol craze might save them."

From the looks of things, it hasn't. True, they still see the big houses that belong to folks who own the land, usually set back from the road in a grove of pecan trees, with broad verandas and a Cadillac SUV parked in the circular driveway alongside a pickup truck that shines like it just left the showroom. True, the little shotgun houses where black laborers used to live beneath tin roofs that radiated heat like a griddle when the sun was out and leaked buckets of water when it rained are nearly all gone. But they've been replaced by tiny prefab homes whose foundations are sinking, big cracks running up the walls, some so big you could stick your hand in.

"So how'd you keep up with all these changes," Ella asks when they stop at the intersection in Belzoni, where a once-famous BBQ shack named The Pig Stand seems to have disappeared. "I mean, you haven't even been in the country for nearly twenty-five years, right?"

Caroline looks both ways, releases the brake, depresses the accelerator. "Well, I was writing about the place in the first part of the book," she says. "When I couldn't remember something, I checked. The internet made that easy enough. And sometimes I read on past my point of interest."

"Of course," Ella says. "That makes sense."

Caroline waits for her to say more. But when she does, it's to ask if she ever once, in all the years since she left, missed home and wished she'd lived her whole life down here.

"No," Caroline says, "not once. What about you?"

374

"No."

"Were you ever back down here after you left for Boston?"

"Not a single time. Martin came down here once without telling me until several years later. He wanted to see where I came from."

"That speaks well of him, I'd say. That's the kind of thing . . . well, it's the kind of thing I could imagine Alastair doing."

"Then can I give you some advice, Baby Sister?"

"Make sure I hang onto him?"

"With handcuffs, if need be."

49 North now bypasses other little towns they remember, Isola and Inverness sliding by unseen. They cross the Sunflower River. Loring, both of them know, is just up the road. As if on cue, about three hundred yards ahead of them, a bobtail pulls into the highway. Caroline wastes no time passing it and keeps her eyes straight ahead, making sure there's no oncoming traffic.

Ella is the one who sees the logo on the side of the tank:

Barkley Petroleum
Loring, Mississippi
Founded in 1956

"Well," she says, "we're home."

•

Home, in this case, is a Quality Inn, the highest-rated motel in town. Like a lot of Delta motels—this is something they both remember—it's shaped like an L, with a swimming pool and parking lot between the two wings. They ask for a room on the second floor at the back, as far from the highway and the pool as they can get.

Ella tosses her jacket onto the bed closest the bathroom, then walks over and draws open the curtains. Beyond a row of pines, she can see the façade of the Academy. "My, my," she says. "Come take a look."

Caroline stops unpacking and joins her at the window. "It hasn't changed much, has it?"

"Not on the outside. I wonder if it's still all white?"

"I did a little research. In the history of the school—remember, we're talking forty-nine years—it's had a total of eight black kids, all of them between 2002 and 2006. Only a couple lasted a full year, and nobody stayed for two. It is what it was. And what it was wasn't good."

"No, it was not."

They stand there a moment longer, each of them wondering what thoughts are going through the other one's head, what hidden memories they might be recalling. Ella is the first to turn away. She walks over to the luggage rack where Caroline has kindly placed her roller bag, probably suspecting Ella couldn't lift it. She unzips it, then reaches under her clothes until she feels the bottle rolled up in a pair of jeans. She pulls it from the suitcase.

Caroline is still at the window, her back to her sister.

"Don't turn around just yet," Ella says.

"Why?"

"There's something I want to ask you. And something I want to tell you."

So here it comes. "Okay," she says.

"How did you know that stuff about the older sister in your book?"

"What stuff?"

"I think you know what stuff."

"Could I just say that she's an invented character?"

"You could."

Caroline keeps her gaze focused on the tall columns that support the entrance to the school. Just beyond those doors Coach Raleigh used to sit with his homemade paddle. She wonders if he's still alive. She has never tried to check. She's afraid she'll find out that he is and that he's even worse than she remembers. She prefers to think he changed, that he became a better man. She prefers to think she became a better woman. But she has hurt her sister, and she knows it. The fact that she did it to save herself is no excuse. Nor is the knowledge that she's only done what writers do. A novelist is just a cottonmouth with a laptop.

"I didn't *know* anything," she says. "But I did pick up some vibes."

"When?"

"Around the time when you were hanging out with Kim. And that made me realize that I'd picked them up before but discounted them."

"Did it bother you?"

"Of course not."

"I wouldn't have thought so. You were more accepting of me than I was of you."

"Well, I was harder to accept."

"But after Kim and I went to Jackson, did people ever . . ."

"If they did," she hedges, "they didn't say it to my face. And they would have said it to my face if they'd had any real ammo. That way, they would have figured, they could have hurt both of us at the same time. To them, we were throw-away items. We didn't belong over there"—she points out the window at the school—"and we don't belong here. And I'd just as soon be gone."

Her sister says, "As for what I wanted to tell you?"

"Yes?"

"My later life, the parts you couldn't have known anything about, you imagined them almost exactly as I lived them. The nature of my marriage. The way I spent my days. The aimlessness that set in when my husband died and left me alone. How was this possible?"

There are a lot of things she could say. She could tell her that she didn't know her husband had died when she was writing the novel, that she didn't know anything about him and had probably used Alastair as a model, that she didn't know anything much about the town she lived in except what she could recall from her brief trip there years ago, that she knew nothing about how she spent her days. She could try to explain that the internal logic of the story dictated its development, that it was almost as if it told her where it wanted to go and getting in its way was useless, unless she wanted to give up on writing, which for her would have meant giving up on living. She could say she wishes she hadn't written so close to the bone, but that would be untrue. Writing close to the bone is all she knows how to do.

Instead of answering her sister's question, she asks one herself. "How did you feel? When you were reading it, I mean."

"Sometimes I felt one way, and sometimes I felt another. And sometimes I felt every way at once. Now I want you to turn around."

When she does as requested, she sees that Ella is holding a large bottle of Four Roses. But it's not the kind of Four Roses you can buy these days, it's the kind you could buy forty or fifty years ago, when it had ceased to be bourbon and turned into something called American Blended Whiskey. She drank it a few times, and she remembers the taste. It was godawful. Worse even than Old Crow, which their father used to drink. "Where did you get that?"

"Right here."

"When?"

"The year I moved to Boston. I've kept it all this time." Ella stands the bottle on the desk, pulls the wrappers off the two plastic cups next to the ice bucket, breaks the seal, twists the top off, pours half an inch of whiskey in each cup and hands one to Caroline. "I want to propose a toast," she says.

"You know you shouldn't drink."

"It will be the last time I ever do it. And I intend to do it with my sister. So, here's to us: to who we are and who we never were." She bumps her cup against Caroline's. Both of them take a sip, each of them finding that it no longer tastes anything like they recalled.

"This is a better ending," Ella says, "than the one you wrote."

•

Tomorrow, they've agreed, they will go look at their old house, and they'll visit the cemetery where their father is buried. And then, because Ella insists, they'll go find the house where the Paces used to live, where he and Grace drew their final breaths. After that, they will drive across the river to Pine Bluff, and they'll place flowers on their mother's grave and then spend the night in Little Rock before driving on to Memphis the next morning. Caroline has booked them for one night at the Peabody Hotel, where Faulkner used to hole up when he went to Memphis. After that, back to Boston.

But now, they need food, and the desk clerk tells them the best place is down on Main Street, that it's a diner called McKenzie's Good Eats. So while neither of them has particularly high hopes, they climb back in the car and pull into the highway. "Can we drive along the bayou?" Ella asks.

Caroline doesn't ask why. She doesn't have to. Once she turns onto Bayou Drive, she slows down, so that her sister can achieve a good, long look at the house where Kim Taggart used to live. As she suspected—though her guess is that Ella did not—the once-grand home does not look at all grand now. The front steps are crumbling, the porch columns are badly stained, and the yard can't possibly have been mown for at least a month. There's a newish Lincoln in the driveway, though. Some appearances must be maintained. Ella looks but says nothing.

It's Monday, and McKenzie's is closed, Main Street all but deserted. They park in front of what used to be the Piggly Wiggly but is now nothing at all, its display window boarded up along with the doors. They walk past the Bank of Loring, which is still in business but closed now since it's almost six o'clock, past some kind of fabric shop that was not there before, a florist's, two more empty buildings, one of which used to be considered the top dress shop in town.

"Remember," Ella says, "when Momma bought us those skirts in there?"

"I sure do. We thought we'd joined the cream, didn't we?"

"They probably cost her a week's pay."

"More like two or three, I'd say."

Ella reaches down and grabs her sister's hand. At first Caroline thinks she must be feeling faint, but she's not. She just wants some human touch. "Momma didn't often do things like that," Ella says, "but I'm sure she would have if she could have."

No, Caroline thinks, she would not. That just wasn't her nature. She was born in the '30s and held frivolity suspect.

To their surprise, Loring Hardware is still right where it always was, just a few shops away from the store where their mom worked for so long. As they pass it, Caroline sees a customer step out, a heavyset man around their age, who is puffing on a cigarette and carrying a bucket of paint thinner. Though neither of them knows it, it's Irwin Majori—the same Irwin who kissed Ella in the cotton field nearly forty years ago.

He stands on the sidewalk watching them from behind, two grown women walking down the street holding hands. He got a glimpse of their faces and didn't recognize either of them, and he's lived here all his life. Those ladies either don't know or don't care that in this town, people still don't behave like that. Delta Blues tourism is a thing now, and it draws folks from all over. They must be from a whole other world, he figures. Someplace like New York or Boston.

Acknowledgments

My thanks to the following people who provided friendship and support during the three years it took me to write *Stay Gone Days*: Ewa Hryniewicz-Yarbrough, Lena Yarbrough, Antonina Parris, Gordon Parris, Linnea Alexander, Kathy Barwick, David Borofka, Christine Casson, Stu Cohen, Erick Garnick, Julia Glass, Joanna Gromek-Illg, Edmund Jorgensen, Margot Livesey, Deane Marchbein, Greg Michalson, Pamela Painter, Wyatt Prunty, Alex Rainer, Ron Rash and Dan Tobin. Sloan Harris, of ICM, has now been my agent for twenty-four years, and every writer should be so lucky. Elizabeth Clementson and Robert Lasner at Ig Publishing believed in the novel and have given it a great home. I am indebted to all of them.